PLANTING THE ORCHARD

FALL OF THE CITIES – BOOK I

BY
VANCE HUXLEY

© 2015 Vance Huxley

Published by Entrada Publishing.

Printed in the United States of America.

TABLE OF CONTENTS

DEDICATION

To my Noeline and to the Joy of my life

ACKNOWLEDGEMENTS

Thank you to my editor Sharon Umbaugh,
for turning my words into a book worth reading.

Chapter 1:
No Finesse

"Hey, it's soft lad. Blimey, what are you doing on the Iraq border, up on the sharp end?" The wide smile took the sting out of the words as the corporal punched the arm of a soldier stacking boxes in the front of the lorry. The soldier turned showing that he was also a corporal but his uniform was a lot cleaner.

"Hey Stones. Why are you lot running away? Now the Mad Mullahs have come to play in Kuwait, us office weenies are getting nervous. We've been sent back to Camp Bastille with the pay records but I thought you'd be out there slaughtering them with both hands." Corporal Harry Miller punched the SAS man in the shoulder in return, then looked over the corporal's shoulder.

"Are your lot going native?" Four of the eight men climbing into the back of the lorry were wearing robes and looked a lot like locals except for the pale, shaven faces smiling out from under the headgear. That and the Army kitbags they were throwing into the lorry or sitting on.

"No, somebody in Bastille is getting worried and needs a few bods to poke around the neighbourhood. That's us, but are those really the pay records?" Stones was peering at the boxes stacked in the front of the lorry. "Can you bump me a grade?"

"Sod off. How come you've got the stripes back?"

"Clean living, Harry. Oy, you lot, we've got protection on the way back." Harry winced while Stones turned to the rest, now sat on kitbags holding a variety of weaponry.

"What, the pay corps? Will he buy them off?" The speaker pulled off his helmet and rubbed his almost bald head. "He can swap hats so I get one without sand in it?" There was a little bit of curled lip and a little sneer in the words.

"Be careful, Tez. He can shoot that thing of yours a lot better than you can." Stones pointed to Tez's rifle and the fat scope on top of it. "Bastard used to beat the crap out me at the rifle club before he joined up."

Harry resigned himself to this because Stones thought the story was funny and loved to tell others. "The little sod was only sixteen and it was a bit bloody annoying when I came home from the Army full of piss and vinegar. Went down the club to show them how Army do it and Harry had joined, and I got my ass whupped."

"So why is he a bloody clerk then? A pay clerk. Is this another sodding wind-up Stones, because I'm not in the mood?" This soldier was laid on one side rather than sat.

"That's because you've got a bullet in the ass rather than a sense of humour Ferdy. You should get down lower when there's incoming. Though the rest of us were safe hiding behind that big arse of yours."

"He likes pizza and chips too much." There was some more banter and the men forgot Harry which was fine by him.

Though after a few miles of bumping along the dusty roads Tez was bored enough to return to the subject. Stones and Harry were catching up on who was doing what back home when Tez interrupted. "So if he can shoot this thing, why is he a pay puke?"

"In case some rough sod like you runs off with the cash box?" Stones nudged Harry. "Tell them Harry."

"I can shoot targets but I really don't like shooting at people." Harry braced himself for the usual disbelief and ridicule.

"He didn't even like shooting those targets with the pictures on. Drove the bloody instructors crackers. He's a better shot than most of them but gets all wobbly about what he shoots." Stones was having a wonderful time. Harry wasn't but he knew Stones wasn't being malicious, the idiot truly did find this really, really funny.

"So why are you in the Army then?" The rest were interested now.

Harry sighed. "Because I joined up, and then found out about my little problem. It was a bit late then."

A third voice joined in from under a robe. "What did you score on the ranges? What are you classed as? Marksman?"

Harry smiled because he found this bit funny himself. "I'm a crap shot according to the Army."

"What?" The robe was pulled open and a thin, suspicious face peered out. "So Stones is just winding us up?"

"No I'm not. Harry here shot lovely little neat groups, the sort you dream of Dobbin. He just shot them in the outer target ring, or through the top right shoulder of the target figure." Stones had his big grin back. "Always the top right shoulder. Then he'd put enough holes dead centre to get a pass. Harry spent more time painting rocks and polishing toilets than all of the rest put together." Stones pointed at Tez. "When we get back we'll get him on the range and I bet he whups you. I'll want four to one odds though."

"You're on at two to one." Tez lifted his rifle briefly. "No civvie target range asshole can outshoot me at a proper distance." The soldier scowled at the rifle. "I wish we hadn't had to leave our real gear back there. Why have we been issued with outdated crap?"

"Because the ones we left need the modern rifles and these were good enough the last time we did this shit. We'll get decent gear again once we get to Bastille. Now stop griping because this isn't exactly a bloody combat patrol." The thin-faced man pulled his robe around him and turned his back. "Bloody prima donna," he muttered.

"Is that an excuse for backing out Tez? You're going to blame the weapon?" The sneer in Stones's voice brought another scowl from Tez, aimed at Harry.

"Not a chance. I can beat a pay clerk with a bloody catapult."

"Sorted. Ah, I forgot to mention the ranges he can get those little groups. Naughty me." Stones leant back, happy to have got the bet confirmed. "The instructors were curious as well so he's used one of those sights Tez. Tough titty."

Tez opened his mouth to reply but a giant picked up the entire truck, shook it and threw it down the road. That's how it felt anyway.

*   *   *

Harold never could remember the actual blast, only the lovely soft sand. A glance to the side told him the sand was better than the big rocks some of the others hit. Harry noticed papers scattered about and was wondering how long it would take to file them properly when he realised what had happened. IED. Improvised Explosive Device and a really big one. Harry started to get up.

"Get your head down you bloody idiot!" That was Stones, and he sounded a bit shaken up. Which was another stupid observation considering the circumstances so Harry shook his head to clear it. A rattle of shooting and a big clang on metal behind him encouraged Harry to stay very still for a few moments.

"Here you bloody moron. Get in here." Harry glanced over towards the voice and rolled over that way. That left him sliding down the sides of a big hole. Harry grunted as he found the rocks on the way down and he looked around properly. This was a bloody big hole and the front of the lorry hanging over the lip had been very badly mangled.

Then Harry saw a figure in robes with blood staining the sand around his head, and Tez who was unconscious or dead. Tez had lost his sandy helmet and his arm was twisted out of line with white sticking out of the break. "Christ, Stones, are you all right?"

"No you silly bugger. My leg is screwed up." Broken, Harry realised when he looked at it. "Which means I can't crawl up there and shoot those bastards." Harry put his hands up and caught the weapon Stones threw to him. "Stick that over the top and send a few down-range will you? Then I can sort this out." A pale-faced Stones gestured at his leg.

Harry looked at the rifle and hesitated but he could shoot near enough to make them duck. Kill the bastards some part of his mind encouraged, because they're trying to kill you, and Stones. Harry gritted his teeth and started up the side of the hole. "All right. I'll just stick it over the top and pull the trigger."

"Be bloody careful." Stones pointed at the figure with blood around his head. "One of them can shoot. That was a single shot." Stones's voice hardened. "For fuck's sake Harry, just shoot the bastard. Through the fucking head."

Harry looked at the big fat scope on the rifle Stones had thrown to him and realised why Stones had done it. He took a deep breath and Stones spoke again, quietly. "Poke the barrel up nice and slow between a couple of those rocks on the lip. If there's no response slide up a bit and look for him. If you can't see anyone I'll get his attention." Stones grunted and when Harry glanced over the soldier had got a rifle tight against his leg and had tightened his belt round it. Then Stones leaned back and shut his eyes.

Harry did as he was told. "Can't see anybody like that though there's some blokes loosing off bursts from the rocks." Moments later there was a puff of smoke up on a bluff behind the other shooters and a thump nearby. Harry jerked his head sideways.

Stones waved the helmet on a rifle barrel. "He just shot my stupid friend here. Now kill him Harry. Otherwise when the others decide to come over here and finish the job we won't be able to do fuck all about it." Stones glared. "I could do it so you can. If I wasn't stuck here dicking about with my leg I'd smack you silly. Just shoot him."

Harry looked through the scope at the little lump where the smoke had come from. Stones spoke up again. "Get ready Harry. My stupid friend is going to take another peek over the top." Harry looked at the wind and it was barely fluttering the paperwork scattered about. Then he fiddled with the sights and settled down. That lump was just a target, same as at the range.

Crack and thump and a puff of smoke, and then the hump lifted a little and Harry tightened his finger just a bit. The hump dropped until it was almost invisible and stayed there and Harry got his head round it. Harry was sure if he'd missed, the bloke would have rolled aside or pulled back. If Harry had hit the hump then the man was dead. There aren't any other sort of head wounds from rifle bullets unless the victim was insanely lucky. "Got him."

"Good. Now you've got over that, kill some more of them while I sort out Tez and get up there to give you a hand." Stones sounded about a thousand miles away because there was a funny sort of buzz or something in Harry's head and then it cleared. He adjusted the sights and started to shoot at the men in the rocks who were loosing off bursts.

Harry was in some odd place now, where he knew these were people but now he'd got really bloody mad at them. They'd killed that bloke with blood round his head, and who knew how many more, and were trying to kill Stones. Bastards.

Harry moved the sights from one to another and took the time to do it right. Just like being on the range even if there were whining noises and clangs now and then. When the fourth tribesman fell the return fire almost stopped. Now there was just an occasional gun barrel round a rock and a quick spray of bullets.

Harry looked back at Stones. The corporal had rolled Tez into the recovery position and was now inching up the side of the hole with a rifle in his hand. "Why have you stopped?"

Harold shrugged. "I shot some and the rest hid."

"So keep them there. It's called suppressive fire, you prat. Don't worry, I'll be there in a sec. How many did of the others did you shoot."

"Four."

"Ha. Four shots. I knew you could do it." Stones heaved himself up a bit more and peered over the lip, then slid his rifle forward and settled it against his shoulder. "If we're lucky they'll piss off. If not it'll get very exciting. Have you got over the problem with shooting people?"

"Yes, I think so." Harry thought a moment. Yes, he was still mad enough to do it. "I just have to lose my temper."

Stones looked across for a long moment. "Yeah, you never lose it do you? Christ, so that's the trick. Remind me not to tease you so much." He grimaced. "Ah shit, the pain relief isn't working as advertised." The two of them watched the rocks and Stones put a couple of rounds into them now and then. That kept down the number of times someone over there got ambitious. Harry did wonder if any of the other soldiers had survived, but climbing out of the hole to look wasn't really possible.

Afterwards Stones said it was because the tribesmen found out their sniper was dead, and were very fond of him. Whatever the reason the group of them burst from the rocks, shooting as they came. Harry got two with the scope but that was useless as they came nearer. The view was too limited so Harry used the rifle as a shotgun, looking over the barrel with both eyes open. Men were staggering and falling so either Harry or Stones were on target. A big bang announced the grenade Stones had thrown but there were still some men advancing when Harry's rifle ran out of ammo.

Harry didn't have any ammo on him, because he was a pay clerk. There was a moment when Harry was thankful that the tribesmen had also run out of ammo and then he saw the bloody sword. The man running towards him was waving the damn thing and screeching like a banshee. As the man came over the edge of the hole Harry backed off and raised the useless rifle, and fell over.

The robed figure stumbled on the slope and dropped towards Harry and onto his knees, sword raised. Though he stopped before getting down to his knees or swinging the blade. The swordsman's mouth opened in an almost perfect O and his eyes bugged out, and he dropped his sword.

The man curled up and dropped away and Harry realised why as his rifle barrel came free of the man's groin. The bloke had no interest in Harry at all, and was now curled in a ball making high-pitched yipping noises. Harry looked round for the source of the screaming and yelling.

Stones was rolling about with another tribesman, and making most of the noise. Later Stones claimed it was his battle-cry, but Harry was fairly sure it was the pain from the broken leg being banged on the floor. Another robed figure was trying to get a clear cut at Stones with a sword. "Oy, you!" Harry threw the bloody useless rifle at the standing man and it hit him on the back of the legs.

The man turned, raised the sword and started for Harry. "Oh shit." A bayonet wasn't going to be any bloody good now the rifle was over there. Harry saw the sword his own victim had dropped and picked it up. Unfortunately that meant he was on his knees as the advancing swordsman started to run up the slope. Harry threw himself forward and took a bloody great two handed swipe sideways.

The man screamed and came down to his knees and, having lunged, Harry tumbled into him and the pair rolled down the slope. Harry was panicking now as well as still being bloody angry. He lashed out sideways as both of them tried to get up and the man dropped backwards to avoid the stroke. "Fucking stop still!" Harry raised the sword over his head, double-handed, and brought it down on the bit still in range.

That was a leg but the man screamed anyway and Harry shuffled forward, raising the sword and hacking down again and again. "Fucking. Lie. Still. Bastard. Fucking. Lie. Still. Bastard. Fucking. Bastard."

"Harry! Harry." Harry stopped and Stones continued in a quieter voice. "I think he's had enough, Harry." Harry looked at the gory mess in front of him and threw up over the man. He sort of thought it was disrespectful but couldn't help it. In the background, Harry could still hear Stones. "Christ, Harry, why didn't you stab him? That's why it's got a pointy bit you know."

There was the sharp crack of a rifle made his head ring and Harry turned, wiping his mouth with his sleeve. Stones had a rifle again and must have put a clip in. "Just making sure since I don't want a rematch." Despite the banter Stones was sheet white and had blood spattered over his uniform. His erstwhile opponent was also bloody and now had a hole in his head. Another bang and Harry's opponent jerked. Stones raised the rifle again as both looked to where Harry's first victim was still curled up, moaning softly. Stones shot him through the head as well.

"Here." Harry took the proffered rifle. "Get up there again. Stick that over the top and have a look. Anyone still standing or moving, shoot them through the fucking head. Here's a spare clip." Stones laid back as Harry took the spare ammo. "I'm going to need a minute and then I'll join you. Now piss off and give me some peace."

Harry was still in a really odd place in his head, all very clear but not quite real. He was also still both frightened and angry as he climbed back up the slope. So Harry shot anyone still moving, through the head. Nobody was standing though one was sat up and one on his hands and knees, and Harry shot them first. Stones's voice came from behind after Harry stopped shooting. "Is that it?"

"Yes. Nobody's moving."

"Good. I'm on the way up. I'm not up to walking, so will you nip over and get the rifle off the sniper?"

"What! Are you fucking crazy?"

"No, that's you. That's a good rifle and I don't want anyone else shooting it at me." The voice said Stones was closer. "Go on. I've got the scope now so if anyone wakes up I'll flatten them. Now piss off."

Harry would have argued, and should have argued, but he was still in a really odd frame of mind. So he stood up and walked through the bodies, through the rocks, and scrambled up the low bluff. His mind was going round and round because Harry was calming down and trying to fit not shooting at people with shooting the wounded through the head. Harry reached over the lip with a hand and heaved himself up, and was met by a startled yell.

One look at the bearded face crawling towards the sniper's body and Harry threw himself over the lip, dragging his rifle round. The man coming onto his knees and raising the sword double handed was sort of déjà vu but from the wrong end. Harry got the rifle round across in front of him in time to block the strike. He thanked something that this bloke didn't use the pointy bit and brought the barrel round.

The man flinched even as his sword came up, then grinned as Harry's rifle simply didn't fire. Harry pulled the trigger twice more and then threw the rifle up to block the next blow. As it landed Harry pushed forward, hard, and started swinging the barrel and butt double-handed into wherever he could.

One clear opportunity and Harry jabbed the barrel at the man's face. The man jerked back and Harry dived after him, and then they were both rolling about. Harry used his knees and elbows and helmet as well and the sword flew free. Then Harry was hammering down again and again, and then the noises stopped. Or they did once Harry realised he was the only one yelling now.

"Oh shit." Harry tried to be sick, but there was nothing there. He realised that he'd settled the argument. The plastic butt on the obsolete SA80 was strong enough to kill a man but it was messy, and didn't do the rifle much good. Harry noticed the two big gashes in the metal of his rifle where the sword had gone through it. Crap. He hoped he wouldn't be charged for it. There was noise again, shouting.

Stones was waving like a lunatic so Harry tried to wave back but his shoulder hurt like hell, and was bleeding. Harry used the other hand to wave. Then he collected the sniper's rifle and ammo and brought both weapons down the bluff. It did occur to Harry that wrecking his rifle wasn't a problem because the new one was a beauty. Harry trudged back to the wrecked lorry and the hole in the ground.

"You dumb bastard. I nearly shot you." Stones grinned up at Harry. "I was just going to shoot him and up you popped." Stones looked at Harry's rifle. "Christ Harry, you've got to learn how to do this shit properly. Here." Harry clambered into the hole and took a long drink of water, and Stones plugged up the hole in his shoulder. After a breather Harry climbed out and checked the rest of the soldiers, both drivers and passengers.

Five were breathing but Harry couldn't do much more than try and tie up anything bleeding and put them in recovery position. Between four minutes and four hours later, difficult to guess because things got a bit blurry, a drone appeared and had a good look. Both Harry and Stones waved, then Stones passed out again. Five minutes later two trucks arrived and there were squaddies everywhere. One was trying to improve what Stones had done to Harry's shoulder when Harry lost consciousness.

*   *   *

"Come on. It's a surprise." Stones was still limping and Harry's shoulder was sore, but even hobbling wounded weren't getting a lift home these days. Not as the Mullahs tightened their grip on Kuwait. Saudi Arabia had gone up in flames and internal strife so there wasn't much left to stop the fanatics gathering to deal with the remaining Westerners.

Harry was apprehensive. Even more so when they headed into the gym. Stones had persuaded him in there a couple of times in the past to try and teach Harry how to fight. That didn't work. If it got down to close and nasty Harry went to knees and elbows and head the same as he would in a pub brawl. The line of SAS lads with big grins didn't help. "Hun."

Attention was a joke since half of them were wounded and most were laughing. "Get up on there Harry."

"Piss off. What's this about?" Harry wasn't getting up on a box to make a better target.

"We can do it here." Harry stared at Tez. Tez had his arm in a sling but was smiling. "We've got a present for you. Sort of a prize for shooting."

Harry stared blankly and another voice spoke up. "My arse has healed but the ribs are still strapped up so I get to do this. It hurts when I laugh so I'll stay serious." The smile wasn't serious as Ferdy held out a thick wooden stick with a big brass knob on one end. He turned it and pointed to the end. "That's a pen and an inkpot for the heathens who can't speak Latin." Ferdy turned the stick to show engraving around the boss. "This says Stilus Gladio Fortior, which means The Pen is Mightier than the Sword." Laughter echoed in the hall.

Stone produced a similar stick from behind a vaulting horse. "Mine has the dagger and that on the top of course, but the same words round the outside. Just to remind us not to be so fucking full of ourselves."

"So has mine." Tez waved it. "The seven of us that made it home chipped in for yours but me and Stones bought our own. Sort of penance." He grinned. "But although the pen is mightier than the sword?" He raised the stick like a baton to the rest and they chorused "if you also have a sword?"

Stones nudged Harry. "Here, look, si tamen habes in gladio, which actually means But if you also have a Sword? Better still we've fixed up some lessons so you can use this. Three of our lads threw up after clearing up your bodies so you need more finesse."

"Stop taking the piss." Harry was bemused. The bloody sticks were real enough and actually he really liked that inscription. "How much do I owe you? Because I really do like that thing." Especially with that inscription.

"Depends on how many lessons you take. The stick is a freebie because the lads reckon they'll make it back in free drinks when the story gets round."

"Story?"

"Not the real one, not quite, but enough so you'll be on TV. Or at least an Army picture so nobody will ever recognise you." Harold accepted the stick. "Now come for a pint with us so we can have a laugh." Harry realised that this lot were having fun but he was inside the joke, not the target. Anyway, Harry really fancied a pint and a laugh.

"Isn't this thing illegal?"

"Our lot say they'll square it somewhere, so don't worry about it. One of them knows your CO. They probably went to the same poncy school." Stones used his stick to limp to the door and so did Tez despite having no limp, so Harry smiled and pretended to limp after them.

Chapter 2:
Homecoming

"Forget that shit, Miller, get to the plane."

Corporal Harold Miller CGC (Conspicuous Gallantry Cross) stared at the CO (Commanding Officer). Not only did the CO never use that sort of language, but that shit was the pay records for the units based here. Here being Camp Bastille because the French UN troops built it before the UN pulled out of Kuwait. "But…"

A corporal and two squaddies came through the door with jerry cans and started spreading petrol about, and the CO waved a grenade. "Phosphorus, Harry, now get the hell out. They'll string me up if I lose the most famous pay clerk in the British Army."

Harry winced about that bit because what he did really hadn't warranted the medal. He had been frightened and angry, and very, very lucky. Now Harry was paraded like a prize bull for any visiting brass and dignitaries. Though that pop star had been dead impressed and she… Harry snapped to attention. "Yes sir!"

"Don't forget your rifle, or that." The CO waved at Harry's walking stick, a thick length of wood with a brass end, and a big round brass boss on the top. Harold scooped up both, and his pack, which was sitting by the rifle as per the standing orders. Orders instituted when the Mad Mullahs decided that Kuwait was suddenly on their to-do list and sent in the fanatics.

"You might need that rifle because they're through the fence. We can't stop them now." The corporal wasn't joking. If the mad bastards were through the fence there weren't enough men left here to stop them. Not after the numbers who had been sent home already. The base was huge, with buildings and machines and heaps of stores scattered over several square miles. "If you get to the plane, try to keep them off the runway until the rest of us join you. Don't worry, we won't be far behind."

Harry crammed his helmet on, left the office and started running. There was nothing of his in the barracks worth dying for, so Harry headed straight for the runway. Sure enough a big old Hercules was sat there. Engines warmed up, and the tail ramp down, and there were figures in Army kit running that way from all directions. A few fell and not all got back up. Now that he was outside Harry could tell that the shooting was coming nearer from the south. He legged it across the tarmac.

"Corporal, throw your pack in there and pick a place. Shoot any raghead that shows. Forget all the identification shit, kill the bastards." The sergeant stopped and took a double-take. "You!" He turned to a corporal laid on the tarmac, looking along the runway.

"Give me that." The corporal looked up in surprise as his rifle with its big scope was snatched away.

"What the... Sarge?"

The sergeant turned to Harry. "Get up to the nose wheel and keep them off the runway. If anyone blocks it, we're all dead." Harry checked the weapon and accepted the extra clips. Déjà vu. Just in case it really was, Harry took his stick.

Behind him the sergeant was talking to the corporal. "Use his rifle and back him up. That's Miller, the pay clerk. Yes, that one."

Luckily for his peace of mind, Harry didn't have to shoot very many tribesmen. Apparently frightened and confused worked as well as getting angry, since he shot anyone going for the runway. After the first three who ran out of the buildings dropped in their tracks, none of the others fancied it. Then one of the attackers found a Jeep but Harry shot the driver, and then the front tyre when the vehicle kept going with a dead foot on the pedal. The Jeep flipped and rolled, ending up on its back short of the runway. The corporal shot the two surviving passengers as they staggered to their feet.

Harry tried very hard to pretend they were all just paper targets, but paper targets didn't crumple like that. Though since he shot them properly neither did they thrash about or scream. One of those the other corporal shot did move afterwards and needed a second burst, which spoilt Harry's mental games.

"Oy, you two. Miller, Menzies, get your arses back here or learn Ayrab."

"About bloody time." Harry agreed with the other corporal but saved his breath for running because the engines on the Hercules were winding up. He didn't fancy being blown down the runway to meet all those maniacs with guns. The pair swung round the end and jumped onto the ramp, which had already started to lift.

"Here, give me that back." The corporal swapped rifles. He grinned. "Else some pay clerk will take it out of my meagre earnings."

Harry smiled back, because there was no sting in the words. "Doubtful. The CO just torched the records."

"Shit. That's about it for Kuwait then."

"Kuwait, Iraq, all the sandy bits I reckon. Not that it'll make much difference now because every bloody oil well and pipeline is a bonfire." The squaddie who had chipped in didn't look all that sorry.

A mystery voice sounded from in the crowd. "Is that why we're leaving? Because the oil is gone?"

Another voice answered. "Either that or we forgot to pay our rent." The laughter was probably more relief than anything, relief at actually getting out. It died as the aircraft banked steeply and men tumbled.

"What the hell?"

"There's a tank or some sort of armour. Something's shooting at us from the runway." The man was clinging to the side and peering through a small round pane. Harry clawed his way up to look through the one above him and sure enough a squat shape had come out of the buildings. "Who left them a working.. Shit!"

Harry knew that was because a tongue of flame had suddenly sprouted from the shape, though the rest would have no idea. The Hercules continued turning and climbing so the shell had missed. "It missed."

"Where are the Yanks? They're supposed to shoot the shit out of any armour."

"Not this time, because the Gerry is in trouble." Everyone shut up and looked at the speaker, a private.

"You do mean the Gerald R Ford, the flattop?" Someone asked the question everyone was wondering. Wondering and hoping the answer was no, because that was the only offensive air power left in the region. Apart from a few Tornados dug out of some aircraft mothball programme, the ground based aircraft had left or been shot down.

"Yes. It was on our comms. There's been hundreds of suicide boats and missiles trying for the ships and something big got through. From the screaming on the radios it must have been on the bottom and come nearly straight up because it blew a big hole underneath. She's losing way, and the list is getting worse. Kiss goodbye to air cover." The man's grin was ghastly. "God help anyone left behind."

Harry looked through the window again in time to see that flame lick out of the squat shape once more. Still a miss and the Hercules was getting higher. Lower to the side a small executive style jet came out of the hangars and didn't piss about with the runway. The pilot already had the throttle pinned back and the small plane clawed its way off the taxiway and shot across the camp. As it gained a little more height the jet came around to follow the Hercules, low down and jinking and weaving in ways the manufacturer probably never envisioned.

A streak of smoke shot across Harry's view and the armour turned into a bonfire. "There's somebody still out there on our side. They've nailed that tank." Cheers burst out. A Tornado came into view and another line of smoke went into the buildings and something exploded. Then the plane was twisting and climbing, shedding flares as lines of smoke leapt from the ground and closed in. Surface to Air Missiles, a lot of them. "Crap, they've got SAMs."

Too many. Before the SAMs struck the aircraft steadied and volleyed every missile it had towards the abandoned camp. Several dots fell away and then the Tornado came apart in mid-air. There was no parachute because aircrew no longer ejected over enemy positions. They preferred being blown up to being caught, after the videos of captured pilots came on the internet. The deaths were slow and horrific. Moments after the Tornado died, flame blossomed among the buildings as the napalm landed.

Harry couldn't speak, but someone else was relaying the view. Then he stopped as well, for a moment, before continuing. "Time to bend over and kiss it goodbye lads. I reckon they saved the SAMs to catch the Tornado. They've got plenty left over for us and the bastards just launched."

There was cursing, scuffling and some praying behind him, but Harry was held by the view. He couldn't tear his eyes away from the eleven lines reaching up and curving towards him. Flares fell away or arced out to the sides and no doubt below, but they didn't seem to be having any effect. Then five of the lines curved away after decoys, but that wasn't enough.

All six remaining missiles drove in much too close then twisted in the air and moved towards something to the left, out of sight. Not out of sight for long. The small helicopter came into view, dropping down past the Hercules between the transport and the missiles. A Puma, usually a scout copter but now heading into harm's way and shedding a continuous storm of flares. Not out to the sides as decoys, the flares were bursting all around the craft as it fell towards the missiles and then led them off to the side.

The Puma never had a chance. Harry didn't think the pilot thought so either because there was no real attempt at evasion. The pilot just concentrated on luring the missiles away from the Hercules. Whoever was in there wanted every missile in the sky chasing him and it worked. By the time the latecomers went through the cloud of smoke and debris and looked for an alternate target, the Hercules was clear.

The mood in the hold was sombre, and stayed that way as Camp Bastille dropped further behind. There was little celebration even when a trio of Viper Helicopter gunships spread flame and devastation and huge plumes of smoke rose over the distant buildings. Four American Lightning II fighters with long range tanks, probably from the doomed Gerry, took position around the Hercules.

Another Hercules moved in alongside and the pair were joined by an AWACs (Airborne Early Warning and Control) plane. Then a mid-air refuelling tanker arrived followed by another four large planes, all of them transports. Another four Lightning IIs arrived as well.

"Hun!" There was a scramble as everyone made it to their feet and got organised.

A second voice spoke up. "I won't beat about the bush. That's it. We are the last troops out of Kuwait unless the Americans can pick some up in their surface craft. That isn't likely because the last sorties have left the Gerald R Ford. Once they ditch or head for friendly skies there'll be no air cover. The Gerry's list will prevent her retrieving or launching more aircraft and she will be destroyed after the crew are evacuated. Those sailors will take up most of the space on the surface vessels, which will then fight free of the Gulf."

Harry was stunned. Firstly by an officer admitting just what was happening, and then by the scale of it. A storm of queries and protests rose but a sergeant, that voice had to be a sergeant, re-established order. The officer continued. "We will be flying straight home and there will be a proper briefing there. Please make yourselves comfortable. There will be water and rations later." Then he was gone.

*   *   *

An elbow dug him again and Harry grunted and opened gummy eyes. He scrubbed them and looked sideways to find the smiling face of Corporal Menzies. "Wakey, wakey, rise and shine. We're nearly home."

Harry stretched and groaned. The floor had bruised his ass, and the wall had pummelled his shoulders. Wonderful. Outside the opposite window was darkness, except for a few stars. "How do you know?"

"I had a peek out of the window. The lights down there are London. I've come in on enough package holiday flights to know what it looks like." He looked at the other soldiers, now being roused and mumbling and complaining. "I hope there's some hot grub."

"Coffee. I need coffee."

The tannoy struck up to confirm Menzies's news. "We will landing at Heathrow shortly. Please gather your kit and be ready to disembark immediately."

"That was nice and polite. Why Heathrow?"

"Maybe we'll all get a night in the West End as compensation for the crappy catering?" Several smiles answered that. Then everyone set into looking as smart as possible without a shower or shave. They were coming home, into a public airport, and the Army wouldn't be happy if they trudged off here like a bunch of deadbeats. Sure enough, the sergeants were soon pointing that out.

Though everyone had their weapon. It had been that sort of evacuation in the end, where the priorities got narrowed down to survival. There were very few wounded because those had already been flown out. Presumably anyone wounded while running for the plane was still back there, and hopefully dead.

Stones and most of the Special Forces nutters were still there but they might not be either dead or captured. Everyone, even a pay clerk, knew the Mullahs were coming for Camp Bastille. Harry knew Stones's lot had gone out to try and spot the build-up and direct some serious air onto it, but all hell broke loose before they were back. Harry only knew because he had friends among them, mainly because of knowing Stones from before joining up. More to the point the rest knew about the medal and some treated Harry as an honorary member of the nutter club.

The sergeant got the squaddies all sorted out and lined up by the time the Hercules finished taxiing from the runway to wherever. By then Harry had made sure his stick was invisible inside his pack because it wasn't allowed in public. The men were organised purely by their remaining gear with no reference to what unit they belonged to. Because he had a full set of kit, Harry was in the first thirty off. They started off as soon as the back door lowered into a ramp even if the view didn't help.

Harry couldn't see where they were going since the ramp pointed back towards the runways. The first thing he noticed was the puff of vapour as everyone breathed out. Then the cold bit through his clothing, reminding Harry, and the rest, that it was January and they were no longer in a desert. The soldiers wheeled as instructed and came around the end of the plane, and into view of the terminus.

The view of the terminus wasn't quite as expected. Harry didn't actually think there would be a cheering crowd, but nobody at all in one of the busiest airports in England was eerie. Nobody seemed to be in any of the parked planes outside the terminal, and nobody behind the terminal windows. Not even staff or Army brass to greet them.

There was plenty of debris around the planes as they marched past and a lot of noise somewhere ahead. There weren't any footprints in the light snow. The place really was deserted, though still warm inside. The soldiers marched into the main hall and came to attention in ranks, and an officer appeared.

As soon as he spoke it was apparent from his voice that he was the one from the plane. "There has been a breakdown in law and order. Martial Law has been declared in London and the other major population centres, so we are unable to take you to your barracks yet. First the streets must be cleared. There are no shields or batons available, so we will use fixed bayonets."

"You are the British Army, and I trust you to uphold the traditions of that Army. Turn in your ammunition so there are no accidental discharges, and try to minimise casualties among the civilians. We will organise cover if firearms are used against you." He left and headed back through the terminal, and the sergeants began to split everyone up into squads.

"What about bricks and stuff, Sarge?" Harry had seen riots on the TV and they always included rocks and bricks. "Without shields we'll get beaten to death even with helmets."

"Move your packs round to the front if possible. Take some gear out to lighten them, but nothing essential. I don't know if we're coming back here though your kitbags will catch up eventually." The solution spread down the line and a very small pile grew behind them. Most of what was in the packs was essential if they weren't coming back to collect it. The pack felt weird hung in front but was probably capable of stopping a brick.

"Right, you lot. Outside those doors are the taxi ranks and access roads. We go left, to where a fairly thin line of London Bobbies is trying to stop the citizens storming the planes."

"Why do they want the planes, Sarge?" Which was a good question since there were no pilots in evidence. Though another two planes had now landed.

"Since I'm a mushroom as well I wasn't told. Presumably because one of them thinks they can fly one of those bloody planes. Which they will not be allowed to do. Am I clear?"

"Yes Sarge!" From most of the throats present.

"Let's get at it then, because there's another two planeloads coming through here to sort out any other little problems. Turn in your ammunition, now. " Harry really started to worry. What sort of unrest needed three planeloads of squaddies with bayonets?

*   *   *

It was full daylight when Harry was finally allowed to sit on the kerb at the edge of a rubble-strewn street and take a proper breath. They'd all been pulled off the line for a breather and water, but never for long enough to really recover. It was the sheer savagery of the rioters that had shocked Harry. Faces distorted with hate, pressing against the bayonets and trying to drag someone forward into the mob. That had happened twice and when the soldiers had pushed forward and recovered their badly beaten comrades, attitudes behind the bayonets hardened.

"It might be lucky they took our ammo. I might have been tempted when we pulled that copper out of the crowd." Menzies sucked on the bottle of water.

"Not just coppers either. The bastards got a couple of our lads as well. I couldn't tell if they were alive or dead." Harry drank water as well, because like all the rest he had a raging thirst after hours of this crap.

"At least the brass got their heads out of..." Menzies realised there were officers wandering about. "The officers realised the true situation. The bloody petrol bombers lost their sodding enthusiasm when a few got shot."

Harry almost spat but with his luck he'd hit some officer's boots as he came past. "Only after the third planeload were disembarked. There's some bad burns from before then. This riot is supposed to be about fuel shortages and the idiots are throwing petrol bombs. It's sheer lunacy."

"Not completely lunatic, some of that lot were trying for the rifles." Menzies grinned. "Our shooters must have been primed for that because those bastards went down sharpish."

"Yeah, I felt the wind of a couple of those rounds, I reckon." Harry continued to clean his bayonet. "Getting a bayonet bloody because the fool in front keeps pushing is bad enough, but shooting civvie men and women is a really bad job."

The other corporal grunted agreement. "See you found one as well." Corporal Menzies gestured to the riot shield Harry had claimed.

"I picked it up when one of the wounded coppers left it, and used it to push people away." Harry shrugged. "That didn't work because I needed two hands for the rifle. So on my next break I fixed it across my pack. It's a lot more effective than the pack. It's wider and even those bloody wooden poles they're using to stab with just bounce off it."

Menzies was re-shuffling his shield to make it more secure. "It wasn't the shields that turned it though. It was the bayonets and that's just wrong against civvies. The lunatics at the back just kept pushing those at the front onto the points." Menzies spat into the gutter. "The rifles should have shot those bastards at the back and let the front ranks pull away." He shook his head. "The poor sods were being pushed over and through the wounded and into our lines, what did they think would happen?"

"Until enough wounded got back for the rest to get the message, then they stopped. Will we ever know how many were wounded, because they're gone, someplace?" Harry inspected his bayonet again, because he really didn't want any blood left on it.

"Christ knows. They had their own bloody riot when enough started fighting to get away. God knows how many of them injured other bloody rioters. It might have been a blessing when we were ordered forward." Both winced, remembering that. Trying to step over injured men and women, pushing the bayonets forward until the fighting ahead broke up. Then the crowd was just that, a crowd of civilians running as fast as they could while the marksmen shot those stopping to throw a last missile.

"This isn't our job." Harry waved his hand at the street with its scattering of still shapes among those still writhing or moaning. "Bayonets against civvies is just wrong. What happened to the police?"

"Half of them are dead or in an ambulance, and the copper in charge had to ask for an Army escort to hospital. Our wounded aren't going to hospital, unless they actually need an ambulance. Only really serious cases go to hospital because the place is full." Menzies capped his water and looked around. "Or so I was told when I took a wounded copper back there. God knows when we'll get to the barracks."

"Soon, I reckon. After all we broke this lot up. Surely they don't want to try that again?" Harry gestured to a young woman being helped to her feet and led away. Her arm and side were drenched in blood. Many wounded had limped or staggered away once the soldiers were ordered to stand fast, but some weren't able to.

"You lot. From you to you, that's about twenty. Get into that hotel and throw out any civvies who aren't cooks. No cleaners or office staff and no customers. Then sit down in the dining room and get some hot food down you." The men in question looked at the officer. "Christ, look at you. Get some sleep after that. Leave some decent rooms for the officers and sergeants, and squeeze up tight. We've got to cram you all in there if possible."

The lieutenant looked closer. "Well, well, well, we've got the bloody hero with us. Right, you're in charge so I'll know whose arse to kick if it isn't done."

Harry sighed. "Yes sir." The lieutenant turned and headed off, snapping out orders to get the tired men up and moving.

Harry looked at Menzies and gave a tired smile. "Or maybe we won't go to the barracks." He stood and offered the other Corporal a hand to help him rise. "I just hope the staff are willing. Don't fancy the food otherwise."

"My aunt used to make fag ash sandwiches, but it wasn't deliberate. Just what dropped from the one in her mouth. After that I'm not too fussy about what I eat." They gathered the weary men together and headed inside.

*   *   *

Clearing the hotel of residents was easy. "We've only got four guests, er, sir?" The desk clerk, a young woman in a smart dress, was completely out of her depth. "Are the Army wanting to book the rest?"

Harry sighed. "Sorry, but no." He tapped his arm. "These mean corporal so no need for sirs, and we've been sent in to commandeer the hotel under emergency powers."

"Emergency powers? One moment sir, er, corporal? I'll get the manager." Harry stood there with a crowd of dirty, tired soldiers while she did, and it didn't take long.

One look at the rifles and bayonets and the man who was standing in for the manager just shrugged. "Not my problem, though you'll have to evict the guests." He looked pointedly at the bayonets. "What about staff?"

"Just enough to cook for eighty men. Though we could do with someone showing a couple of the lads where the laundry is." If they were here for a while Harry couldn't see the usual services being resumed. They'd all need somewhere to get the blood and muck off the uniforms and clean their boxers.

"Right sir. I'll let the staff know. Those who remain will be in the kitchens, down that corridor and through the door marked no entry." The man turned to the receptionist. "D'you want a lift home, Kathy?"

"What, now? My shift's another three hours."

"No shifts now. This lot are taking over and I for one will be pleased to get the hell out of here. Do you want to stay and risk getting a lift later?"

"Christ, no, Jacob. Thanks, I'll just clock off and get my things."

"See you in the car park."

Harry looked at Menzies and the other man shrugged. "Maybe we'd better get into the kitchen and make sure they don't all feel like that?" Menzies smiled. "You won't like my cooking."

"Right. I'll get the kitchen, you split this lot up and sort out these guests." Harry headed down the passage and into chaos. Though this chaos wasn't because they were all fighting to get out of the door.

"Do we all have to go?" The young woman looked decidedly unhappy about that. "We live in." There were some sideways looks among the others about that, but nobody argued.

"I don't care what the rest do, I need to get home." The middle-aged woman in white clothing glared at Harry. "My kids won't feed themselves but you lot are old enough to manage."

"I need enough to feed eighty soldiers. Well, some are officers and I'll need someone to show us the best rooms for them. Simple food but filling and the first twenty are here and hungry." Harry looked round. "We've got to have enough staff for that." He shrugged. "Orders, so don't blame me."

"You don't need me for that. I cook the fancy stuff so I'll be gone then." The woman headed for the door and Harry hesitated, then let her go. He really didn't fancy stopping a mother going home to her kids. A dozen more followed but there seemed a good few left. Especially when the door burst open.

"There's soldiers all over and they're taking all…." The young man stopped. "Oh."

"Did you get the message?" Harry hoped so because there were others in the passage behind him.

"Yes, we've all got to go home even if we don't want to. Why? Do you know what the streets out there are like?" He looked at Harry's stained uniform and the rifle. "Oh. I suppose you do."

"Yes, even though we only arrived last night. That's why we need beds and food. You can stay if you're catering staff. Kitchen staff, cooks, or whatever it's called."

The youth looked worried, then his face cleared. He looked behind him. "We can stay if we're catering staff. From the kitchens." He turned back with a big smile. "I work in the kitchen, don't I Cullen."

A portly man with a white apron and one of those cook's hats looked at the youth for a minute. "Why yes, of course you do. You'd better get your apron on. In that cupboard." Ten more people of all ages came out of the corridor behind him and four young women were kitchen staff and happy to stay.

"Right sir, food for twenty coming up. Quick and simple." Cullen smiled. "In the dining room in ten minutes, OK?"

"Lovely, I'll get the lads organised." Harry was relieved because all those in here were smiling and none were making for the door. "Can someone show us the best rooms, for the officers?"

"There's someone showing the other soldier with those on his sleeve." The young woman pointed.

"Brilliant. I'll get out of the way then." Because Harry was covered in all sorts of crap, and stood in a kitchen surrounded by people in clean white aprons. Health and Safety wouldn't be impressed.

*   *   *

The meal was bangers and mash with gravy and bloody wonderful. Hot cooked food, real English food and exactly what the men wanted. The meal was served by half a dozen women who Harry had assumed were kitchen staff. Two were definitely waitresses, their expertise in handling the dishes and plates was clear. The others had smocks but theirs were pale blue unlike the kitchen staff.

After finishing his meal Harry went to find out who they were, because he knew some bloody officer would give him grief sooner or later if they weren't cooks. The four in question were missing. "Who's in charge and where are the rest of the kitchen staff?"

The portly man with the hat spoke up. "I'm the assistant cook, Cullen. This is all the kitchen staff."

"Plus those two waitresses and then there were at least four others. Don't piss me about, Cullen, because I'm the reasonable sort. Some officer or sergeant will be a lot more bloody annoyed and then give me crap as well. So who are they?" Cullen's eyes went round the kitchen while he worked on an answer.

"Cleaning staff sir. They daren't go home."

Harry turned to the young woman, one of the waitresses. "Why not? The riot is over. Is that why you and her have stayed? The rioting?" Harry realised that he was tired and probably sounded angry when the woman flinched back. He gentled his tone a bit. "Who are you?"

"Janina, sir. We're all frightened to go home. Some of us have been here three days now, expecting the place to be wrecked. Then you all turned up. Is the Army here to rescue us all?"

Harry stared. Rescue them? "We've just landed at Heathrow and there was a riot, so we were told to stop it. Nobody said anything about rescues. Why can't you go home?"

The young woman looked embarrassed. "It's the rioters sir. They go back to the estates at first light, but, well, they're still there. Some of them look out for women. They caught Lucja on her way in on Wednesday, sir. The manager took her to the hospital but we haven't been home since."

"What about the others? The ones who left?"

Cullen spoke up at last. "They are the ones with houses or flats in the better areas, the ones that only get rioters at night. Most of them have got families. We're the ones who live in digs or on the estates." He sighed. "The manager didn't come back after taking Lucja."

Harry sighed as well. He'd been totally stuffed. "How many are actually kitchen staff?" There was a lot of hesitation and then people started shuffling about. Six kitchen staff and four not, plus the missing four. The orders were to send them home, but Harry just couldn't do it. Not after what the lass, Janina, had said. "Can you manage to feed us with six if the place fills up?"

"Not really. I'm a trainee cook, though we're called assistants. None of the real experts are left. We can cook basic food but with six?" Cullen shrugged.

Harry looked at the worried faces and sighed again. He would get so much crap if anyone found out. "Can you manage with fourteen, if they peel spuds or whatever?" Tentative smiles appeared on four faces, two of each sex. "Go and bring the other four in for God's sake. They'll be worrying."

"They can hear, sir."

"Stop the sir. Anyone with stripes is in charge of those with nothing, but isn't a sir. The ones with fancy badges are in charge of us and are all sirs." There was a scuffling and a big cupboard opened to show four apprehensive faces. "Come out here. Can you help this lot to cook?"

"Yes sir." That smile was three parts relief and two parts cheeky, and all five parts were very pretty. "I'm Cynthia, sometimes known as Cyn, and I can make cheese on toast."

Harry laughed, he had to. "Good. If you can cook porridge as well it sounds as if you're on breakfast duty." Harry looked round them. "The Army will want three meals a day, and possibly something for those on duty at night, so organise yourselves. If you are all sorted by the time anyone else asks, they won't bother to mess you about. You'd better show me which are the staff rooms so I can make them off limits." Harry looked round. "Do you all live in?"

There was a lot of feet shuffling and glances one to another. "There aren't any staff quarters. Some of us have been staying but we're supposed to go home after shifts." Cullen looked defensive. "If we go home we might not get back."

"Only the manager lives in. Lived in because he left. He's got a flat and there's two bedrooms in there." Cynthia smiled. "We know because we have to clean them as well."

Harry made a quick decision. The officers wanted staff, and this way there would be cooks here twenty-four seven. "Are there settees in there, or maybe room for a mattress on the floor? If not you need to take over the nearest room and make it look like a staff bedroom." Harry smiled. "Throw out the flower vases and posh soap and hang up some undies in the bathroom."

There was a mixed response to that. "What's wrong?"

"Most of us haven't got any more clothes so we sleep in separate rooms. We've been washing clothes out at night, but if we're all living together?" Cullen looked around. "Your soldiers might like the idea of seeing them running around while their undies are hung up to dry, but I doubt they'll return the interest." He patted his large, round stomach. "I doubt they'll appreciate this either. Not exactly the body beautiful." Cullen was trying to make light of it and some were smiling but some were still very worried.

"The manager's family must have left clothes, and what about the last guests? Those we told to leave didn't all take suitcases." Most of the faces looked happier but one went scarlet.

Cullen glanced at her but spoke to Harry. "Some of our customers don't have suitcases. They only rent for a few hours and don't leave together."

Harry looked at the red-faced one. "On the game?"

"Yes." It was a whisper. "Do I have to leave? I'm in here because none of us are walking the streets now. Those bastards don't care why you're out there, and they don't pay either."

"Don't look for business in here. This lot are fresh back from Kuwait and you'll start a bloody riot. Then some officer will throw you out. Now all get into the proper uniforms and raid the rooms for whatever you need." There was still some hesitation. "What now?"

"Martial Law. We can be shot for looting."

"Requisitioned for Army use, just don't list exactly what clothing you take." Harry caught the sparkle in Cynthia's eyes. "Especially you, I reckon." He hesitated. "Sort out the uniforms, tunics, whatever, and I'll get a couple of sensible blokes to stop anyone else asking difficult questions."

*　　　*　　　*

"Christ Harry, I'm knackered." Maynard was Harry's usual darts partner. "You'll get to see a bunch of girls raiding the panty store?"

"Will they be trying them on?" Maynard paused a moment. "Hey, these are English girls, right?"

"Keep quiet you idiot. But yes. Well, some Irish and maybe Polish as well."

"Yeah, but with real legs like the ones who served the grub? Not all covered up and likely to stick a knife in me?"

"Well they might if you misbehave but yes, they wear skirts. But they are also respectable so keep your bloody hands off." Harry put on a scowl.

"I know. Christ, you know me Harry, all mouth."

Harry did know Davie Maynard which was why he had picked the man. Maynard might look with longing but the soldier was shy when he actually met a decent looking woman. "Yes, I do. I also know where your mother lives so you keep your trap shut to the rest."

"Ooh, low blow. Come on then, before they've finished trying them on?" But Maynard was grinning as he said it. He'd got the message. Harry explained to Menzies as well and between the three of them they escorted the staff around the rooms. The tired soldiers who were already in some rooms weren't best pleased to be disturbed, but much too pleased when the young women came in.

"Shut it, you lot. This lot will be cooking your breakfast so behave."

"Please miss, can I have breakfast in bed?" That brought a round of laughter but the two staff with Harry got out of the room before it got much worse. The other staff with the other two soldiers were coming out of rooms being pursued by laughter, and some fairly crude comments.

Maynard gestured at the embarrassed women. "This won't work, Harry."

Harry looked at the faces of the women, and even the oldest was definitely blushing. "You're right Maynard, but us sorting through women's underwear won't go down too well either."

"We could take the lot." Menzies shrugged. "If we take the male staff to help collect it up the women can sort through it later."

"Good idea. You ladies had better scarper and sort out those staff rooms, and ask the rest of the men to come up with any bags they've got." The women scarpered, smartish.

Harry and the other two soldiers told the rest of the soldiers that all the civvie clothes had to be taken away and saved for the owners. Two hours later the three of them were slumped in the room they'd picked, the nearest to the staff rooms and the manager's flat. They'd told the staff to call out if there were any randy sleep walkers. The door handle rattled and opened.

"This is where you're hiding. Why aren't you idiots asleep?"

"Come on Sarge. We've been getting the staff organised and making sure you and the officers have pretty bedspreads and smelly soap." Menzies grinned.

"Well hard luck though I'll check my bed carefully after that comment. Now you get to come and tell the officers what a wonderful job you've done. Not only that," Sarge produced a wicked smile, "but there are a couple of top coppers down there to discuss tactics. Guess who the brass want to show off" Harry groaned. "Don't bring that poncy stick though, just make sure you've got your ribbon nice and clean." Sarge turned to go. "Dining room in fifteen."

Harry turned to Menzies. "Sorry. Look, they only want me so you and Maynard get some sleep."

"Not a chance. Sarge didn't give me a pass and he's got a bloody good memory. Though when we've had a kip I want to know the real story."

"About the medal? I lost my temper."

"Yeah right."

"It's true. Harry is known as soft lad by anyone who really knows him." Maynard shook his head. "Now we're all frightened of upsetting him again." Menzies looked from one to the other.

Then he shrugged. "Later. First I need a swift shower so I don't keel over and fall asleep."

*   *   *

The brass showed off their clerk, and assessed their rooms, and set a guard rota as the rest of the men stumbled in and were shown their rooms. About half of the soldiers decided that sleep came before food and the rest were organised into shifts for the dining room.

"Well you managed that all right. Must be the office training." The lieutenant sneered. "Must have been a shock for you, getting in among the muck and bullets where the real soldiers live." Harry let it wash over him, because the Army seemed to be split in two camps. Many were dead impressed by the medal, and often wanted the story. The rest assumed it was all bullshit to cover up for Special Ops or something similar because after all, Corporal Miller was a pay clerk. A desk weenie. Though all the clerical brass liked to show Harry off to visitors.

"Now you can report to Sergeant Wilson, and he'll keep you out of mischief. Though you'll turn out with the rest if there are any more riots. Understand, Miller?"

"Sir."

Sergeant Wilson was lurking nearby, waiting. "Lieutenant Symonns told me to deal with you, Miller, since he's got real work. You're already awake and know how this place works, so you get the job of organising the food." Sarge had a smirk when he said that, the bastard. Menzies apologised to Harry and headed for bed, promising to be back in four hours.

The waitresses all had black skirts and white blouses now, and there were four of them juggling plates and cups. The first shift was going well enough when the first man tried for a handful of waitress. The woman yelped, twisted away and two plates of egg and chips hit the floor.

"Stop that shit, right now."

The man, a corporal, looked round and noted the two stripes Harry wore, identical to his own. "Else what? I was only being friendly-like. After all we've not seen a friendly face in a tight skirt for three years." There were several voices pointing out it wasn't the friendly face they were pleased to see.

One of the other men at the table grinned. "I didn't get a Christmas present or a New Year kiss out in Kuwait. Maybe we can get both. I don't mind them being late."

Emboldened, the corporal carried on. "Since you've only got two stripes, same as me, who put you in charge?" Harry cursed the decision that, because there were very few officers, the sergeants could share the grill room. That had been declared the officer's mess.

Harry opened his mouth to reason with the man, though he thought it wouldn't work. The scrambled retreat, then the riot, had shattered morale and, apparently, discipline. Then a voice spoke up from a nearby table. "You might not want to get Harry annoyed, Suggs. You won't like him when he gets angry." There was a ripple of laughter and the corporal looked around, scowling.

"He don't look that hard to me. Does he turn green and split his pants or what?"

Harry knew what was coming. Several of this lot knew him, even as just a nodding acquaintance. Sure enough. "Look at the ribbon, Suggs. How many pay clerks do you know with a CGC?" There was more laughter. "Though look on the bright side, he hasn't got a sword or a rifle."

The corporal, Suggs, narrowed his eyes and looked closer. Then his eyes rose to meet Harry's. "Shit. That really is the CGC. You really are him?"

Harry shrugged. "Says so on the pay records."

"Harry would know." There was some more laughter and Suggs subsided. He turned back to his meal, though an intense discussion started at the table and Suggs occasionally glanced at Harry. The waitress cleared up the mess and went back to serving, though she also gave Harry a nod of thanks. Eventually this shift finished and left the dining room.

Suggs paused on the way past. "I'm not frightened of you."

"Didn't expect you to be."

"Lost it a bit back there. Bad night. No hard feelings?"

"None. We've all had a rough night."

Suggs nodded and carried on but Harry wasn't so sure it was over. In Suggs's eyes the corporal had backed down in front of all these men, and he looked the type to want to even up somehow. The next shift were better behaved, or at least there was no trouble. When one or two did start to take it beyond light flirting with the waitresses, it quickly died out. Nearby soldiers made a point of leaning over and speaking to the offender, and they subsided.

News of Suggs would have spread by that subtle magic infecting all gossip, ensuring that it moved faster than light. By morning all the men in the hotel would know that the pay clerk, the corporal, was that one. They would get a gory version of the medal winning which to be honest Harry didn't remember very well. Then they'd all want a blow by blow and treat him like a live hand grenade until they knew him better. The sooner all the units were sorted out and the brass found Harry a nice cosy pay office the better.

Four hours later, as promised, Menzies turned up. He looked a lot better and had managed a shave. "You get six hours according to the rota Sarge gave me. It's in our room. I've let the kitchen know the meal shifts and our shifts so they know who to annoy. Apparently we, you and me and Maynard, are the catering corps for now."

"Why?"

"No good deed goes unpunished. We sorted it once, so it's our job." Menzies shrugged. "Look on the bright side, we get to go to the kitchen for a cup of coffee whenever we can find an excuse."

"So what else are we supposed to do, if there's no riot? Because that lieutenant seemed to have it in for me so he won't want me bloody well skiving."

"Find food, bread and milk or whatever, organise dustbin emptying and laundry, all the fun stuff. It's on the list. Sarge seems to think it's funny." Menzies curled a lip. "He's got an odd sense of humour."

"Sorry, some people don't like this." Harry tapped the ribbon. "Why has Sarge got it in for me? I never served under him at any time." Because Harry didn't know the sergeant at all and sergeants were usually fairer about the decoration.

"Because a bloke with a medal should be a proper soldier, not a pay clerk. You offend his sense of how things should be." Harry stared but Menzies wasn't joking. "I still want the down and dirty some time," the corporal continued.

"Maynard can tell you." Harry headed off for a shower and a long peaceful sleep.

* * *

"Good morning sir. This is your early morning call."

"Wha? Mmm, coffee." Harry got an eye open and confirmed coffee and that the voice really was female. "Cynthia?" He quickly checked that the blanket was over him. "What are you doing in here?"

"We have a list of your shift times. The other corporal, Menzies, left it in the kitchen. See, I've remembered the ranks. We've been learning them." Cynthia giggled. "Maybe not morning, it's nine o'clock at night."

"Twenty one hundred."

"It said two thousand one hundred or twenty one point double zero. I didn't fancy trying to say that but it's nine o'clock on the kitchen clock."

Harry's head slowly caught up, not helped by the bright chattering voice. "You should knock first. Just in case, er, we're washing our boxers or whatever."

"It can't be worse than the last three days where we all managed with one of everything." Her eyes widened. "Unless you lot are commandos? I've heard all about them."

Harry laughed. "No, I'm a pay clerk."

"Well, the pen is mightier than the sword." That twinkle was in her eye again.

"Only if there's a line of blokes with swords or rifles to back up the man with a pen." Harry glanced down the room and the other beds were empty. Bugger, he'd better get her out of here sharpish. If Sarge caught him with a woman in here? "You'd better get out of here before you get me into trouble."

Her eyes flashed again. "That's supposed to be what I say." Cynthia pouted. "In that case I'll put your coffee here and leave. I'd been hoping to find out if what they say about soldiers is true."

Harry wasn't falling for that lead-in. Though it was tempting with those eyes because it had been a long time since he'd been close to a pretty lass. Well, one he'd dare be alone with and didn't have a horde of fanatical relatives. "Scat. I'll be down in half an hour."

"Yes, Corporal Menzies said it would take you half an hour to get yourself fit to be seen." She sniggered. "That must be why you've got those covers pulled up so high." Then Cynthia twirled and left, but not before Harry saw the smile on her face.

Harry sat up and picked up the coffee. Mmm, lovely. Though Cynthia had better be careful about wandering into this room since either of the others could have been showering or getting changed. Harry mused briefly on that smile. Then regretfully decided that since she was living in a room with three or four others, and so was he, he'd never find out just how interested Cynthia was. Though his early morning call had definitely put Harry in a good mood.

Right up until just after midnight. "Move it, move it!" Soldiers stumbled out of rooms as the fire bell went off. They assumed this was a call-out and not a fire since an officer had decided to use it as an emergency alarm. Though Cullen turned up to check, just in case there was a fire.

"The walking wounded are staying to mind the store so you've got to be a real soldier for a change. See if you remember how." Harry ignored the lieutenant and found Menzies and the others who were now in their squads, then got into ranks. Harry had kept his shield but now it was strapped to his chest instead of to his pack.

Menzies was scowling. "We've got a few more shields now, but no bloody batons or rubber bullets."

"Is it another riot? Against bayonets? Are they bloody stupid?" Harry couldn't believe it but sure enough they were soon marching to where two single decker buses were waiting. It was cramped inside but not for long since they hadn't far to go. Then once again it was bayonets against civilians.

*   *   *

"Shit! Sir, man down. He's been shot." Harry, along with a lot of others, looked at his empty rifle and muttered unkind and profane comments about officers.

"Don't worry. The sharpshooters will get them. Just keep your heads down a bit."

"All right for that bastard. He's not trying to fend off a sodding lunatic while keeping his sodding head down."

"Shut it!" Sarge stifled further anonymous comment. A rattle of shots from behind and overhead announced the sharpshooters.

"How come you aren't with them?" Menzies was puzzled. "You being so shit hot with a rifle?" Maynard must have given him the story, or enough of it.

"Glad I'm not. I'll shoot a bloke with a gun but I'm not even keen on that. I'm bloody pleased I'm not shooting some woman throwing a petrol bomb, because I wouldn't sleep well." Harry still dreamed of some he'd shot and they were lunatics with guns.

Menzies grinned. "You won't sleep well if the bloody thing hits you. How come though, because they've picked out all the marksmen."

"I never qualified since I didn't want to be a sniper. What about you? You had a rifle with a big scope and looked the part."

"Picked it up off a body. I didn't want someone using it on me as I ran for the plane. I was damned glad you took it." Menzies glanced up and crouched. "Oh shit, here we go again."

The rioters had quietened for a moment as the gunfire echoed in the street, but now they were back and petrol bombs were coming up and over. By the time the crowd broke the bayonets were red, and three soldiers were down with gunshot wounds. Two went to hospital and one into a body bag. Two of the civvie corpses had holes in their backs where their own had shot them, by mistake presumably. The Army rifles killed six shooters but only three handguns were recovered.

The soldiers marched back to the buses, and were taken back to the hotel. The hotel staff produced tea, coffee and bacon sandwiches for those awake enough to eat. The rest staggered into their rooms.

*   *   *

This time good morning was in daylight. "Eight thirty hours." A smiling Cynthia informed Harry, because the shifts had been altered. "Now you are on shift from nine hundred to seventeen hundred, and Menzies from then until oh one hundred. Maynard has the night shift."

"Unless there's a riot."

Cynthia's smile faltered. "Then we have nobody to feed so we don't need a supervisor." Cynthia's smile brightened again. "That means that I get to bring your morning coffee *every* morning. So maybe I'll eventually find out the truth about commandos." She made a mock attempt to peek down Harry's covers.

"You could be very disappointed."

"You could risk it?"

Harry looked down the room. "Where are the other two?"

"I told them to leave so that you wouldn't be embarrassed if I peeked." Just for a moment Harry thought she might have, until he caught the mischief in her eyes. Then Cynthia laughed. "Nearly got you that time. Now I have to go before you ruin my reputation." She gave Harry a lovely smile and turned. Just as she left her voice added, "though I'm a bit disappointed you haven't even tried."

No, thought Harry, but I surely would if you pulled this stunt anywhere I thought might stay private long enough. Cynthia was safe with her teasing while Harry was here, sharing a room with three others and with Sarge likely to turn up at any time. If he ever got any leave, Harry would offer to take her to a dance or pub, and try to find out how much was tease. He sat up and reached for the coffee.

*   *   *

"Oh, corporal, just the man. Are the Army organising more supplies? Bacon, eggs, sausages, potatoes, all that sort of thing."

Harry stared at Cullen. "There isn't enough?"

Cullen shrugged. "Your soldiers are going through the usual stocks of simple but filling at speed and there have been no deliveries. There weren't many the week before that but we haven't had many guests." Cullen smiled. "You don't want me to start experimenting with what's left. I told you, trainee."

"But we had bread? And milk?"

"We're using frozen milk and really need more soon. The bread is made here so we need more flour and yeast."

"Damn. Make a list and I'll see what I can do." Harry headed towards the front of the hotel, officer country.

Plywood was being fastened over the ground floor windows. Even those not already broken. The captain overseeing that had obviously been anticipating Harry's query at some time.

"This is a list of supermarkets and discount warehouses in the immediate area. Over there on the reception desk are the keys to the truck out front and an A-Z map of London. Take a lance-corporal with eight soldiers and make sure they are all armed to the teeth." The captain smiled at Harry's look. "That's a war zone out there so treat London the same as any other city you ever fought in." Harry collected his rifle and helmet and signed out an ammunition belt. Once he'd got his escort armed, Harry gave the lance-corporal the list and map.

The streets did look like a war zone, and Harry did actually know what a war zone looked like. It wasn't just the rubble and broken windows. There were also burned out cars and buildings, and here and there were other signs of how serious the situation was. Patches that looked too much like old bloodstains, and items of clothing. Torn and stained shirts, or single trainers, were laid on the footpaths and tarmac. The lorry went around the largest lumps of masonry and over the rest.

* * *

"This is the first supermarket on the list." 'This' had two holes where the door and window should be. The ground outside was covered in broken packets of pasta, cereal, flour and sugar. Mixed in were other crushed packets and boxes, and even some squashed cans.

Harry sighed. "Two men on the back of the lorry, one on the street out front, one in the cab. We'll go in and see if there's anything we need."

"The place has already been looted." The lance-corporal, Tredwell, was looking at the mess on the pavement.

"Opportunists. They'll have grabbed what they want and left. There'll be no booze or prescription drugs." Harry looked along the street both ways. "They grabbed the expensive or alcoholic and ran so there'll be beans and suchlike left. Anyway I'd rather take the food from a wrecked shop than somewhere the local families get their food from."

"Fair point, Corp. You two, with me." The three men stepped into the shop with their bayonets fixed and a round up the spout. Nobody wanted to take chances after the last few nights. Within a few minutes Tredwell came back out.

"One body in the back office and there's a floor safe. It's open and empty and so is the till. There's a room at the back with a big padlock on. Someone hit it with a fire extinguisher but the lock is still holding." Tredwell grimaced. "You're right about grab and run. There's still a lot of food laid on the floor, and there are plenty of cans of beans and suchlike.

"That door is probably either a big fridge or the storeroom. Have we got anything to open it because I don't fancy stopping a ricochet?" Harry smiled. "If it's a fridge I reckon we're sorted for bacon sandwiches."

"There'll be something in the toolbox, Corp."

"Which means you just volunteered." The squaddie sighed dramatically and climbed out of the cab. He rattled about in the big box bolted to the truck and turned, waving a selection of tools including a lump hammer.

"Hang on." Tredwell sent one of the other men into the cab and then the volunteer locksmith headed into the gloom. Harry and Tredwell followed. While he waited for the door to be opened Harry had a look in the office. The body had been beaten before his throat was cut, presumably to persuade the man to open the safe. This wasn't just rioting and looting.

Within minutes the padlocked door opened to reveal an apprehensive middle-aged woman. Her face cleared as she saw the uniforms. "Thank God, the Army. But where is Silas?" She was trying to look past Harry and her face tightened as she saw the state of the shop beyond.

"Who is Silas?" Harry had a horrible suspicion that he knew.

"My husband. He was going to give them the keys to the safe so they would go away and leave us in peace. But he swallowed the key to the padlock so even if they searched him, it wouldn't be found." She looked slightly embarrassed. "I was expecting to wait a little bit longer while he, you know, retrieved it." The woman moved out a bit and looked round. "They've wrecked it. Why didn't they just steal the food and booze, why wreck it?" She turned towards the little office and Harry stopped her.

"Mrs?"

"Yes, Mrs. Imberg. Betty."

"I need to talk to you before you go in there. What did your husband look like?" Betty wrenched herself out of Harry's grasp and lunged towards the office. She stopped in the door way and gave a strangled gasp, before moving forward and dropping to her knees. Then she looked back at Harry, her tears already starting.

"Why?"

Harry had no answers. "I'm sorry. I don't know."

Behind him Tredwell tapped on Harry's back and whispered. "That store is full, and there's a cold store at the back. We can get most of what's on the list. Should we start?"

Harry turned and spoke quietly. "Yes, get it loaded quickly but take loose food from the floor first. Then we can lock the rest back up. Try and find something for the body." Tredwell looked past Harry, startled. "Would you want tell her we're leaving him here?" The LC shook his head.

"I'll get on it. Will you?" He gestured.

"I'll explain requisitioning. Just make sure you've made a list." Harry turned back to the weeping woman. "Mrs. Imberg. Betty. Is there someone you can contact?"

She looked up, her eyes already red and swollen. "Yes, we have family."

Harry picked the phone up off the floor and remarkably, after replacing the hand-piece for a few moments, got a dialling tone. "Why don't you call them? Then we can give you a lift." Her eyes went to her husband. "Yes, him as well." Harry held out the phone.

In the end Harry had to talk to the family himself because Betty couldn't really put everything into words. Tredwell found a roll of big rubble sacks and some tape, and with one of the squaddies made Silas Imberg into an anonymous parcel. Meanwhile the soldiers loaded the lorry. Once they had finished Harry picked a big padlock off a shelf and put it in the clasp. He handed the three keys to Betty Imberg.

"What's the point?"

"The point is that you and your family can live a long time on that food. It might get a bit boring, but hopefully you'll all stay alive and well until this all dies down." Harry looked at the rest of the shop. "If you come in daylight, maybe your family can help you take the other useable food."

"But it isn't going to die down, is it? Not with all the oil gone."

Harry shook his head. "It hasn't all gone, there's billions of gallons still down there. Anyway, all the wells can't be gone. There'll be some left, especially the ones out at sea."

Mrs. Imberg shook her head at that. "The TV explained. The oil is all useless because the refineries are all gone."

"They'll rebuild. It'll just take a bit of time." A chill went up Harry's spine. All the refineries? Was that possible? The Army wouldn't allow live TV in Kuwait and he hadn't really had the chance to catch up since coming home.

"But what happens during that time?" Betty Imberg took a deep, shuddering breath. "I'm sorry. You have been very kind and I don't want to seem ungrateful. It's just." She waved a hand around to take in the shop, the lorry, and no doubt Silas. "I really would appreciate a lift, and then we will see."

At least Harry felt a bit better when the house door opened and a big man with grey hair swept Betty into an embrace. He nodded to Harry and his eyes narrowed as two men brought the body round. The man moved the grieving woman aside, gently, as Silas was taken into the house. Then Harry lifted a hand in farewell and told the driver to head for the hotel.

*   *   *

"What the hell has been happening? I just met a woman who said all the refineries were gone, everywhere." Harry had cornered Menzies who was up and about but not yet on duty.

"Christ! No, surely not all of them? The bloody TV is in the officer's mess so none of us have seen sod all. Hang on, someone had an old newspaper. You go round the lads as well, borrow any magazines and papers." Menzies was back in ten minutes as was Harry, and they sat and read in silence for a while.

"Crap. We're screwed."

"The Yanks have still got oil and South America is still pumping the stuff out." Though Menzies didn't sound optimistic.

"A lot of places are still pumping it out according to these. There's just no bloody refineries left. According to this," Harry waved a newspaper, "someone even blew up the little one in the north of Scotland. What the hell sparked this off?"

"Christ knows, or maybe Allah. The reporters can't decide if it started in Russia or the Middle East. Then suddenly Milford Haven and the big Dutch refineries were going up, and there were groups lighting bonfires under oil pipelines all over the world." Menzies looked from one publication to the other. "But why? Nobody seems to be protecting their little bit and asking for a lot of cash."

"These are old news, so maybe they have now." Harry grimaced. "Because it's not all over the world. Just Asia, Europe and Africa which leaves all the Americas with all the petrol."

Menzies waved a magazine. "The map in this showing destroyed refineries looks like over half the world got measles, and add Australia to the list." Menzies hesitated. "Some of them reckon it's a CIA thing, so that the Yanks have all the oil. That it got out of hand."

"Not according to this." Harry lifted the magazine. "Their article reckons if it was the CIA they'd have picked on Venezuela, since they aren't the USA's best friends." Harry sighed. "Betty was right, we really are in the shit. I can't remember where I saw it but years ago some TV bloke said Britain only has enough petrol for a week, and enough gas for three days."

They stared at each other and let that settle in. "Let's hope the special bloody relationship includes the Yanks filling up the national petrol tank." Menzies grunted agreement. "We should get a radio at least, or maybe a TV."

"The officers would nobble it. Otherwise there'd be a TV in the dining room. They're not exactly stopping us finding out, just making it difficult. Mushroom syndrome." Menzies waved the newspaper. "These are all old ones, so we need to get up to date." Then he smiled. "Maybe Cynthia has a TV in her room. Nip in there and find out, or have you already done that?"

"Crap, no. Don't even breath it. Though what about whoever wakes you up?"

"She's nice but definitely hands off. A quiet lass with a lovely smile but I reckon you got the firecracker." Menzies looked at Harry and grinned. "We could requisition a TV from somewhere? A little portable and give it to the staff?" He laughed. "You could maybe get into her room after all."

That reminded Harry of a question over the wakeups. "Hey, Menzies, how come you pair are missing when I get woken up?" Harry grinned. "Well I know Maynard is on shift, but you're always gone as well. I don't mind but it's bloody tempting when that lass turns up."

Menzies laughed. "There's nobody there when I get my call, so where are you?" Harry was trying to think why he was never in there. Not for Menzies because Harry was on duty, but not when Maynard was woken up either. Menzies laughed again. "I wondered so took note, and there's always some sort of query. From the kitchen staff and it's never serious. Just enough to get me out of the room or occupied for about ten minutes."

"So Cynthia, er, the staff are making sure they get us alone?" Harry frowned. "That's risky."

"They don't care, apparently. I daren't make a move but you're right about tempting because the same bright smile wakes me up every time. Though mine isn't more than a smile. I reckon I'd be lucky to get a kiss if we did find a quiet spot." Menzies grinned. "You've got a smile as well from what you said. Cynthia?"

"It might just be because they're on duty at the right time?" Harry laughed. "But it isn't, is it? Christ, now I really do want some leave and someplace to take Cynthia dancing."

"Me too. Since we get diverted Maynard must be getting the same treatment." They both laughed because Maynard was known for being shy. Trying to talk to a woman while in bed he'd be dumbstruck. Harry was now curious enough to try and find out how interested Cyn actually was.

*   *   *

"Good morning Harry Corporal Miller." After a week that was the usual style of address from Cynthia, ever since Harry tried to explain his rank and name. That and a wicked smile. Harry woke up slowly as usual, then smiled.

"Just hang on a sec while I sit up. Don't peek, will you? In case this blanket slips." Harry started to sit up and got his partial answer. Cynthia didn't look away. Instead she watched with a little smile and the tip of her tongue peeked out. Then she pouted.

"Spoilsport. You never let it slip at all." Cynthia put down the coffee and then slowly looked over the exposed parts. She sniggered. "Though now I know you don't wear a shirt, so I'm really curious."

"It's a good job I'm not as curious. Your roommates might not be happy if a soldier charged in there every morning." Harry did wonder if he could organise a diversion for her roommates sometime.

"They might not be there if they knew you were coming." Cynthia let her tongue come out just enough to wet the middle of her lips.

"Yes curious that, there's never anyone here when you arrive."

Cynthia sighed dramatically which tightened her blouse front in a really attractive way. "But still you never take advantage. It makes me wonder what a girl has to do to get noticed."

Harry laughed, he couldn't help himself. "God almighty Cyn, everyone in the hotel notices you." That was true. The young woman was happy to indulge in a little light banter with most of the squaddies. Those who got a bit crude were simply ignored, not just the comment, but permanently.

"Mmm. But there's noticing, and there's doing something about it."

"What, like barging into your room?"

"You might get a bit of a shock if I sat up." Cynthia smiled again, "You might lose control."

"Well you don't seem to have that problem." Harry grinned at her. There was definitely something between them, now if only he could get some leave. "If I ever get some leave, I'm going to take you dancing, and then find out how much control you have. Maybe find out how much Cyn there is in Cynthia."

Cynthia's eyes lit up. The young woman stepped in close and bent over the bed. Her lips met Harry's, very firmly, and her hand ran down his chest although it stopped short of the covers. Then she stepped back fast enough to avoid Harry's arm. Instead of capturing her, his hand ran down her back and round her thigh. "There. Now you you've got a hint. So when do you get leave?"

"Damnation, I wish I knew. Not soon enough after that." Harry took a grip of the covers. "In fact I'm half tempted to risk a visit from Sarge. More than half tempted."

Cynthia giggled and headed for the door. "I wouldn't want poor Sarge to have a heart attack. Drink your coffee, it'll get cold."

Harry's brain kicked in. "Wait a minute. Have you lot got a TV or a radio?"

"Just a little radio. One of those you say is an officer came and took the manager's TV. Why?"

"It's just that we're a bit behind on the news. So if a portable TV turned up, maybe in your room or someplace?" Harry grinned.

"Ooh, I wish. Cullen would insist it went in the manager's flat, in the lounge. I daren't take you in there, on the settee." The wicked grin was back. "All those soft furnishings, I wouldn't want to shock the rest."

"We could sit and hold hands?"

"Boring, but you're on." A bright smile and then she was gone.

Harry didn't drink his coffee until it was luke warm because he was sat there thinking about those hot lips and Cyn's hand. Damn. He'd been out in Kuwait too long. Then Harry rushed his shave and shower and made it downstairs on time. He spent the rest of the day very aware of every time Cynthia was nearby. Twice he caught her watching with the tip of her tongue peeking out.

*   *   *

Three nights later Harry sat and held Cynthia's hand while the other off-duty staff sniggered. They thought it was hilarious that he sat and watched the news, but once it started they were all riveted, and really worried.

Harry looked around the room. "Don't mention this lot to the other soldiers, all right? Then it will get to the officers, and you'll lose your TV again."

Cullen was worried. "Will this get us into trouble? The telly?"

Harry smiled. "You haven't been told you can't have a TV, and we haven't been told not to watch it, officially. Just as long as everyone keeps quiet?"

"What about Santos? Corporal Menzies?" The quiet girl with tanned skin and a Spanish accent ducked her head when Harry looked her way.

"I'll tell him." Harry smiled. "He might want to watch the morning news." There were a few sniggers but the girl didn't reply.

Though Menzies did go to watch the morning news once he knew.

*   *   *

The news was truncated and definitely being censored, but still confirmed that the world was in a bad state and getting worse. Harry and Menzies talked to the staff while watching their separate servings of daily news and collected the background as well. Harry at least really did hold hands while watching.

Harry was always walked back to his door by Cynthia, which she thought funny because the boy was supposed to walk the girl home. The goodbye kiss at the door was getting a lot more friendly though, and Harry was glad that his room was up here away from the main rooms. There weren't so many soldiers were wandering about here though the pair had to break off sharpish a couple of times.

*   *   *

"It's a real mess. Nukes?" Menzies had been catching up as well.

"The ones on the Israeli border were maybe dirty bombs, not proper nukes. Enough to make the country uninhabitable though." Harry was shaken by that. Poisoning the land with radioactivity just so your enemy can't live there was a whole step beyond scorched earth tactics.

"Got it wrong though, the stupid bastards. A shift of wind and now Gaza glows in the dark as well. D'you reckon the Iranians really gave Hamas or whoever the materials?" Menzies looked at another paper. "This one reckons the Pakistanis sold some."

"The Israelis thought it was Iran, and they certainly lashed out before leaving. Iran is back in the stone age, and will be lucky to find anywhere to live that isn't radioactive. Maybe they'll have the same problem as the Israelis." Harry paused. "Crap, that was deliberate then. Eye for an eye is definitely Old Testament and the Israelis go for that. Egypt isn't much better so maybe the Israelis thought the Egyptians did it. Though the Egyptians haven't got nukes, have they?"

"There's no proof it was Israelis who put a nuke in the Aswan dam. Though the radioactive flood pretty much wiped out Egypt as a viable nation for a thousand years or whatever. All the fertile land along the Nile is poisoned, and every town along the route flooded with radioactive water." Menzies hit the bed with his fist. "I know they were pissed, and could understand them blowing the locks on the Suez Canal, but not that, not the dam."

"It might not be them, the Israelis. It might be whoever dropped a nuke on Mecca and both that and the dam happened after the Israelis had evacuated." Harry frowned. "Those who could evacuate before the lunatics ran over them. Mecca could be the Indians since they were truly wound up when the Pakistanis started. Maybe they decided to thin out all the Moslems, not just their neighbours."

Harry looked at the notes he'd jotted to help him remember. "You mean the limited nuclear exchange? Whatever idiot coined that has never been in one. Though India and Pakistan have still got enough soldiers to plough Kashmir into mud."

"Did you get anything on China? Russia's supposed to have come apart with Army groups declaring independence and trying to grab oil reserves or military bases." Menzies had notes as well. There had been a lot of catching up to do.

"Not much on China. Just the rumour that all the satellites and mobile phones going down was them, launching ball bearings into orbit of all things. To stop their own people talking to each other. Then unconfirmed reports of Army units rebelling." Harry grimaced. "As long as them and the Russkies don't decide they like the sound of limited nuclear."

"They wouldn't have the fuel to take advantage." Menzies rolled his eyes upward. "Please Lord I hope not. There sure isn't much fuel here at home. D'you reckon the cities here are as bad as they say?"

"We've seen London. I've finally got a letter from my sister, Sharyn, and she's worried about shortages and riots. The bloody phones don't work to actually talk to her." Harry was really worried about that. He really didn't want Sharyn and the kids caught up in something like this lot. "The bloody letter had those black lines in it so she told me something I'm not supposed to know. It's England, for Christ's sake."

"Not just you. Now some mail has come through a lot of the men are complaining about bits being censored. I know we're Army, but there's also free speech." Menzies glowered at the floor. "My parents are moving out of Sheffield. They're heading into the countryside. To someplace in Lincolnshire called Market Rasen where nothing ever happens according to them."

"I'll tell sis to do the same if it gets worse. If the bloody Army don't cross it out." Harry wondered about that. Since he was back in England, he should have been able to stick a letter in a post box. Not anymore. The Post Office had stopped collections and deliveries which it never did, not even in wartime.

Catching up and the news each day gave them food for thought. Though a lot of the news was enough to give them indigestion. Cynthia was definitely a distraction, a really welcome and pleasant one.

Chapter 3: Riots and a Broom Cupboard

The nightly riots dealt with keeping Harry distracted from the state of the country. There wasn't time to think of much else in the next week except the constant barrage of bricks and lumps of timber. That was bad enough, but the constant threat of gunfire was causing a trickle of really serious injuries or deaths.

A sergeant stopped on the way past. "We've got gunfire again. Next street this time." Harry's squad were having a drink as there was a break in the assault.

Harry looked around but everything was fairly quiet. "The snipers will sort that. As long as nobody here gets brave while they're gone." Tonight the first two rioters throwing petrol bombs had gone down hard. The Army shooters were supposed to wound petrol bombers if possible. Too many nights under attack and too many squaddies burned or crippled or killed had lowered definitions of what was possible. "The bloody bricks are bad enough."

The sergeant moved on but another voice rang out. "Right, Miller, get your lot back in line. If you've got the breath to natter, you're rested." The squaddies rolled their eyes and got up, quickly draining the bottles of water.

"Right Sarge. Where?"

"Relieve Menzies. Someone tossed a lump of concrete with reinforcing bars sticking out and two of his lot need patching. Watch out for whoever it is." A snarl entered Sarge's voice. "If you see him shout out, and we'll snatch the bastard."

Harry winced. That meant a squad charging into the crowd, using long batons to force a path to the target. Then the bloke would be hammered into submission and brought back to, presumably, prison. "Right Sarge."

Menzies even had a description of the bastard, sort of. "Big bloke with a black balaclava."

"That's easy then." Harry looked at the sea of rioters, and every third one had a black balaclava or something close.

"Sorry, but if you see a big bloke and he's got a black shirt as well, jump forward and smack him sharpish. He chucked that from about three rows back." Menzies gestured to the chunk of concrete and Harry winced at the lengths of steel jutting from the block. Then the squad was changing places with Menzies and his men, and there wasn't time to think.

Right up until a sharp scream and Harry turned to see Pinter go down and roll on the street holding his face. The chunk of concrete studded in spikes told the story. Harry's eyes moved across the crowd and he saw the retreating back topped by a balaclava. The world went a bit fuzzy around the sharp focus on that retreating head. "Willis, with me," and Harry was moving. He closed the short distance to the nearest rioter and kneed him, then threw him to one side.

Someone at the side snatched at his arm and Harry whacked whoever someplace in the head with the rifle butt. He didn't look where, just kept moving. The next rioter flinched as he was suddenly faced by six feet of rapidly advancing soldier and Harry body-checked him backwards. The soldier then shouldered the woman next to the rioter the other way and went into the gap, angling across towards his target. Sarge was shouting but Harry couldn't hear what was said so he kept going.

A slash sideways with the bayonet and the man raising a lump of timber as a club screamed and dropped it, blood spurting from his forearms. The man stumbled back and went down and Harry trampled over him, keeping his eyes on that balaclava. Harry was now three rows deep and the next rioters were totally shocked to see a soldier.

He punched one in the face then slapped the woman who tried to grab his rifle. Something rang off his helmet and a hand grabbed his arm. Harry gave whoever it was his arm, elbow first as hard as possible, and grabbed his rifle two-handed again as the grip slackened.

Another hand took hold, then let go as quickly as Harry bulled forward, hitting the man hard in the chest with his rifle butt. Harry had nearly caught up with the bastard and the man must have heard something, because he turned. The eyes behind the balaclava flared in shock and his hands went up to defend himself. Before Harry could get through the gap and drop the bastard, two men hit. One grabbed at the rifle and another struck at Harry with a cricket stump. Luckily on the shoulder though it hurt like hell.

Harry butted the one going for his rifle and his helmet smashed the rioter's nose, judging by the spray of blood. The man reeled back and Harry wheeled, bringing his knee across. It wasn't perfect but the man with the cricket stump doubled over a bit and went backwards. Harry glanced up and the big man in the balaclava was backing away. This balaclava had a mouth hole and Harry saw the smile as the gap between him and that smile widened. A man and woman surged into the gap to confront Harry.

Harry snatched the cricket stump from the winded man and turned sideways. One foot went forward and the cricket stump went out, one end on his hand. With the turn and lunge as well, suddenly Harry could reach over three feet further, plus the length of the stump. Right between the two blocking his path.

The stump's blunt point struck beneath the bastard's smile. Far enough beneath to hit his Adam's apple and the whole of Harry's weight was behind the thrust. It crossed Harry's mind that his tutor would have been pleased and then he dropped the stump and pulled back. Hands grabbed at him and Harry swung and kicked.

Harry thought they'd got him as more hands struck or grabbed hold. He lashed out and at least one got the point of the bayonet instead of slashes. He butted a woman, and used his knees and elbows but the crowd was squeezing in. Then the pressure eased and the savage faces around him changed expression. They were suddenly frightened and trying to back off, and then some were reeling away and falling. "Lose your way, Miller?"

"Sorry, Sarge." Squaddies were pushing past in a tight group.

"Have you finished, or were you enjoying the view?"

"All done Sarge." The squad started to retreat and nobody pushed them. This was the snatch squad with decent riot armour and shields and real batons. Long ones that would break limbs if applied ruthlessly. These soldiers were always ruthless after arriving too late for some of their comrades.

"Sorry Harry. I couldn't keep up." Willis had a black eye coming up and was having a bleeding hand tended to so it wasn't for lack of trying.

"It's OK. I lost it a bit."

"Miller, a word." Harry stepped to the side with Sarge, who gave him a once-over. "Bleeding marvellous. Not a scratch." Harry could have argued because he could feel where he'd have some lovely bruises. "Did you get him?"

"He won't be back."

"How come?" Sarge wasn't happy with that, but Harry was facing up what he'd just done. Anyone else could call hitting the man there a fluke, but Harry couldn't because that thrust was training. For a moment Harry had been back in that bloody hole in the sand, and he'd lashed out and killed a man.

"He won't be back, Sarge. I promise." Harry needed to go somewhere quiet and possibly be sick like the first time, but that wasn't going to happen. Not with Sarge lurking. "I could murder a pint." It was out without thought.

Sarge laughed. "Me too. If you weren't that Miller I'd push this, but I just saw how you got that bloody medal. Did you go apeshit then?"

Harry sighed. "Yeah, but I had bullets as well then."

Sarge gave a low whistle. "Remind me not to argue over my pay. Have a minute and a drink. Of water." Sarge moved off with a friendly nod. The first sign of civility Harry had seen from Sarge since they met on the plane.

"They were wrong. You don't go green or split your trousers. I'm supposed to see if you're OK." Menzies grinned. "We're having a quiet moment since some savage just trampled the poor citizens in front of us underfoot." His face sobered. "Did you get him, because Pinter's maybe going to lose that eye."

"I got him, but not official. Right?"

"That'll do. We'll sort a squad from our two, because Willis isn't great so we lost two each. Though Willis will be fine tomorrow, and so will at least one of mine." Menzies left a bottle of water and went. Harry followed him after a drink, but the rioters weren't pushing now. Within the hour they gave up and backed off.

Then it was time to load up bodies and send the badly wounded civvies, those not rescued by their friends, to the camp. The camp that had been set up outside London, allegedly. The wounded civvies would receive treatment in the camp, apparently, but even the worst of them travelled in a truck, not an ambulance.

Pinter went in the ambulance with the other badly wounded soldiers and an armed escort. The ambulance escort now had loaded rifles since several emergency vehicles had been ambushed by gangs looking for drugs. London was coming apart at the seams. The squaddies drank their tea and staggered off to bed.

*   *   *

"Good morning Harry Corporal Miller." Harry smiled before opening his eyes and started to sit up. He winced and paused. Cyn's eyes went wide. "What happened to you?" Cynthia moved closer, looking at the bruise on Harry's shoulder where the cricket stump had hit him much too hard.

"Careful." Harry grinned. "Though if I sit up and you see the rest, will you come even closer?"

Cyn was back on balance. "Sit up then. I'll try to resist." She sniggered. "I'm still wondering just what a soldier wears in bed." Harry sat up, carefully because a couple of those bruises were sore. Cyn's eyes went wide, then twinkled. "Are there any more?"

"I could show you, but not until I'm on leave. They'll probably have faded by then but you can see my scars?" Harry picked up the coffee. "This smells lovely."

"What do you put on them. The bruises?" Cynthia was serious.

"Nothing. We're rough, tough soldiers and the Sarge would have hysterics if we even complained about them." Harry was grinning as he said it but Cynthia's eyes narrowed.

"Oh well, it'll have to be the old fashioned remedy then." Harry had a hot cup of coffee in the hand towards Cynthia or he really couldn't have resisted catching her. She stepped in, ducked her head, and kissed the bruises on his shoulder. A real Cyn smile blossomed and her lips quickly met Harry's before she stepped back. "Does that feel better?"

"It makes me consider getting more bruises. Then waiting before picking up my coffee." Harry put the coffee down. "Do you want to kiss this one now?" That one was on his chest, just below the kissed ones.

"Just the one." Cynthia stepped in again and bent to kiss it, and Harry's arm closed round her.

"Gotcha."

"Oh dear, help. What can I do? Scream, scream." Cyn was smiling happily and not attempting to escape, and Harry really was tempted.

"If I wasn't due on duty, I might take a chance on Sarge right now." Cynthia brought her head down and forward as Harry hugged a little bit. This time her kiss was hot, and definitely full of promise, and went on much too long for Harry's peace of mind.

Cyn was smiling as they both broke for breath. She sniggered. "If you do that again another morning, I might jam a chair under the door handle and not take no for an answer." The next kiss was shorter but just as full of promise. "It's been much too long since I was kissed like that by a big strapping bloke." She pulled a face. "Much too long since I was kissed properly at all."

"Really?" Harry had to let go soon, because Cyn really felt lovely inside his arm like this. "Are the blokes round here blind or stupid?"

"Ugly, dirty and usually belong to a gang so they don't believe in asking if you get in range." Cynthia shrugged. "The decent ones on the estates leave or keep well out of sight." She looked Harry over. "Maybe into the Army?"

She pulled away a bit and Harry let her go. "Marvellous. I find a bloke I don't want to get away from, and he lets me go." Cynthia pouted. "Get some leave soon, Harry Corporal Miller."

"I wish. I really wish."

That apparently deserved another very short kiss and then Cynthia was at the door. "I'd better go, or you won't have time to find your undies."

Harry looked at the clock as the door closed and swore to himself, then smiled. That had been worth a bit of rushing about. Then he started rushing.

* * *

The following morning the kiss arrived before the "Good morning Harry Corporal Miller."

"I could recommend that sort of an alarm clock." Harry opened his eyes as Cynthia broke lip contact.

"That was happy Valentine's Day, except I have to hurry this morning" Cynthia sat on the edge of the bed. "But first." She pulled the cover down a bit and leaned over, kissing each bruise. "Sometime I really want to see the rest."

Harry had both arms round her by the time their lips met and both were breathing heavily by the time they stopped for breath. "This really is dangerous, Cyn. Definitely Cyn when you kiss like that."

"Whenever we can find the time and place we'll find out, Harry Corporal Miller." A quick kiss and Cynthia was on her way. She had to hurry "because someone mentioned how long I took yesterday."

* * *

More riots followed but a week later some of the sheer rage had gone out of the crowd. This time the crowd broke early which meant Harry got some decent sleep. The knock on the door was a shock. So was another voice in the room. Menzies? What had happened to early morning coffee?

The door opened even as Menzies finished his mumbled complaint. Sarge stepped into the room and looked at Harry. "Get up and dressed, sharpish. How easily do you go apeshit?"

"Takes a bit of doing." Harry knew it sounded defensive but he didn't like that side of him. It had never happened before he joined the Army, but twice since. While he was thinking that Harry was already pulling on his clothes.

"How about a mate getting beaten up and maybe a girl getting a bad time?" Sarge was dead serious. "I can't make this official because if what I hear is right, the girl shouldn't be here."

"Cyn?" It was out before Harry's mouth got organised.

"Probably sin, but voluntary with your mate Maynard. Now a big nasty bastard says she's on the game and he wants some. He can't get to you or hasn't got the balls." Sarge gave a little smile. "Some of us have reassessed you."

"Shit, Suggs."

"Corporal Arsehole Young seems to have forgotten he is in the British Army. I can do this officially, but then I have to look closely at who the staff are and I'm guessing it's a bad idea." Sarge still had his little smile. "You'd better hurry."

Menzies butted in. "Go on, Harry. I'll explain the staff and follow." Harry started for the door.

"Where is he?"

"Car park because your friend is taking a non-smoking fag break, if you get my drift. There was mention of carving up so you might want to take something, but I'd rather you didn't kill him. Not too bloody either or the questions will be persistent." Sarge had a question in his eyes but Harry wasn't sure what it was.

Carving, so a knife or bayonet. Harry smiled though it probably wasn't pretty. "Will my poncy stick do?"

"It will be perfect." Sarge eyed the big brass end. "No blood at all. Right, you have some news for me, Menzies?" Harry got out of the room while Menzies was still working out how to explain the staff arrangements. Harry ran down the stairs and into the kitchen.

"Where's Maynard, or Marcie?" There was a lot of hesitation and a couple of glances at the back door. "Shit." Harry opened the door and stepped out.

He stopped two steps outside as the door shut and let his eyes adjust. There was some light from the windows at the back of the hotel, but the car park was gloomy. There were a lot of deep shadows around the outbuildings and waste skips and as his eyes adjusted Harry caught movement. "Maynard? Or is that you, Suggs?"

"That's a shame because now I'll have to wait for my freebie. Unless you just want a share of the whore?" Suggs gave a little laugh as he stepped out from the shadow by the waste bin. "She's been persuaded to give free samples so I've put my name down for the first." Suggs had an arm around Marcie and a bayonet in the other hand.

Harry looked at Marcie, but she appeared unharmed though definitely frightened. "Where's Maynard?"

Macie started to answer but the bayonet came round in front of her face. "I told you, your mouth isn't for making a noise, right?" Suggs looked at Harry. "Maynard will be keeping out of this, so it's you and me."

"So let her go."

Suggs made a point of looking Harry over. "Just that poncy stick, as Sarge calls it? The medal won't help you now, pay puke, and you've forgotten your rifle. Step clear of the door and I'll consider it."

Harry took four steps, covering half the distance between them. "So let her go." Harry was starting to get that edge but he wasn't going to lose it this time. He didn't need to, not for one asshole with a knife. Stones and the training had seen to that.

Suggs considered for a moment, then threw Marcie back behind him, into the shadows. "You try to come past me, whore, and I'll cut you. You just stay there until I come back." Then he smiled at Harry. "According to the rumours you don't like this riot control shit. So you are going to desert tonight, puke. I'm sure anyone with a brain will get the message, but nobody official will."

"Oh dear, help, I'm going to be bored to death." Harry grinned at the other man's expression. Suggs really didn't like Harry taking the piss.

Suggs's shock turned to anger. "You shout for help and I'll carve the whore real good. You keep quiet and I'll just get my dick licked and keep her for the future. I'm sure a straight type like you will go for that."

"I wasn't going to shout, Suggs." Harry took another step and put his stick up to rest over one shoulder. "As long as you don't cry when I spank you." He might not like killing, but Harry had been on the town with Stones and other squaddies enough times to know how this was done. Annoy the other prat, then crack him good and hard when he loses it a bit. The trouble was this one had a bayonet, a seven inch bladed knife, so Harry had to hit him good and hard first time.

Suggs moved forward and crouched a bit, and Harry took a long step. He swung the stick over and down and Suggs moved his head back beyond reach. So Harry bent forward and twisted his waist so his shoulder went forward. The end of the stick poked Suggs hard in the eye because Harry had kept going, taking another step. Then he swept the stick down to the side and knocked Sugg's knife hand wide. The next step wasn't one because Harry used the leg swing to kick Suggs hard on the shin with his Army boot. Easier than getting at his nuts but Suggs's open eye went wide with shock and pain.

A good crack on the shin always got someone's attention, this time long enough for Harry to turn a bit. One more step and he shoulder charged

Suggs in the chest. That put Harry with his right arm conveniently poised to grab Suggs's knife arm, and bring the stick in his left up and down smartly. "Oops," Harry murmured, "might have broken that." The crack as the stick hit the base of Suggs's thumb certainly released the bayonet. Harry stepped clear and kicked the bayonet towards the hotel door.

He faced Suggs, who was trying to decide between putting his left hand to his eye, using it to cradle his broken right hand, or hopping because his leg was on fire. "Enough yet, Suggs?"

"He might have, but we haven't." That wasn't Suggs! Another squaddie stepped out, holding Marcie, and from near the outbuildings came another with a bayonet to Maynard's throat. A rag was tied round Maynard's mouth. The man with Marcie curled a lip at Suggs. "Fucked that up pretty good, didn't you? Now we've got to kill these two to be sure of getting him. Fucking hard man?" He spat.

Harry put his right hand on the stick just below the boss, and the left slid down just below the fancy trim. Harry tensed. He could probably kill these three if he went a bit apeshit, lost it, and remembered his lessons. But it would have to be kill to get them all, and Maynard might die, and Marcie. "Trade you Suggs's knife back for you letting that pair go? A private and a young lass against a corporal and two privates, who will a court martial believe?"

"Nice try but no. Though if you toss away the stick and kneel, I'll let the girl go when we've done. Nobody will believe a whore."

"I've got another suggestion." Two figures came from the shadows to the side and Harry recognised Sarge and Menzies. They'd come round the side of the hotel and Sarge couldn't have waited for much explanation. Harry smiled a little because Sarge had a bayonet as well and it looked very comfortable in his hand.

"How about Suggs goes up for pulling a knife on an unarmed soldier. Bayonet against a poncy stick." Sarge grinned. "The fact Suggs got the crap kicked out of him won't count. We're under Martial Law so I reckon I can get you shot, Corporal Arsehole Young."

Sarge swung his eyes to the other two. "If you stupid pricks wave those blades this way, you've threatened a sergeant in front of witnesses. I can maybe get you shot as well if you push it." His face hardened. "Now drop the fucking things!"

Both bayonets hit the floor. Suggs was staring wide-eyed and even in the dim light Harry could see how pale he was. His eyes darted about, looking for a way out. "No Suggs, or I'll let Corporal Miller hit you again. I want to see what he does next." Suggs settled for looking from Sarge to Harry and back again. He'd decided to cradle his hand, and one eye was swelling up nicely.

As he was released Maynard stepped away and then turned and swung, a total haymaker. Telegraphed and a big wide swing, gathering speed all the way, and the man should have easily ducked it. Unfortunately he was looking at Sarge and simply didn't realise until much too late. The soldier went over backwards with a short yell and then rolled about with both hands to his face. Maynard gave a short exclamation as well and doubled over, clutching his hand.

"You two stay where you are." Sarge glared at Suggs and Private Forbes, who had released Marcie. "Let me see that, Maynard." The private made for Sarge still nursing his hand, with his face twisted in pain. He yelped as Sarge inspected it while Marcie more or less danced around behind him, wanting to help or something.

"You are an idiot, Maynard. If you're going to protect the honour of young ladies you should take some lessons. Don't hit people in the head with your fist or you'll break things. Take a tip from Harry, use a poncy stick." Sarge seemed to be enjoying that bit, which was a bit odd since the poncy stick thing was his own doing. "Get that seen to. I think there's a nurse waiting if you turn round."

There was, Marcie darted in and the first part of nursing was a kiss that might have anaesthetised Maynard's brain. Then she carefully cradled his hand and stroked it. Harry smiled and Sarge caught it. "Before we discuss that sort of nursing, let's deal with these three." The Sarge's smile wasn't understanding at all.

"You three have been a wart on the Army's backside for a while, but a careful wart so I never caught you. Now listen up because there's two choices. One is that I have Corporal Young shot or he goes into the glass-house for a long, long time. You pair will join him for a lot of it as accessories, kidnappers, and general arseholes. Understand?" There were two sullen nods though the one now sitting up still had his face in his hands and might not really be listening.

"The other alternative is that you all volunteer for the Border Protection Detail, stopping the bloody refugees from storming the port of Calais and stealing the ferries. Before you do that you will sit down at breakfast so everyone can see the state of you pair. Just so everyone realises why you want to run away, and that they should all remember their manners." Everyone was staring at Sarge now because that was letting them off!

"There is a proviso of course. If I hear the slightest hint, the very breath of a hint that the staff here are not all kitchen staff, we go to option one. I for one have got used to happy smiles and decent grub, and will be truly pissed off if it stops. Do you understand, Young?"

"Yes Sarge."

"Forbes?"

"Yes Sarge."

"Gallaher?"

"Mmph Pharw." The third man's head nodded since his smashed lips weren't working too well yet.

"Piss off and get cleaned up. You can buy new bayonets when you arrive with your new unit because you lost these. You can also be walking wounded with them instead of cluttering this place up." The three left, Gallaher still holding his face and Suggs limping and nursing his hand. Harry, Menzies and Maynard were looking the question at Sarge.

"No, I've not gone soft. We've been asked to send our troublemakers to Calais. The new unit really will stop refugees, but with just a shield and baton since it's technically France. For that reason, even when the refugees chuck petrol bombs and bricks and try to stick them with knives, nobody can shoot. The bullet would go into an allied country so it's not allowed." Sarge had a wide smile. "They'll look like that most of the time and will be expected to stand to even with black eyes and broken teeth."

He sobered. "Even so, I might not have let them off even with that, but for the effect on morale. Since now I know just how many bloody staff we'd lose." Harry got a glare for that. Then Sarge glared at Maynard. "How did they know you'd be here?"

"Er, well."

"I asked him." Marcie had her head down. "Maynard has been very nice so I wanted to say thank you. Privately." Even in the low light her face had darkened with a blush. "For Valentine's Day, because he never tried, to, even though?" She shrugged.

"Really? Did you like thank you, Maynard? Exactly how often did you go AWOL out here?" Sarge was unhappy now, and Maynard suddenly thought he knew why. What Sarge thought he'd been doing to Marcie.

"Just five minutes, maybe ten? Marcie asked me to look at something out here last night, and then she wanted to kiss me." Maynard was almost wriggling in embarrassment. "She, well, then I wanted to kiss her again tonight." Maynard looked at the others and then at Sarge. "Don't blame her. I won't kiss her again?" Harry didn't think that was going to be down to Maynard or Sarge either.

Sarge's smile was certainly a lot happier. "Just don't let it interfere with your duty. Light duty supervising the kitchen but you don't get sick leave. I don't believe I'm saying this but next time you need a kiss find somewhere private inside. The bloody broom cupboard or something. Somewhere nobody will see you. Right?" Two heads nodded rapidly. "Now go and get your hand looked at, Maynard. Find a broom cupboard for ten minutes first so Suggs and his mate aren't with the medic."

The remaining three men watched them go, two heads together with Marcie's arm round the soldier. "Christ Almighty. Innocence and a hooker with a soft heart, fair makes me weep. Is he a virgin?"

Harry stared. "What? Christ Sarge, how would we know?" Though most of the men thought yes.

"If they find a big enough cupboard I don't reckon it'll be in question any more. Pick up the bayonets will you, Menzies."

"Oh, right Sarge." The change of subject caught him out but then Menzies put away his own bayonet and set off across the car park.

"Can I test the weight of that poncy stick, Miller?"

Harry sighed. "Yes Sarge." He handed it over.

Sarge weighed it in his hand, then tapped it with his bayonet before putting the blade in its sheath. "I thought it did too much damage for the force you seemed to use. The damn thing is way too heavy but it explains a broken hand. What's it made of?"

"Steel tube."

Sarge looked closely at the wood grain effect along the length. "Good work that. I wouldn't want to arm wrestle after seeing you handle it, but then I saw you throwing people about when you went after the concrete thrower." Sarge had his little smile back. "Though I didn't see you do what I thought you might. Or rather I think I did but in his eye. Someone was puzzled by Mr Balaclava's body. So was I when they told me he'd been found." Sarge's little smile broadened. "I'd asked them to look out for him since you were so sure he wouldn't be a problem."

"Body, Sarge?"

"Hah. Yes, body. What was it, he won't be back Sarge? Not likely since someone had stuck a cricket stump into his neck."

No I didn't, Harry thought. "Cricket stump?"

"Yeah, it was laid nearby and I reckon it was that or a poncy stick, maybe. Just a jab in the Adam's apple that left a round mark but it did the job. Barely broke the skin which was why the body squad was puzzled. I suppose if you'd jabbed Suggs like that instead of in the eye he would have ended up the same way?"

"No idea Sarge?"

"Fair enough. I still don't like the idea of you as a pay clerk, but you'll do, Miller. After all, if you'd been a sniper or in a proper unit instead of a pay unit, I'd have had to find another way to fix that bastard Young. Now piss off, and don't let me catch you coming out of a broom cupboard with a big smile."

"Right Sarge." Menzies arrived and handed over the bayonets and the pair of them scarpered back up to their room.

Neither of them could work out what had really happened, but it seemed they'd done Sarge a favour. Menzies was really curious, having seen some of the fight, so Harry promised the highlights if he could get some sleep first. Though he wanted an answer to one question. "Did your good morning mention Valentine's?"

Harold smiled. "Oh yes, and I really want some leave or a broom cupboard to follow that up. What about your bright smile?"

"Ah. Well, you know I said I wouldn't get a kiss? I don't think she's had a lot of practice but Valentine's seemed to be important, and sort of surprising in a very nice way." Menzies shook his head. "Bloody hell, I'm glad that fear of Sarge is keeping me honest because I was damn tempted to sort of, well as you said, follow up a bit."

"Broom cupboard?"

"Christ, no. Not this one. Holding hands and a few kisses will probably be as far as it goes until we leave." Menzies sighed. "Nita is really sweet and I wish we were staying longer."

"Me too."

*   *   *

Good morning went on a long time and Harry pulled her down on top the bed, even if she was outside the cover. Cynthia giggled. "Should I put the chair under the door handle Harry Corporal Miller?"

"If you wake me up like that again put the chair under first, because I'm not likely to let go." Harry meant that because after the tension of last night that kiss had really got to him. No, sod it, that kiss didn't need help from last night.

"You'll be late on duty?"

Harry grinned. "I might not care. Which will be a shame because apparently I'm to get you in a broom cupboard."

"Really?" The tip of Cynthia's tongue peeked. "I'll look for one that's big enough."

"Better knock first."

"Marcie? Oh God yes. She's sort of fascinated because Stevie treats her like she's made of china. Virgin china. She really wants to get into Stevie's pants but doesn't want to look easy." Cynthia giggled again. "We've all sworn not to tell him, you know, what she does. Did, because Marcie reckons she's coming off the game. She likes how Stevie treats her."

Cynthia became much more serious, "It was getting really bad out there before this, with the gangs getting worse than ever. The coppers don't even go onto the worst estates now. How long will the Army stay?" She hugged tightly and giggled. "I don't want to be left wondering."

"I don't know. Really. We were supposed to go back to barracks but never got there. I suppose if the riots die down we'll go." Harry sighed. "I don't fancy leaving you here if it's bad as that."

"That definitely means you're going to have to rush about this morning." Cynthia's lips descended. When she finally pulled her head back both of them were breathing heavily. "If you leave, I'm hiding in your rucksack."

"If you don't wriggle about, I won't tell."

That was worth a bit more rushing and then Cynthia, and Harry, really did have to hurry so that nobody asked awkward questions.

Though the curious soldiers when Harry was a bit late for breakfast were more interested in the trio sat in one corner. On had a big patch over one eye and his hand was strapped up, one was having a lot of trouble eating through swollen lips, and one just kept very quiet. None wanted to make eye contact with anyone else. Harry could feel the eyes of everyone else looking to see if he bore any signs of combat, and ignored the whole thing.

Though Harry had a quiet smile when the plates of breakfast landed in front of the three soldiers. Burned breakfast in a mixed heap in the middle of the plate. Harry reckoned it was probably scraped from other plates when they went back to the kitchen. Cynthia gave Harry a big smile on the way back. The trio left the food, and the dining room, and a lot of chatter broke out. Though nobody asked Harry anything. It was the last time any of the squaddies saw the trio in London.

*   *   *

After another ten days the riots eventually died away a little, though the troops didn't leave. Some men started to hope that the worst was over, and Cyn promised a broom cupboard soon in case the soldiers were leaving. Instead the sergeants came round in daylight with instructions for everyone to collect ammunition. Then the buses turned up but three this time with steel plates on the sides to supplement the heavy wire mesh on the windows.

"Where are we going, sergeant?" Sergeant Wilson grimaced.

"The police have a serious problem with criminals. Something over and above their firearms squad or maybe they're busy." Sarge looked round the bus. "Be really careful this time because we've been told this lot are armed, really armed. Forget being in England. Treat this as a raid on some nutter's compound in Kuwait or Iraq or Syria. Take no chances and shoot without hesitation."

"What is it, some gang headquarters or what?" Sarge glanced at the speaker.

"You should be so lucky. This is a council estate. Social housing and the chances are most of them have never left the place in years. It's their own little country where even the coppers don't go. Now we're going to invade. You'll get it all at the briefing but this is the highlights."

"Christ Sarge, will there be women?" Harry had spoken without thought because if it was an estate?

"Yes, Miller, and kids. Everyone be very, very careful what you shoot at. But remember if you identify a shooter it doesn't matter if she's someone's Grandma. Shoot her dead." Sarge looked around the bus. "Don't piss about or you'll kill one of your mates as sure as putting the gun to his head." Then he reached down and handed Harry a fat scope. "I know you'll be careful so you are covering us today." He held Harry's eyes. "Keep them alive, Harry."

A big pair of binoculars went to LC Tredwell. "You're a crap shooter, so spot for him. There'll be snipers with proper rifles and suchlike covering the operation, but I want a pair of eyes I trust over our lads. With our own personal cover."

Harry put the big scope on his rifle. "Tredwell?"

"Yeah, Corp?"

"Find me a big bit of concrete or such like, three or four hundred yards out with some distinctive marks on. Something where the bullet won't go through and kill someone watching telly."

"OK. Why?"

"So I can make sure this thing is working properly." Harry tapped the scope.

"It's the real thing this time, isn't it?" Tredwell sighed. "In England. That's never right."

*   *   *

This wasn't at all like Kuwait and not only because of the style of buildings. Light snow covered the ground and breath plumed as the men dived for cover again and again. The opposition was different as well, and not because of their clothing. These people had never fought troops or anyone with a lot of rifles. The defenders thought that blazing away with handguns from fifty to a hundred yards away would stop the soldiers.

They certainly didn't think of taking cover at a hundred yards away and were being shot down in droves. That didn't stop more of them picking up the weapons. That sort of fanatical lunacy was definitely like Kuwait. Unfortunately some had rifles, and they did know how to shoot. Though they still didn't understand taking cover properly.

"Got another one, Miller." Tredwell's voice had lost its earlier excitement. That had died as nine times he watched while men with guns died. Smashed down by bullets Tredwell had personally called down on them.

"Where?" Harry was numb. This was exactly what he didn't want to do, exactly what he'd tried so hard to avoid. But now he had got to know the soldiers ahead. The squaddies who were being shot at were personal friends. There were too many guns shooting from the buildings and the official backup snipers were being overwhelmed by the sheer number of targets. They were also trying to respond to targets called in by a lot of different units. So Harry squashed his reservations and pulled the trigger time after time.

"Tower block, the one with the big yellow graffiti. Four floors down, sixth window from the left. That's a rifle." Tredwell cursed. "It just fired so it really is a solid target. Oh shit."

"What?"

"Never mind. There's curtains so you'll have to shoot at where you think er, he is. The shooter." Tredwell sounded a bit flaky, but he'd gone that way after the third so Harry ignored it.

Harry moved his scope onto the window and there were flowered curtains billowing in the wind at the open section. Beneath them a long tube was aimed downwards. Harry carefully adjusted his sights as Tredwell gave him the range. Harry used a flag over one of the tower blocks to estimate the wind and it was still about the same. The curtains billowed and Harry caught his breath.

"Tredwell. It's, she's." Harry couldn't say it.

"She's a shooter Harry." Though Tredwell's voice was very quiet and not totally convinced. Harry pictured that face as the curtain obscured it. Not a Grandma, but old enough for a mother, maybe a few times.

The rifle spat flame again and the radio asked plaintively if someone could kill the bastard snipers please. Not sniper so not necessarily this one, but Harry hardened his heart. He followed the line of the rifle barrel up and settled. Then moved the point of aim just a little.

Harry couldn't guarantee a kill anyway, but this way increased the chances of just wounding. If he smashed her shoulder then she wouldn't be shooting again. Harry fired. The rifle in the window was snatched backwards suddenly and didn't reappear. That was a hit because the jerk was involuntary, not a reaction to a near miss.

"Hit. Probable but not confirmed." Tredwell didn't sound happy either.

Silence fell around them though the rattle of gunfire continued just ahead. Harry was only keeping about fifty yards back from the rest of his mob because this wasn't a specialist weapon. It wasn't that accurate if the range lengthened too far. Then more complaints on the radio led to Tredwell finding another target and the bearded face in the scope was almost a relief. More targets followed and then the Army were falling back. Mission accomplished though nobody was saying what that meant.

* * *

Harry couldn't sleep. He had, briefly, but tossed and turned. In the end he quietly put on his trousers and a tee-shirt because Menzies was fast off. Then he wandered downstairs and sat in the empty dining room, thinking. Nine men hadn't come back on the bus, though five of them were expected to return eventually. There was still no talk of when everyone would be split up to find their own units. There was no hint of when they'd go back to the barracks.

Harry went to the kitchen for a coffee. Marcie smiled and brought him one and a doughnut. "Why are you up?" She grinned. "Cyn will be disappointed if you aren't there for wakeup." So would Harry, he was having to hurry with his shower about one morning in three and was seriously considering looking for broom cupboards. The stunned look and big smile that Maynard had two mornings ago hinted that one was available.

"I'll be disappointed if I'm not there." He sighed. "I can't sleep. It was a bad day." Harry gave her a small smile. "I keep seeing people who are now dead.

I need to think of something else and it's hard." Marcie put a hand on his arm and went off, doing whatever. Harry took his coffee through to the dining room. It did cross his mind that coffee might not be a good idea, but caffeine wasn't the problem.

*　　*　　*

"Corporal Miller." Harry looked up at Marcie.

"Hi there, what is it?" He'd been here half an hour and was tired but still nowhere near sleep.

"There's someone wants to see whoever is on duty. Dav… Maynard is already busy so I thought maybe you would go. Maybe it will take your mind off other things?" The young woman looked anxious.

"Sure, no problem. Who is it and where?"

"Second floor, near the top of the stairs. There was no name, just a message." Harry thought about that but there was no reason for alarm. Not in the hotel itself in the middle of the night. The rooms weren't exactly soundproof so one yell would rouse the lot. Why was he thinking like this? Because he was tired and kept seeing dead people.

Then Harry turned the last corner and could see who was at the top of the last short flight of stairs. "Cyn?"

Her eyes sparkled. "I was told you needed something to catch your attention." She was dressed in a raincoat which was odd. "Do you really want to dance with me, and find out about how much of Cynthia is Cyn?"

"Christ yes, but I can't leave the hotel."

Cynthia took his hand. "Come with me, Harry Corporal Miller." Harry took her hand and followed. Those faces in his head were already fading a bit. He wondered if Cynthia was taking him to her room, but that was on the third floor.

Cynthia stopped in front of a blank door and took a key out of her pocket. Then she put it in the lock. "This is the broom cupboard. It took a while to get it ready." She giggled as the door unlocked and pulled the key out.

"Shouldn't we have knocked?"

"If the key goes in, nobody is inside." They stepped inside and Harry had a brief glimpse of a single mattress with a thin strip of floor alongside. Then everything went black as the door closed and the key rattled again. "There, now we're private." Harry captured the figure moving past and pulled her close, to be rewarded by a fierce kiss. "Just a few moments, Harry Corporal Miller."

"Harry. Just Harry in here." Harry let her pull through his hands, but reluctantly. Bloody hell, he'd actually had a couple of interesting dreams about Cyn but not in a real broom cupboard. "Where are the brooms?"

"Stationery cupboard because it had to be big enough for the bed, but we renamed it because Sarge was so certain." There was a giggle in her voice and some rustling, and then a dim light appeared. "Just a moment." Cyn pulled out something from under her coat and then a sheet was spread on the mattress. "I'll collect it later for the laundry."

Cyn's voice was a bit breathless and Harry felt the same way. There was no tease here, because Cyn had just locked them in and put a sheet on a bed. She was definitely Cyn not Cynthia right now.

"Just the music, then we can dance." Harry was just wondering how to get away with someone hearing that, and if she was wearing a dancing dress under there, when the music started. "Let's Marvin Gaye and Get It On" whispered quietly in the small room. Cyn turned with a big smile and slipped off the coat.

"Can I have this dance please sir?"

"Christ yes, but the dancing might not reach the end of the record." Cyn was dressed in a lace Teddy, and a big smile, and nothing else.

Cyn slipped into his arms and began to move to the music. "We can still dance even if we aren't stood up. Though I had hoped for one upright dance." She giggled and moved slowly against him. "Just so you don't think I'm too easy."

"After all the good mornings where you left me frustrated?" Harry's hands were already exploring the edges of the Teddy, and started on the flimsy garment itself. "In any case, I'm the easy one. If you'd used a chair the second morning?" He bent his head and Cyn tipped hers back.

The third time they broke lip contact to breath Cyn ran her hands down under the top of his trousers. "Considering what your hands are up to, I want to find out what's under here."

"I'm sort of interested in what's under this." Harry's hands went on another trip over the Teddy.

"You know what's under it." Harry moved back just enough for Cyn's hands to get to work on unfastening his trousers and they slid down. "Oh. Not a commando then?"

"No, and even though I know what's under this, I'm still interested." Harry's hands came round the front to show just how interested, and pull at the little bows.

"Not yet." Cyn wriggled as Harry got a hand inside. "Or not all of it. Not with your shirt on." Harry released her to help strip off his Tee-shirt. Then he pulled the straps off Cyn's shoulder and the Teddy came down to her waist. Cyn put her arms round him and cuddled up close. "Oh God yes. Now this is a real dance."

It was and somehow they both got to the end of it still on their feet. The track changed. "Can we sit this one out?"

Cyn giggled and sat on the mattress, pulling Harry down beside her. "I got my dance. The standing one."

Donna Summer began to sing "Love to Love You Baby."

"Now that's what I call mood music." Harry pulled at the last bows on the Teddy, then paused. "Oh, damn. I haven't, er, got, um." Because he hadn't got a bloody condom with him.

Cyn laughed and rolled away from Harry, reaching towards the light and the little MP3 player. "But we have an um, the rubber ones? We raided the machine in the toilets." Harry looked at the curvy ass now pointed at him and began to strip the Teddy off it. Cyn giggled again and rolled back over, bending her legs one at a time to help him get the bit of lace off. She waved a foil square between finger and thumb. "My turn." Then she reached for Harry's boxers.

*   *   *

"Good morning Harry Corporal Miller." Cyn kissed Harry long and soft, and cuddled in with a happy sigh.

"Not morning yet, and it's Harry in here." Harry gave a happy sigh as well. The Donna Summer track had been the album version and went on and on. "Je t'aime" followed, then one breathy track after another that had drifted through his head and mixed with their own heavy breathing and happy sounds.

"No. You'll always be Harry Corporal Miller to me." Cyn gave a little wriggle. "Though I still need to check what you wear in bed." The giggle was silent and felt wonderful.

"I might sleep walk and return the favour after this."

"Ooh, I wish you could." Cyn sighed. "But there are five of us in there, and the others would be jealous. Well two would because Marcie and Nita have a key as well." She sniggered. "Santos will be answering a mystery message in the next few days I think. Once Nita finally works up to it."

Cyn rolled partly over on top of Harry to look down at him with a serious face. "You must think we are sort of a bit loose." She kissed Harry gently. "Luring you in here and such." Cyn gave a little smile. "Marcie really is a loose woman I suppose, but not with freebies."

"Not really. Startled and really, really happy, but I didn't exactly drag my feet." Galloped happily towards her, Harry thought

"Ah, but you're a bloke." Cyn gave a little smile. "The thing is, the world is going to hell. You three are really nice blokes compared to the assholes where we live. Lived, because the place will be stripped bare by now." She gave Harry another little kiss. "We all decided that we wanted a really nice memory before you leave."

Cyn sighed. "Well actually Nita has gone a bit daft over Menzies. She's got it bad. Marcie wants a bloke who treats her really gently and is truly sweet on her. I want the memory of a clean, decent bloke who I genuinely fancy. Something to last us through the shit, because the government can't stop it now. Not until the oil is sorted and that might be too late." She put an arm right over and round Harry. "Hold me tight Harry Corporal Miller. Give me nice memories."

"I won't be forgetting this myself Cyn. Heh. A night of sin with Cyn." Harry chuckled.

"A whole night? Yes please. I'll work on it."

"Oh yes. Though I'll have to get back soon."

"No, not yet. The little electric alarm over there will tell us when, so you're there for your good morning. Now the idea of this was to help you sleep." Cyn kissed him gently. "So sleep, Harry Corporal Miller." Harry slept and there were no dead faces waiting for him in dreams.

*   *   *

Three days later Menzies walked past Harry, gave a big smile and said "Broom cupboard? Sarge would go crackers." Then carried on walking.

Though neither of them were smiling after watching the news the next day. "Maybe it was the CIA, since they finally got around to Venezuela?"

"Christ no. Surely they wouldn't do that? The morning news said that cloud was once the third biggest refinery on the planet, and the explosion had registered as an earthquake." Menzies looked grim. "The CIA might have done that I suppose, but not with the city next door. The fireball ate a third of it eventually. Not the CIA, for God's sake."

"If it was they left it too late. The USA is on fire from one end to the other. No, I reckon it was just whoever organised the first lot finishing the job." Harry thought a minute. "All right, not actually organised. Started, then stepped back and let the local nutcases finish the job. Hamas have been making sugar rockets for years and that's all it needs, apparently, to burn a refinery. Or to screw up the repairs."

"The glories of the internet. There'll be step by step instructions on there. I'm sorry for the Yanks and all that, but it leaves us really in the shit. No friendly tanker to fill up the national petrol tank now." Menzies looked at Harry. "I've got to get Nita out of here."

"I'll look into it, since I'm Sarge's blue-eyed boy at the moment."

Though everyone was much too busy for five nights as the news re-ignited the riots. This time mornings didn't bring relief and the riots continued well into daylight. The soldiers were dead on their feet by the time the streets quietened down again.

*   *   *

When the riots finally subsided the soldiers went back to raiding strongholds to help the police out. The first was a huge concrete tower block. Another six men didn't come back though three of them should recover in hospital. The little force was being slowly whittled away.

"Flash-bangs? They should have given us real grenades." Menzies came very close to spitting.

"It's to do with Human Rights. I asked Sarge. We are not allowed to use explosives inside civilian structures with innocents present." Harry tried to keep the disgust out of his voice.

"The bloody gangsters or whatever use explosives and petrol bombs!" Menzies threw his hands up. "Then we've got rifles when they're in our faces and can't get the bloody barrel round fast enough." Harry threw something onto Menzies's bed, and the corporal stared at it. "Where did that come from? We'll be in deep, deep shit if anyone sees that."

"We'll be in good company. Nearly all the corporals and sergeants will be carrying one if we collect enough." Harry threw two clips across to join the handgun. "Fifteen rounds a clip should give you breathing space. It's up to you to keep it in working order. The damn thing will need cleaning for starters." Harry gave a grim smile. "Luckily some of the assholes don't know that so their weapons keep jamming. Work fast. We've got two days if we're lucky, before the next one. So be ready."

"Christ, Harry. What's happening?"

"The world's going mad, Menzies." Harry sighed. "Worse than that, we can't stop it. If the Army decide to send us someplace else, we can't even save the girls."

"Christ Harry, we have to." Menzies looked stricken. "I can make her a dependent. Put in to marry her."

"Nita?"

"Yes. I'll see Sarge."

"It won't work. Apparently there's been a lot of it and the Army has put a block on it. No permissions to marry until the emergency is over." Harry had asked because Maynard was completely lovesick. He wanted to marry Marcie, and rescuing had nothing to do with it.

"But if she's a dependent? I'll get her pregnant if I have to." The last was a whisper.

"Won't help because Sarge gave me all the news. Fully, legally married and your wife gets married quarters. If you've already got a kid and the woman is registered as your next of kin, she gets married quarters. That's already got a kid, Menzies, not bun in the oven." Harry sighed. "We'll have to watch Maynard or he'll go AWOL."

Menzies muttered but Harry didn't catch it. "What?"

"I'm her first. Her first bloke. For fuck's sake Harry, there has to be something." Menzies had his head in his hands and couldn't see Harry's stunned face. Cyn had said Nita was working up to it and was daft about Menzies, but he hadn't thought that meant losing her virginity. Christ!

"Well you'd better bloody well stay alive then. Clean that damn thing and make sure you can use it." Menzies looked up, startled. "How do you think she'll feel if you end up in a body bag? Make some really nice memories for if that happens." Harry shrugged, a bit uncomfortable at the next bit. "That's what Cyn, Cynthia wants. Some good memories at least for when things get shitty."

"Christ. So you'll just walk away with thanks for the memory?" Menzies wasn't startled now, he was getting angry.

"No, you daft bastard. If it would get her out I'd put her down as a dependent as well, but I can't. Think, man, you could be dead next time round. Give her a lot of nice things to remember about her first bloke, and no moping and shit." Harry thought hard. "Come on the next supply run and find her something, a keepsake. A brooch or frilly knickers, whatever."

"That's looting."

"That's requisitioning. What do you think she's wearing?" Harry stopped and gave a slow smile. "I'm damn glad someone lost what Cyn looted."

That certainly changed Menzies's mood since he also gave a slow smile and took a trip down memory lane. Harry wondered briefly if some prostitute had left her undies here and they'd been shared round, then didn't care. They weren't Marcie's because that Teddy wouldn't have fitted Marcie like it had Cyn.

On the next trip Harry had a fairly good idea what sort of keepsake Menzies got because he disappeared into a jewellery shop. One with massive steel shutters that hadn't been looted which was impressive these days. Since there was someone still inside and no argument broke out, presumably Menzies bought the whatever.

*   *   *

"We, the Army, will go in the end. What will you all do then?"

Cyn hugged closer. "I don't know. We can't go home, any of us."

"You could stay here? The Army has put up sandbags and fixed up the windows." Harry wasn't sure how much they'd help though.

"No, this place is too near the airport. The rioters will come to loot that and include this place. They'll think a hotel has booze." It did, firmly under lock and key so the soldiers didn't neck the lot and get disorderly. Cynthia was thinking hard. "We need an old library, or something like that. Maybe a church. Something solid enough so those bullets don't come through the walls." That was Harry's fault, explaining that a high powered rifle would shoot through a brick wall.

"I'll keep my eye open, and ask the others. Will everyone want to go the same place?" It would be safer, probably, but Harry didn't know how well they got on.

"Probably. We weren't really friends before but this has sort of pulled us together. It would be safer." Cyn grinned. "Don't check your rucksack, Harry Corporal Miller."

"Not until I find a broom cupboard."

"Now you've reminded me, why are we in here?" Harry could see the tip of her tongue in the low light.

"You've forgotten? What can I do to remind you?"

*   *   *

"That's a bloody library, and definitely not on our list."

"Shush, Tredwell, you'll get all hot and bothered. My books are overdue? I need some midnight reading?" Harry smiled and headed up the steps to the solid stone building with the big wooden doors. It also had small windows with pointed tops where there had been an attempt to make it medieval.

Tredwell was right behind. "You don't need midnight reading according to rumour." Harry whirled and Tredwell went back a step. "Christ man, what do you expect? One girl gives you bloody great smiles every time she sees you, and an extra egg or whatever. Half the blokes are sure you're at it somewhere, and the where is driving them crazy."

"Why?"

"Because more than one would make a run for one of those girls if there was somewhere private. From the bloody smiles you found one, you jammy bastard." Tredwell was smiling. "Not me, I've got a wife and anyway, if I was you I sure as hell wouldn't share." The LC looked beyond Harry. "Now why a library?"

That was said in a low tone and Harry looked past him to the puzzled men on the lorry. "Looking for a cookbook, lads. I fancied a Chinese for a change." They laughed. Harry looked at Tredwell and spoke lower. "Come with me but we'll leave a couple of men at the front, and put two round the back, right?"

"Done." Tredwell turned. "You two guard the back, you two guard the door, and the rest of you make sure nobody nicks the lorry. What sort of reading do you fancy?"

"Cowboys." "Sci-Fi." "What you got?" "Any dragons?" "Military of course." The last had a big grin.

"The rest think about it, for when we check what's in here." Then he turned back to Harry and hefted his rifle. "After you corp."

Harry stopped just inside the door. "Quick thinking, and actually a good idea."

"If I ever have another idea, do I get another stripe?" Tredwell smiled. "I'm bored bloody stiff so yes, I'm going to requisition a book or two. Now why are you in here?"

"I'm looking for a good strong place to leave the hotel staff when we get pulled out." Harry watched the shock hit Tredwell, and then watched him rally. "Yes, do you want to leave them to what's on the streets."

"So why here?"

"Big stone walls. I told Cyn, er, Cynthia, that rifle bullets go through bricks so she wants stone walls if possible."

Tredwell's eyes lit up. "Sin. You've got a girl called Sin?"

"Her name is Cynthia to you and Cyn is a shortened version, OK?"

Tredwell was trying not to laugh. "Yeah, no problem. Christ, I'd love to have that to drop out over a pint. Oh yes, I once had a bird called Sin. Does she sin?"

"Shut it."

"Yes corp. So why are we in here? Oh, we're in here for sin."

Harry had to laugh. "Yes we are. I want to check for gas, electric, toilets and suchlike. To see if they could all live here for a bit until it dies down." Harry sighed. "It could be a while."

"How long? I'm a bloody mushroom as well and that sigh knows more than I do. Give."

Harry gave, and answered questions.

*   *   *

"The rumours among the men aren't completely right but if anyone put them all together they point that way. Though not well enough for anyone to realise how bad it is." Tredwell looked really worried now. "Shit, I've got to get back to the barracks. My missus is there, and two bloody kids."

"They're safe enough there. It's the ones who aren't married who are in the shit and the Army aren't allowing marriages just now. No more dependents, but this is all supposed to be kept quiet."

"Crap. I won't say because some of those with serious girlfriends back home would go AWOL." Tredwell looked round. "This place needs a couple of freezers, a generator, a couple of fridges and some decent furniture. Beds as well."

"What?"

"If we tell the lads it's hush-hush they'll keep quiet. Especially if we let them sort out some books. Even more especially if we let them take more next time, to sell to the rest." Tredwell looked at Harry with a big smile.

"I doubt that will actually work, but why are you even trying?"

"Because you mentioned not being able to get married or take dependents. That means you asked, Corporal Miller, so it matters to you. If we can we'll fill the fridge and freezer, and throw a few cartons of beans in here." Tredwell laughed. "Now I'll be able to tell the lads over a pint back in quarters about this bloke who had a girlfriend called Sin. How he fitted up a Sin Palace." Harry had to laugh as well.

The two of them looked at the small room with a stove and sink, and the larger toilet area, and agreed this would do. Harry looked out the back window. "That's a bonus."

Tredwell looked out of the window as well. "Too true, no neighbours and it's a decent neighbourhood anyway. Those look like the playing fields for a school out there. Since next door is a church, the only neighbours are that little block of flats the other side and there's the car parks in between." The LC thought a moment. "Damn, I was thinking of fields of fire and suchlike and they won't have guns. Though it will be easier to defend these narrow windows if they have to."

Harry realised he'd been thinking the same way. He scowled in disappointment and frustration. "Better still if they're boarded up and everyone makes like a mouse for a while. The government will have to sort it out eventually."

"Still good enough?"

"Good as we'll get." Harry sighed. "Now we need to square the lads."

Tredwell laughed. "Not a problem because I've been thinking about it as we looked round. This stripe means sod all authority so we learn to get things done willingly." He looked around. "Would you be astounded to learn that the Army were leaving squads to keep an eye on things? Very quietly of course because we're mushrooms so it'll be a tiny rumour."

Harry looked at him and started to smile as Tredwell continued. "The men setting it up might think they're the ones being left. They'll want it nice, won't they, though without telling some nosy officer."

"So what they put in here will be tucked away out of sight." Harry's smile grew. "I'm not playing cards with you, ever."

"Nobody does. Just to make sure the location stays secret, they get to sell a few books on. Then if this gets out the blokes are in deep shit for looting and selling stolen property."

The result over the next few weeks wasn't luxurious, but it would be a good start. Not chairs and settees, but some mattresses and bedding were installed. One squaddie suggested solar panels in case the electric went, and a camping stove with a supply of gas canisters went in as well.

The lorry was backed up to the door so nobody could see what went inside, but some of the boxes of books were carried round to the cab in plain view. All of them in fact since not many books were taken. Though that looked to the occasional spectator as if the Army were emptying the library. Since the place was boarded up and the door nailed shut when the squaddies left, and was still intact when they returned, nobody was very curious.

*   *   *

Sergeant Wilson looked at the boxes and then at Harry. "A TV and a video player?"

"Yes Sarge. The shop was gutted but we dug these out. We thought the lads could watch videos to stop any more fights over cards." Harry smiled and waited. One of the squaddies wanted a video player in the hideaway as they were calling it. Another had mentioned that one of those would be popular back at the hotel since the men still couldn't watch live TV. Though rumours of the troubles both home and abroad were getting stronger and unrest was spreading.

Sarge sighed. "I'll ask in officer country. Where will you get the videos from?"

"A looted or empty video rental shop? All the porn stuff will be gone, and probably a lot of the really violent ones so maybe it will educate the men. Broaden their horizons."

Sarge had his little smile back. "Good luck with that. Though a good few seem to have taken up reading?"

"We bring back a few."

"For sale?" There was an edge in that.

"No, though you know the men. They'll sell after they've read them. Can't stop it unless we open a library." Harry crossed his mental fingers because if there were any rumours about libraries Sarge would jump on that mistake.

"All right but get a video player for the officers as well. The TV is crap these days. Really crap." Sarge paused. "Collect a selection of books as well. Something highbrow so they can feel superior. Otherwise some of them will confiscate what the men are reading." He sniggered. "Then a few for the sergeants, a bit more lowbrow. I like spaceships and tight spacesuits on buxom wenches if you find one."

"Maybe you could mention this directly to the captain? Because if Lieutenant Symonns thinks the idea is from me?" Harry shrugged, then smiled. "Maybe the staff could have one?"

"Possibly." Sarge grinned. "Though not for the broom cupboard. I assume from some of the looks that Maynard finally found one big enough?"

Harry let his own smile widen. "How would I know? Though since someone gave them the idea?"

"Oh, I think that lass might have worked something out in time. Though there's not a hint she's taking customers in there?" There was a definite question in Sarge's voice.

"Retired. When I asked about marriages? That was for her and Maynard."

Sarge stared. "Really? I thought it was you."

"Maybe, to get a lass out of this shithole. But that's been stopped." Neither were smiling now.

"Fair enough. Now piss off while I corner the captain in a good mood. Organise the videos because from the moaning through there I reckon this idea will fly." Sarge headed for the officer's mess.

Harry was right, all the porn was gone when he found a shop by using a yellow pages directory. So were a selection of others, but a good few of the remaining videos were requisitioned. Some went into the hide-away but the men didn't see how many chick flicks were in the bottom of those boxes. Harry had a good reason to raid the chick flicks since the permission that Sarge relayed included the staff. The receiver for the men wasn't allowed an aerial so it couldn't get TV broadcasts but morale improved anyway.

Morale needed improving, because the forays into social or other housing, and the occasional riots, had reduced the eighty to fifty-nine. Seven more were in hospital. Several of those still on the strength had been injured and were recovering, and it was obvious that the situation was getting worse.

*   *   *

The group of soldiers parted and Harry looked down and then around. "Get a bloody medic."

"On the way, corp." The nearest men flinched away as Harry looked up but he wasn't angry at them. He was angry at the nameless arsehole who'd put a bullet through Menzies. It was a bad wound, the bullet path was half from the side through Menzies's chest and already there was blood on the corporal's lips. Blood that bubbled as Menzies tried to speak.

Harry knelt. "Don't speak you prat. You'll make it worse."

"Get her out."

"I'll try."

Menzies coughed and bright red spattered his lips and chin. "Get her out."

"Done. Now shut up."

"Promise."

Harry couldn't, but? "I promise I'll get her safe."

Menzies subsided and moments later he was being assessed, stretchered, and carried away. To the ambulance so maybe there was a chance. Harry had no trouble pulling the trigger for the next two hours.

When he got back to the hotel Harry wanted to go out and pull a trigger a few more times, because Menzies was now in a body bag. Harry went to find Cynthia, because this wasn't a Cyn visit.

"Santos? Um, Menzies? He's dead? Oh Christ." Cynthia looked absolutely stricken and tears were already starting. "Oh Christ. This will kill Nita. She'll think it's a punishment."

"What? How the hell does that work?"

"She's a Catholic, really old-school. What she did is a sin and she really was worried about it. The thing is she was bloody smitten. As bad as Davie, er, Maynard." Cynthia gave Harry a worried look. "You know that they were both, well, virgins? Nita and Davie?"

"Not for sure with Maynard but it was a good bet. Menzies told me about Nita." Cynthia's eyes narrowed. "No bragging. He was stunned, in the nicest possible way." Harry sighed and hugged Cynthia. "His last words were to get her safe."

"That will get harder the longer you're here. She might not be able to walk too far if you're here another four or five months."

"What! You mean, er."

"Up the duff, one in the oven, in the club, pregnant. She already missed her period, a fortnight ago, and she doesn't mind." Cynthia gave a faint smile through the tears. "Because contraception was a step too far. Sex before marriage was really scary for Nita but she thought God would understand love."

Harry was horrified. "Menzies didn't insist?"

"Oh yes. We told her he would so she asked how to give God a chance." Cynthia sighed. "She wanted to know how big a hole in the condom God needed so it was down to Him. If God wanted a baby, she'd have one."

"You showed her?" Harry was incredulous because that was lunacy. An illegitimate baby in this bloody shambles of a city?

"A tiny, tiny hole but either God was insistent or she didn't think that was enough and made the holes bigger. That's why we provided the condoms but don't worry, Nita always carried her specials." Cynthia cuddled. "Now I've got to tell her God's price was she could have the baby, but not the father. Oh shit." Harry returned the gentle kiss. "I know it's bloody rubbish, but it's how she'll see it. Will it matter if nobody sees Nita for a while?"

"No. If it's noticed I'll invent something."

"Period pains. Blokes never ask for details. That's a bit sick under the circumstances." Harry was kissed again. "Now we'd better stop snogging in the corridor. I'll see you in the morning."

* * *

Nita wasn't on duty for several days but nobody asked. Before she came back to the dining room Harry had another problem. He was short-handed.

"I'm not madly keen on someone filling Menzies's boots, but we need another one to cover the catering. Sorry Sarge, but all day on the raids or all night on riots as well as keeping the grub coming is killing the pair of us." Harry wasn't joking because Lieutenant bloody Symonns wasn't cutting the catering staff any slack. Harry was out scavenging some nights because he'd been fighting all day. That was no fun at all since twice they'd had to drive through a gathering mob to get away.

"It won't be for long, but you may as well have Tredwell since you get on so well." Sarge scowled. "I'll mention it to the captain while your friend is busy someplace. This is getting bloody ridiculous now."

"Right, ta. But what do you mean, it won't be for long?" Harry had suddenly lost interest in getting help.

"It's not official yet, but I can see the signs. They'll either bring in more troops and rotate us out, or pull everyone back to regroup." Sarge looked at Harry's face. "That serious? Then find her somewhere safe before you go. Don't even think of trying to get her out with us." Sarge curled a lip. "You don't want anyone you give a shit about in the camps. That's rumour, but a strong sergeant rumour." Solid gold then, Harry thought.

"I might find a place. But how do they get there? This place will get trampled when we pull out and the mob head for the airport." Harry paused to let that sink in. "Maybe we could load the lot into a lorry and drop them a few miles away."

"Found somewhere? Near a library or a bookshop?"

Sarge hadn't narrowed it down which was a relief so Harry went for flippant. "Of course not Sarge. Perish the thought. But what about some transport?"

"I'll ask. Now piss off before you find some more work for me. That's not the way it works."

* * *

"This is ridiculous." Though Cyn wasn't smiling, let alone laughing. "I've got a bloke on a bed with his pants off and he's got me stripping. A bloody gun."

"I waited until after all the good stuff?"

"Too bloody true or I really would be pissed off. Just how serious is this because it's frightening me."

Harry hugged her, then tried to get his mind back on the bloody gun because Cyn was still undressed after good stuff. "The thought of you left out here without a gun makes me very afraid. You told us about the estates? Well they're worse than that now. When the refineries went up over in America, something snapped and they've gone crazy."

"Can't you get us out at all?"

"Yes, into a camp but I won't do that." Harry hugged her again. "Sarge says I wouldn't want someone I care about in there."

"Bad boy, saying things like that. Now you've said you care, I'm going to have to kiss you, and then try and remember where we were up to. With the gun thing I mean." Moments later Harry was thinking he should have said he cared a lot more if the result was this. Then he got his mind back to teaching Cynthia the basics of using a hand gun. It was one of the captures and this one came from Menzies. Harry had removed it so his friend didn't get into trouble when the weapon was found in the hospital.

*   *   *

A week later and after quite a lot of missed sleep in pleasant company Cynthia could reload quickly and smoothly, and take the weapon apart to clean it. "But I'll never be able to shoot someone."

"One of you will if it gets bad enough." Harry sure as hell hoped so.

"But what if I miss? People shoot off hundreds of bullets and the man comes out of it untouched." Which was how films worked. That or the hero hit one target per bullet with deadly accuracy.

Harry relaxed a bit. "I told you. Close up only and use both hands. Come on, assume the position." They both grinned. "That one later."

"All right, but you behind me." The grin was pure Cyn. "For this position."

"There, now let the asshole get close. Aim at his belly because this will try and kick up. No heart shots and no head shots. Definitely no trying to shoot the bloody gun or whatever out of his hand."

"He'll have his whatever in his hand?"

"Possibly, but in that case aim for that." The giggle was definitely enough to spoil Harry's concentration but he gathered it up again. "Shoot the bastard more than once, until he falls down and drops whatever's in his hand. When it's over, if he's still moving, shoot him in the head."

Harry felt her go still and tense. "You never said that before."

"Sorry. It's just that, well, it was the thought of what he'll be coming for. But what I said is true all the same." Harry hugged her. "I don't know how long we've got."

"Will LC Tredwell teach Nita?"

"What?"

"Well Marcie sort of persuaded er, Maynard to teach her." Cynthia tried to call Maynard by his surname but obviously the women used the soldier's first names with each other.

"She did?" Cynthia sniggered and so did Harry. That really did feel much too nice. "I suppose it wasn't that difficult."

Cynthia turned her head and smiled. "Not really. But Nita wants to know as well. So she can look after her baby. To be honest I think she's more likely to shoot someone than either of us."

That shook Harry, because Nita seemed to be so quiet and shy. "Really? I thought that with the religion she'd be peace and love."

"A bit more angels with burning swords smiting the sinner I think. Any sinner threatening her child could get a hell of a shock." Cynthia seemed sure, and Nita's baby costing her the father because she sinned was definitely that mind-set.

Harry thought about it. "Maybe. At least Tredwell won't try anything because he's happily married."

"We know. Nita said she owed it to Santos to look after his replacement and took him morning coffee. To offer coffee, not anything more. We couldn't stop her without getting crude but Tredwell told her he was married right off." Cyn had put the hand gun down now and turned in Harry's arms. "Two of the girls were considering being Tredwell's wake-up girl since you three turned out so well. They would have been disappointed." Her tongue peeked out and her arms went round Harry's neck. "Now about assuming a position."

*   *   *

"The Army is pulling back to reposition. Please make sure your kit is ready and your rucksack packed for transport." The colonel looked over the assembled men. "You will deal with any rioting tonight but only if it threatens the route out. There will be no combat tomorrow. We aren't going back in there until we have more men." He looked over at the captain. "Carry on."

Harry made a beeline for Sarge when the men were dismissed. "Yes, I've found a place but it's three miles. They need transport."

"Christ. I'll try, but they may have to walk." Sarge looked around him. "It's a bloody battlefield round here. Maybe the lieutenant will let you take them the first mile to get clear. All of them?"

"Yes, they want to stick together for safety."

"Good idea, I'll try."

*   *   *

"You really have to go?" Cyn was hugging very close and had lost her smile for once.

"I told you it would happen and now we know. We go the day after tomorrow. Tomorrow we pack up and get ready, and the following day the buses will arrive with an extra lorry for our kit." Harry was hugging hard as well. "I tried Cyn, but you'll be left. Though you know where to go. It's three miles but if you stick in a group?"

"I hope so. There's too many women, Harry Corporal Miller. We'll be carrying our cases and obviously refugees." She hugged and shook Harry a little. "Though at least there's someplace to head for. You really put food in there?"

"Yes. If you get there, nail the door shut and don't answer it."

Cynthia smiled. "Is there a broom cupboard?"

"No but there's a mattress. Let me try to get you a lift again. Really hard this time." Harry had already tried and the answer was no.

"But the lieutenant said no."

"I've got a secret weapon. Now this might be our last night so I don't want to talk about him, I want to explore." Cynthia giggled as Harry started his exploration of an entirely different very frilly nightie.

"Mmm, yes please. How come you always do that? Lots of exploring even when the girl is already nekkid?" Cyn giggled and looked down. "Or soon will be at that rate. I'm not complaining but usually, in my admittedly limited experience, blokes tend to skip that once the panties are history."

"This sort of exploring?" Cyn made an appreciative noise and Harry smiled. "I was trained."

"What?" Cyn was having trouble speaking through her giggles. "As a gigolo?"

"Not quite." Harry carried on exploring, gently. "My second girlfriend told me a bloke has two sorts of sex, good and fantastic. A girl varies from a non-event to bloody fantastic." He chuckled. "She said that if the man does this sort of thing, then the girl will have a much better time." Harry kissed Cyn thoroughly. "Then she might ask him to do it again and make sure his experience is fantastic."

"Ooh yes, Harry Corporal Miller. Do it again, please."

*   *   *

"What do you want, Miller?" Lieutenant Symonns looked up from a small heap of paper he was working through.

"I've come to ask if I can take the lorry to find the staff a safer place, sir."

"To tuck your girlfriend away? Is that how you got into her pants? I told the sergeant no and I assume he passed on the message." The lieutenant leant back and smiled. "There's a petrol shortage."

"But keeping them here meant they can't go home. Their flats will have been stripped, sir." Harry knew Sarge has presented the arguments but didn't want to go the next step.

"I heard it all, about this being near the airport and suchlike. Well they can walk someplace else in that case. Without petrol they'll have to learn to walk." Lieutenant Symonns smiled.

Harry sighed. "I'd like to speak to the captain, please sir."

"No."

"I insist, sir. These people have put their lives on hold to care for us. They did it cheerfully and now we're going to dump them. They deserve a chance." Harry was still trying to get through but the lieutenant was more interested in getting at Corporal Miller. "I'd like to speak to the captain please, sir."

"You don't want to go over my head. It will cause you a lot of trouble and I'll just advise the captain to say no." The bastard was smirking.

"Then I'll go higher. Sir."

"The captain won't allow it."

"Yes he will." Harry took a deep breath and tapped his ribbon. "This will get me to the colonel at least if I push it, and I will. Despite what you say I have never used this to get any special treatment. Well, this time I will. Sir." Harry let the arse see his little smile because it wouldn't make any difference now. Harry was going to pay for this, repeatedly.

"You jumped up little bastard." The lieutenant settled back but the smile had gone. "All right. Go for it. See the captain. I won't even come with you but I will be waiting. I'll be waiting every time you turn round now, smartarse."

"Sir."

* * *

"You're not supposed to do that where others can see." There were four squaddies in the corridor, all with big grins.

"Well I can't get you in the broom cupboard again, if we've got to pack up and leave." Cyn's tongue peeked. "Are you coming? Is there a broom cupboard there?"

"I'm coming, but no broom cupboard because a bunch of big strong soldiers will be watching and they are supposed to bring me straight back." Harry sighed. "I feel a total shit anyway."

"Don't worry. We'll make like mice. I'll let the rest know."

When the staff came out of the hotel the soldiers were busy loading food and bedding, cutlery and cooking pots and plates. "Thank the captain, please?" Cullen looked at the soldiers heaving gear into the lorries. "We might have trouble getting more food to start with."

Cyn hadn't told the rest of the staff about what was at this new place, so that nobody told the wrong person and got Harry into even more trouble. Except Marcie and Nita of course. There again Cynthia didn't know everything that had been put in place.

Cullen looked up at the back of the hotel. "I should thank him myself."

"He's too busy, Cullen, but I'll pass it on." The captain might not agree with Harry's interpretation of taking the staff and their stuff.

Marcie and Maynard came out hand in hand while the rest was being loaded, and she was the last aboard. Before that Marcie gave her Davie a goodbye kiss that raised a round of applause from the squaddies and sent Maynard bright scarlet. "All aboard?"

"Yes corp. Are you travelling in the back?" Tredwell had a big grin as did several of the squaddies.

"Cheeky. There's no room." It would be too tempting as well. Seeing the corporal deliver that sort of kiss would definitely get back to someone. Harry climbed into the cab.

"Where to corp?" The driver had a little smile.

"Hideaway." The man's smile grew a little bit and he put the truck in gear.

* * *

The men were laughing and joking as they unloaded at the other end, though they backed up tight to the door again. First for the passengers to get out so nobody got a clear view, and then they unloaded the goods.

"The squaddies might talk once we've left." Tredwell was worried.

"I'm already as deep as I can get. Just use the same old answer. The corporal said it was a hush job." Harry laughed. "It was."

"Is she worth it?"

"All of them are worth every shovel full I'll get dumped on me." Harry looked round. "I need a few private minutes."

"You haven't got time for Sin."

"What have you been teaching Nita?"

"Shit. I don't want to see so I can honesty deny all knowledge. I thought it was so if they could trade for one, they could use it." Tredwell actually seemed to be shocked.

"So that's what you still think now. Now go off and do LC things, and I'll do corporal things." Harry headed for the lorry cab and pulled out the steel box with the handles each end and a big padlock. He put it in the toilet and went to find Cyn.

Harry unlocked the padlock and opened the lid. "Six? Oh Harry Corporal Miller! Are you sure there isn't time – no, I suppose not." Cyn delivered a kiss that tried to compensate.

"There's ammo as well but keep the box out of sight until we are long gone. If one of the lads mentions the other gear we put in here someone might come to look. Whoever looks won't be happy if you're carrying these about. I doubt anyone will actually take bedding and a bit of food off you, but hide the box for a bit."

"If the men say something, will you be in trouble?"

"I already am." Harry grinned because right now he didn't care.

"More trouble, idiot." Cynthia thumped him lightly on the chest.

"Probably."

"Leave it with me. Don't go out of that door without a goodbye." Cyn gave Harry a brilliant smile and was gone.

Harry checked that the rest of the food and bedding had been unloaded, and that the fridges were now stocked. A voice, Tredwell he thought, called from the main library. "Corporal?"

Harry came out of the kitchen to find the men and Tredwell lined up in the main library. There was a small stack of books by the door. "We're ready to go but the young lady wants to say something." That was Cynthia.

"We just want to say thank you to all of you. We want to do so person-ally because with all this we can hide. Then maybe we will be safe until the Army come back." Cynthia paused. "I know Harry Corporal Miller didn't tell you." There was a ghost of a smile from a few of the men. "That was to protect you. We want to say thank you for not saying anything and not get-ting him in trouble."

Cynthia stepped back and Nita stepped forward and held up her hand. A tiny diamond sparkled on her third finger. "I want to say a special thanks. I will have Corporal Santos Menzies's baby when the time comes. It's all right because I want his baby. The baby will be safe here. Thank you." Nita stepped back and Cullen walked up to Tredwell.

He stuck out his hand. "Thank you, Lance Corporal." Then Cullen worked down the line saying thank you to each man, followed by the men.

Marcie went up to Tredwell. He got a peck on the cheek with his thank you, as did the rest of the men. Nita went next and a few of the men congrat-ulated her. Some of the young women who followed kissed lips, and a few kisses were a bit firmer, but the men behaved very well. Some looked a bit stunned. Cynthia went last and they all got a little kiss on the cheek. Then she came over to give Harry his kiss. That got a round of applause as well.

The men filed out looking very thoughtful and bemused, but Cynthia stopped Harry at the door. This kiss made the applause version almost staid. When Harry looked round the staff had all disappeared while his brain was on holiday. "That was thank you from everyone, Harry Corporal Miller. Come back if you can?"

"I will if I can, Cyn."

There were a lot of little smiles when Harry came out and got into the cab. "Hotel, please."

"Right Corp."

*   *   *

Tredwell cornered Harry as soon as they were clear of the men, back at the hotel. "Did you put her up to that?"

"Cyn? No, why?"

"She should be a bloody Lance Corporal. That lot, the lads, were talking outside. Anyone opens their mouth and the rest will beat him senseless." Harry stared and Tredwell laughed. "It's all right, I can guess why your brain is still in shock if you got another goodbye, but your Cyn played it dead right."

"But the staff really are grateful."

"Which is why it bloody well works." Tredwell sighed. "I hope we're going to the barracks because the goodbye you got reminded me of how long it is since I saw my missus."

They headed upstairs but when they opened the door to their room it was full of soldiers. "What the... sorry sir." The captain turned and sighed.

"I suppose we have to search you as well, and Lance Corporal Tredwell, but you aren't carrying an illegal weapon, are you?"

Harry looked round the room where his kitbag, pack, and every cupboard and drawer had been emptied out. "No sir." It had been a close-run thing though. Harry had intended giving Cyn a spare he'd picked up and the one Menzies had sort of bequeathed. Then he'd decided at the last minute it wasn't enough.

Tredwell looked puzzled, but that would be because they hadn't found his. Harry was going to have to explain that later. But first Harry needed to know what this was about. "What made you think we had illegal weapons in here, sir? Is everyone being searched?"

"No. Why, should they be?"

"Not as far as I know, sir. I don't know why we're being searched."

"There was a firm report that you had taken civilian weapons and been trying to sell them to the men." The captain was definitely annoyed, but Harry thought he was also not completely ticked off at Harry. "Obviously a mistake. I really will want to talk to the source of that information. Sorry about this." The captain waved his hand at the heaps of belongings. He gave a little smile. "Gives you a chance to sort it out and pack properly."

Harry grinned, at least partly from relief. "Very kind sir." The three squaddies who went out after him were definitely puzzled. No doubt they had spare weapons themselves and had thought the extras were sort of sanctioned. Only up to sergeant, apparently, or only unless they came to official attention.

Tredwell was looking round and then at Maynard and Harry. He turned to Maynard. "Full marks for bloody fast reactions, but how the hell did you hide them and the ammo."

"He didn't, Tredwell. I did."

Tredwell turned to Harry. "Why, and where?"

Harry took a deep breath. "In a box in the library now, and I took yours because there weren't enough. It was a last minute decision. I was going to buy you a replacement from one of the lads who has a spare spare, if you get my drift."

"You might have asked." Tredwell stopped and gave a little smile. "I would have said no before that bloody show the staff put on. Why didn't you just collect some extras?" Tredwell looked at the mess. "Though I can't complain. Did he nick yours as well, Maynard?"

"Er, well, no. Harry said it was for Marcie so I gave him both of them." Maynard was pink now. "So she'd be safe. You've seen all the weapons out there, Lance, there's hundreds of the bloody things."

"Two?"

"Yeah, well, I'd been teaching Marcie to use one, so I'd got a spare to sort of stick in her pocket at the last minute or something. Then Harry had this box, so I put them both in."

"With a shitload of ammo. He was saving up for a war so I'm not sure her pockets would have handled it. Before you ask, I threw in the one from Menzies. I thought it was right, for Nita." Harry waited while Tredwell digested that.

"Fair enough. It's done now and seems to have saved my bacon as well. Though I'd dearly love to know who decided to turn us in. I would have thought all the men have their own by now, so they should be keeping quiet." Tredwell was trying to come up with a name. "Hell, the officers must know, though the captain would have to go official if his nose was rubbed in it. Who have you upset lately?" Tredwell stared at Harry. "It's in your face, you know."

"I reckon it is now, after you just asked that." Harry's grin was a little bit feral. "I reckon Lieutenant bloody Symonns is going to have trouble finding a name for his bloody informant."

"Christ. I am so glad we're leaving. No offence, but I've got family and don't want to be caught in the fallout if he's that keen to get you. Why?"

Harry's grin was even wider. "I went over his head about the staff. I told him my medal would get me as far up the tree as I needed so he backed off."

"Ouch. Well, let's get this lot sorted, because he'll probably pull a room inspection just to give you more crap." Tredwell started to sort out his gear. "I really do want to get back to the barracks and out of this."

Chapter 4:
Parlez Vous and Goodbye

"So why do they get to go on leave, Sarge?" Harry was watching the bus leave from the temporary camp set up for the troops pulling out of London. One of several camps, according to rumour.

"Because the brass want to reassure the men with wives and families that their nearest and dearest are being looked after." Sarge looked after the bus as well. "Morale was a bit rocky just after we pulled out."

"What about the blokes with steady girlfriends?" Harry grinned. "Some of them are married according to some cultures." Then his face sobered. "What about the ones who aren't in quarters? My sister lives back where we grew up, near her hubby's family. He's a lieutenant with the Rifles, in Ukraine."

"Don't ask me, I'm a mushroom as well. Though there's something up because I was asked if I wanted to leave. Not buy out, just resign, honourably with a pension." Sarge snorted. "Not a bloody chance, I'd be lost out there."

"I thought they'd want more of us, not less. With all the riots and such."

"I was told it's because we're all being brought home, every unit from every-where. So they'll have plenty for the UK." Sarge shrugged. "Makes a sort of sense."

"So what will us single blokes be doing while that lot are all having fun?"

Sarge pulled a face. "Manning roadblocks, to stop the civvies from fol-lowing us out. We're supposed to keep everyone inside the M25 London Or-bital Motorway. It's the perfect place to stop them according to some genius."

"They'll go round the roadblocks." Then Harry stared. "We're pulling out of London entirely?"

"No we aren't pulling out, there'll be strong presences in the Tower and various convenient places. According to sergeant rumour." Sarge smiled. "As for civvies going round the road blocks, well that's what idle squaddies are for. Patrolling."

"Oh joy."

*   *   *

Harry was on duty every hour the lieutenant could arrange it, and crawled into his sleeping bag exhausted every night. Oddly, that turned out to be a favour. One blessing was that being on the patrols meant he was mainly intercepting people who ran away rather than tried to kill him. That meant Harold had to shoot very few people, and those were shooting at him.

The Army had accomplished one thing in London, Corporal Miller could now pull the trigger with a human in the sights. But he wasn't in that numb trance brought on by the endless riots and forays into the estates, so Harry had time to think. Which meant that Harry was facing up to just what he'd done.

All the bullshit about not shooting live targets, and now he'd lost count of how many nameless people he'd killed. Not really, because Harry could remember every face, but he refused to count them. It was bad enough watching them die, over and over, in his dreams. Although Harry hadn't realised it at the time, Cyn had kept those dreams, and the faces, at bay. Now total exhaustion was almost doing the same, but only almost.

The married men had two weeks leave and came back a lot happier. Right up until they saw the road blocks. "Concrete blocks? Steel plates? A bloody tank!" Tredwell stared at the burnt out vehicles on the sides of the road leading to the road block. "What the hell is happening?"

"It's got worse in there, inside London. Someone went through another roadblock with a bus covered in steel plates and we had a couple of cars try to crash through. After the bus, the tank turned up." Harry lowered his voice. "Help me keep an eye on Maynard will you? He's going crackers over Marcie being in there. If he goes AWOL the Army will shoot him when they go back in. If they catch him running, I'll be on the bloody firing squad."

Tredwell looked startled. "Shoot? I thought that was only in there, with the Martial Law thing."

"Extended indefinitely all over the country. There's already been a few executions though not here, thank God. Else that bastard Symonns would put me on the firing squad." Harry sighed. "Keep clear of me, mate. I'm a lightning conductor, but for shit."

"Still?"

"For as long as he's in my chain of command I reckon. Did you hear when the old units are being put back together?"

"No, not yet." Tredwell gave it some thought. "Maybe the brass are waiting until everyone gets back home. Right, I see brass coming this way so I'm going to pack my gear away like a good little soldier."

* * *

Harry read the notice and a voice from behind him asked "Are they serious?"

"Yeah, they asked some sergeants already." Harry looked over at the speaker, a squaddie. "Just like it says, there's too many soldiers for what we have to do. Everyone's coming home. Well, not all of them." Harry had just had a letter from his sister Sharyn. Freddie, her husband, wouldn't be one of those coming home.

"Christ, there'll never be room in the barracks."

"So they send a lot of us away. The simple way is this, giving us early retirement. The married quarters are being cleared out already." Harry grimaced. "I just heard from my sister. Her husband is in a body bag, and there's only quarters for the families of serving soldiers." Sharyn had tried to get out of the city because that was turning into a war zone like London, though not as bad yet. According to the words between the black lines, life for all civvies was getting worse.

"I'm not sure I fancy it, going into a mess like that without a rifle and a bloody Army behind me." The squaddie turned as another voice piped up.

"I might. My Mum and Dad are in one of those messes. So is my sister and her hubby and kids. Though I'd prefer to take my rifle."

"Not on the list, mate." There was a list of equipment any departing soldiers could take in lieu of pay. "Though this might be the only way to get any pay."

"The back pay is piling up now. Maybe the cash box is empty?" There was a lot of muttering from the group now gathering.

"On the bright side we've got food and clothing and a roof." The speaker paused. "And a rifle which might be the important bit."

"If this crisis doesn't get better, the pay will be useless but we'll be safe in the Army. If it is all sorted out, we'll be rich." There was a muttering as some agreed and others were more worried about relatives if the worst happened. A few were pointing out that with a rifle the Army could get anything else.

"Shut it. There's an officer coming." The group broke up. Harry left with the rest and he was torn. Harry didn't fancy leaving the Army, but he didn't really like the idea of Sharyn in a bloody mess like he'd left Cyn and the rest in. Not on her own. He toyed with the idea of resigning and going into London and joining Cyn, and that was tempting.

Then there wasn't time to think because it was time to go on another bloody patrol. Harry knew he'd get broken ruins or one of the places where the sewage system had collapsed and caused a swamp. Lieutenant Symonns was still getting his revenge.

*   *   *

"What's the panic, Sarge?" A good half of those on the road block were throwing their gear into a truck. Packs but not kitbags so this wasn't a permanent move. As usual Harry had slid his stick into the pack in case it went Déjà vu.

Sarge grinned. "We're going to France, so better polish up your manners. Voulez vous couchez and all that."

"Why? Have we declared war?"

Sergeant Wilson's face sobered. "No, though it's a bit tense. The Border Protection Force is being overwhelmed and last night the refugees broke through. None got onto the ships, but there's supposed to be hundreds more refugees arriving from Lille. When they get there, it'll be bloody chaos."

"Christ. I know the news said it's bad in the French towns, but what are they marching to Calais for?"

"There was a big riot in Lille. Now the survivors are marching to Calais and the Frogs are letting them. These aren't refugees, or they weren't. There's been some ethnic cleansing going on and this lot lost." Sarge looked at the men loading into the buses. "We're heading for a ferry and there'll be more units joining us. The officers don't know why the Frogs aren't stopping the marchers and there's a flap on, which is why the brass have been so bloody talkative. Now move it because you don't want to be last aboard. Not considering who is in charge."

Harry saw Lieutenant Symonns heading towards the bus and got the message. He was aboard long before the officer got there.

*   *   *

Three hours later the soldiers filed off the ferry in Calais. The first fifty or so were forming up when voices started shouting. "At the double, at the double. Leave your packs, follow the Land Rover."

Since that was blaring over the ship's tannoy everyone got it, and started moving faster. Harry did wonder for a moment if the gangway would take it but the running men weren't in step so it just swayed. Those on the lorry ramp wouldn't have that problem. Within minutes three hundred men were jogging after the vehicle with just their rifles as luggage. The men went straight through the warehousing and past the custom's inspection points until they reached a wide, clear area.

"Form a line, double rank. Forget units. Move, move, move!" The urgency infected everyone, as did the sight ahead. The mesh fencing was still down in places and beyond it a sea of humanity was coalescing into a mob. The broken bits of timber, lumps of rubble and shoes mixed with stains on the concrete explained the urgency. The captain in charge had a split lip and had lost half the sleeve of his battledress.

The remaining Border Protection Force didn't look much better, and Harry realised that the body bags on the quay probably weren't dead refugees after all. Not with civvie bodies still laid outside the fence. "Come on, move it. Line up and fix bayonets."

Lieutenant Symonns stared at the captain in horror, and seemed determined that he wasn't going to end up the same way. He turned to the soldiers. "If one of you backs up I'll shoot him."

There were a few mutters at that but nobody was actually against getting ready for what was coming. The battered captain headed off down the line, waving his arms and shouting as more men arrived.

"Crap, we should have brought more blokes."

"Someone was on about another ferry. It must be late. Probably the crew are on strike." The anonymous comedian would have been funny any other time, after the number of strikes there had been on the ferries. Right now he didn't raise a laugh.

"Here they come." That statement wasn't necessary as the crowd started forward, towards the partially wrecked fence and the thin line of soldiers.

"Load your rifles." A chill went up Harry's spine. Symonns wasn't going to open fire, was he? This lot hadn't thrown a brick yet.

"One in the air I reckon." Whoever said that certainly made Harry feel better. Though he wasn't happy since how the line formed up left him with his back against a stack of pallets. Retreat wasn't an option even if they were only about four feet high. Though he'd have a lot better view from on top. Then, Harry realised, Symonns would shoot him for retreating.

Everyone looked up at the scream of aircraft, coming in low. The crowd of refugees crouched but the planes were further back. Black dots fell from the jets and then they were gone, hurtling off and out of sight, still low and without altering course. Behind them plumes of black smoke with flickering flames at the bottom rose into the sky.

"Oh shit, oh no. That's the camp. They'll kill us all." The man in front of Harry was one of the battered Border Protection Force and for a moment Harry thought he'd run. Then he straightened and braced. "The bastards. The bloody stupid bastards. They've only gone and killed the women and kids."

Unbelieving faces turned towards him, and then wrenched their attention back to the front as a guttural roar rose from the crowd. The whole mass broke into a run and the first missiles arced up towards the soldiers. "Fire. Shoot." The soldiers froze because there had been no sign of firearms, there weren't even any petrol bombs. "Shoot them you stupid bastards!" That sounded like Lieutenant Symonns!

A long burst erupted from somewhere to the left and refugees went down and then weapon after weapon joined in. Harry tried to hit those with weapons though after the second shot he paused. The tops of lorries showed over the men still running to contact, and they were coming at speed. Not down the road towards the barriers. These were bouncing cross-country, intent on smashing through the fence. Then they'd go straight through the thin line of soldiers! Men waving weapons were hanging from some of them.

The marchers from Lille had arrived and this lot had firearms and a plan. Harry couldn't see to shoot the bloody drivers so he turned and climbed up the pallets. Then stood and raised his rifle. When the three lorries coming his way finally stopped, one actually overturning, there was no shortage of targets with firearms. Harry was never sure how long the chaos went on but it probably wasn't very long.

Then there were calm voices calling from behind and more soldiers were pushing into the line, firing short bursts into any men still advancing. The remaining refugees stopped, and then began to run, leaving a carpet of dead and wounded. Rifles cracked and some of those with firearms dropped, but in a remarkably short time they had all gone.

"You, Miller, where do you think you're going?" Harry turned, open-mouthed, to see Lieutenant Symonns pointing at him. "Running away? I always thought so, you're gutless."

"No sir. I needed to see, to shoot."

"You couldn't see a target?" Symonns swept a hand out across the mass of casualties. "Everybody else could." His eyes narrowed. "You're under arrest."

"What started this?" Harry and Symonns both looked over at the speaker, a captain. "Who ordered the troops to open fire like this?" The captain looked at Symonns.

Symonns looked around and then back at Harry. "This man opened fire sir. A full burst and the rest just followed. I was just arresting him for running away." The captain's eyes looked at Harry and where he was, stood behind the line of soldiers.

"Well?"

"Needed the height sir, to see the lorries. So I could shoot the drivers."

"Makes some sense. If he was thinking like that, are you sure this man fired first?" The captain's eyes moved to Symonns but it wasn't him that answered.

"I can confirm that sir. I was looking straight at this soldier, and he was the first to fire." Harry's heart sank as he saw the speaker. Corporal 'Suggs' Young. His hand had healed but his other eye was black and swollen now, and he had a split lip that was still healing.

"You are absolutely certain?" Symonns had a triumphant gleam in his eye as he asked.

"Yes sir, I'll swear to it."

"Corporal, you will hand over your rifle and come with me. You two as well because this needs sorting out right now." The captain looked at Young. "You, corporal, take this man's rifle and ammunition."

Harry looked around desperately and saw a familiar face. "Sergeant! Sergeant Wilson." Sarge looked round and Harry beckoned. "Here, quickly please." Then he turned back to the captain. "The rifle and ammo clips are evidence sir, so they should be kept by the sergeant. He's not involved so there'll be no doubt about the condition of the weapon."

"Is it broken?"

"No sir, but I can prove it wasn't me?" Or reasonable doubt, Harry hoped, if the Army were still reasonable.

"Very well. Sergeant, take this man's rifle and ammunition and come with me. He is under arrest for panicking and starting this bloody massacre, and for attempted desertion." The captain turned on his heel.

Sarge looked at Harry and opened his mouth then shut it at a glare from Symonns. That was followed by a malicious smile at Harry from the lieutenant. "I knew I'd get you, but this is perfect. Hand the rifle over."

Harry did. "Don't clear it Sarge, it matters. Don't change the selector either, please." Sarge looked down at the weapon and then very carefully kept the barrel facing skywards.

"You should make it safe sergeant." Symonns was smiling happily.

"Evidence sir. I will point out that you interfered if the sergeant touches anything about it." Harry kept his voice level. He could get out of the first charge except for bloody corporal arsehole Young. That made every tiny thing important.

The march back to the colonel, busy supervising the rest of the men from the second ferry, was a short one. One that took about a year, from Harry's point of view. The captain spoke briefly and the colonel came across with another captain. The colonel looked at the four of them.

"Are you sure, Lieutenant?" He was looking at Lieutenant Symonns.

"Lieutenant Symonns. Yes sir. This man opened fire first, and was trying to get away at the end."

"Are you certain, very certain, Corporal?" This time the colonel was looking at Corporal Young."

"Corporal Young. Yes sir. We used to be in the same unit."

"So what's your answer, corporal?" This time Harry was the object of the attention. The colonel's attention fastened on Harry's battledress. "What's that on there for?"

"Corporal Miller. My CO said I had to wear the ribbon. I didn't fire any bursts sir. I got onto the pallets to be able to hit the lorry drivers, and pick out those with firearms."

"Pick out? That's not a sharpshooter's rifle."

"A moment sir." The new captain wanted a word. A captain without unit badges and Harry suddenly felt a bit happier.

The new captain looked at Harry. "Did you do the same as when you got the medal, Corporal?"

"Yes sir."

"How many did you get?" The captain was enjoying this, though the rest were looking baffled. Though Sarge had a little smile at mention of the medal. "How many rounds?"

"Twelve but fifteen rounds because I used two for the lorry drivers." Harry wasn't religious, but he would stick a few quid in the box outside the next church he passed.

The captain grinned at all present. "As I understand it, this man was supposed to be firing uncontrolled bursts. I'll bet the rifle says not, unless it's been altered. I'll also bet there's fifteen rounds left in the clip. Any takers?"

The colonel looked at him for a moment and then turned. "Captain Akers?" The original captain, the one who'd marched them all over, stiffened. "Check the rifle please."

"Still one up the spout sir, and I didn't alter the selector since the corporal insisted." Sarge still had that little smile, with a bit of anticipation now.

The captain checked. "It's on semi." He worked the bolt to eject the rounds. "I make that fifteen." Harry's webbing was checked and all his clips were full. The captain looked at the colonel. "Good job I didn't take the bet."

"Yes, isn't it? Well, Lieutenant?" The colonel had absolutely no humour on his face or in his look.

"I was sure it was him, and he was on the pallet. Then this man confirmed it." Corporal Young flinched. "There was a lot of confusion, so perhaps I was mistaken. Though I'm still unsure why this man was on the pallet."

"So he could shoot better." The mystery captain turned to the colonel. "I can explain?"

"Good. I'm a bit lost myself over the leap of faith. Do you know Corporal Miller?" The colonel looked over at captain Akers. "Take the Lieutenant and Corporal Young somewhere private, please. Make sure they're separate. I'll be really interested in comparing what they say."

Captain Akers hesitated. "What about Corporal Miller, sir?"

"He'll be coming as well, but not until I've had a little chat." The colonel turned back to the mystery captain. "I suppose this is top secret or some such?"

"Not really, but nobody believes the truth. I don't know the Corporal personally, but I'll bet he's a pay clerk." The captain took Harry's rifle from captain Akers and handed it back to Sarge, then the officer turned back. "Remember when the Mad Mullahs decided Kuwait was on their to-do list?" The captain was talking to the colonel but Harry remembered all right. "There were a lot of convoys and single vehicles ambushed, and a lot of very nasty fire fights, and a few made the news. One concerned some clerk and a group of mysterious chaps who were the only ones out of the lorry who were still breathing when relief arrived."

There was a spark of recognition in the colonel's eyes now, as the captain continued. "There was a lot of fuss and the clerk ended up with the medal, and most people assumed it was to keep the other conscious man out of the limelight." The captain nodded towards Harry. "Meet the clerk, and believe me he actually earned anything he got. The other man put him up for it." That was news, that Stones had put him up for a decoration!

"One shot per man, mostly through the head except for when they charged and he had to double up on a few. Then his rifle jammed so he beat or chopped a few more to death. This man doesn't run which is why that's the CGC. His CO really is proud of that and insists he wears the ribbon, since it's a bit unusual for a pay clerk." The captain looked over at Harry. "Our lot think it's funny, being rescued by a pay clerk, which is why most of us who were out that way know about Corporal Miller. Now I've got to go and sort those other things?"

"Yes, thank you." The colonel turned to Harry. "Now you give your deposition, and then you tell me exactly why you ended up with a CGC because I'm really curious." Harry noticed Sarge following behind, trying to be inconspicuous.

*   *   *

"Then the relief turned up and took us all home. The relief counted up bodies and when they found out who shot who, gave Stones a lot of stick about being shown up. So the CO really did insist the bloody thing is on my uniform." Harry indicated the ribbon.

Sarge leant back and laughed. "Crap. I thought the same as most people I suppose. Right up to when you went after that asshole in a balaclava." He chuckled. "Suggs never had a chance."

Harry smiled. "The last one had a sword."

"So the poncy stick?"

"Stones and his mates didn't think much of my technique up close and personal, so they wanted me to have something handy next time. It's even got a pen and inkpot inscribed on the top and Stilus Gladio Fortior, The Pen is mightier than the Sword."

Sarge sobered. "You'll get off the hook on this, because you weren't guilty and a proper investigation will find that out. They'll pull the bullets out of the lorry drivers if necessary. Your problem is that Lieutenant Symonns is a nastier piece of work than I thought."

Sarge sat for a few moments, visibly thinking hard and then his face cleared. "You may as well know. The arse is connected. Best thing you can do is take the Army offer and get out. Go and rescue your sister. Get her out of town and into a country cottage someplace."

"Christ, are you serious?"

"Symonns will use his connections to wriggle out of this and drop the lot on Young. Who thoroughly deserves the crap. But then you'll find some other, more senior officers here and there, looking for you." Sarge shook his head. "Bloody marvellous. You start acting like a bloody soldier and you've got to go."

Harold was thinking fast. "I might go and get my sister, though I might collect some passengers first?"

Sarge shook his head. "No you won't. If you go into London you won't get out. Leave that lass with whatever help you managed, and come back later if you have to. Save your sister before the government seals off the other cities."

"What?"

"It's been mentioned. But you sure as hell never heard that from me because to be honest I'm not sure. I can't see why, or how the country can function like that." Sarge stared at the ground. "There again I'm not some bloody high-powered brain with a bright idea and the ear of the Prime Minister, am I?"

"Thanks, Sarge. I'll do it. I don't like leaving but I can't leave Sharyn and the kids in something like London. I could write and warn them?"

Sarge's snort of derision confirmed Harry's own thoughts on that. "They'd cross that part out, then give you shit for suggesting it." Sarge stood up. "Now get your arse in gear and start the paperwork. I'll square it over you pissing off before the enquiry's done now that the colonel's onside. Though this enquiry won't be done in my lifetime so that won't be a big problem."

*   *   *

Harry stared at the ticket. One way, bus leaving in two hours. "Why can't I sort out my own transport?"

The corporal behind the desk grimaced. "Petrol shortages. You take the official bus to wherever you told the Army you're going. I might mention that this only came in after about a dozen of the squaddies who took discharge headed into London."

"So what?"

"You think the brass want trained soldiers waiting when we go back in? Just my humble opinion." The clerk looked down. "It says here you're going to your sister's. Is that true?"

"Yes, but I did intend a diversion."

"Not now. Get on the bus, Mr Miller, late of HM Forces." The corporal glanced at the heap by Harry. "You'll need a bus to carry that lot."

Harry laughed. "I tried to get my pay this way because I don't reckon the balance in cash will ever turn up. Good luck Corporal."

"Good luck, Mr Miller."

*   *   *

Harry stared out over the city from the top of the by-pass. Miles of empty dual carriageway tarmac disappeared in front and behind the bus. In front, at the bottom of the up ramp, was a road lined with burned houses. "Is this it?

How do I get home from here?"

The driver, an Army reservist, shrugged. "I'm not allowed to go down there, mate. Sorry. Maybe you can get a cab or leave some stuff with the guard post." As Harry looked around for some sign of a cab, the bus door sighed shut and he heard the gears engage. Harry looked down at the full sized Bergen kitbag and two packs, all stuffed with Army kit. Accepted in lieu of pay, or some of it at least. There was no way he could carry them to Sharyn's flat and the bloody mobile phones were still screwed up.

Harry shrugged and headed for the guard post. The post was sandbags and a corrugated iron roof, sat at the top of the ramp so they could see anyone coming up. The down ramp was sealed off with concrete blocks. "Hello. Is there any chance of getting a lift into town? Is there a phone so I can get a cab?"

The squaddie had been watching Harry approach. Now he shook his head. "Not a chance mate. Have you got any civvies? Clothes?"

"No. I've been out of the country over three years and civvie clothing wasn't a lot of use over there. Not a lot of social life outside the bases." Harry looked round. "Crap. I've got a ton of gear that I took instead of pay."

"Running out?" That came with a sneer.

"No, my sister's down there with two kids and I came to get her out." Harry nodded out over the city.

"Too late mate. You can supposedly still get a pass but once you're in, don't bet on it." The squaddie waved at the burned houses. "There's a lot of that going on, and we've got to keep it bottled up." He looked Harry up and down. "Still going in?"

"I've got to. I told you, my sister and her kids are waiting for me."

"Hang on, because you'll have to square it with the sergeant." Harry stood there trying to grapple with that as the squaddie went into the shelter and voices were raised. He needed permission to go into an English city, and couldn't come out? Sergeant Wilson's rumour mill was running slow. Harry was also grappling with the government sending him home into a sealed city. Yet they wouldn't let soldiers into London?

"Are you serious about going down there dressed like that?" The sergeant's voice jerked Harry out of his thoughts.

"What else can I do?"

"You'd be better off stark naked. They don't like us down there." The sergeant looked Harry up and down. "You shouldn't be wearing proper Army kit anyway if you've left."

"Surely it's OK with no badges or stripes? Anyway, it's all I've got, seriously."

The squaddie came out and the sergeant nodded at him. "He says you've got family down there."

"Sister and two young kids. She's worried so I came to get her out."

"Luck with that. We've been turning back at least five of every six that try to leave. The rest have a pass. Though even they have to leave most of their possessions." The sergeant looked Harry up and down. "I can't do it. It would be as good as murder to send you down there dressed like that." His eyes drifted past Harry. "Hellfire, how were you intending to move that lot?"

"Taxi, bus? Nobody mentioned this." Harry swept his hand out wide to include the shambles below. Most of the small estate that came within three hundred yards of the motorway was intact, but a wide swathe of housing beyond was burned or damaged. To one side of the estate was a caravan storage park with about a dozen of the big mobile home types parked up. To the other was a huge empty car park with less than a score of cars in it. Most of them had luggage heaped on the roofs.

"Tell you what." The sergeant pointed to the big empty car park. "Several coaches full of drivers turned up and took the cars from there." He looked at Harry's baffled expression. "All new cars, waiting to be sold or for delivery I presume. Those have parked on there because they weren't allowed out here." The sergeant glared at Harry. "Keep your trap shut, right?"

"Yes? What about?"

"About going down there and looking for a pair of jeans and a shirt that fit you. Then taking one of the vehicles if there's keys in one." He smiled. "Unless you can hot wire a car?"

Harry laughed. "Not a bloody clue."

"Nor me. Then bring it to the bottom of the ramp. Just to the bottom, or we will shoot you." There was no humour in that.

"Christ!"

"You haven't seen what we have." The sergeant looked at Harry's heap of kit. "Then cart that lot down and piss off. I never want to see the motor again, ever. OK?"

"Really? It's stealing."

That brought some humour, but the bitter kind. "Hah, who cares down there? My authority stops at the three hundred yard mark, unless you wave a firearm. Then we'll do our level best to kill you at any range." The sergeant watched Harry's face as he absorbed that. "Sorry, but this is city living 1-0-1. Take one of the pickup trucks if you can because the roads are rough in some places."

"Rough?" Harry realised he sounded a bit dumb, but this was a hell of a shock.

"That mess, where the houses are burned? That sort of rough. The mob that did it was pissed off because the RAF spotted them coming and we had a couple of armoured cars waiting. That damage was pure spite since they couldn't break out. Be off the streets by dark."

Harry stared out over the city. "I thought London was bad. Well it was, we were in a bloody war."

"Then you know what it's like down there. Still want to go?" Harry realised that the sergeant was hammering the situation home to give Harry a chance to back away.

"Sorry, I left someone in London I couldn't get out. Can't do the same to sis."

"Fair enough. Your gear is safe while you go shopping, since we shoot anyone stealing on the Queen's Highway." Harry stared and the sergeant nodded. "All the motorways and dual carriageways are private property now. They belong to the Ministry of Defence and the MOD will defend them."

"I'll go and get a motor." Harry set off in a daze.

He hadn't gone four steps when a voice called "and jeans. For God's sake get out of that uniform." He raised a hand to acknowledge the words and kept going.

Chapter 5:
Sister and Rug Rats

"Harry!" Sharyn hugged him tightly. "Come on in."

"I've got some gear, downstairs. I'd rather not leave it in the truck."

"Do you need help?"

"Not really ta, it's just a kitbag and a couple of packs. Is there anywhere I can park up?"

"Basement garage. I'll go down in the lift and open up. How did you get in without buzzing me?" Sharyn frowned. "Is the lock all right?"

"Yes, some old bloke sat in the foyer let me in." Harry grinned. "He wanted me to take him for a pint."

"He would. That's Clarence, and he's always doing that." Sharyn caught herself and the frown was replaced by a smile. "He's a bit doolally but we've got to stop him letting strangers inside. Though this time he got it right." She hugged Harry again. "Go on, the garage door is round the side. Then you can bring your gear up in the lift from there." She pushed him. "Round the side, just follow the little road and it's just off the car park. Hurry, it's getting dark."

Not really, there was barely a hint of dusk, but Harry hurried. He was wearing a big relieved smile because at least Sharyn seemed all right. He wasn't so happy about the two burnt out cars in the car park, or the big dents in the garage door. Once inside Harry went back to look at the door. Sharyn came out of the lift and joined him.

"When this did happen?"

"Three nights ago. It's getting worse, Harry. The police barely patrol at all now, and never get out of the cars. The coppers carry guns, now, which is scary all by itself. We can hear the gun battles every night on the big estates. The yobs come and steal everything that's not nailed down at night, which is why we lock up." Sharyn smiled. "We don't let Clarence down there at night or he'd let them in."

"Can't you fix the door so it won't open even if he tried?" Harry didn't like that idea at all, doors a doolally old man would open to anyone with a pint. This place didn't sound as bad as things were round Heathrow but then the place he'd taken Cyn to wasn't that bad either. Not yet, hopefully.

"Maybe. I'll ask Finn. He's an electrician so maybe he can do it? We thought of jamming something under the door to stop it opening, but some of the residents are worried about a fire." Sharyn was chattering happily as Harry carted his kit into the lift and they set off up again.

"What about the landlord, or the council if it's them? Can't they give you a master key or something?" Harry wasn't keen on the idea of a fire and doors that were jammed either.

"The landlord is the council. It's months since anyone from there came round. We've got a caretaker, but Mr Blunder can't get a straight answer from them either. That's if the phone works." Sharyn laughed at Harry's look. "Sorry, Harry. We call him Mr Blunder but it's really Baumber. He tries his best but if they won't talk to him he's stuffed. It's a good job we've got Finn and Rob living here. Rob's a plumber."

"All mod cons. Why haven't you boarded up the doors and bottom windows?" That was out before Harry thought properly. "Sorry Sharyn, but if you're worried about the yobs, that would stop them." Harry had been thinking of the front doors, and the big glass panes that allowed Clarence to see him, and his brain had slipped to the Cyn palace.

"I don't think anyone thought of it. Then there's the damage nails will cause to the frames. The council will go crackers. They still reckon we should pay part of the cost towards fixing the damage in the kid's playground, and that was yobs." Sharyn was thinking it through now. "You really think we need to do that? Board the windows?"

Harry decided to be honest and calm Sharyn down later if necessary. "After what I saw coming here? Yes, it might be a good idea."

"But where would we get the boards? I suppose B&Q or one of the other big DIY places might still be open, but who pays?" Sharyn firmed up. "Anyone who doesn't want yobs in through the windows I suppose. Where are you staying, Harry?"

"On your lounge floor?"

Sharyn gave a big beaming smile. "Wait until the rug rats get up in the morning. As I remember, you aren't that great at mornings."

"Bloody hell, the last time I saw Daisy she was firmly anchored down in a cot. How big is Wills, he's what, two now? That'll be a shock for both of us since I've only seen pictures." Harry suddenly realised just how long he'd been abroad. Over three years of sand.

"Daisy is nearly four. I was going to remind you in the next letter." Sharyn's voice wavered. "After all, no present from Daddy this year."

"Lots of Uncle Harry spoiling instead."

"That will be new for her. I've never thought of you playing with kids, though I did wonder if you'd come back with a girl." Sharyn had her smile back. She loved teasing little brother.

"Not allowed." Harry realised that had come out a bit sharp and moderated his tone. "No girls until we got back because Kuwait wasn't a safe place to go courting the locals. Then there actually was a girl. She was lots of fun and when it came time to leave her behind, I sort of suddenly didn't want to. The Army put the blocks on it. She's still in London." Harry smiled. "You nearly had a surprise sister-in-law."

"She must have been a hell of a lot of fun! Seriously?"

"Yup. Not because it was undying love. It might have turned out that way eventually but there wasn't time. The thing is, none of us wanted to leave any young woman in that hellhole. The Army put the blocks on it all." Harry laughed. "Davie? Maynard? He found a girl and he really, really did want to bring her with him."

"Maynard, Davie, found a girl? Blimey, did he actually kiss her? Did she tie him down? What does she look like?" Sharyn knew Davie Maynard and the squaddie was tongue-tied round her, let alone a single girl.

"He got a pretty one, and she really was determined." Harry laughed. "They ended up locked in a broom cupboard together and Marcie had the key. He's absolutely smitten."

Davie's love life kept them laughing up to the fourth floor and in through Sharyn's flat door. "I'll dump this lot in the corner for now." Harry turned from putting down his kitbag and suddenly had his arms full of sister. A sister who was sobbing her heart out!

"Thank God you're here Harry. Nobody knows what to do." Sharyn looked up through the tears. "Some of us want to leave but we've no idea where might be safe. Freddie said he'd get us into quarters when he came back and now he's not coming." That was all the talking since Sharyn buried her head in Harry's chest and cried. Big wracking sobs and he could feel the damp spreading on the shirt he'd stolen.

Harry was completely thrown. This was Sharyn. Big sis. The one who had sorted out the strife her little brother got in, slapped his ear for getting out of line and taken the piss out of his friends and girls. It had been a good few years since she'd stuck a plaster on Harry's knee or patiently listened to his heartbreak over some girl, but it was always that way round. She never needed anyone, not Sharyn.

When Dad left, and eventually Mum hit the bottle a bit too hard, Sharyn always made sure there was food in the cupboard. She sorted out the money and made sure Mum kept the council flat and Harry had a home. When Sharyn got married, Harry stuck it for a year. Then he joined the Army at the grand old age of sixteen. Mum had signed the papers without hesitation and then moved with no forwarding address.

Now Harry stood and patted Sharyn's back, and made little sympathy noises, and tried to work out what the hell to do next. He'd expected Sharyn to know what to do, not be waiting for him to arrive and bring a solution. Eventually the storm subsided enough for Sharyn to back off and try a smile.

"I've sogged your shirt. Not much of a welcome."

"Don't worry, it's stolen."

"What?" That straightened her up a bit, as Harry had hoped. He couldn't deal with a soggy Sharyn. Sad Sharyn, yes, Harry had expected that after Freddie dying, but not a sobbing mess.

"Jeans as well. So is the truck." Harry smiled and put on a terrible fake American accent. "I'm on da lam, sis. I gotta lay low or da Feds will get me."

"Piss off. The Feds?" Sharyn sniffed. "I'm a mess."

"A mess I'm very happy to see." Harry looked round. "Where are these rugrats? Did you give them a knockout drop or sell them to slavers?"

"Two doors down where I dropped them off when you went to get your stolen truck. Now give. Stolen clothes and jeans? I thought the Army let you go?"

Harry settled down in the kitchen and an hour and two cups of coffee later the bare bones of catching up was done. Then Harry got to meet a very shy four-year-old girl who looked just like the pictures he'd received, but without the cheeky smile. The toddler with her was big-eyed and overwhelmed. They were collected from Susan, a happy, bustling woman in her thirties who lived in the flat literally two doors down.

"Is the chippy open?" Harry grinned. "I could murder real fish and chips."

"Not at night. How about fish fingers and chips?" Sharyn smiled, happier now that she'd got her little brother and kids all together. "Did the Army teach you how to peel spuds?"

"Not a chance. It's all modern now. Dead cushy, like a five star hotel." Harry smiled back because Sharyn was an Army wife. Army widow, ouch, that hit Harry hard. Sharyn was twenty five, too young to be a widow.

Sharyn smiled at the cushy part. "Well it's time to learn how to be a civvie again. Let's see if you remember all those handy lessons I taught you. C'mon Daisy, bring Wills in the kitchen and you can watch Uncle Harry making a mess of the chips."

Wills made the biggest mess in the end, but on the little tray at the front of his high chair. The first glimpse of cheeky appeared when Harry pinched a chip from Daisy's plate and she pinched one back. Better yet, Sharyn seemed to have relaxed. The TV afterwards was just as depressing as usual so Harry did learn to draw a pony. Apparently a pony, drawing wasn't his strong point. Harry relaxed as well.

Daisy went off to bed at eight, and Harry was introduced to the bedtime book and The Amazing Talking Pig. Daisy remarked on the fireworks starting up early and Sharyn made a shushing sign at Harry, finger to lips. Once clear of the bedroom Sharyn turned and shrugged. "I don't want to tell her it's gunfire."

"Well it does sound a bit like fireworks. Have you heard enough to know the difference?" Sharyn had never been in an official war zone, but now Harry was wondering if this qualified.

"Every night. I'm not sure when occasionally became every night because the volume sort of worked up from now and then." Sharyn gave a little smile. "I thought the noise was fireworks at first but Freddie was home on leave once and said not. Though the firing was only now and then two years ago."

Sharyn gave a big sigh and looked at the other bedroom, the one where her son was already sleeping. "I'm sad that Wills will never remember Daddy, but maybe that's easier on him?" That needed another brother hug. Sharyn was definitely fragile at the moment.

"None of this is easy. I intended taking you out of here but the Army are only letting people with passes leave." Harry smiled. "If I'd known I would have applied."

"Have you got a trade? The only people I know who were offered a pass were Finn and Rob. Finn won't leave his mother, and Rob is sweet on Susan." Sharyn produced a real smile. "Yes, that Susan. Rob is divorced as well and we're all waiting with bated breath for the first real move from either." Gossip cheered Sharyn up but not for long. "If you go up to the roof, you can see the flashes."

"Seriously?"

"Oh yes, those are very serious people out there. We assume one lot are the police shooting back, but there's never a proper report on the news. Just some vague reference to unrest." Sharyn waved a hand downwards. "There's a lad with a CB radio on the second floor, Toby, and he talks to kids on the estates when he can get through. It's definitely not all police, because Toby's friends say that sometimes the lunatics are shooting at each other."

"Do you mind if I nip up there, just to look? I'd like some idea of how bad it is." Already Sharyn's description was worse than the TV or sergeant rumour had suggested.

"I'm fine, honest. Though I do feel better now you've arrived. Daisy likes you as well." Harry was nudged. "You'll be drawing ponies every day now. Or cats or pirates." Sharyn glanced at the TV. "You can help to keep Daisy occupied. There's two hours of kid's stuff on that in the morning. All repeats but Daisy didn't see most of them the first time round. No preschool now and those with kids at school aren't happy because of the violence. Half the teachers have left." Sharyn sighed. "I'll give you the gory details later. You go and watch the fireworks. They'll get louder nearer midnight."

"So I'll look then. Until then we can watch boring TV or you can fill me in on city living."

"Oh boy, have you got a treat coming." Sharyn smiled. "You can make the coffee since you're dossing here. Cheap coffee because the good stuff is in short supply now."

*   *   *

Harry stood on the roof of the flats and watched the flashes of gunfire here and there in the cityscape spread out on all sides. He was worried about the sheer volume of fire in some places, though those were a long way off. What worried Harry more was the line of tracers out of the night sky into the middle of one of the firefights. There was a helicopter gunship up there, firing on a British city! He assumed the same must have happened in London, but he'd been fast asleep or in the middle of a riot most of the nights. Harry smiled. Or locked in a broom cupboard.

Maybe the answer was still to get out and try for that place in the country. He should be able to smuggle Sharyn and the kids past the guard posts, especially if the Army were only guarding the roads. Harry hoped he could, and that there'd be a motor he could steal out there nearby. After all, there were lots of places that the housing spilled over outside the ring road.

Harry remembered London, but there the place was completely sealed and the housing outside the M25 had been evacuated. Here there were still passes, and no tanks. There was still some normal life. Harry watched a long line of lorries making their way out of the city. He could see each blocky shape in the light of the vehicle behind. Supermarket deliveries? That was reassuring, the normal nightlife of a city.

Sharyn was dozing when Harry came down, so he chased her off to bed and settled down on the settee.

*   *   *

Harry jumped a mile when he opened his eyes. A pair of serious dark brown eyes were looking at him from only a few inches away. They jumped back with a squeak as Harry reared up, startled, and then there was a peal of laughter. Drawing and bedtime stories had dealt with shy, sort of, and Daisy had come to see if Uncle Harry wanted to draw. Harry groaned, wrapped the cover round himself, and staggered to the bathroom.

"Good morning." Harry groaned again as he came out of the bathroom to meet Sharyn's smiling face. "You got a lie in. She's usually up before eight."

"What!"

"Cheer up Harry. I've already fed Wills. You still sleep soundly and missed it. I sent Daisy in to wake you up before she drove me crazy, because she's been on the go for over half an hour. It's gone eight thirty and she wants to play with her new toy. Uncle Harry. Welcome to married life, without the benefits." Harry did his best to smile over his cornflakes. "Do you mind if we go shopping, Harry?"

Harry tried to imagine Daisy helping him shop in a supermarket and pictured chaos. "All of us?"

Sharyn laughed. "Not this time. I'll leave them with Susan but I'll owe her."

"Owe her? Is Susan a childminder then?"

"No, she's a neighbour without a job. Susan will be very happy with food as pay since the dole doesn't always arrive either. Which is a bitch since she worked in the dole office before the redundancies. They got rid of everyone with short service so it cost the miserable gits peanuts, or will if they pay up." Sharyn sighed. "There's a lot of that about, redundancy and places shutting down."

"Do you want a ride in a stolen vehicle then?"

"Shush." Sharyn rolled her eyes towards Daisy. "Big ears and bigger mouth." Daisy recognised the description and giggled. Then put both hands over her mouth. "How much petrol has your new ride got?"

"Three quarters of a tank. It's a diesel."

"Who cares what sort of fuel? Three quarters of a tank, where did you?

Um. Never mind, but petrol and diesel are very hard to get. Don't leave the thing parked up anywhere without a guard."

"Difficult while shopping." Harry knew there was a shortage, but having fuel tanks drained if the vehicle was left unattended was a whole different scale of shortage.

"So far so good in their car park, because there are people about. Daisy, you're off to play with Susan while we go shopping. You be good." They left Daisy chanting Coco Pops which was both her favourite cereal and not always available.

"How do you survive? With Daisy and Wills as well." Harry was smiling but also a bit stunned. Whole days of that sort of onslaught from Daisy was going to be wearing.

Sharyn sniggered. "She'll calm down a bit when the novelty wears off."

"I'll have to go to the pub for some peace and quiet."

"Not after dark." Sharyn looked at Harry and reassessed. "You might get away with it. You've filled out a bit, little brother."

"Bloody hell, are you serious about that, the pub?" Harry thought about the fireworks and Sharyn's comments about lack of a police presence. "Maybe I'll bring a few cans back."

"Maybe I'll pinch one."

*   *   *

The trip around the supermarket was a revelation because there were gaps on the shelves. "I've never seen that before."

"Probably because the Army don't think it's a good idea to upset the soldiers? The shortages are getting worse, and mainly named brands. Especially foreign food. I suppose the ships haven't got the oil to sail all over the world and import the exotic stuff. Though coffee isn't exotic, not really." Sharyn was looking at the coffee on sale, and Harry could see there really only were the cheaper brands and mainly powder or granules.

"I hope it's not that."

"What, the imports stopping? Why, are you a fan of foreign food now?" Sharyn smiled at him. "Mr Bacon Egg and Chips Please used to be your unofficial name."

"It still is, but the UK can't survive without imports. We don't grow enough." Harry thought again but he was sure that old TV programme had said so. "Blame late night TV but it does tell you odd facts. There's too many people in the UK for us to feed, even if we plant up all the farmland that's been left unused under the eco scheme."

Sharyn looked startled. "We'd have to go back to the old war films, with everyone planting up their gardens. Though we can't plant spuds and carrots in a window box."

"Then we need a house with a garden."

Sharyn stopped the shopping trolley and gave Harry a long look. "Seriously? Did you just win the lottery?"

"No but it's just another step up from the pickup. All these people have left, so the houses are empty?" Harry laughed. "Your face is a picture."

"Grand theft auto to grand theft house is a big step. Anyway, the houses will be up for sale."

"To who? Look, it was a joke but now I think about it, why not?" Harry looked round. "Not the best place to talk, so wait until we're home." Harry picked up a cereal packet. "What's a Coco Pop look like?"

"They're expensive now."

Harry smirked. "Uncles are supposed to be stupid and treat kids, aren't they? Anyway, while she's stuffing herself with Coco Pops I get a rest."

"Fat chance. Here, they're not the right ones but as near as we'll get. They turn the milk brown with chocolate which is apparently the main requirement." Sharyn picked up a packet with a garish picture of a bowl of mud and a happy face. A bowl of chocolate according to the blurb.

Harry put three packets in the trolley. "Right, what's your favourite, apart from a big bar of chocolate?"

"Small bar, the big ones are extinct. Hey, look, your favourites. How many cans do you want?"

"Not many. I don't fancy a hangover and Daisy combined." Harry kept throwing extras in the trolley because that would pay his way. "You let me get this lot, right?"

"All of it?" Sharyn was taking milk off the shelf and hesitated. "You really are flush?"

"Yes, so cash in. Take extra of everything. I didn't spend much pay in Kuwait even while it was still going into the bank on time. Even if they still owe me a lot of back pay I'm OK for a while." Harry took an extra couple of big plastic bottles of milk. "Better cash in before I find a girl and spend it on her."

"You just did, I reckon. Her name's Daisy." Sharyn was looking at a plastic horse with a rider that had somehow appeared in the trolley. She looked almost shy for a moment. "Um, just how flush are you, Harry?"

"I'm comfy for a while. Why?"

"Because we can get some real fresh food, but only for cash. Black market except it's not. It's a real market but the veggies are fresher and they have fresh meat, even joints. The meat in here looks a bit tired and is usually only fit for stewing." Sharyn smiled. "We could get free range eggs that way." Then she looked embarrassed again. "I can't afford to get much usually since the good food is expensive. Freddie's payments just haven't come through. His pay stopped but nothing else has started."

"Lead me to a cash machine. Bacon, eggs."

"And chips," Sharyn finished.

* * *

Six eggs and two cans of lager paid for babysitting and the Daisy on-slaught started with a delighted squeal at the sight of the horse. It was gone eight and Daisy was in bed before Harry had a chance to talk sensibly to Sharyn, and she'd been waiting as well.

"Here." Harry accepted the can Sharyn offered and popped the tab. "Now just how serious were you about us moving?"

"Well I'd like to board up the windows and door first, and sort of weigh up the situation here. If things get even close to like where I was in London, we need a library or bank or something similar. An old solid place, with small windows and stone walls, and car parks each side." Harry thought about the Cyn palace. "Maybe a playing field out back. If the schools are shut we can plant spuds."

Sharyn narrowed her eyes. "That came out much too pat. When did you work this out? It wasn't with a chance remark in the supermarket."

"I told you about the girl in London, Cynthia? Well." Harry explained about the Cyn palace.

"Did you get it bad for this girl?"

"Kinda. Yes, probably if there'd been time. It was all sort of riots and broom cupboard. I would have liked to take her for a pint, and to a dance, and then who knows? Then as I told you, I couldn't get her out."

"Yes, I thought it might be that way. You're acting all casual about Cynthia but you gave her a box full of guns. Most girls expect flowers but under the circumstances that sounds a much better idea. I'm beginning to wish Freddie had been one of those who brought back that sort of souvenir." Sharyn glanced at Harry's pack. "Did you?"

"No, because we all had our gear searched before we left London. Luckily the sergeants sort of leaked the information up-front. Anyway, I gave them all the spare guns, the staff." Harry knew he sounded defensive but Sharyn had a big smile and a raised eyebrow. "They weren't a personal gift to Cynthia."

"Whatever you say, lover-boy. Seriously though, the gun maniac didn't bring one itty bitty popgun home?" Sharyn sighed. "That might have been comforting if the fireworks came closer."

"I'm not a gun maniac. I just like shooting rifles. It's sort of peaceful. All your attention has to go into the shot, and with the ear defenders on you're in a little world away from all the rest. Though shooting is nothing like peaceful in the Army when someone shoots back." Harry fell silent for a while.

"Want to talk about it?"

"Not now, thanks sis, and maybe not ever." Harry looked around. "Let's talk about boarding up windows and cheerful things like that. While I was being catted and pirated and generally abused, did you mention boarding up to anyone?"

"Susan likes the idea but has no money for boards. Rob is sort of for it, probably because of Susan. Finn isn't sure that boarding up is necessary but if he thinks his Mum is in danger he'll be out there with a hammer and nails in a nanosecond." Sharyn smiled. "Finn won't move unless we bring his Mum. She's in a wheelchair and he's sick with worry because the ambulance didn't turn up for her last visit."

"Why!"

"Steady on. Staff shortages, why?"

Harry sighed in relief. "Sorry. We had to put armed guards on ambulances in London. Some were hijacked for the drugs."

Sharyn stared. "Christ. It's not that bad here, or maybe it is and the hospital wasn't saying. Finn did say the A&E, Accident and Emergency reception, was overflowing when he took his Mum in the car. She hates that, being lifted in and out and using a hospital chair."

"We could strap her wheelchair down in the back of the pickup?"

Sharyn laughed. "Mary might enjoy that. She's cheerful most of the time, but takes tons of pills to stay that way. Because of pain, not depression. The drug dealers should raid her cupboard, not an ambulance." Sharyn looked at the kitbag again and sighed. "Not one?"

"If it worries you, I could nip down to the rifle club." Harry smiled at Sharyn's startled expression. "I kept up my membership with a good old standing order. My old rifle should still be there if it isn't worn out." Harry shrugged. "Not mine, technically, but I paid for it and the club said they'd only loan that rifle to people who could really shoot. To people who would treat it decently. Not that I could bring a rifle home anyway."

"You could steal it?" Sharyn laughed. "Gotcha. Your face is a picture. Revenge for the house suggestion." Her face straightened. "But you might want to check if the gun club is still open."

"They'd better be. They've been taking my bloody money for over three years because I kept thinking I'd get leave." Harry pulled out his wallet and then stopped. "I didn't keep the card. Did you keep my old gear?"

"Your Sci-Fi paperbacks and little black book? Plus the first love letter or whatever was in that box. At least it didn't smell." Sharyn relented. "Yes, in the back of my wardrobe. Though you said a year or so until you had a chance to sort yourself out."

"I was only seventeen when I was in the country the last time, so I didn't work up much of a black book. Though the book does have the number of the gun club. If the phone is working?"

"Hang on." Sharyn lifted the receiver and listened. "There's a dial tone so I'll go and get the box."

"Good, because I couldn't get a connection from London."

A few minutes later Sharyn tried to peek while Harry slid out the address book. There was a garter in there, and a picture of a girl wearing it with a big red lipstick kiss and not a lot else obscuring her. Neither were something a big sister should see. Then Harry dialled the phone number.

"There's an answerphone message saying they're not open without an appointment, and another phone number. Have you got a pen?" Harry tried the number again once he had a biro and a pad and wrote down the contact.

"Right, I'll try this one. I wonder why they're closed? You'd think more people would want to join or at least practice on a range, what with the fireworks." Both were referring to the gunfire, which was now clearly audible again, as fireworks. That took the edge off how serious the reality was.

"Harry Miller. I'm a member. Yes, honest, look me up." Harry sat with the phone to his ear and waited. Sharyn was curious so he covered the mouthpiece. "He doesn't know me, never heard of me, and doesn't want to talk about the club." Then Harry took his hand away and spoke into the phone. "Hello? Did you find me?"

Sharyn listened to a one-sided conversation as Harry persuaded the man on the other end that he was that Harry Miller and had been in the Army, and was home now. The phone went down and Harry really looked worried.

"He won't meet unless it's in the pub up the road, in broad daylight, and he wants to see my ID. Not only that but it's got to be on Monday, after the weekend. Otherwise he won't show me where the range is or let me in. Christ, I could drive right to the place but Mr Pilsworth nearly had a bloody fit when I offered to do that."

Harry looked over at Sharyn. "There's all of six members left and he's only seen two in the last month. He's worried about some toerag finding the range and nicking everything. If I was a toerag I'd be round there with a crowbar."

"You are a toerag. Are you going in your stolen motor?"

"Ouch, low blow. Yes, and wearing my stolen jeans though at least I've now got some shirts and a civvie jacket."

"You could have more?" Sharyn gave a sad little smile. "Some of Freddie's clothes would fit."

"Thanks, but that would feel weird, and won't it upset you?"

"Not really, I don't think. If it does, then you can clear them out for me? Please? I can't do it." Sharyn sighed. "I went to the service and scattered his ashes and yet somehow getting rid of Freddie's clothes means he won't be coming back. That's all screwed up, I know. Maybe if you wander round here in his trousers and maybe wear his coat, it will sort of close things down?"

"OK. It will still seem weird but I'll try with the coat." Harry smiled. "I doubt I'll fill his trousers." Freddie was a hero to a younger Harry. The big, cheerful soldier who swept sis off her feet. Even now Harry still felt a bit of that hero-worship. Freddie, and Stones, were the reasons Harry joined up but sis didn't need to know that.

"OK. Another beer?"

Harry recognised a change of subject when it hit him between the eyes and went for two more cans.

*   *   *

They watched the news, and the mounting list of cities and large towns where there was civil unrest. "This place never got a mention. Doesn't that count?" Harry waved at the window where sporadic fireworks sounded.

"Wait until tomorrow, Friday. The weekends are worse for some reason. That makes no sense because the TV says the unrest is the unemployed and gangsters." Sharyn watched the news a bit longer. "Be careful when you go to the rifle club. I've got a baseball bat you can take."

Harry was startled, then smiled. "I've got something better. A poncy stick."

He laughed at Sharyn's look. "A little memento from Stones and his mates."

"Has it got a cannon in one end, or bloody great spikes on it?" Sharyn was staring at the pack as Harry opened it. "What did those idiots give you?"

"Stones did it really, I reckon. When I got the medal." Harry turned with the stick.

Sharyn gave low whistle. "That's definitely as good as a baseball bat. I thought it was your shoulder and hand that were hurt, not your leg?"

"It was Stones who had the broken leg so he has one as well. Watch this." Harry cavorted around the room waving and jabbing with the weapon while Sharyn fluctuated between disbelief and hilarity.

"Stop it or I'll end up waking Daisy and she doesn't need to see that demonstration. She'll want a toy version and Wills will lose an eye." Sharyn sniggered as Harry propped the stick against the kitbag. "That should do the job. Was that prancing from films or have you really practiced?"

"This was Stones, remember, so we had to practice a lot too bloody hard. He's still in Kuwait as far as I know." That took away Harry's smile.

Sharyn glanced at the TV, the source of all knowledge these days. "Well the news said everyone, the Army, is home now. Except for the Falklands, for the oil, and Gibraltar which is probably just to keep sticking it to Spain. Or maybe because the Navy needs the parking space. Stones might not be coming back." She paused. "Tessa will be gutted."

"Yeah, that'll be no fun for her. She won't get married quarters if he didn't come back."

"She married him?"

Harry laughed at Sharyn's expression. "No, not Stones. But he does refer to her as his missus and put her down as a dependent. Told me he sent her part of his pay to help with Eddie. You do know she had a boy and Stones is the daddy, all official on the Army records?"

"Yes, I used to see her shopping now and then, but she's moved across the city to live with her dad. You should look her up." Sharyn smiled. "Though there's that girl in London so maybe not."

"Stop it. Stones might still be alive." Though a seventeen year old Harry did have a bit of a thing about Tessa when he saw her with Stones. Lonely dreams of a frustrated teenager sort of thing.

"Of course, and the last thing she needs is pestering by a pimply youth." Harry didn't have pimples now, but Sharyn had once again tweaked him nicely.

"Where's the best place for plywood?"

Sharyn also understood a change of subject when it hit her on the head.

*   *   *

"The Dog and Stoat looks a bit rough." Harry eyed up the boarded windows on the pub.

Mr Pilsworth glanced at Harry. "How long is it since you saw it?" His eyes narrowed. "You can't have been old enough." The tall, spare man with grey hair had relaxed a bit after seeing Harry's ID but still wasn't comfortable about showing a stranger the rifle range.

"Seventeen when I last saw it, but I was a tall seventeen. After all, it's not that far from the range." Mr Pilsworth twitched so Harry continued. "I really can drive straight there, so I'm not trying to rob the place."

"I looked it up. You really did buy the rifle for the club. Why?"

"I was sixteen so I couldn't get a licence. Mum was a bit keen on the bottle so she certainly wouldn't get one. This way I had a decent second hander that wasn't as badly abused as the other club rifles." They were inside now and Harry waved at the pumps. "A pint please."

"Sorry mate. That one doesn't work. Not many of them do because the deliveries are a bit iffy. We've got a crackin' home brew."

"Pint of home brew please, Sam."

Mr Pilsworth didn't seem to have any hesitation so Harry took the plunge. "I'll risk one as well, please. Is it brewed in a bathtub then?" Harry thought that through as the pints were poured. "How does he produce enough for a pub?"

"Her and him, two of them. They've got a microbrewery that supplies a good few places and that's all you find out." Sam smiled to take the sting out of his reply and rang in the cash.

"Blimey, most producers like advertising."

"Not since two microbreweries had midnight visitors and all the bloody stock went missing. One was trashed and the other poor sod was working late. The savages killed him." This time Sam didn't hide the sting. "Where have you been?"

"In London, with the Army."

"Bunch of wankers. They sit on the bypass and watch the assholes burn the place down." Sam didn't think much to the Army. Put like that, those left in London probably weren't keen.

"They aren't allowed to help. I left to come and help my sister, since they've got too many soldiers now." That didn't match up with pulling out of the population centres either. This trip wasn't making Harry feel better about the situation. "You've still got police though?"

"They won't stop unless there's actually a murder going on in the street in front of the car." That was Mr Pilsworth so it wasn't just Sam who was bitter. "Can we sit down because I'd like to check something?"

They sat and in a quiet voice Mr Pilsworth asked. "Do you genuinely know where the range is? I'm sorry, but I'm absolutely paranoid that someone will get what's left and kill some innocent."

Harry told him, and briefly described the inside. "Now you can tell me just how bad it is here. This area sounds worse than where my sister lives." Mr Pilsworth explained, and it was a lot worse. The smashed windows in most of the houses on their way to the range, and several burned out cars, bore mute testimony to that.

Mr Pilsworth got out of his car, glanced around and then unlocked the gate, and both drove into the yard. As soon as he got out Harry had his first question. "When did the gate go up?" Mr Pilsworth turned from locking them in.

"Two years ago when one of the members was mugged while getting into his car. Luckily he wasn't someone with their own rifle." Mr Pilsworth went down the three steps and the door now had a steel plate across the whole front. The engraved plate on the old door that had announced what was inside here hadn't been refastened. There were two locks, and as soon as they were inside Mr Pilsworth drove two big bolts home.

"Has anyone tried to get in?" Harry was a lot more worried now.

"Twice though I don't think they knew what was in here. Just someone with a crowbar looking for an empty lockup to rob." Lights came on as Mr Pilsworth flicked switches. "Don't come here at night, and don't tell anyone where it is or bring them with you."

"I can't come anyway without you."

"Yes you can." Mr Pilsworth unhooked keys from a board. "The rest have their own keys and since you know where the place is you may as well have a set as well. Please be careful to shut all the doors before shooting, Mr Miller, because that means nobody can hear you. Unless you've got some sort of big cannon you're going to bring here?"

"No, I just wanted to keep my hand in. What about buying ammunition?"

"The charges are up there, for air pistol and two-two rifle ammo. That's all we have. There again, you know that." He looked at the lockers and a list. "There's the rifle you want." He unfastened the locker. "There are club rifles in those three, and the air pistols in the end one. The rest are empty now. The ammunition is through here in a floor safe." Mr Pilsworth laughed. "Under the rug of course. Make an entry in the book and stick the cash in the box in the safe."

After showing Harry the safe and the combination, Mr Pilsworth stuck out a hand. "Well I'll be off. Please bolt the door after me, and get out before dark." Harry shook the man's hand and bolted the door as asked. Then he sat for a while to digest the news on how bad this area was. The whole place was definitely edging towards a London scenario.

Harry popped off thirty rounds just for the relaxation, and the cool quiet of the range worked its magic and relaxed him. Then he locked up and drove home.

Sharyn had bad news. Three of the four living on the ground floor weren't willing to have their windows boarded up because they wouldn't live in a cave. Worse still, the news announced that a second city, Glasgow, was being sealed off the same way as London. Army engineers were shown putting up mesh fences and bulldozing a clear zone along its length. The pictures also showed a mob with firearms trying to storm an Army checkpoint.

That night Harry's dreams started again. The screaming faces charging him and the hate-filled ones pointing rifles at his friends, and one after another he shot them.

*   *   *

Five days later Sharyn was waiting as Harry came into the flat. "Can you come to a meeting please, Harry? Susan will be looking after Daisy and Wills because I want to be there as well." Harry was nicely chilled. He was just back from his second visit to the range and a pint of home brew.

"What's the panic?"

"A group of yobs chucked a brick through Mr Bungle's flat window, and tried to throw petrol bomb after it. Well, they did throw one but he's got a proper fire extinguisher for emergencies so he put it out." Sharyn threw up her hands. "Now everyone wants their bloody windows boarding up, right now."

"A window? What about the main doors?"

"They threw a couple of bricks at that but the glass is tougher. Health and Safety regulations. At least Finn fixed them so Clarence can't open the doors now or he probably would have." Sharyn was collecting toys for Wills.

"Organise Daisy will you, because otherwise she'll complain because it's Uncle Harry time." Daisy did complain and was mollified by promises of an ice lolly later.

Harry waited in the corridor while Sharyn peeled Daisy off him and then handed her to Susan. "So where is this meeting?"

"Thank you Susan. I'll cast your vote." Sharyn turned. "In the foyer. It's the only place big enough since some will sit on the stairs. We'll take the lift this time." That was a dig at Harry for using the stairs to keep fit.

Harry hadn't seen so many people at one time since arriving. A quick look round and he made it thirty-four now he'd arrived. "Hi Sharyn. Is this the soldier boy?" A short, balding, portly man in blue overalls waved as they came out of the lift.

Sharyn laughed. "Harry, meet Rob. Rob, meet Harry." She looked around the assembled residents. "In fact, everyone, meet Harry my little brother."

"Little? Cripes, have you got a big one? A jolly green one." That was a dark haired woman in her early twenties who was wearing an apron with scorch marks on it. She wasn't exactly tiny herself, only just under six feet Harry thought.

"No Liz. Just the one and he's only just over six feet. He just looms a bit next to me."

"Hi Liz. Hi everyone. Sharyn said there's been a fire." Harry didn't need Sharyn taking the piss in front of everyone, and she'd start if there was a chance.

"There was but Mr Blu... Mr Baumber put it out." The lady with the blue rinse smiled and shrugged off the slip of the tongue. "But if that was my window I don't have one of those big extinguishers. By the time I'd got the one from the corridor the while place would have been ablaze."

"Worse still, what if they'd come in through the window?" The arms the elderly man had around the woman with him were a clear indication what he was worried about protecting.

"We need the windows boarding up, and Sharyn said that was your idea the first time round, Mr er?" That was blue rinse and Harry wondered if she was the yes or a no the first time round.

"Harry."

"Oh, that's informal. Harry. Can you board up windows?"

"If I've got the plywood and some help."

A stout man had another worry. "What about the damage to the window frames?"

"Better than having the flats on fire Mr Baumber."

The mystery voice made the objector, a stout man in a brown smock, pause for a moment. Mr Baumber then continued. "But the council will insist on being paid. I can't make it official." He hesitated. "I can forget to report it? Blame the phone?"

"Good man" and various other comments came from the company.

"We need to go and buy the gear before dark. Has anyone got money because I'm not sure how much it will cost?" Harry looked round. "Though I'll chip in because being up on the fourth floor I don't fancy the first floor catching fire." Initial reluctance gave way to offers of money as people thought that one through.

"I've got petrol in my van though we might need two vehicles." Rob smiled. "I don't fancy taking my gear out of it to make room, not if we've got to get moving by dark."

"I've got a pickup." Harry shrugged. "It's got diesel as yet. Who's got tools?"

Finn stuck up a hand. "I reckon between me and Rob we've got enough drills and such. I'm sure a lot of people have a hammer or a screwdriver but we'll need screws or nails." Other hands went up to volunteer tools or help and then the crowd was moving.

"Come on, soldier boy." Liz smiled. "I've got plastic but no cash so I'll need a lift to Homebase." She noticed Sharyn's little smile and lifted eyebrow and laughed. "He's safe with me. I like my men with a lot more muscle. Body builders, weight lifters," her eyes opened wide and she put more expression into the last word. "Blacksmiths."

A hand squeezed Harry's bicep. "Plenty there for me, dearie." Harry looked down startled and Blue Rinse smiled and headed off up the corridor.

"She does that." Harry looked at Sharyn as she spoke and his sister was grinning. "Karen has got Mr Baumber running scared. She keeps inviting him in for a night of gin rummy, gin, and debauchery, and nobody is certain she doesn't mean it." Harry received a sister-hug. "Now go and do your thing, solder boy."

Liz was chatty but really did like muscly men, and especially blacksmiths, and bemoaned the lack of medieval fairs and the like in the last few years. Harry did find out about the apron. "If you want a twee little bit of metal scrollwork to fasten to Sharyn's door I'm the go-to person."

Liz smiled. "Or some real Twisted Sister artwork, all twirly bits of wrought iron and brass? No big brutal stuff like that stick, though I could probably make one. Might not manage such a good job on the crest or the engraving.

What's it say?"

"The pen is mightier than the sword."

Liz laughed and pointed at the stick. "Maybe if you've got a pen that size. Turn left at the traffic lights. Don't wait because they won't change." Sure enough the other traffic was ignoring the red light. Harry pulled into the car park and the first thing that was obvious was that Homebase had been dipping into their own stocks. All the big windows were boarded up.

Harry was a bit worried about that so he found someone with a name badge straight away. "Have you got any plywood left and where is it, please?"

The young man glanced at the group behind Harry. "Maybe. It depends on how much you need because everyone's got the same idea. Down there, at the back." He headed off, obviously determined not to be commandeered into the loading.

"We've got the transport." Rob and Mr Baumber had a low trolley each and the group soon found the plywood.

"How much do we need?" They looked at each other.

"All of it? We can always sell any that's left over." The rest glanced at Liz, at the heap, and agreed.

"Hey, you can't take it all."

"Because? It is all for sale." Harry looked at the two men and wondered if he should offer them some. Then he thought of the number of windows on the ground floor.

"But what will we do? What about our windows?" The older man wasn't giving up.

"Take some off an empty building." Everyone turned to the young man coming past with a basket containing boxes of screws. "If they're empty, who will stop you?" Then he was gone towards the checkout.

"That's stealing." But the younger man was now pulling the arm of the older and talking quietly, eventually leading him off towards the nails and screws.

"So why aren't we stealing ours? Though it doesn't actually seem right." Rob was definitely unsure now.

"Because we can afford it, we've got enough here, and we haven't time to run around for the amount we want." Harry was pleased that Sharyn wasn't here or she'd be raising an eyebrow to mock him or asking where he got that lovely motor.

"Screws are over here." Liz was done with the discussion and she was right, they needed to get moving. Not only that but the nails and screws were taking a beating as well so the group loaded up with a good selection. On the way out Harry picked up the three remaining pick-shafts.

"What are they for?"

Harry smiled at Mr Baumber and hefted one. "For the first toerag who climbs through a window?"

"Go soldier boy." Liz liked the idea. "Why not a big hammer?"

"Because only a blacksmith could swing it."

She laughed. "I'll look out for one, and a hammer." The woman on the checkout wasn't happy at taking part cash and part payment from three separate credit cards, but couldn't find a reason to say no. The ply and lengths of timber were loaded and the convoy reversed their course.

Liz was still very cheerful when they arrived back, and actually told Harry why. "I've been worried sick because nobody would actually do anything. Now you've arrived and suddenly we're getting organised."

"Not really. This is because some yob broke Mr Baumber's window."

"Not really. After all they nearly broke into the garage before you came. But one or two of us like the idea of the Army, a soldier boy, on hand. We'd been discussing your idea of boarding up but only Karen was up for it." Liz sniggered. "Even now we'll probably have to cut a hole so Mrs Burren-Croft can let her Fluff in and out."

Harry had to ask. "Fluff?"

"A bloody great hairy cat with a name as long as it is, so we all call it Fluff. Her objection is that Fluff can't get out the window to do dirties. Hang on, I'll get the garage door."

An additional dozen men and women were perfectly happy to help saw, hammer and screw plywood into place though it was decidedly dusky by the time they'd finished. Fluff did have a hole in the boards, which had a door in it and a bolt for when he wasn't out doing dirties. A lasting effect of the boarding up cooperation was an agreement to have a resident's meeting every week, in the foyer.

Harry was torn over the following days. At least partly because of a reluctance to believe that the area he grew up with could get like the streets near Heathrow airport. He did take the time to look for a suitable place to fort up. There was nothing unoccupied and defensible where he looked. After trying to buy diesel, Harry was wary about using what was in the pickup to just drive around looking. Both Rob and Finn confided that they took fuel as part payment for the work they got. That was drying up though, both the fuel and the work.

Everything was drying up. The fresh food at the cash market became scarcer, and cost more. There was no sign of Sharyn's pay from the Army Compensation Fund, nor Susan's redundancy pay. Harry's back pay didn't arrive and it became clear that only long-standing payments for unemployment or sickness were being paid. Something had to happen soon because more and more people were running short of money for food.

The next block of flats was two hundred yards away across a now abandoned and overgrown children's play area and the two car parks, one for each block. Following a night where the residents in Sharyn's block could see flames in a lower window, there was a visitor. The man went off with the advice that had been given in Homebase, steal plywood from empty properties.

Chapter 6:
Forting Up

"Christ, what the hell." There was hammering on the flat door and the phone was ringing and Harry was trying to get his head working. At least it had stopped the bloody dream.

"Harry, Harry!" That was Finn.

"Coming." Harry staggered to the door as a bleary-eyed Sharyn headed for the phone and a sleepy complaint announced that Daisy was awake.

"There's someone breaking into the garage." Harry sharpened up as Finn continued. "There's a gang of them."

"How many?"

"I don't know. Karen can hear them because they hammered on her boarding first. Said they were coming to get her." Finn looked past Harry. "Can I have a pick-shaft please?" He was clutching a claw hammer.

"Yeah right, no problem. How many more are awake?"

"Everyone because we're ringing round or hammering on doors. In case they get in or set fire to the place." Finn was interrupted by Sharyn.

"Louise is on the third floor right above them. There's seven and they've got hammers and crowbars." Sharyn had the phone to her ear and held up a hand for a moment to listen. "She says should she throw things?"

"Big heavy things she doesn't mind losing. That'll slow them up because they'll dodge." Sharyn spoke into the phone while Finn pulled on Harry's arm.

"Won't that stop them?"

"No. She might get one but if they're determined they'll just step aside. We need enough people to scare them off."

"I'll see who will come. What should they bring?" That was Susan, now in the corridor wearing a big fluffy dressing gown. "Rob says he's got a crowbar and he's on the way here so you can go to the garage in a group. In case they're already inside."

Harry shook his head. "We don't want them in the garage. If they break the door we'll never fix it. We'll have to go out and chase them off." Silence greeted that.

"Go outside?" Finn wasn't happy and the six pairs of eyes now in the corridor weren't either.

"Unless you want a broken garage door and the next lot lighting bonfires in there?" The eyes didn't like that either.

"Right. Er. I'll start phoning. What do they bring?" Susan was firming up nicely.

"Clubs, and the longer the better. We want to be able to threaten them before they can start punching or anything like that." Like knives Harry was thinking, because it was odds on that the yobs would have some.

"You need shoes at least, even if you're doing a Hulk impression in boxers." Sharyn's voice brought Harry up with a jerk. He glanced down.

"Er, right. I'll get dressed first." He retreated into the flat and headed for clothes.

As soon as the door closed Sharyn asked. "How serious is it?"

"If we stop them breaking the door, not too bad. Enough people waving things and they'll back off. Can you get people to look out of the other sides and make sure there's no more lurking?" Harry had suddenly realised that a few luring the main doors open would be a neat trick. Hopefully the yobs weren't tacticians.

By the time Harry was in the foyer the answer was no, there were no other yobs in sight. There were also sixteen determined residents gripping walking sticks, some golf clubs, a couple with baseball bats, and several with claw hammers. Karen had a single crutch and Harry remembered how slowly she actually walked. "You guard the door Karen."

For a moment Karen was about to object, then subsided. "Very smooth. Just my type."

Harry smiled then turned to the rest and held out his spares. "One baseball bat and a pick-shaft. Those with muscles please apply." Liz took the baseball bat and passed her long shafted lump hammer to someone with a kitchen knife.

"I've got muscles from pounding iron." She twirled the bat. "Right, what the plan, general?"

Harry looked at them and got a little bit ambitious. Not completely, but they outnumbered the yobs enough to try. "We'll try and get the hammers and crowbars off them. Who are fastest and fittest?" Hands went up, some hesitant. "Right, when I start running you come with me and we try to get level with them. Not surround them or they'll fight. We want them to drop the heavy stuff and run to avoid being surrounded."

"Will that work?"

"No idea but if we can get the tools they won't come back."

"I'm with that." Rob did have a crowbar and a wicked looking nail bar nearly the length of a baseball bat. Liz claimed it and handed the baseball bat to another less well armed man, one who said he could run. "You keep them occupied and once I finally get there?" Rob swished the crowbar. "We can't let them get at the women."

Harry hoped they all kept the act up, and that enough would firm up if it came to a fight. Rob was certainly determined. Liz grinned. "I'm protecting the men."

"Right, come on." The crowd exited and Karen stood inside the door as it closed, with her implement ready and a determined expression. She would look through the peephole, and open up when the residents came back. The group walked to the corner, from where the clang of hammer on metal and the creak of the door under strain sounded clearly. So did a sudden crash and swearing, and the sounds of breaking in ceased for a few moments. Louise was on the job.

As soon as the next crash sounded Harry said "now" quietly and the group went round the corner. The seven were looking up at the balcony where Louise was shaking her fist at them. Harry was relieved because most of this lot were low teens, maybe sixteen or younger. The two older men were perhaps Harry's age. Even as the group of residents closed the gap one of those looked over and swore, and the rest turned to look.

One man held up a hand. "You stop right there or you'll get it." Sure enough, knives appeared in several teenage hands.

Harry just kept walking. Most of the youngsters weren't confident because they were looking at numbers, not the type of people behind Harry. He spoke to keep them in place just a bit longer, because Harry wanted to be near enough to clobber one of the older men if it all went wrong. He thought the youngsters might scatter if that happened. "We'll get what? Big long clubs against bitty little knives? We'll beat you to death." Harry hoped that would reassure the ones behind him.

One of the older men was speaking urgently, but the other one shrugged him off. "Bunch of office workers and shop assistants. The first sight of blood and you'll wet yourselves."

Possible, Harry thought, but a few seemed up for it so. "Run." Harry said it calmly and set off at an angle. If he'd run towards them, the yobs would have come to meet him, but running at an angle threw them. Especially since half the residents stayed were they were. Harry took the dozen long strides to get level with the first couple of them and then stopped.

Harry stopped and went very still. The speaker had pulled out a handgun. Crap. "That's better. Now you can all throw down those crowbars and baseball bats. You, mouthy, can throw that fancy stick over here."

Harry played for time. "Poncy stick. It's a poncy stick."

"What? Hey, I told you, put that lot down." The handgun pointed briefly off towards the other residents before coming back to line up on Harry. Harry took a deep breath of relief. Never again, he promised himself. Never come into a fight without a bloody gun.

Something clattered to the ground off towards the rest of the residents. "Pick that back up. You'll need it to beat the crap out this lot." Harry took two steps as the man watched, puzzled. "Because when this prat uses that air pistol it'll be empty, and I'm going to make him eat the bloody thing." Harry heard footsteps following him.

"I'll shoot you."

Harry took the other two steps so he was almost level with the last one of the group round the garage door. "So what? After I've jammed it where the sun don't shine I'll put a plaster on the hole and have a pint."

"It'll kill you."

"No it won't, and I do know that." Harry knew it was unlikely to do so, which was near enough right now.

"He should know, since he uses the real thing."

"What?" The man's eyes moved towards Liz's voice.

"He's a soldier. The real thing, asshole." There was pure sincerity and real malice in that.

Harry wished Liz had kept quiet given the antipathy the other people he'd met had towards the Army, but this lot used a different script. The youngsters were impressed and worried, and there was a definite drift towards their escape route. Still, now it was out in the open, he may as well act mean and soldierly. "Which means I'll run you down before you reach that corner." Harry hefted the stick by the bottom so the big brass boss was waving about. "Then guess what?"

"Hammer time." That was Rob. Harry nearly sniggered because it was ages since he'd heard that. The man facing him hadn't heard of MC Hammer, so he got the literal meaning. So did the other older man and he tugged on his friend's arm again.

The leader glanced at where the rest of the residents were. "Next time, soldier boy."

"No. This time. That's my garage door so you pay for the damage. Drop the hammers and crowbars, and that poncy little gun, and you can go. If not we take payment a bit more personally." Oops, Harry realised he'd got a bit carried away there. Maybe he should have let them go because the residents weren't really up to a proper fight. He'd got annoyed again.

"I want him that keeps tugging your sleeve, Mr gunman. I'm going to smack him silly." Liz might be all right then.

"I want the bastard who's been using the big hammer on my garage door." Rob sounded genuine as well.

A crowbar hit the floor, and then two smaller hammers. The front man whirled. "Pick them up. They're bluffing."

Harry took a long step towards the group and the man saw the alarm in the eyes of his friends. He turned back and Harry took another step and grinned at him. "Bet you don't get four steps now."

"Fuck it." The other older man started moving away and then the sledge-hammer hit the floor, and the remaining small crowbar. "Leave the hammers. We'll get more." Then he was walking backwards, away from trouble. The front man took a step backwards and Harry matched it.

Just this one to deal with and Harry was confident that he was close enough now. If the barrel came up to fire, Harry would go for it and the chances were the yob couldn't get it up fast enough. "No, you leave that or you eat it." Harry ducked aside as the air pistol flew towards him and the man was running, followed by the rest.

The yob stopped at the corner, briefly. "We'll be back for you." That wasn't unexpected and was swamped by the cheering from behind Harry. He turned and Liz suddenly had her arms round him. Then she burst into tears!

"You are a lunatic. You scared me shitless." Harry patted her on the back and Liz sniffled a bit and straightened up. "Sorry, but my legs were going wobbly when the arse pulled a gun and you just sneered at him. My whole bloody life flashed before my eyes and it wasn't long enough." Liz thumped Harry lightly on the chest. "I've never been so pleased to be with a macho bastard."

Then she smiled and squeezed Harry's bicep. "Pity you're such a skinny macho bastard." Liz turned and walked towards Rob, holding out the nail bar. "Here. I don't know why we bothered to come with him."

Rob smiled. "I wouldn't have missed that for the world. Were you in the bloody SAS or what?"

"No. If it had been one of them he'd have insisted on beating a few up."

Harry opened his mouth to say he was pay corps and shut it. They needed confidence, and a pay clerk wouldn't inspire it. He smiled at what Liz had said because it was true. "Though I am a soldier, the real thing." People were moving forward now and collecting the tools and someone swore.

"They got the bottom bent up at the corner. It'll never go back flush because the frame is torn and twisted."

Harry wanted to know one very important thing. "But they can't open it?"

"No." The man grimaced. "But they can chuck a bottle of petrol under there or lever it up a bit further and maybe get a kid through. Some of that lot were skinny."

"We need sentries." Finn was actually smiling. "One in the garage and one in the foyer. Maybe sort out a rota to watch out of a window each side." He looked round, "Since we've got a soldier to organise them."

Harry walked back round with a chattering crowd and hands patting him on the back, and a definite feeling of impending doom. He'd scared off some second rate chancers, and this lot thought they were fireproof. The cheers and hugs inside didn't help and Harry was relieved to get inside Sharyn's flat. A roused Daisy wanting some Uncle Harry and a bonus story was a really welcome bit of light relief. So was the lack of dreaming the rest of the night.

*　　　*　　　*

The sentries didn't need a soldier to organise anything really. They were perfectly capable of agreeing what was necessary and sorting it out, though someone always called round to see that Harry agreed. Harry did find out that there were fifty-one people living in the thirty-six flats, so most were single. A score were elderly and some needed a good bit of medication and were unhappy about the problems with getting an ambulance.

"How did they manage before?" Harry had just agreed to another hospital trip. "If Rob and Finn weren't still scoring some fuel and sharing I'd have run out by now."

"Either an ambulance or their relatives used to organise everything. They feel safer with you." Sharyn was puzzled as well. "I can understand that some relatives would stop coming because of fuel, but not the visitors to others. Not the ones like Mrs Burren-Croft because her son is some sort of bigwig in the council offices. Civil servant type. One of the others has a daughter who is a headmistress. There's three or four who I would have put money on arriving with goodies and sympathy."

"Well someone needs to sort this out so at least they all go the same day." Harry sighed. "It's getting worse at the hospital as well. There was a burnt out ambulance there last time, for God's sake."

"They'll have to keep going because the doctor's surgery has closed down."

"What? When?"

Sharyn shrugged. "I don't know. Finn went to get another prescription for his Mum and the doors are locked. There's a notice with a number, and the number says go to the hospital or find another doctor." Sharyn snorted. "Fat chance. Finn tried three out of the directory and they were all giving the same message."

"All closed?"

"Worse than that. Finn went to one where the phone didn't answer and it was smashed wide open. I suppose whoever did that went after drugs. Worse than that, he was shot at in broad daylight."

"Crap. I'm going to bring my rifle home."

"What about the poncy gun?" Sharyn sniggered. "Liz liked that." Then she gave Harry a long look. "Stealing a firearm Harry?"

"I bought it, technically, and everyone who still goes to the range has their own rifle. I doubt they'll ever know since there's no sign they're still going. The next time someone pulls a poncy or any other sort of gun on me I want one as well." Harry smiled. "I'll bring some pellets for poncy gun as well but I'll pay for them."

"You'll ruin your reputation. Why don't you steal the lot?" Sharyn had a little smile and Harry thought about it.

"Not yet. That will be noticed and I don't own them in any way. If it really gets bad I'll consider that, if only to stop someone else getting them." Harry waved a hand at the fireworks punctuating the night. "Those are getting worse." Then he gave a rueful smile. "I might end up stealing all sorts soon because flush for money is now becoming strapped for cash. Nobody wants to talk about paying me anything, especially back pay."

"Good news little brother. The bank finally agreed that as I'm his widow and Freddie did leave a will, and there is a ton of paperwork confirming it, I get his money."

"The payment?"

"No, just the other account. Freddie had one that was for him to use abroad. In case some foreign toerag nicked or ripped off his card. So that I wouldn't be stuck without a card or money while it was all sorted out." Sharyn sighed. "It's not a fortune, but if you need new boxers or a couple of beers? I owe you more than that."

"Not yet, but I really need some trainers, and a second pair of jeans."

"Sorry about that but the clothes were too much. Not the coat, that suits you, but the rest was a bit near to home. Thanks for clearing the rest of Freddie's things."

"Not a problem. The coat is a beauty." It was, a long leather one that Harry was surprised to find did fit him. He always thought of Freddie as being a lot bigger. "What will you do if the kids need the doctor?"

"Get an Army escort to the hospital."

*   *   *

Sharyn met Harry as he returned from the hospital. "They've all gone." Harry looked blank so she continued. "The ones we talked about, like Mrs Burren-Croft." Sharyn wasn't going to remind Mrs Turner, the passenger, that her sons never visited.

"Tell me upstairs." They took Mrs Turner to her flat and Sharyn started talking on the way to her flat. "Susan is in my flat so I could catch you alone. I don't want the kids hearing, or Daisy at least, because this is worrying. A bus turned up for all the ones we talked about and a couple of extras."

"There aren't any buses."

"Well someone found diesel for this one. There were already people aboard, all old ones, and a couple of burly men to carry bags." Sharyn stopped because they were nearly home. "Those leaving turned in their keys. They left the furniture and everything that wouldn't go in suitcases. Mrs Burren-Croft has a lot of those china figures and they're worth a fortune. She left them." Sharyn gave a brief smile. "Though she took Fluff."

"So are they coming back? When things get better?"

"No. They turned in their keys and told Mr Baumber they'd cancelled their payments for rent."

"We should do the same." Harry had spoken on impulse but it immediately made sense.

"We can't do that, stop paying. Where did that come from?" Sharyn frowned. "That's a long step from nicking an abandoned truck."

"This isn't going to end soon and some of those people were related to people who would know before we did. People in government. Maybe those people want headmistresses for their children but with tradespeople being allowed to leave this is getting scary. The government and council won't do repairs or pay out sickness or dole or provide a doctor so why are you paying rent? How long is it since the kids' playground was wrecked?"

"Two years. It must be close to that since the last time a council plumber or anyone else came. You're right." Sharyn smiled. "There are a few feeling the pinch who won't be sorry, but most of us have to agree. Otherwise we might be used as examples. I can't see us all being thrown out at once. I'll call a meeting."

"While you do, I'm going to get my bloody rifle. If someone was shooting at Finn in daylight, I'm not wasting time." As Sharyn opened her mouth Harry interrupted. "I don't have a vote on this because I'm dossing on my big sister's sofa. See you soon."

*   *   *

Even with the keys Harry felt like a sneak thief. He bought ammunition for the two-two and more for the poncy gun, putting the cash in the safe. Harry locked up the empty locker and put the rifle under his coat. All the way back home he had an itch, waiting for the sound of a siren, but nothing happened. When he came in, the resident's meeting was breaking up.

"All for one, Harry. There were a couple who wanted to keep paying but Mr Baumber said his pay is late and voted to stop the rent. He says that anyone who wants to pay can give the money to him and he'll help to keep the others fed." Sharyn laughed. "That sort of settled it." She glanced at the shape under Harry's coat. "Are you on the lam again?"

"Yes, and I want to see Mr Baumber because if there's empty flats I want to put this in one. Away from Daisy."

"Crap, yes. She hasn't put anyone's eye out but she loves marching round with your walking stick. Where's the poncy gun?"

"Finn has got it. Sort of love-hate because he's a bit frightened of the damn thing but wants to be able to use it. I explained that I wasn't quite truthful about harmless and he doesn't want to play cards with me."

"Nor me from what Liz said. She's a fan, though your fair body is safe. Liz showed me a couple of pictures of ex-boyfriends and you are a bit skinny." Sharyn squeezed Harry's bicep. "But watch out for Karen." Then she turned Harry and pushed. "Good, he's finished. If you're quick you can catch Mr Baumber on his own."

*   *   *

When he arrived back in the flat Harry called Sharyn into the kitchen and gave her a key. "Next door, I didn't realise it's empty."

"Has been for about six months. Are you moving in there?"

"Tempting but Daisy will just hammer on the door in the morning, or the wall. Do you want to throw me out?" Harry did feel as if he was underfoot sometimes, with his gear still cluttering up a corner of the living room.

"Not a chance. You keep amusing Daisy and I'll wash your socks. Deal?"

"Deal. Now I'll nip off and give Finn the pellets, and these."

"Targets?"

"Mr Baumber says Finn can pin them to a door in Mrs Burren-Croft's old flat for target practice. Then her son can pay for the damage if anyone ever inspects the place. Late pay has made Mr Baumber very bitter."

"Yes, one or two feel that way. There were some strong feelings aired in that meeting and a few were wondering. What happens when the money runs out?" Harry had been wondering that as well.

He smiled. "We sell the good china. Not ours though."

"Then go on the lam."

"See, dead simple." Except both of them knew it wasn't.

*   *   *

"That's our hospital." Sharyn and Harry stared at the TV. That was definitely the local hospital, one of only four that still had a functioning Accident and Emergency unit. "Where does Finn go now? Where does anyone round here go?"

Harry stared at Sharyn and then back at the TV. She'd nailed it because Finn would have to take his Mum halfway across the city to find another place for her to get medication. "It's a war zone. We have to leave." Harry was watching the report as he spoke. There were people running about with weapons, standing off the police. Fire was belching out of some of the windows on the lower floor of the hospital.

"Where are the patients? Where is the evacuation?" Harry was baffled. "Why isn't the fire suppression or whatever kicking in?" The police were trying to regain control, but seemed to be out-gunned and out-numbered. More were turning up, lights flashing, but still not enough to evict the gunmen.

Sharyn was baffled by something else. "Why don't they just rob the place and leave?"

Harry thought, and remembered London. "Because they want a war. That lot want to shoot the police rather than steal drugs." Sharyn stared at Harry as he continued. "I remember asking the same question when the rioters pushed onto bayonets just so they could punch a soldier. They're crazy with hate. We have to leave."

"How and where? The Army have sealed the whole place off."

"I reckon I can get the four of us through the wire." Even as he said it Harry had a pang. Leaving Karen and Finn, Liz, Susan and Rob to this sort of chaos didn't sit right. Harry should have just picked up sis and the kids and run. If he hadn't stayed so long, then the rest of the residents wouldn't have mattered to him.

"No you can't. I won't leave my friends to this, Harry. Anyway, according to the TV it's worse out in the countryside."

"How can it be worse than that?" On the screen the police were pushing the gunmen back, but not before the criminals had overrun four police cars. Now the police were trying to break into the hospital and the flames were spreading. "Patients are burning to death in there." Harry paused. "Patients and staff. The very people those idiots will need if they get sick or are wounded."

"We have to make this place safe. So if they come for us, we can stop them. A big crowd won't bother with a few flats because we have no drugs." Sharyn looked round. "Where else can we go anyway?"

"I don't know and you're right. At the very least we have to make this place stronger. Tomorrow we steal ply from wherever we can and strengthen the doors and windows." Harry sighed. "Then I'll get the other rifles."

Sharyn gave him a big sister-hug. "Thanks little brother." They sat and watched the hospital burn until the view changed to an atrocity in another city. Then another, and another.

*   *   *

"But what about Mum?" Finn was frantic the next day.

"How long has she got meds for?" Sharyn was asking and Karen was right alongside, blue rinse nodding

"I get mine monthly so I've got two weeks' worth left." Karen looked round and it hit everyone how many more residents were in the same boat.

Finn steadied down a little. "Nearly three weeks. But then what does she do?"

"We fix this place up first. Then we've got a fortnight to find an alternative." Harry wanted the place safe before Finn or anyone else went running off trying to source drugs. Harry had a nasty idea about just where he'd find them. Some bloody drug dealer would sell pain relief and with a bit of luck the stuff would be clean. Dealers would have morphine, dihydrocodeine, pot, anything habit forming.

"You can get drugs from the internet. Maybe, if the internet works?"

Karen spoke gently. "Toby, the post has stopped."

The teenager with the CB and an occasionally functioning PC link to the internet lost his excitement. "I forgot. Sorry."

"No, thanks for trying. Let's get the windows seen to, because Harry is right." Finn sighed. "If we don't keep the place safe, drugs won't matter."

"In that case, we need teams. At least half a dozen fit people in each group, and at the first sign of trouble, head for home." Harry looked around them "If one voice shouts 'oy, what are you doing' we get out. Before we find out how many friends they've got."

"We'd better load as we take boards off then, in case we have to run." Rob was looking round. "Who is with me because Harry, Finn and me are the ones with the load-carrying vehicles and fuel? We've got fuel for now anyway." People began to move towards one man or the other, or head off to get their baseball bat or golf club, or tools for actual work.

*   *   *

"It's getting a bit late to fix this lot. I'll drop you off at the door and put the pickup in the garage, still loaded." Harry smiled at Toby. "You can get your fix of CB before tea."

"Brilliant." Toby had worked hard even if he didn't really have the brawn for this work yet.

"I'll tell his Mum it's his pay." Liz ruffled his hair. "Keep this up and you'll be building muscles and getting a tan and none of the girls will fancy you. Thin and pale is today's look, isn't it?" Toby wriggled, embarrassed, and was off like a shot when Harry pulled up. The rest of the crew climbed out of the cab and headed in and Harry went round to the garage.

As he stepped out of the cab to open the garage, Harry heard the chink of metal and turned. Three shapes rose from between the two burned out cars in the car park and started towards him. Harry turned the other way and four more came out from the twisted remains where the big plastic waste bins had been partially burned before Harry arrived. Harry had been going to run but the keys for the front doors were in the pickup.

He snatched up his stick and headed for the nearest three at a run. They took another two steps and stopped, startled, and Harry saw who it was. Mr poncy gun had found a machete or cutlass. A big crude blade for hacking down vegetation and he was aiming to hack down Harry. Harry kept running and as the blade came over and down the man's face moved from a grin to shock. There was a clang as instead of biting into wood, the machete bounced to the side. Harry kept going and literally knocked his opponent over and trampled him underfoot.

The baseball bat across his shoulders hurt but at least Harry was moving with the blow which softened the impact a bit. Then he slashed across to the left as hard as possible. The grunt of pain meant the blow had landed but Harry was turning away. He smacked the baseball aside with the stick as the other youth tried for another blow and stuck the blade in him. Then kept turning and hit Mr poncy gun upside the head as he sat up. That was backhanded with the stick and dropped him. The youth Harry had hit first was doubled up, holding the line of red across his bicep. Harry hit him hard over the back of the head.

Then Harry bent to wipe the blade and put it away. He stood and twirled the stick as the other four skidded to a halt. These were the cautious man from before and three youths. Two of them had baseball bats and two still only had knives. Harry grinned and nudged the machete with his foot. "Anyone else want to try?"

"It's fucking Rambo."

"SAS you twat, I told you." With that two of the youths legged it, and the other two yobs immediately followed.

Harry stood for a few moments getting his breath. His back hurt like hell and he was glad the others hadn't kept coming. It had been all right while the adrenaline was pumping, but the pain would have come through in a prolonged fight. He looked down at the three on the floor and Harry's face hardened.

A glance upwards and the sentry was still back out of sight. They kept inside the rooms so anyone sneaking up wouldn't spot them, but that meant their own balconies blocked the view straight down. The assumption had been anyone approaching would be spotted before getting here. Which had been a big mistake. Another glance and so far nobody had seen the fight.

Harry took a two-handed grip and hit each of the downed attackers once, on the soft bit where the skull was thin. The big brass boss crunched home and Harry put the stick down and stripped them of wallets and knives. Then he dragged them back to the burned out cars. He would have to decide on the best person to give him a hand to shift them. Harry didn't want the residents to start considering him as their local pet superhero.

Harry also wanted to sit down for a bit because he'd done it again. He'd lost the plot and left bodies. It wasn't something he wanted to share. Definitely not with his sister. He was worried about that, what Sharyn would say if she ever found out some of the things he'd done in the Army. Or here, now.

Harry snagged his pack as he came in the flat and headed for the bathroom. "Need to get changed." Then he threw his jeans in the bath and washed out the blood, most of it, with two rinses. His socks and tee shirt went in for a quick wash as well, and some wet loo paper sorted out his boots. Then Harry came out in his boxers. It was a good job he was living with sis.

"Got some stinky rainwater down me so I didn't want it in the wash."

"Typical. Give them here and I'll put a load in the washer." Sharyn waved at the kitbag. "Put on your battledress trousers. Nobody in the flats will mind."

"Ta. I'll just nip next door and do soldier things." Harry put on trousers and a tee and gave Daisy a hug. "Back in fifteen minutes, poppet."

"I can count them now." She could as well, but Harry really needed all fifteen. Even the second class yobs were arming up which was worrying. Worse, Harry couldn't pretend those three were the heat of the moment. Maybe they would have died anyway and maybe one or two were dead, but Harry had made sure in cold blood. Maybe he really did belong in the nutters, or at least as a regular soldier? Oh crap. Harry took his time, cleaned the blade and the stick properly, and accepted his scolding from Daisy for taking nineteen minutes.

*   *   *

The next day Harry went for the rifles. On the way he tried to work out who was the best bet as an accomplice. Harry kept deciding and rejecting names because the person had to be strong enough to help move bodies, yet keep quiet. He still hadn't decided even after putting all the loose powder, the loading kits and spare brass, and even the bars of lead in the crew cab. Harry loaded the rifles and the air pistols before putting them in the cab and hesitated. Then he took the cash box as well, since there was only his money and the float in there.

Harry had loaded the weapons because on the way here there was gunfire in the nearby streets, and a brick bounced off the pickup. This was in broad daylight and Harry was pleased he'd brought his own rifle with him even if it wasn't actually needed. There wasn't time for a pint this time. Harry noticed in passing there was fresh plywood on one window of the Dog and Stoat. Another brick came from the same alley on the return trip. Someone had a new game. Harry kept driving.

Harry came round a corner into a street of terraced houses. Old houses with no front gardens, just a footpath between the front door and the roadway. He almost stopped because the narrow way was half blocked. A knot of men was spilling off the footpath and they were fighting. Then one waved him past but on the far side of the road and Harry kept going. As he approached he realised that they weren't fighting, not now. A big man had gone down and now there were six of them kicking him while he curled up in a ball.

Harry pulled across the street and drove past. Then he couldn't, not with six of them on a man who was down. Crap. The man who was down might be a complete asshole but Harry was already slowing. He ran up the kerb and swerved away onto the road, then reversed until the back hit the house wall at an angle. At least they'd have to come over the truck bed or round the bonnet.

Harry was chanting "stupid bastard" to himself inside his head, but that didn't slow him up. His stick was quickly propped against the back wheel and Harry stuck the two air pistols in his belt and grabbed two rifles with each hand. One of the men was watching and then another as he put the weapons in the truck bed, nice and handy, and brought the first rifle up.

"Quit that now." Harry thought two of them were going to ignore the shout but the others prodded them, and all six looked across. Then one shouted, a door opened, and two more came out of the nearby house. The "stupid" chant in Harry's head went up in volume. "Just piss off and leave him be."

"You a queer lover? Or maybe you're his boyfriend?" Laughter rippled among the men. Young men, probably late teens and not second class yobs at all. They all had baseball bats and probably knives but obviously preferred kicking the bloke on the floor.

"Neither. If you'd been fighting one on one I'd have driven by. Now just leave him be to stagger home or whatever."

One of the pair who had come out of the door gestured back towards the opening. "Home isn't up to much now."

One of the kickers who had been reluctant to stop stepped forward. "Toss the rifle down and you can leave."

"That's not how it works. You walk away and I drive away afterwards."

"No, because that's a little gun. Some sort of target job." He pulled at his belt. "So is this but a bit bigger than that." The man waggled the barrel on the pistol. "So it'll put a bigger hole in you. That one looks like something from a fairground so it'll be crap. Give it up and walk away or I'll get angry and come over there. You won't like me when I'm angry." The group laughed at the Hulk reference.

"But this will hit you from here, so you won't get over to me. If you point that thing you won't even get to fire it." They were too damn close, all of twenty yards away. Harry thought he might get his shots off but then it was four to one and all armed and biggish lads. Crap.

"Really?" The man looked from side to side. "This one reckons he can get all of us with one bullet. He's watched too many films." Even as the man started to look back at Harry the pistol came up smoothly so Harry shot him through the throat. First shot with lots of time to aim and Harry didn't even look at him again to check the bullet had hit.

These were target shooting rounds so Harry aimed at soft spots and since they were coming straight at him, their throats were easiest. The other three rifles came up one at a time and three more men clutched at their throats. Harry dropped the last rifle and did a sort of fast draw as the first two came over the back of the truck. One fell back and the other yelled and clutched his face when both air pistols went off. As Harry stooped to pick up his stick the man in the truck bed caught him by the arm and the stick clattered to the floor, out of reach.

Harry tried to wrench free, turning to face the last two unharmed opponents. The wounded man's other arm came over and pulled Harry back against the truck bed so the bastard wasn't very wounded. The other two were now around the front of the pickup and moving in. Harry got a foot up and the first man reversed quickly so the kick missed, but the step back fouled the second yob. Harry managed to free the grip on his arm but the other arm from behind was now around his throat.

Twisting a bit to scrabble in the truck bed, Harry found an empty rifle and pulled it up and over the low side. He threw it at the advancing men as they started forward again. The first one ducked and the one behind was struck by the rifle and staggered back a couple of steps. The first man brought his baseball bat down.

Harry got his forearm in the way and bit back the yell. Maybe the arm wasn't broken but it was on fire. So much for a bloody deflection. The man raised the baseball bat again and the second one had recovered and was manoeuvring to get in a swipe as well. Crap. Harry let go of the arm around his throat to try and grab his opponent's weapon this time.

The arm around his neck went slack! Harry lunged forward, out of the embrace, and lowered his head to avoid the baseball bat. Not so much a head butt, more of a duck that went offensive as the top of Harry's head got his opponent in the face. The man reeled back with blood spraying from his face and Harry had a free moment. A somewhat dazed moment after the impact on top of his skull. Harry ducked down and scooped up his stick but before he could do anything with it, the men in front of him were running!

A shape lurched down the outside of the pickup truck, too late to catch the runners, and threw a baseball bat at their retreating backs. "Come back, I'll give you fucking pouf!" The man stopped and bent over, fighting for breath, and Harry glanced behind. The man in the truck bed wasn't moving and there was blood on the back of his head. Two of those laid in the street were still moving, but both were kicking and writhing and clutching their throats.

"Thanks mate." Harry was leaning on the truck as well, then he had second thoughts and lurched towards the cab. He felt marginally better with a round in one of the rifles.

"Thanks mate as well." The grin was ghastly, with a split lip and both eyes coming up black and blue. There was also a cut on his head and Harry realised. This was the victim.

Harry sniggered, he couldn't help it. Some victim. "Pouf?"

"Us poufs can't fight. The assholes said so but they had to team up. Bastards." The man straightened and he was a bit taller than Harry and definitely better built.

"Us? Are you really gay, or whatever today's name is?" Harry had been out of the country for a while, and sometimes such things were rebranded.

"Gay still works. Yes, but no frilly panties. Is that a problem?" The man tensed up.

"Not to me, but Liz is going to be heartbroken."

"Liz?"

"She likes big muscly blokes and reckons I'm too skinny."

"I'm Casper and I have similar tastes in men. Do you think she'll bond with me?"

"She'll kill you if she finds a blacksmith and you get him first." They were both grinning like idiots and laughing as they spoke. "I'm Harry and hoping like hell I'm not your type."

"You're safe. Even if you were, I'm in no fit state to take advantage."

"That was what was worrying me, I'm in no state to fight you off." They both gave up and laughed properly. "I think I'm a little bit drunk on survival." Harry looked back and his eyes sharpened. "How many ran off?"

"Two. Why?"

"We're one light. I only see five of them down."

"Not a problem." Casper limped back along the truck and kicked something on the floor. "Damn, I don't think he felt it. What the hell were you shooting with?" Casper was looking at the four spread back to where he'd been laid, who were all still now.

"Four of these." Harry waved the rifle. "I had two air pistols but had to shoot too fast to make them count."

"This one took a while to mop his face and recover. That gave me time to get up." Casper gave another ghastly smile. "He was busy watching you so I picked up a baseball bat and brained the bastard. Then that one there had his back to me."

"Thanks for that. I was about to get brained myself."

"No problem, Harry. Entirely my pleasure." Casper looked down and stamped. "No, he's really out and can't feel a thing. With luck he's dead."

"Do you want a lift home?"

"Not much point. I live right there." Casper pointed at the open door and sighed. "Or did. I'll have to move now. Damn, I've been here three years without any strife."

"Liz might put you up if you swear off blacksmiths." Harry thought this bloke would be a definite asset. He'd climbed off the floor after a kicking and was pissed he didn't get all of them.

"I like my blokes a bit cleaner. We could compare scandalous stories and such? Will she put me up just like that? Until I get sorted?"

"Get your gear from in there and we'll load up the hardware. Since it's scattered across the street and a hazard." Harry looked at the fallen. "We can leave these for traffic calming."

"First you've got to step into view. For my peace of mind." The ghastly grin appeared again.

That really did puzzle Harry. "Why?"

"So I can see if your underpants are on the outside. Then if you aren't a superhero, I want to know why you're driving round with a car full of rifles looking for assholes to shoot." Casper looked around him and laughed. "Or is God gay and you're an angel?"

The big man shook his head when Harry didn't have y-fronts over his trousers. "You owe me the story sometime."

"When we're safe I'll tell you. Get your stuff." Harry limped across the street to collect whatever weapons the deceased or insensible were carrying. Especially the ammunition for that target pistol because it was a decent calibre. He was trying to remember if that bloke hit his leg with the bat when Harry tried to kick him. Possibly, or he'd pulled something. At least his arm wasn't broken or not properly. Maybe cracked because it bloody hurt. So did Harry's throat.

Harry was dragging the one off the back of the pickup when an arm came past to help. "We've got one good arm each." Casper gave his hideous grin. "Something hit my shoulder and only one arm works properly. My batting arm, luckily."

"A baseball bat hit mine. You might have to change gears while I steer?"

"No problem. Are we good?"

"Yes. Um, Casper. I'd rather not make a big thing of this. Cut down on the numbers and the dead and all that if anyone asks?"

"Damn, it's a good story. Never mind, fair exchange. If you ever need anything?"

"Help with getting rid of three bodies?" Casper looked around but Harry shook his head with a little smile. "No, three others. I don't want to frighten the neighbours."

Casper laughed. "You're frightening me. Are they secret bodies as well?"

Harry shrugged. "Sorry."

"I'll survive. Shit, I survived tonight didn't I?" Casper climbed into the cab. "Home James. Sorry, Harry."

*   *   *

Casper felt like crap when they got back and so did Harry. So he put the big man in the gun flat, with the weapons, and went home for a soak.

"Is it safe? Him in there with the guns and such?"

"No problem Sharyn. The man just saved my life, and then didn't even demand the traditional kiss of gratitude." Harry shrugged and winced because that hurt. "I don't know why, I just trust him."

"What? A kiss?"

"He's gay."

Sharyn had a big smile. "So how come a limp wrister saved my big rough brother?"

Harry laughed. "Ouch, that hurt. Tell him you said that tomorrow. He's got a sense of humour." He tried to work his arm a bit. "This might be a bit broken, so I'll need a beer and sympathy after a bath."

"You'll get a sling so Daisy takes it easy, and then twenty questions."

Harry came out after his bath and had his sling fitted, but went to sleep after about the tenth question.

*   *   *

"You'll never sleep tonight."

"Wah?"

"Tea time or you'll sleep straight through and be up at four in the morning. Then you'll be in a crappy mood all day." Sharyn waved the mug of coffee. "Is your hero up for burgers and chips?"

"I don't know. Bang on the door, gently. If he's awake, ask him."

Sharyn came back with a grin. "He wanted to know if I was Liz. When I said I was your sister he asked what my taste in men was, so he didn't screw up." She sat next to Harry. "He also fancies burger and chips and isn't worried about rugrats. So what's with Liz?"

"I told him that if a blacksmith turned up, he should let Liz have first pop at him." Harry grinned.

"What, seriously? Where did you meet?" Sharyn giggled. "In a drunken gay bar fight because you sounded drunk when you came in? You still do."

"Sort of. It was an odd sort of conversation and we were both a bit high on life." Harry sniggered. "Ask him. He's got a real sense of humour."

Casper still had his sense of humour, especially after he had surrounded a plate of burgers and chips. Then he topped up the fridge and food cupboard. Half Casper's luggage was edible. Just to fill up his bags since someone had pissed on a lot of his clothes and he didn't want them after that.

Sharyn promised to wait for the full story until they were recovered and she could threaten to beat them if anyone didn't come clean. She also didn't want to tell Liz that Casper was gay because he was built just like the ex-boyfriends. Sharyn reluctantly agreed in the end that letting Liz flirt with a gay bloke really would be mean.

Daisy was very happy to have another pony and pirate drawing assistant, and insisted on two stories. Casper managed to produce a story without a book which impressed the hell out of her. Then Harry took Casper next door so they could clean the weapons, gloat over the new aluminium baseball bats and knives, and count up the cash in the wallets. They also got their story straight. Harry staggered back to Sharyn's flat and went out like a light until morning. He didn't even dream.

*   *   *

"Hi Liz. This is Casper, and he's made a solemn promise about you." Harry was grinning.

"Really. What's that?" Liz was eyeing Casper with a little smile.

"If you find a blacksmith, he'll stand back while you have first crack at him. If you bounce, then he'll make his play." Harry watched Liz try to make sense of that, and then her face change as she did.

"Ooh, that is mean. Did you scour the whole bloody city to set this up? Or was it that sister of yours?" Liz gave Casper another look. "Were you trying to fight him off or kidnapping him, because neither of you look great."

"I was rescuing his honour, then he was rescuing me so it sort of seemed sensible to team up." Harry really did enjoy some light relief because he'd been thinking about the state of law and order, and that had upset him. He'd actually thought about the aftermath of the fight. Despite gunfire, beatings and bodies, nobody stuck a nose out of a door and no police turned up. That wasn't a good sign.

"What? I thought you were, er, straight?" Liz made a mock swipe at Harry's head when she saw the broad grins. Casper's still looked ghastly and Harry wasn't shaving his scraped cheek until it healed up. "Ooh, you bastard, stop that. Now the pair of you get in here and give me the story instead of winding me up." Liz gave a dramatic sigh. "I suppose it's safe to invite Casper in, unfortunately."

Liz hadn't been joking about Twisted Sister ornaments. "Where do you sell these?" Harry went to pick up a collection of bent metal and spikes that might have been a vaguely human figure. Then he decided against it in case the thing cut a finger off.

"Nowhere now. They used to sell at craft fairs, and a few on the internet. Now the internet is usually down and there's no delivery services anyway." Liz looked at the collection of sculptures. "I've got the materials and the tools in the basement to make more but why?" Then she brightened. "Hey, next time someone tries to break in, we can throw these."

"Throw them?" Casper wasn't sure if he was being wound up.

"From the third floor, there's a flat on each side which has a stack of bricks on the balcony just in case." Liz was looking at her surplus stock from a different viewpoint now. "I could improve these a bit, maybe add some spikes."

Casper winced. "Ouch. Remind me why I'm here instead of safe in my flat?"

"Nobody will piss in your undies drawer?" Harry shrugged. "It's rent free?"

"It is?"

"Oh yes. We've got a commune, if only I can get the free love started. Go and clean your gun or whatever, soldier boy, while Casper and I work out the rules of engagement for blacksmiths. Then he can tell me how you got beaten up." Liz smiled happily. "Then I'll give Casper the dirt on you just by way of revenge."

As the door closed behind him Harry heard Casper's voice. "Soldier boy?" Harry headed for Rob's flat. As soon as Rob realised what Harry was driving at he phoned Finn, and the three of them discussed the possibilities.

"I don't want to move if we can keep safe here. Mum is in a bad way, and I'd have to find another supply of medication. At least I know the roads around here." Finn was unhappy but resigned. "I could try to make a run across to one of the other hospitals in the van."

"Paint out your sign on the side. Otherwise the assholes think you've got cash." Rob looked a bit embarrassed. "A customer advised me. Advertising that you're carrying anything that might be worth cash or that you've got cash is a bad idea now, he reckoned."

"I'm more worried about the shooting in daylight. Would one of you mind coming as shotgun?" Finn gave a nervous laugh. "Literally if I could get one. That air pistol won't be enough if I run into some real nasty sods."

"I've got something as good." Harry explained.

"So we should be safe here?" Finn was a lot more hopeful.

"Not if real bad bastards turn up. Those aren't really nasty guns and we haven't got enough people who can shoot." Harry sighed. "Do either of you know of a bank or library, a big stone place with little windows?"

"Some churches are stone, but they've got big windows. Why?" Harry explained the benefits of thick stone. He was disappointed because this pair got around more than he did and couldn't come up with somewhere.

Finn sighed. "So we stick here. We should meet with this new bloke. Are you sure of him?"

"In a mutually saving life sort of way."

Finn gave a little smile. "Good enough these days." Rob wasn't quite so sure but went with the other two.

*   *   *

Casper curled his lip. "They smell a little bit ripe."

"Luckily the weather has been cool." Harry showed him the roll of plastic bags and the duct tape. "If we slide them into the rubble sacks, one over each end, they'll be no problem."

"Done this a lot, have you?" Casper was a bit wary as he asked.

"Last time I gave the job to a couple of squaddies, and I didn't actually kill the bloke. It was a good grounding though."

"Liz said soldier, though she didn't say you were bossing them about." Casper looked again at the bodies. "You didn't shoot this lot."

"I used this stick and a blade. This is where I won the machete." Harry glanced back at the flats. "If we slide the packages into the truck bed and then chain one of the wrecks to the back we can drag it away."

Casper eyed up the two burned out cars. "Why?"

"That's our excuse for being out here. Not only that but these three snuck up on me using these wrecks while I was opening the garage." Harry waved across at the part melted plastic. "The others came from there but ran away."

"So would I." Casper grinned because Harry's look showed he didn't believe it. "So exactly why wouldn't the rest like knowing these three are dead?"

"They'll rely on me too much, and get too confident. One of them might push it at the wrong time. Then if I go down they'll break and get slaughtered." Harry bent over the bodies. "Whew, take a breath before you get nearer."

Casper took a tentative sniff. "This will cost you."

"What exactly?"

"That machete thing. I've never used a gun but the next bastard who comes for me with a baseball bat is going to get a hell of a shock." Casper's grin was still ghastly, and more so now with the evil leer.

"Deal." Harry thought that Casper with that blade would be a big comfort at his back. At least he knew Casper would actually use it if necessary.

Chapter 7:
Breakout – On the Lam

Sharyn and Harry were watching the late news when once again the local area made the headlines. "That's the big junction to the motorway. They can't be serious."

Harry agreed with Sharyn's sentiments, but those were Army engineers putting down wire and installing concrete blocks. "Necessary because of the breakdown of law and order? Why not send the soldiers in?" Harry waved at the TV and winced. He'd got some lovely bruises and his arm and leg were still very sore. "There's a pattern and I'm wondering if someone has a list. A list that the engineers are working down, because we are the seventh big population centre to be sealed off."

Sharyn was startled. "You mean it's pre-planned? Why?"

"I don't know but I'm going up to the roof."

"That's a better view." Sharyn pointed at the TV.

"Not of what the rest of the city is doing. They are going to go crazy out there according to what happened elsewhere." Harry heaved himself to his feet and took his stick to lean on. "Do you want to come? We can get Susan to sit in here."

"No, I'll watch this." Sharyn smiled. "Susan might have a visitor and want some privacy."

"Really?"

"Rumour is strong that Rob was seen nipping in there. But he didn't have a toothbrush, so they might just be watching TV." Sharyn lost her smile as she looked back at the TV, where a crowd was confronting the Army. Then the scene cut to a flood of vehicles pouring over another section of the by-pass and heading into the countryside. The helicopter camera zoomed in on a guard post with no soldiers in evidence. Hundreds of people on foot were also streaming past.

"The Army will seal that off with prejudice." Sharyn glanced up, startled at Harry's tone. "When anyone overran an Army post round London, the brass sent in tanks."

"Oh crap."

"Yes, exactly. I might be a while depending on what's happening." Harry limped out of the door and made his way to the roof.

Casper was already up there, as were a dozen other residents including Rob and Liz. Harry looked around the horizon and his attention was drawn south. There was a hell of a battle going on that way, with tracers hammering down from aloft into the middle of the melee. "That's where the news showed the first wire going up."

"Though nothing is happening yet where the lines of cars were pouring through. Which seems strange." Rob was puzzled and Harry agreed, because around London any breakout was a priority for the Army. "There was some shooting up north as well for a while, and a hell of a firefight in the city centre. That was cut short because there were some big explosions."

Everyone ducked as two aircraft came over very low, heading south, and then explosions echoed in the fighting there. "Those sort of explosions," someone pointed out. "Bombs for Christ's sake."

"I was considering trying to join that stream of cars after seeing the TV, but I'd have to get past that." Liz pointed at a patch of light where flames were leaping into the sky. "That's a big council estate and there must be a war breaking out there. Their own personal hell." She looked around the horizon. "There isn't a clear way out from here."

Harry looked around, as did the rest, and they started to compare notes. The conclusion was chilling when he voiced it. "All the big housing blocks, the social housing, are either on fire or there's a battle going on there. There's fighting in between, but they are the most serious. Down south it's spread, joined up, and presumably the inhabitants tried to leave."

A storm of tracers erupted to the west. "One of those escape routes on the TV has just been cut off." Flames leapt into the air. "What the hell is that?"

"That, Obe, is napalm." Harry looked back at the staring faces. "They've burned a section of that stream of people to stop the rest. Think Beirut, Gaza, Ramallah, any of those Middle East war zones."

"But they're English, the refugees. They didn't burn refugees in the Middle East." Obe was a solidly built man with a tight mop of pure white frizzed hair but he looked frail, shrunk in on himself. His eyes and teeth were stark in his dark face as he looked from one person to another. "They can't do that."

The latter was a whisper though, because flame gushed skywards in the middle of the fighting to the south.

"What happens now? Now that we've been penned in with the rioters and criminals?" Casper looked over at a fresh outburst of firing, once again out towards the new city boundary. The wide strip of tarmac making up the ring road encircled most of the conurbation and was now a ring of steel. "How on earth do the shops get food?"

"How do the markets get any more fresh produce? The allotments can't provide enough." Susan had arrived and went across to Rob, then put an arm round him. The gravity of the situation was driven home by nobody even mentioning the first public display of affection between them. Not even when Rob hugged her close.

"The TV said there were arrangements in the other places that were sealed in." Several heads nodded, but nobody could remember details. Then they tried to remember what was actually said, and there hadn't been details.

"We could phone them, one of the other cities." Louise looked round. "If anybody knows a number? Or phone up a shop of some sort." Three people headed off downstairs.

"We should get as much food in as possible." Harry remembered having to scavenge in London, and the number of supermarkets closed and usually looted. If that happened here food would get scarce, very fast.

"We'd better go together. Both vans and the truck?" Rob was looking at Harry, who nodded. "What about a chemist? To buy as many plasters and cough medicines as we can."

Billy, a redundant clerk, looked around. "Maybe we can get some for Finn's Mum, and the rest." Mary was always Finn's Mum to the residents. "We should get a list of everyone's prescriptions and try to buy it."

"We'll need to pool money for that, and to build up a stock of food." Liz put a hand in her back pocket and then waved something. "Here's my card. Abuse the hell out of it and I'll argue with MasterCard if we survive."

"Maybe we should all abuse the plastic. It's not like they're going to arrest us, is it?" That was a stunner from Louise, who was generally considered a quiet type. Except for her brief foray into hurling furniture. "They didn't even send the police round when I tried to brain that moron using my bedside cabinet. I hereby donate whatever meagre resources Visa will part with before they shut me down." A round of agreement followed.

More sombre news came when the three attempting to phone other cities came back. The landlines were accepting local calls only. Any prefix outside the immediate area simply didn't make a connection. Harry remembered that he hadn't been able to phone Sharyn from London. A quick round of discussion confirmed that nobody had managed to phone out for a couple of months. Everyone just assumed a temporary problem since the internet and mobile phones weren't working at all.

When Harry finally limped downstairs the fight to the south was still going strong, and fires were burning here and there across the city, big fires. There were numerous smaller ones and no sign of the gunfire ending. Sharyn came for a hug when he came into the flat. "The TV showed a mob attacking the refugees at one of the crossing points. Then there were explosions and flame and the refugees were caught up in that. The camera didn't show the place after that."

She shuddered. "Another hospital burned and I don't know if it was the one we are supposed to use. I usually complain about the TV closing down so early, but not tonight."

Harry told her what had been said on the roof, and they went to their beds. It might have been because he was thinking over tonight's chaos, but Harold didn't dream. Maybe bad things cancelled each other out?

*　　　*　　　*

Finn shook his head in despair. "You warned us, Harry, but this is so quick." This was the second supermarket the little convoy had visited and the place was a shambles. The windows were smashed and there were scattered and broken packets and tins all over the car park. Even at that it was better than the burned out shell of the first.

"I came here yesterday. What if they're all gone? All the shops?" Mr Baumber looked around at the mess. "How do we eat?"

"There will be food inside. In fact, if you look round some of what's been dropped will be useable. Load up and don't be fussy." The rest looked at Harry. "I saw this in London. The first lot are a mob and just grab and run. All the booze, fags and fresh meat will be gone. There'll be spuds and cans of beans in there, batteries and tissues and maybe milk. Maybe even frozen food since this happened last night." A man and woman came out with full carrier bags, took one startled look at the four vehicles and the group, and ran.

"That's stealing." Rob didn't sound totally convinced.

Liz laughed. "We were going to use credit cards we can't pay off. This just cuts out the middleman." She headed over towards the shopping trolleys.

"Who's got a quid for a trolley? Bloody marvellous. We're going to rob the supermarket but I can't unchain a trolley without a quid in the slot." The rest were laughing now because Liz was right.

Rob stayed with the vehicles after a bit of thought, because they obviously had fuel and that might be a target. He had a rifle and an air pistol which, as he pointed out, he couldn't use. Though the rifle and the van hooter should let everyone else know there was a problem. Inside the supermarket there were about a dozen people, in pairs at the most, collecting food. All were looking furtive and kept well clear of the chattering group of six.

*   *   *

"That's it. We can't fit anything else." Finn looked round at the almost empty shelves where he was stood. "You were right about the drugs. Someone has taken the lot."

"Not the plasters and antiseptic cream and suchlike. Just the bottles and pills. I have visions of someone trying to get high on some of that stuff." Casper was smiling.

"Cough medicine will do it I was told. Though it probably takes dedication. I've taken a lot of condoms and birth pills just in case we have an orgy." Liz smiled at the startled faces. "I'll be really pissed off if I find a blacksmith needing shelter and have to stay platonic." She scowled at her trolley full of milk containers. "All this milk is skimmed. Drinking that except in coffee will take real dedication."

"Tinned milk here. Evaporated and condensed." Harry grinned as Liz promptly unloaded some of her milk and threw in tins instead. "Skimmed is good for you."

"My gran had a book that said it was only fit for pigs." Liz headed for the doors. "Come on Casper, use all that muscle to help me get this outside." Casper obliged as each trolley was manoeuvred over the lip of the broken door.

Rob reported that two separate cars had come in, looked at the vans, and left when he'd let them see he was armed. More people were drifting across the car park as the small convoy left after a second trip inside. Some arrivals headed inside but others were picking over what was scattered outside.

*   *   *

Finn took Harry to one side when they arrived back. "Were the chemist shops looted in London?"

"Yes, every one." Harry realised where this was going. "Sharyn wasn't sure which hospital caught fire."

"Not caught fire. It was attacked, robbed and burned down. That was the wrong one for Mum. Can we look for pharmacies please, Harry? Before it gets urgent?" There was an edge of panic in Finn's voice.

"I'm up for it if we can raise an escort." Harry raised his voice. "Who's up for a pharmacy run?"

"We should do as Billy said. Get a proper list together." Rob looked at Finn. "If you can wait."

Finn smiled. "Tomorrow will be fine. No problem. I'll use the directory and ask Toby to try the internet so we've got a list of possible places." Everyone went back to carrying bags and boxes into the lifts.

*   *   *

"We're too late. That's the fourth and that isn't smash and grab. They've been deliberately emptied except maybe the burned one." Finn kicked at a few packets on the pavement. "The real painkillers, the prescription stuff, is all gone. So are the headache pills for Christ's sake. This mess was just looters coming for the dregs afterwards." He looked at the rest of the group. "What if we can't find anything?"

"Then we make a run across town to a surviving hospital." Harry didn't fancy that.

"After last night? There wasn't such a big fight down south, but we could see fighting all over the city. Then there were the attempts to break out." Those were easy to see. Tracers, a lot of them, and then planes or helicopters and fire blossoming, all in concentrated areas out near the city perimeter.

"There's five shops more on the list. Let's go." Rob was nervous because a small crowd was gathering at the end of the street. The convoy had already found two roads barricaded off by determined residents.

Everyone was getting really worried when the seventh shop had been gutted. The next to last on Finn's list was a small place with heavy iron shutters that seemed to be intact. The sign above the shutter had been spray painted to obliterate any hint as to what the shop was. "Are you sure it's a pharmacy?"

"Yes, according to Toby though this one wasn't in the directory. I reckon the spraying is self-defence." Finn shrugged. "I'll go and bang on the door."

The small convoy stayed back as Finn walked down the street and banged on the door. There was some shouting that nobody could make out and Finn beckoned. "He wants to know who is in charge. I told him you were."

Harry stared, then decided to let it ride. No point arguing here so he shouted at the door. "Can you fill out prescriptions if we pay?"

"Who are you lot?"

"Residents of a block of flats. We've got old folk in there."

"Just prescriptions. You have to pay."

"No problem." Harry turned. "Sharyn, your card is needed." Sharyn had volunteered her credit card for this one, for the medicines.

"Just four of you, two women and two men. Leave those guns outside. Wait two minutes and then open the door."

Inside the place was gloomy because only the lights at the back were on. There was a large young man stood by the counter with a cricket bat, and an older man behind him who spoke up. "Give me the prescriptions please."

There was some shuffling of the papers and then most went back onto the counter. "Most of these have been used so I can't fill them. You'll need new ones from the doctor."

"There is no doctor!"

Harry put a hand on Finn to calm him. "Let the man do what he can." They waited as the chemist went through a door and the young man watched. The older man came back with the familiar paper bags with the prescriptions stapled to them.

"I have given you a substitute for two of these because we haven't the exact medicine in stock. Unfortunately there aren't any deliveries any more." He took the credit card and put it in the slot, and waited for the contact to go through. Which it did which was weird given the restriction on calls.

"What about the rest?" Finn gestured at the heap of rejected prescriptions.

"Get current ones and if I've still got any stock, I'll fill them." The machine beeped and the card was handed back to Sharyn. "Unless we are discovered before then."

"No. You fill them now!" Finn pulled the air pistol from the back of his belt and pointed it at the chemist. "We'll pay but my mum isn't dying while I try to find a doctor."

Harry opened his mouth to object, to point out there was time to find somewhere, and the young man raised his cricket bat. Before anyone else could react Liz brought her air pistol out from under her coat and put it to the young man's head. "Just stand very still please." The young man froze and the chemist raised his hands.

Harry sighed and took the cricket bat from the man's unresisting hands. "You'll get it back when we leave." Then he turned to Liz. "Why?"

"The pistol? Because I wasn't coming in here unarmed even with a soldier boy. Then when Finn started it seemed the simplest thing to do. To stop a fight." She gave a sad smile. "You're a bad example."

Sharyn spoke up. "Fill the prescriptions please and I'll still pay. Enough for a month for each one and more if you can do it." She put her card back on the counter. "One of us will come back there with you, so you don't lock yourself in. We don't want to have to smash your door. Does that sound reasonable?"

"For an armed robber, yes. You won't hurt anyone?" The chemist was looking at Liz.

"I'm not going to hurt him. I just wanted to stop him hurting Finn. If I move back a bit you won't start trouble?" The last bit was to the young man who shook his head very gently, while watching Harry with his bat.

"Finn, you go in there but don't panic. The chemist will do his best, won't you?" This time the chemist nodded.

This wait was longer but eventually Finn came out with carrier bag full of boxes and bottles and jars. "Everything, or substitutes. I offered him a safe place if he brings his stock but he won't come." Finn was a lot happier. Rob was outside and wasn't happy. He had already banged on the shop door to tell them a crowd was gathering.

"Run the card and then we're gone. I suggest you take all the stock somewhere else and lock it up. Then sell for cash or better still trade for food or fuel." Harry watched the shock hit the chemist. "We found you on the internet and someone less civilised may come next time." The chemist looked at the weapons. "Seriously. You were eighth on a list of nine and someone is stripping pharmacies bare. Get out. I was in London and it's going to get worse."

The machine accepted the card again. Harold tried to warn them again. "I'll leave the cricket bat by the door but it won't even slow them up if a mob arrive, or drug dealers."

Liz looked at the young man. "Is the pharmacist your relative?"

"Uncle."

"Persuade him. Or someone will kill you both. Get out of the building because the bastards will torch it for fun. Two of the places we found were gutted by fire." The young man nodded and watched as the four of them left. Harry tossed the bat onto the floor, slammed the door and jumped into the pickup.

Rob was right about the crowd. About thirty adults, mainly men, had moved to within twenty yards. Rob and Billy with a rifle each and Casper with the machete were keeping them back. Ahead of the pickup half a dozen people were being deterred by Mr Baumber carrying a rifle. Two bricks hit the back of Rob's van, on rearguard, as the three vehicles pulled away but the men ahead scattered.

Finn apologised, but it no longer mattered really because he did the right thing. In retrospect, if that was the last chemist, a new prescription would be scrap paper. None of them expected the place to be open, one way or the other, by the time anyone got another prescription. That was underlined by a determined attempt to break into both blocks of flats that night. A van rammed the garage doors which only held because Finn's van was backed up tight inside to reinforce it.

Bricks from above broke the windshield and then Harry started shooting into the front seat from the first floor. Someone in there screamed and the van left in a hurry. "Harry, Harry."

Harry turned from watching the van race away and Billy was pointing to the other block of flats. The ply over several ground floor windows was alight as a crowd threw petrol bombs at them. "If they've wet them down, the ply should hold." Harry hoped so because he wasn't leading this lot in a rescue attempt. They'd get swamped.

"I'll let Susan know, she's got one of them on the phone." Billy left.

Harry seriously considered shooting at the crowd but in the dark, lit only by the flames, he'd be lucky to do any damage. Then the crowd might disperse, or they might set into this block instead. Harry watched as three youths tried to use a van to try to climb onto a first floor balcony and a table and then chairs rained down on them. Petrol bombs arced up and the balcony up there was soon ablaze. Tomorrow the residents here would have to reinforce the first floor windows, Harry realised.

Eventually the crowd dispersed and the fires were put out as dawn broke. Tired people from both blocks scoured the surrounding area for ply and fastened it up, and then many of them slept through the afternoon.

"Susan has been talking to those she knows over there, in the other flats. That lot last night wanted young women." Sharyn was picking over the knives taken by Harold and Casper. "They said they'll be back tonight. They're not getting me, Harry."

"I'll do the dancing and prancing thing. They won't get you, sis." Sharyn needed a long hug before she went for her nap. Or tried, because Daisy and a colouring book went with her.

*   *   *

As the light began to fade those catching up on their sleep were roused, and Harry and Casper collected the weapons from the gun flat. The residents gathered in the foyer, some staring at the rifles and knives being placed on the stairs. Sharyn spoke up because Harry said he wasn't starting this discussion. "We have to make a plan, or everyone will be in one place while they break in another."

"What do you reckon, Harry?" Rob spoke but all the other faces turned his way and Harry sighed. "Did everyone make sure the balcony doors with ply on will open?" The ply had been fastened to the outsides of the outer sliding doors onto the balconies so residents could still step out there.

"Yes, but it doesn't make sense to me. That means someone from outside can open them." Billy shrugged. "Just saying."

"Last night some yobs tried to use a hi-top transit to get to a balcony in the other block of flats and were driven off with furniture. That won't work if they are determined." Harry looked around everyone. "We have to be able to drive them off those balconies or they'll make holes and burn us out."

"We can't go out there and meet them with knives and clubs." Obe sighed. "We aren't fighters, Harry."

"Who will actually pull a trigger if they have to? I mean it. Don't freeze on me or you might kill us all." Frightened faces looked back at Harry.

"I will because I'm not letting them get the women. Though I will probably miss." Rob looked grim. Public hugging had translated into a fierce determination to protect Susan.

"Not at this range. There's a hole cut in every window on the first floor and a little hole in the ply. You can't miss across the width of the balcony. No heroics, shoot them in the gut." Harry handed Rob a rifle and a box of rounds. "Keep shooting until they are very still or fall off the balcony."

"I'll be there by then." Casper hefted the heavy chopping blade. "I'll go out and clean up or deal with anyone getting in."

"I'll turn up where the attack concentrates, if it's concentrated. We need two more for a rifle, and one for a pistol, a real one." Harry showed the target pistol he'd taken from Casper's assailant.

"I'll take that. I've practiced with the poncy one and can hit something across a balcony." Finn sighed. "They aren't getting Mum, nor are they stealing her medicine." He gave a wan smile, "now I've stolen some for her."

Harold handed Finn the target .38. "This will kick back harder and make a hell of a noise. Shoot for the bastard's belt buckle and I promise the bullet will stop a man. It isn't even a tiny bit poncy. Take your time to be sure because there's only seven loads."

"I play shoot 'em up on the computer? If I squint and pretend I'll pull the trigger. For Mum." Toby received a big hug from his Mum as well as a worried look as Harry showed the lad how to shoot the .22 rifle. "Hey, some of the shooting games have sights like these."

"Then you won't miss. This is the lever for the bolt. Just up and back and the old case pops out. Slide a new round in, make sure that locks home, point and pull gently." Harold pulled the butt into Toby's shoulder. "Tighter, so nothing jumps about." Harry tapped Toby gently on the head. "Keep one thing in mind. Do not, even for an instant, point this at anyone who lives here. Even unloaded. No joking, no games."

"OK soldier boy, er, Mr Miller. Sorry."

"The soldier boy thing is my fault." Liz shrugged. "I tried the poncy gun but I look away when I pull the trigger. I'll take it though, and aim before I look away. If that will be any good?"

"The more weapons pointing if it gets to a stand-off the better." Finn handed the air pistol over and showed Liz how to reload.

"I'll take a rifle." Obe looked grim. "Many years ago I was caught up in a couple of race riots that scared me to death. I think I'll be able to do it if I just remember what happened then. I was watching what you did with Toby but give me the quick and dumb lesson anyway." He took the last rifle. Billy took an air pistol because he'd done a little bit of practicing with Finn and could load it.

Then Karen stepped up and held out her hand for the last air pistol. She gave Harold a little smile. "Give me that. I'll pull the trigger though they probably won't need to duck."

"But they will duck, Karen, which gives those who can aim just a bit more time. Thank you." Harry spent time going through how to use the weapons until the users could stick a reload in and send it out of the barrel.

Mr Baumber appeared with five long poles and a lot of duct tape. "If you tape some of those knives to these, will it help keep them off the balconies?"

Harry grinned. "Too bloody true." The knives would probably come free once they were used, but most of the residents wouldn't stick a knife in a person anyway. The blades on poles would look dangerous and give the defenders a reach advantage. "Thank you Mr Baumber."

"I also found these safety gloves, for those who are throwing ornaments. They should be tough enough to protect fingers? I am willing to throw things?" Quite a few people smiled or winced because the ornaments were

Liz's entire Twisted Sister stock, which she had donated. They were now with the bricks behind the third floor windows.

"Right. Does everyone know where to go for throwing, fire-fighting and shooting?" Murmurs and nodding heads confirmed they'd all got it. "Billy is watching the front door in case someone actually breaks it, so we get warning. The babysitters and the children are assembled away from windows and the ground floor flats are empty. Try to doze if nothing is happening though the lookouts must keep wide awake. Tea and coffee will be provided through the night."

Harry looked around them all and put all the confidence he could into his voice. "These are just yobs and if we look too hard to take, they'll go after someone else. Let's go." At least a dozen sketched a salute of some sort.

"You look the part, little brother." Sharyn gave a real salute because she knew how.

Harry glanced down. "I'm not really in the Army now."

"No, but the reason I want you in battledress is because that firms this lot up." Sharyn gave Harry a little hug. "I like having a soldier about again and anyway, you'll scare the shit out of some of those yobs."

Harry smiled. "I need a balaclava."

"Heh, yeah. SAS. All those bloody films." Sharyn sighed. "I'd love to have Stones and a half dozen of his mates here now. They'd be having a bloody ball."

"Too true but I'll settle for a quiet night, sis." A last hug and Sharyn headed upstairs to join the throwing squad. Harry chose the first floor window nearest the front door and ran a quick mental check. There were three watching that hole under the garage door with a fire extinguisher and golf clubs or baseball bats. Harry debated sending a homemade spear down there but those needed to be visible.

For almost two hours the firework noises grew and then a group came around the end of the road and headed for the other block of flats. The flats were surrounded but the mob made no real attempt to break in. Bricks were thrown and there was a lot of jeering, but no petrol bombs or climbing to get at balconies. Not until three vehicles came round the corner with an even larger crowd surrounding them and Harry swore. One had a cherry picker lift on the back, and another was the hi-top van but with ladders fastened to the side and projecting above the roof.

The last vehicle was a pickup with a contraption fastened to the front. A steel bar vee shape that turned the vehicle into a battering ram. The front door of the flats would never stop it. Harry sent word down to the garage to make some petrol bombs, quickly. Bottles of petrol and oil with a rag in the top. If that thing broke the doors he'd burn the vehicle in place. Dangerous, but better than a big hole the mob could pour through. Harry though the fire-arms could stop the other two vehicles, or at least those using them to climb onto the balconies.

There was a big discussion going on among the mob now with people organising an assault on the other flats. "Bethany, phone the other flats and advise them to make petrol bombs to burn the vehicles." Harry heard the phone dialling and low voices behind him.

"These are the first two. How many do you want?" Two wine bottles with rags in the top were given to Harry and he set them down carefully.

"Two at the middle balcony on each side on the third floor. Only to be used if a vehicle actually pulls up and stops. Tell them to break the windscreen with bricks first if possible, and don't miss with the petrol." Harry considered for a moment. "Make another four and be ready to take them where they're needed if the phone goes. Put my pickup or Rob's van against Finn's to help block the garage doors."

"OK, I'll tell them." Isiah limped away.

Harry watched the preparations around the other flats, and the mob were too organised for comfort. Though Harry was fairly certain even the impromptu battering ram wouldn't shift the garage door with both vehicles behind it. Though the door would be wrecked, which would meant that it couldn't be opened or it wouldn't shut again. Even as Harry was regretting not having a heavier rifle, the attack on the other flats started. He shelved dreams of shooting the bastards in charge with a buffalo gun and watched how this attack developed.

Someone had worked out how to do this, or this wasn't the first block of flats they'd attacked. Petrol bombs arced up on all sides mixed with missiles. Half bricks Harry thought since they weren't big enough for full ones. Small enough to throw hard, big enough to be very dangerous. Luckily the windows were now covered in ply. Though soon several balconies were ablaze and then the first two vehicles lurched forwards. They went for the two balconies closest to the doors, and now Harry could see what the plan was.

A swarm of men went up the ladders on the van and onto one balcony. Four men rode the cherry picker straight up to the other balcony and they jumped straight on. More men were waiting as the platform lowered for another load. As figures appeared on higher balconies, throwing bricks, gunfire cracked and some of the defenders staggered or fell. These looters or rioters were properly armed. The barrage of bricks from above faltered.

Those on the balconies started tearing at the plywood over the windows, and the third vehicle lurched into action. There was no hesitation. Either the driver was well strapped in and padded or hopped up to the eyeballs, because the vehicle didn't slow down. The bonnet was buried in the entrance when the pickup stopped, so the doors were gone. The engine roared and the whole vehicle vibrated as the driver recovered and attempted to reverse out of the wreckage.

On one of the balconies there was hand to hand fighting now but Harry's eyes were attracted by a surge in the mob nearest to him. The garage door was opening! A minibus accelerated out as the mob raced forward waving weapons, and was followed by a van and an estate car. A fourth car stopped in the garage entrance as bats and machetes and bricks smashed through the windscreen and presumably struck the driver. The stopped vehicle blocked most of the opening and fighting erupted to either side of it.

The minibus accelerated away and made it, knocking aside several people on the way but shrugging off the missiles hitting it. The van swerved and slowed as the windshield starred, and men were trying to drag the doors open. A side door slid open and two men tried to climb aboard even as the driver recovered and accelerated clear of the mob. The van bounced across the car park and smashed down the wire between that and the old children's playground.

One attacker fell away, rolling across the ground as the van swerved towards the road. The second came off as the van hit the kerb, but as he did two other figures were pulled out of the van to follow him. The van accelerated off down the road because more of the mob had started towards it.

Meanwhile the estate car crashed into the low retaining wall at the car park entrance as a volley of gunfire ripped into it. In moments the mob was all over it and Harry saw limbs flashing and heard the screams. Women. The car was carrying women.

The two who had fallen out of the van staggered to their feet, took one look back and started running towards Harry. The man who had fallen at the same time staggered to his feet, looked around, and then limped after them. Long hair flew as the taller figure ran, though she was slowed by pulling along the smaller, slighter figure. Harry raised his rifle.

Crap. Flickering light, bloody target ammo, and only a two-two. Even if he hit the man it might not drop him and then that lot would know how weak the defence was here. He called upwards. "Third floor balcony, Harry here."

"Yes Harry." That was Mr Baumber.

"When those two get close enough so you won't hit them, start throwing at the man. Sharp stuff."

"All right, Harry."

Harry half-turned. "Beth, get all the shooters and spears here, double quick." About fifteen men were coming from the main mob and Harry wanted to scare them off. Behind Harry the phone was already calling.

Harry was about ready to shoot anyway because that man was getting too close to the two women, and then something gleamed briefly before clattering on the path. The man swerved and stopped, looking up, and Harry could see the shock on his face. Mr Baumber had damn near got him with a real Liz special, all pointy bits of metal.

"Far enough, fella. Back off." The man's attention moved to Harry and he backed off a bit. Below him Harry heard the door open and then close again, so Billy had been watching and was ready. The fugitives were inside.

The rest of the men came charging up waving baseball bats, hammers and more of the machetes. There was even a butcher's cleaver. "Watch it, they're throwing sharp shit and he's got a rifle." The original man's warning stopped the rest.

"One? I'll whistle up a couple of the lads from across there." The man who spoke made sure Harry could hear the reply.

A door opened to Harry's left, then right. "Two rifles." That was Rob and there was no give in his voice.

"Three." Toby was game but wavered a bit.

"It's been a while, but they say you never forget. Which one is mine, soldier boy?"

Harry kept the smile from his face because from what he'd said everyone out there would assume Obe was ex-Army or similar. "You can shoot the bastard with the limp, just for laying hands on the women." The man in question looked startled after relaxing when his friends arrived, and moved to join the other men.

"I've got the fat bastard on the end." Finn was here now.

"Save one for me." Liz sounded totally sincere again, but she did last time when about to collapse according to her.

"OK punks, which one feels lucky?" Harry had to smile, because that was Karen. All the men were staring at her.

"She means it you know." Harry got their attention back. "I'm going to shoot the first one through the left eye, then the next through the right to make it interesting."

"Bullshit." The leader wasn't having that, which was a mistake since Harry had him down as the first target. Though through the throat, not the eye in this light.

"Pure gospel, asshole. That uniform isn't a knockoff. His Majesty gave him it." Liz. Of course. Though this lot didn't look happy about the news. Maybe it was just law-abiding citizens who gave the Army crap.

"True. A real live soldier boy, and HM probably spent a fortune teaching him to shoot." Harry let Rob keep going because apparently someone else telling them worked better than Harry saying anything. About half of the yobs were already wanting to be elsewhere. A cheer went up over at the other block of flats but Harry daren't look.

"That ram will knock down the door and the bloody shooting won't help then. Hand over those two and we'll leave you alone tonight." The leader wasn't backing down.

"Wrong. Our door has steel bars, and we'll shoot the shit out of anyone getting onto a balcony. From inside where your guns can't see us. Then I'll shoot your shooters." Harry let his rifle threaten one, then another.

"If anyone gets up here, they get one of those spears, or I'm going to cut their fucking heads off with this." Casper spoke up from behind Harry and was no doubt waving that bloody great blade.

"Come on, Bas. They're in the other place and we'll miss out."

"Yeah, they'll grab all the bloody women." Men were backing away now. More followed and then the ringleader.

Though not without a last gesture. A hand pointing at Harry and "I'll be back tomorrow, for you, soldier boy."

Harry spoke quietly as the gang retreated and then turned away. "No jeering or cheering. Nice and low key. Don't attract the rest."

"What, we let them just walk?" Rob wasn't happy.

"Yes, because we haven't got bars on the door. Look over at the other block." There were more people climbing the ladders now and they were pouring into the flats through the now uncontested window. More were moving into the garage where resistance has ceased. A petrol bomb went off and the car in the doorway started to burn but it was too late. Men were already inside.

A single petrol bomb went off in the doorway where the pickup had now reversed clear, but the mob simply trampled through the flames with a roar of triumph. Another cheer signalled the second of the balcony windows being forced and men flooded through. The screams and sounds of fighting from inside were clear now and a few of the side balcony windows opened. People came out on the balconies and looked down, but not all the mob were going inside. Some were waiting for escapees.

For what seemed like hours the mob rampaged through the flats, bursting out of doors to attack those sheltering on balconies. Those were cut down, or dragged inside, or in some cases thrown over. The fighting stopped but the screaming didn't and it was different screaming now, mostly women. One partially clothed woman ran out and threw herself from a fourth floor balcony as men pursued her through the doors.

"We have to do something." Liz was sobbing and she wasn't the only one.

"We can't. If we go out there they'll kill whoever I take, then come over here and finish the job. We can't stop them." Harry wanted to go. He wanted to go completely apeshit and kill as many as he could, but there were too many.

"At least they got a lot of the women out." Several people looked at Billy and he dropped his eyes and voice. "Sixteen women and kids anyway, according to Patricia."

"But where will they go?" Susan was clinging to Rob, having turned over child care to the elderly since many youngsters were asleep.

"I'll find out. Call me if any of that lot head this way." Harold went to find the refugees. If they had a destination, wherever they were going might be better than here. He found the long-haired woman, Patricia, sat with a cup of coffee and sobbing her heart out.

Kerry was keeping her company so Harold asked her quietly. "Who was the other one?"

"Hazel, fourteen. Her Dad is in the flats, her Mum was in that van. She's in that bedroom with my daughter and will hopefully cry herself to sleep."

Harold went to the older woman. "Was there a plan, a destination?" Harry tried to ask as gently as possible, because after all Patricia was from that block of flats and must know those still inside.

"No, not unless the drivers agreed something." Patricia tried to stop sobbing and answer. "We didn't expect this, but Christopher said if the doors went down we had to go. He realised what that truck was for. His wife stayed with him to help." Patricia descended into sobbing again.

Kerry took her away to join Hazel while Harry returned to the windows. He looked across at the flats and tried to think of anything that might help. There was nothing. Just after two am Harry came to one certain decision and went to find Sharyn. "Start packing. They'll come back tomorrow, prepared for firearms and a steel barred door. There's too many and we can't keep them out."

"Some won't leave."

"Then they die. You don't, Daisy doesn't, and Wills doesn't. We are leaving with as many as will come with us and as heavily armed as possible. I'm not leaving the firearms. Tell who you can and I'll do the same." Sharyn looked at Harry's face and nodded.

"All right Harry. Where are we going?"

Harry hadn't got a clue, except far away. "Near the Army will be best."

"They'll shoot us."

"No, not if we stay three hundred yards away, but they'll shoot the bastards with guns." Harry shrugged. "I was told on the way in, and suddenly realised what the rules mean. There is a three hundred yard exclusion zone. Outside that the Army won't interfere, except they will shoot at anyone with a firearm. All we need is a place where nobody can reach us without the Army seeing them." Harry gave a little smile. "Open to suggestions?"

Sharyn straightened up, her face determined. "I'll start with Rob and Susan, then Finn because he'll want his Mum out of here."

"I'll start with Casper and Liz. He can fight and she can make missiles."

"Ask Karen." Sharyn sniggered. "If you feel lucky, punk." That story had spread and was one of the few bright spots about tonight. The brightest was that they were all still alive.

*　　　*　　　*

In the early hours four almost naked women were dragged out of the doors and loaded into a van, then driven away. Soon afterwards six elderly men were thrown off the roof. The watchers could see their white or grey hair as the victims fell, screaming until they hit the car park.

Then the mob streamed out carrying TVs and anything else they fancied. By dawn the flats were still burning in places but otherwise silent. The fire in the garage had taken a real hold now. Harry picked up his rifle. "I'm going to look."

"Some of them might still be there." Susan's eyes were dark with fatigue because she had been trying to comfort Hazel, and also start packing.

"Good. I'll kill the bastards." Most of those present flinched from Harry's tone but Casper stepped up.

"I'm good with that. Anyone else fancy a bit of good old-fashioned retribution?" Casper looked around the impromptu residents meeting. Rob kissed Susan gently and joined Casper, then Finn stood up. Mr Baumber and Obe stood, and then Toby stepped forward.

Karen came forward and gave a little smile. "I'll come if I won't slow you up."

"You're welcome." Harry knew that everyone who volunteered needed to do this. They needed to make some effort after sitting here watching all night. He certainly did. "Wouldn't want some punk to get lucky."

Karen actually looked embarrassed. "Sorry about that. I didn't know what to say."

"Wish I'd thought of it." Mr Baumber smiled at her. "I'm Stewart." Little smiles appeared here and there as Karen smiled back.

Twenty residents crossed the gap in the end with Sharyn bringing Harry's pickup. They avoided the garage, especially when a thud and a gout of flame heralded another vehicle catching fire. "Toby and Finn, stay by the main door." Harry beckoned and Sharyn drove the pickup closer. "Sharyn will park that across the door so you've got cover if some asshole turns up."

"I'll have no problem with shooting now, Mr Miller." That murderous look shouldn't have been on a fourteen year old face. Toby knew Hazel, mainly over the internet when she played games or compared homework.

"Harry will do, Toby. Now you've been conscripted." Harry turned to the rest. "I'll take one group up the stairs and Casper will take the rest in the lifts. Then we leave a guard on both and search each floor. Break down any locked doors you find since they've been locked after that lot finished. Shoot or chop any bastard without a really good reason to be in there." Harry doubted many would do so in cold blood, but Karen for one had a grim look about her.

So did others after they found the two women who had survived the estate car crash. Both bodies were naked and they had been raped as they died of gunshot wounds. The others in the car were dead, killed instantly in that fusillade. If there were any survivors the women were gone now, women because all the car's occupants were female. The bodies in the car park and just inside the main door had also put a vengeful gleam in a few eyes.

The ground and first floors were clear of all but the dead, and now most people were angry and determined. Harry was working through the third floor when three shots rapped out and then a scream, cut off short. Harry headed for the sound and found Casper cleaning the machete. "Found one. The asshole was asleep I reckon and came out to see what the noise was."

Liz picked up the slightly smaller version of a machete near the man's body. "I think I can manage to use one of these now, soldier boy. After seeing this place." She kicked the body. "Let's see if he's got friends." Liz's hardened attitude wasn't surprising. Everyone searching the rooms was ready to kill some bastard by now. Room after room told the same story of death and terror.

Dead bodies were scattered throughout the building, some raped and a few of those were men. All the women who hadn't died fighting had been raped including the old and infirm ones. The children were the worst bodies to find, though according to Patricia most had got away in the van with the women. Not the two preteen boys or the babe in arms, or the young teenager, who had all stayed for some reason.

*   *   *

Rob looked back as Harry came out onto the roof. "He's the last one."

"So shoot him." The man was backed into a corner of the roof with a semicircle of armed people penning him in.

"We were wondering about nailing him to the door as a hint to the bastards when they come back. After cutting his dick off of course." Liz was hefting her new weapon and certainly seemed to mean it.

Harry didn't want these people setting off down that route. He looked at the cornered man. "Did you hear that, fella? You might want to jump." Actually Harry would shoot the arse if he didn't jump, but the residents deserved a bit of vengeance. Making him follow those old blokes into the car park would do.

The man's eyes widened. "Oh fuck. It's you." His eyes moved across and rested on Karen. "Oh fuck." Then he dropped his machete, turned, took two steps and jumped. A scream trailed him down and stopped abruptly.

"Damn." Billy spat over the edge.

"No. Because torture is a very bad road to go down. Execution I am definitely in favour of and it gets the message across just as well." Harry looked over at Karen. "You've got a rep. He didn't jump until he saw you were here."

Karen smiled sweetly. "You say the nicest things." She turned to leave and Mr Baumber, now Stewart, helped her down the steps.

Finn picked up the machete the man had dropped when he was cornered. "There's a lot of these about now. That's four we caught and they all had one." He looked round and took a deep breath. "It wasn't much payback, but I feel a little bit better now." The rest were nodding as they headed down to the lifts.

Sharyn had moved the pickup from the entrance when a minibus came around the corner and stopped. The windshield was starred and one headlight was smashed, but Harry was sure it was the vehicle that had escaped. He looked around. "Would any of you be recognised by the residents here?"

"I might." Toby ducked and looked a bit wary, then straightened. "I used to play internet games with some of them and some of us swapped pictures. Nothing icky!"

"Step out there and let them see you. I don't think your love life is a problem now." Harry grinned as Toby went pink. "Put down the rifle though."

"Ah, right."

"Louise and Susan both know some of the women as well. I could go and get them?" Sharyn was in the pickup already with the engine running so she wouldn't take long.

Harry nodded. "Ask Patricia to come as well. Don't tell Hazel until we know who is in the minibus." Harry hoped Hazel's Mum was in there, but this was the wrong vehicle. Sharyn drove off towards the front door of her block of flats. Harry spoke quietly. "I would like the women to the front, please, without waving any weaponry."

Liz handed her captured machete to Casper. "I want it back."

Either Toby or the women reassured the occupants because the minibus drove closer. It stopped about twelve yards away and two women got out. "Where is everybody?" The speaker looked at the bodies in the car park and her face crumpled. "Dad." Then she was running towards a white-haired corpse.

The other woman walked forward, a bit unsteadily. "All of them?"

"Sorry. There were too many for us to help." Liz moved forward. "We got four who were slow to leave."

"Who are you?" Her eyes moved to Harry. "Who the hell are you?"

"If you go to the other block, we'll tell you all about it." The woman's eyes went past Harry to the smashed and scorched doorway behind him. Harry spoke again before she asked. "You don't want to go in there. Whoever it is, remember the last time you saw them." Her eyes tracked back to Harry. "Please. It will save you some bad dreams. I know."

Harry had dreams about bad people he'd killed. It had to be worse seeing someone he cared about hacked to bits or raped to death. "Just go over there. What about the van that got away?"

The woman looked at the car and the bullet holes. At least the women now had curtains thrown over them. "Only the van?" She bit back a sob. "We are late. A road block and a fight in the road. The others should be here." The next sob was stronger. "Oh God."

Harry spoke quietly. "Liz goes over there, put her back inside, and drive them to our door. Nice and steady but don't accept no."

Liz glanced back, startled, and then nodded. "OK Harry."

Harry turned to the rest of his party. "Anyone still want to be here tonight when they come back?" Nobody answered. "Then let's get packed."

"What about them?" Mr Baumber waved at the bodies. "That isn't right, just leaving them."

Harry looked back at the building and the smoke still coming from some windows. "If there's time we put them all inside and make sure this place is well alight."

Rob's voice was bleak. "If we open the fire doors to the garage it'll do that. Those doors won't last much longer anyway, the way the garage is burning. Then the whole block goes up."

"We all pack first, and if there's time we deal with the dead. Now let's move!" Harry put some snap into the last bit and the startled group got moving as the minibus started off. Two of the group collected the woman from the car park, promising they'd deal with her Dad.

*   *   *

By two pm the first group was ready to leave, though they waited to help with the bodies. There was no attempt at laying them out. Each one found outside was rolled onto a curtain or bedsheet and carried inside, then left in the foyer. That was a job for strong stomachs, especially with those who had been thrown from the roof. Any dead attackers from inside were thrown out of the door or windows to rot.

The smoke inside was thickening when Finn went down the stairs to the garage fire door. He reported that the sides were giving way and he daren't get near enough to trip the catch. The other fire doors and lift doors were propped open to help the draught when the flames broke through.

The first group of twenty three were those who were going to find relatives elsewhere and included two from the minibus. The women in the minibus varied from fourteen to early twenties and had been sent out first because of what the attackers had promised the previous night. Four of the ten women left partners behind in the flats, while another three left a parent.

The van contained mothers and younger children, with Patricia because she was a nurse. Trainee nurse but the best there was available for the children. By three pm all hope of the van returning was abandoned. That left thirty-three people who had no place to go. The residents who were coming with Harry's group or possibly staying. A few, such as Isiah and Kerry, still clung to that option.

*   *   *

Harold indicated Sharyn. "Since nobody has a better suggestion, we are heading for where I first came in when I arrived to get Sharyn. There's the best part of a private estate if it's still standing, a big bit of reasonably open ground each side of the houses, and the Army overlook the place. The houses towards the city centre are wrecked and looked deserted. The Army is why I think those houses will still be standing." Twenty six faces looked at Harry because Hazel and Patricia were looking after the four children too young to be here. Even Mary, Finn's Mum, was here to cast her vote.

Sharyn spoke up. "Patricia and Hazel are coming with Harry because they believe he's the best bet."

"I'm with Harry." Casper grinned. "Though he isn't really my type."

"I'm coming too, otherwise you'll find a blacksmith first and then I'll cut my throat." Liz was grim despite the joke. "I've already loaded my gear but there isn't room for the ornaments." That was true. Everyone had to leave all but essentials. Food was more important than clothing or ornaments right now, or even hand missiles.

"I've got to bring Susan or Sharyn won't have a babysitter." Rob smiled and hugged the Susan in question.

Finn laughed a harsh sound. "Mum will be upset if she never gets to ride on the pickup."

"Too true I will."

Toby stepped forward. "I've been conscripted."

"I've got a rep to keep up." Karen smiled sweetly.

"I've got to keep an eye on the residents." Mr Baumber was looking at Karen.

"Just raise hands if you're with Harry." Billy laughed. "No, to make it easier, any idiot not coming raise your hand." There was a moment of hesitation from Isiah, Kerry, and Alicia but no hands went up.

"Then lead us to it, soldier boy." Liz sighed. "Why couldn't you be bigger or Casper be straight, and then this would be perfect. Desperate flight with a big strong hero."

"We leave in fifteen minutes. If it isn't in a vehicle, it ain't coming with us." Harry watched backs disappearing rapidly. "Are we packed?"

Sharyn smiled. "You never unpacked. Anyway you just steal what you haven't got."

"It's a plan."

Chapter 8:
Finding an Orchard

"Thank all and every God for that." Harry could see intact houses beyond the damaged estate.

"Shush, you'll spoil the aura of infallibility." Sharyn sighed. "Though I am very relieved." She looked either side of the approach road. "I don't think much of the neighbourhood." Many of the houses either side were burned and three were total ruins.

"At a guess someone tried to break out over the bypass. At least there aren't many cars and the road is open." Twice the convoy had stopped to push wrecked cars out of the road, and four times they'd detoured around roadblocks. There had been threats but the number of rifle and pistol barrels stuck out of windows got them through.

Harry was looking for the turn and voiced another quiet multidenominational prayer because it wasn't barricaded. "We drive in nice and peaceful with the weapons out of sight, and talk to any residents."

There was a nervous giggle from the back seat, from Hazel. "Sorry, but you said that ten times already, to everyone. You also said the women had to get out so the Army and residents could see us."

"They do have to except Patricia since she is babysitting. Now we hope the houses aren't all full."

"You said that as well." Sharyn grinned. "You really are a fusspot aren't you?"

"Well everyone seems to think I've got all the answers." Harry sighed. "Here we go." He turned in and drove up the road until he could see the last vehicle pull in off the main road behind him.

"Orchard Close. I like it. Sort of bucolic and homely." Harry looked round, startled, and there was a sign on the garden wall. "That looks empty and just your size," Sharyn pointed up Orchard Close to the big house at the end. "Providing it's empty of course, but the garden is a hint." Weeds were showing over the low wall.

"Let's deal with the locals before hammering in claim pegs." Harry climbed out and so did Sharyn and Hazel. Patricia stayed in the back seat with Daisy and Wills. Women climbed out of other vehicles and stood by them.

"Clear off!"

"To where?" Harry turned and an old man was stood in a doorway with a big rifle, complete with a damn great bayonet. "Wow, a Lee-Enfield three oh three. I haven't seen one in years." Harry noted that the man's house backed towards the bypass so the Army couldn't see his weapon at the front door. "Are you going to shoot me?"

The man glanced down at his rifle and back in surprise. Harry's comment probably wasn't the usual reaction to the big weapon but Harry loved the now obsolete World War rifle. Big, heavy, tough and if they were cared for really, really accurate. The Army shooting range had one.

"If you don't leave, yes I will shoot you."

"There are only five rounds in one of those clips. Big ones, but only five. Then these women are going to be angry, and so are the men in the vans." Harry sighed. "Our neighbours were burned out and massacred. There were ten survivors who are with us. We didn't want the same to happen to our flats. All we want are the empty houses and we'll help defend the place."

"The Army will defend it."

"Not if the bastards don't use guns. I'll show you what we can do about that. Casper?" Casper climbed out with his machete. "He hates the yobs but plays with my sister's kids. Not a bad sort of neighbour."

"I can use one of those as well." Liz showed her machete. "We took these off some of the rioters." She sighed. "I've had a bloody awful few days. Can we at least sleep here and talk in the morning?"

"How many are there? Can I see you all?"

"Sure." Harry called down the vehicles. "Everyone out. Don't show the weapons."

The old man looked startled, then wary. "Weapons?"

Harry smiled. "We could have just shot you, but as I said, we come in peace."

Another head appeared behind the man at that and spoke urgently in his ear. The older man spoke up again. "You can pull in there, Orchard Close. The house at this end, number one, has people inside so leave it alone."

"Yes! Perfect. Bagsy the one at the end." Sharyn had a big smile. She waved at the two figures in the doorway. "I'm Sharyn and he's Harry. Give us an hour to settle in and come up for a cuppa. We'll be in the one at the end."

"Er, right. I'm, oh, that's awkward. I'm Harry." The older man gave a little shrug.

"I don't mind Harold."

"We call him soldier boy because he is. Or was until he came to get his sister." Liz turned to call down the convoy. "We'll have to doss on the floors tonight. Any single girls come with me." She grinned. "Me and my girlfriend, Casper." A ripple of laughter went down the vehicles and people started walking forward or climbing back aboard.

Liz walked forward and as she came level with Harry she took a mock swipe at him and spoke in a low voice. "Will you stop doing that?"

"What?" Harry really was startled.

"When someone offers to shoot you, your first reaction is to sneer at them. He's got a cannon and you tell him he can only get five of us? It puts bloody years on me." She looked up Orchard Close. "We need a big place for all us girls."

"None of them are small, but the one at the end is taken." Sharyn waved her hand around. "I've got two kids who need separate rooms and I'm not sharing a room with my brother."

"I'm with that, sis."

"I'll need a room as well." Hazel glanced apprehensively from one to the other. "If I can?"

"You can sleep in Daisy's room if there aren't enough. Come on." Sharyn started walking up the pavement. "Bring up the luggage please, driver." Harry smiled and did as he was told. He was agreeably surprised to find that the house wasn't locked and the keys were hung on a row of hooks inside the door.

Sharyn was truly happy with the kitchen and that the beds had mattresses and bedding. They were a bit damp, but the place hadn't been empty long enough for mould to take hold and there were even some clothes in the drawers and food in the cupboards.

A quick inspection and two of Harry's sleeping bags, taken as part of his Army pay, were commandeered for Daisy and Wills. Hazel stayed upstairs to read a story, since Uncle-Harry had to do soldier things. The first was to find the meter cupboard and turn the electricity and then the gas heating on. Sharyn was soon singing happily to herself and the smell of hot coffee drifted through the place while the driver brought in the rest of the bags.

*   *   *

The knock at the front door was polite, and when Harry went to answer he found three people waiting. The older Harry, a younger man, and an older woman. Harry thought it was a good sign that the other Harry hadn't brought his rifle. "Come in, please. The furniture needs a bit of airing but we've put covers over the chairs and settees for now. Would you like a drink?"

"Thank you. Ooh, is that coffee? We daren't go to the shops because the last two who went shopping didn't come back." The woman looked a bit uncomfortable. "We've been taking food from the empty houses which Harry says is looting, but what else can we do?" She stuck out a hand. "I'm Betty, or Elizabeth if we're being posh, and I live at number one. Your neighbour, sort of."

Harry shook hands. "Pleased to meet you Betty. I'm Harry. Ah, Harold now." Harold shifted his attention to the older man. "That will take some getting used to but I haven't used Harry as long as you have. I know your name and thanks for the place to sleep."

"We've been talking and maybe we can offer a bit more than that." The older Harry looked at the other two. "We've been looking at you as everyone unloaded, and you look like normal people." He gave a little embarrassed laugh. "You know what I mean. We also saw enough weapons going into the houses to know you told the truth. You could have just killed me if your group intended taking over. Matthew here says we need extra people in case there are more of the rioters." He gestured to the side. "This is Matthew. He used to be a Traffic Warden but they were all laid off months ago."

"Last year, and I get the unemployment money but the damn redundancy never came through." The slim young man with bright red hair stuck out a hand. "Pleased to meet you." He looked across as Sharyn came through. "Hello. I'm Matthew."

"Sharyn. Do you want tea or coffee?"

"Coffee please if you can spare it."

"Harry, and I'd like tea if it isn't too much trouble." Harry senior smiled. "Milk but no sugar?"

"I'm Betty and I would love coffee please." Betty looked from Harold to Sharyn. "Are you, well, is he your, um? Significant other?"

"Yes but not how you think. He's my little brother." Sharyn smiled. "Not as little now, though he'll feel a lot younger if he is going to be called Harold again. Mum called him Harold until he left home, and so did I up until he was fifteen. That's when he went all rebellious." Sharyn ruffled Harold's hair. "The milk will be skimmed." Nobody seemed to mind.

Harold sighed. Sharyn was telling the truth and he would feel fifteen again for a while, but it would stop a lot of confusion. Hazel came in as everyone was sitting down and hesitated. "It's all right Hazel. Nip through and get a drink and I'll explain who else lives here." Harold quickly explained that Hazel was possibly an orphan, and that Sharyn was a widow and there were two young children upstairs.

"I feel a lot better now." Harry senior shrugged. "I was still a bit worried, but an Army widow with two young children and an orphaned teenager are a lot less threatening than you and that big man."

"Casper? He's turned out to be a good friend in a nasty spot." Tea and coffee finished breaking the ice.

Harry senior came back to the initial greeting. "We really were worried, because there's only sixteen of us living here."

"We are a bit scattered because we all still live in our own houses, or rather the houses we rented. Most of the rest of the residents left in one night. There were no vans or lorries, just buses and hand luggage." Harry senior looked embarrassed again. "We really have been looting, but just for essentials."

"I don't think it's looting any more. Certainly not compared to the situation further into the city. Supermarkets have been emptied and burned and the police are just trying to survive." Harold glanced briefly at Hazel and she was looking tense but not weepy, yet. "There are organised gangs looting now and they are killers. Is there a chemist's shop anywhere in the area? We have some elderly people with us, and are worried about medication for them."

"There were a few shops on the next estate but they all burned in the riot, and so did the doctor's surgery. Medication is a problem here as well. We asked the Army, and the sergeant said that if someone was an urgent case they would call an ambulance. Whoever it was would go to a camp where there would be medicine." Betty looked at Harry senior. "We sent one person but haven't heard from her since. The sergeant said she won't be allowed back."

"My wife, Sally. She needed oxygen and her bottles had run out." The strain showed on Harry senior's face. "I wanted to go with her, but the soldiers wouldn't allow that unless I had a pass."

"Only tradespeople such as plumbers and electricians were offered passes, or so we understand." Sharyn spoke softly, but there was no way to soften what had happened or ease the man's pain. Harold's knowledge of conditions in the camps certainly wouldn't help the older man to feel any better.

"The rest of the residents who left didn't have trades, not that sort." Matthew had a curled lip. "Most were retired anyway."

"We, the ones who are left, weren't exactly part of the club. Poor relations at best. Some of the residents were sociable enough but they didn't make any close friends." Betty was looking puzzled. "Why would civil servants, managers, and retired judges, that sort of person, get a pass?"

"The people taken away by bus from our flats were all related to that type of person. Someone is rescuing the people who are used to being at the top of the heap. Those who run the place. Though the answer might be simply that they could afford the ticket." Harold was seeing a pattern now and not a pretty one. "Though they've also taken the right people to keep life comfortable, the tradespeople."

"Where to? The countryside is supposed to be full of gangs, and the cities and big towns are being sealed off." Harry senior looked from one to the other. "Where can they go?"

"Maybe Market Rasen." There were blank looks from everyone and Harold gave a short laugh. "A friend of mine said his parents had moved there. It's a little place in Lincolnshire where allegedly nothing happens. Nothing like riots and murder in the streets anyway. If the lot that left here moved there, and brought plumbers, how would we know?"

"But what about the gangs in the countryside?" Matthew's face showed that he was thinking of one answer even as he spoke, an answer he didn't like.

"How much do you trust the TV news?" Sharyn wasn't smiling at all now. "Though what happened to all those who got out? There must have been thousands pouring through those gaps the first night and they didn't look like yobs or rioters."

"From the middle class suburbs, remember? We worked out roughly where the breakouts were, the ones that weren't stopped with machine guns and helicopters." Harold's mental picture was settling down. "Almost all of those will be good solid citizens according to a certain set of standards. Perfect for keeping the milk and eggs coming in Market Rasen. Unlike the nasty, dirty-handed yobs from the social housing and the terraces and tower blocks." Harold stopped and looked at the shocked faces.

"Sorry. I suddenly had a very nasty thought or two. This stinks, but I could be entirely wrong." He sighed. "It doesn't make any difference now because we're all sealed in." Harold looked at the three residents. "We are sealed in, aren't we? The TV showed wire and concrete blocks."

"Yes, completely sealed in. The bypass here is up in the air, a long overpass really, so the roadway is impossible to get to except up the ramps." Matthew sighed. "I considered going underneath but there's wire and there must be cameras or alarms. I was inspecting the wire fence when two soldiers turned up and pointed rifles at me. They told me there was a three hundred yard zone where I could be shot on sight." Matthew sighed again. "I came home."

"The Army mean it as well and they've put up signs now. A group came up the main road and were shooting at the soldiers and then a plane came over. They dropped bombs. Then a helicopter dropped fire bombs." Betty's face reflected the shock she still felt over that. "Between those and the other fights every house along the main road is wrecked."

"Other fights?"

"There have been several more groups trying to get out. They didn't come in here, thank God." Harry senior smiled sadly at Harold. "I would have probably missed you with that rifle. It was my Dad's and looks damn impressive, especially with the big bayonet on the end. We frightened off one car full who were looking for trouble."

"The more serious ones would have shot you from inside their car where the Army couldn't see the weapon, or sneaked back at night and overrun the place. That weapon is an incentive now because I doubt if there are many heavy rifles out there." Harold smiled. "Not good, solid, tough ones like that or ones with a big bayonet."

"He's a soldier, a real one." Hazel blushed when everyone looked at her. "Sorry. Everyone told me that Harry, Harold, him, he's a real soldier and can shoot properly. He can also use a stick, a club, and fight properly. That's why I want to stay here, in this house." Hazel subsided, still blushing.

"So why won't your friends in the Army let you leave?" Matthew was suspicious now.

"He left the Army to rescue me, but we all got trapped. Then Harr... Harold organised our defence, chased off the first attackers, and got us out when things got too bad." Sharyn was apparently a lot more proud of her little brother than she ever told him to his face.

"I gave advice." Harold looked at Matthew. "I can't go up there because I'm a civilian now, just one with an old Army uniform in my wardrobe."

"That's a relief to me." Betty smiled. "Someone who knows what to do about the yobs." She looked at the other two. "We should go and tell everyone, and have a proper vote."

"Yes, we have a sort of committee, but this needs everyone." Harry senior stood up. "Thank you for the talk and the tea." He smiled at Sharyn. "We only have tinned milk left so skimmed was a really nice change." The other two stood up and said goodbye, then left.

"We should let all our people know, and then get some sleep." Harold yawned because it had been a long three days and two bad nights.

"I'll do that." Hazel stood up. "I slept more than you because Patricia gave me a pill, and I want to be useful. Then you can sleep. I want to talk to the rest as well, please, the ones from our flats, the ones I know?" She looked at Sharyn. "I'll sneak into Daisy's room, I promise."

"We'll leave you a sleeping bag in there. Just stick to Orchard Close."

"Oh yes, and I'll run between houses." Hazel headed out of the door.

"You are let off story telling tonight because both the kids are already dead to the world. So you should sleep because Daisy will be up at the crack of dawn and demanding compensation." Sharyn gave Harold a hug. "Go on, little brother Harold. There's a shower up there that might work and if not Rob will fix it tomorrow. Yours is the room with an open door."

Harold brought out the last three sleeping bags and took one. Then he went up and threw the sleeping bag on the three-quarter bed in his new room. The shower did work and Harry didn't really inspect the bedroom afterwards. He just crawled into the bag and relaxed, and then was asleep.

*   *   *

Four days later the refugees were settling in properly. Not only in Orchard Close now because seven houses, even big ones, weren't enough for thirty-three warm bodies. People had spread out and were filling the gaps between the original residents, taking empty houses. The couples and families found new places first, with the single women mostly remaining in numbers three and five.

Though some weren't really couples, or not yet. A few of the single people wanted some space to get over what had happened, but everyone started to relax. Harold smiled over his morning toast and marmalade when the sound of a strimmer came in through the open window. An open window that was a bit chilly, but that and having the heating on was airing out the house very quickly.

"Settling down, Stewart?" Harold smiled at Mr Baumber as he walked past.

"Well it is a mess." The ex-caretaker looked along the other gardens. "It doesn't take long to knock the worst down as long as we've got cord." He gestured at the strimmer. "We are only using electric ones, and then we've got two electric mowers to do the job right."

"Tea's ready, Stewart." Harold left with a little smile because Stewart was cutting Karen's grass first. Sharyn was considering starting a book on the date of the first gin rummy game. Gossip was alive and well in Orchard Close.

Orchard Close was a rather anomalous description already. Those who had moved to other houses still considered themselves part of the Orchard Close gang, as they tended to put it. Liz was still actually in Orchard Close with Casper and ten women in their teens or early twenties. Many were from the survivors in the minibus plus a couple from the flats and those all carried machetes or baseball bats now.

The women also brightened the day for the younger single men by exercising together in the front garden, though carefully covered up. Loose jeans rather than skirts were a trend among the younger women now, after seeing the fate of those caught by the looters. Harold opened the gate and walked up to Matthew's house, because he wanted to investigate the surrounding ruins.

"Hello Matthew. Can you spare me a few minutes?"

"I've got hours these days. What about, Harold?"

"Scrounging and scavenging." Harold smiled. "Or looting in some people's eyes."

"Harry lost that fight when the loo roll started to run out. But where are we to go?" Matthew waved a hand towards the city. "The fighting over there hasn't slowed down."

"No, but none of it has come this way yet. Once they've finished with the city centre, looters and rioters will come this way." Harold gave a little smile. "I had a look in a couple of the houses that were burned or damaged. Some only have broken windows. Even where the roofs are letting in water there's still useable things inside."

Matthew frowned. "Such as? Bedding will be wet, and so will loo rolls." He smiled. "Sorry, but there was a near riot here when loo rolls started to run out."

"Tinned food, and coffee. Tins of milk and plastic tubs of flour and cereal? Loo rolls still wrapped in their plastic?" Harold smiled back at Matthew's sudden grin. "If there's a fridge or freezer in a garage and the electric is still working, it might be full of food." A thought struck Harold. "Where did all the people go?"

"A lot died when a big mob rampaged through there. The rest left, just ran or got in their cars and drove away as fast as possible. Most went off to the south, along the road at the roundabout just down there." Matthew grimaced. "They didn't come this way because the Army was shooting at any rioters heading towards them. The Army actually came down and buried a lot of bodies in a big pit afterwards, but the stink was bad for a while so they didn't get them all."

"So nobody has been in the houses since?"

"There have been people coming back but as long as they stayed over there we let them be." Matthew shrugged. "We assumed they were residents coming to collect any possessions that had survived. They might have been looting?"

"Only one way to find out but I want a combined group. The original residents and some of my lot. Not really mine, the residents of the flats."

"No Harold, your lot. Ask them and they'll tell you. Well not you, but they tell me they're part of Harold's gang, or soldier boy's. Even the ones who've moved next door to me." Matthew grinned. "I'll see if any of Harry's lot want to come. Or Betty's lot, or whatever because your lot are a definite group."

"Matthew's lot will do. Round them up and let me know, will you?" Harold pulled out the bit of paper. "This is the phone number for the house I'm in."

"Your house now, Harold." Matthew gestured at the house behind him. "I used to rent this, but it's mine now it seems. Do we need to bring clubs or something?"

"Whatever's handy. I'm taking Casper and Liz so they'll bring the heavy metal."

"Scary. Good. I'll call as soon as possible."

Harold stuck the target pistol under his long coat just in case, and took his stick for the same reason. Matthew had four people, and Harold brought five plus himself. Harold waved a hand around his group. "Casper, Liz, Billy, Toby, Emmy." Emmy was one of the minibus escapees, a tall twenty year old Jamaican whose husband died in the flats. She was carrying a rucksack and a baseball bat and determined to do her part.

Matthew waved at his group. "Curtis, Seth, Bernie and Sal." All were early to mid-twenties and just a little bit overweight and out of condition. Seth was a lot more so than the others. "They all want to join the exercises if that's allowed."

"Everyone is welcome. If anyone knows any judo or anything like that, they'll be really welcome." Liz smiled. "You haven't got a blacksmith have you?"

"No?"

"Never mind. Everyone look out for one while we scavenge." Everyone who knew Liz laughed and they were soon spreading the joke. That was a good icebreaker.

The group needed something to cheer them up. There were still bones in the ruins, and not all were completely clean yet. Though some of the rest did cheer people up. Definitely loo rolls, and quite a lot of tinned goods. "I've got seeds in here. Do we need, hang on, nasturtiums, poppies, carrots, broad beans and, oh yes, cauliflowers." Emmy appeared at the garage door with a handful of packets. "There's lots more."

"Bring them. If there's no improvement we may have to grow our own. I hope somebody has a vague idea about gardening because I don't." Harold hoped that supplies were re-established before that was necessary

"Christ, surely not. That would mean no food over the winter. It'll be next year before we can grow food." Seth looked horrified, but so did everyone else except Curtis.

"We can sow seeds now, and some will keep cropping as long as we keep the conditions right. Some will need to go in soon for next year. We'll only produce green stuff at this time of year, but that's what we need, right?" Curtis patted his little pot belly. "All right, I haven't worried about it before but healthy diet will be important, yes?"

"Yes, I suppose." Matthew wasn't impressed by a healthy diet but Liz perked up.

"If it's just greens I can do that. As long as there isn't tofu."

Curtis grinned. "Sorry, no idea how to grow tofu or yoghurt." His face fell. "No milk unless someone found a cow."

"We need lots of tinned milk and even if cheese is mouldy it isn't useless." Harold smiled at them. "Honest, that's not just a rough tough soldier thing."

"Yeuk. Cut my mould off before I see it." Toby grinned. "Then stick it on some toast."

"Bread, damn." Everyone looked stricken at that. "Chips, pizzas and take-away Chinese."

"We can make bread." Emmy shrugged. "I'm sure we can. I'll bet what we want is here."

"Beer, where's the beer?"

Sal patted Seth's belly. "Maybe that's not really necessary."

Seth swatted her hand away without any real malice. "Home brew, but we need an expert."

"Yes we do, but for that we need a run into the city. In broad daylight and armed to the teeth." Harold had everyone's attention. "Then we offer a brewer a safe home."

"Seriously?" Seth was a yes vote already.

"England is full of mini-breweries, so it's up for discussion. Now let's take the loot back, divvy up, and make lists of what is most important. We need pads and pens to make lists of what's here, so we can come back for it."

"We want spray paint as well to mark some of these houses." Bernie and Casper had both had close escapes when walls came down because a fire had weakened them.

"Everyone make a list." The group lifted their loads and made their way home.

*   *   *

Five days of making lists and looting houses later a hand banged on Harold's bedroom door. Hazel's voice came through to where Harold was working on the lists. "Harold, Harold, you're wanted."

"On the way, Hazel." Harold happily abandoned the lists. He wasn't so happy to find Matthew and Casper with grim faces.

Matthew spoke before Harold was off the bottom step. "The Army want to talk to the man in charge."

"So why me? What about Harry, or you?"

"Harry says no and actually I've been doing what you tell me." Matthew grinned.

"Suggest, not tell. Others suggest as well."

"Then we look at you to see if you agree. Come on Harold, at least you talk the language." Casper shrugged. "We sort of elected you when we left the flats." He smiled. "I elected you when you recued my fairy ass."

Matthew flinched slightly. He still wasn't used to the casual mentions of Casper's sexuality, or as he'd told Harold, to sexuality being treated as a joke. Gay jokes were a sackable offence for Traffic Wardens. "So will you go?"

"I suppose so. Who is up there?"

"We think about ten of them but it's hard to be sure. The one shouting has three stripes." Matthew looked around. "Sergeant I think?"

"Full marks. Any idea what it's about?"

"No, he just wanted a little chat."

"Little chat means it's probably not totally official. He's either going to bend my ear or ask pointed questions." Harold straightened his shoulders. "I hope he's in a good mood."

"How many packets of frozen chips did Seth drag home?" Sharyn was smiling.

"Dozens? Scores? Hundreds?" Everyone laughed at Casper. Seth's personal obsession with finding frozen chips, pies and beer was already a legend. Though he cheerfully shared them out, since according to Seth the pies and chips would still be there when he'd eaten his. Because everyone else, again according to Seth, was obsessed with healthy eating.

"So if you took a big plate of freshly fried chips up there for our brave protectors?" Sharyn was already heading for the kitchen. "I know enough about soldiers to be certain it will make them all a lot happier. Hazel, nip along the road and ask the girl club to fry some as well, please?"

"OK." Hazel exited at speed and with a big smile because she liked visiting the girl club, the name for the two houses containing single women. Plus Casper, the house mother, allegedly.

"Matthew, can you ask Betty to go up far enough to tell the soldiers I'll be about twenty minutes? I was asleep or something." Harold smiled. "That's a suggestion and request."

Matthew was puzzled. "I can tell them that, it doesn't need Betty."

"Then they might shoot you. I'd ask Karen but she might shoot back." Harold headed back up the stairs because he was wearing his battledress trousers to save his jeans and that was definitely a no-no. That was illegal even before the present stricter regulations came in. Harold took the time to shave as well, since at the moment Harold was only doing so every other day until he scored an electric razor.

"They're in a dish because you'll spill them from a plate." Sharyn was waiting when Harold came down, with a big glass oven dish. The smell of freshly deep fried potato came through the tea towel laid over the top, on which was a plastic bottle of vinegar and a plastic tub of salt. "They get tomato sauce next time if they're nice to you."

As Harold walked down Orchard Close two front doors opened and Emmy came from one and Liz from the other, both carrying dishes with tea towels over them. "We're coming as well." Emmy smiled and waved her dish. "So you don't drop them."

"For protection as well." Liz smiled and wiggled to show off her skirt. "Do the Army have blacksmiths?"

Harold remembered the chemist shop and Liz producing a pistol. "Protection? I really hope you haven't brought anything silly because they will search you."

Liz looked at Harold's serious face and her smile disappeared. "Oh. Sorry. I get a bit nervous without something for emergencies." She pulled an air pistol from inside her jacket, keeping her back to the bypass. "Here, Hazel. Take that back in will you and be careful."

"Er, take this as well, will you?" Emmy put her hand behind her under her jacket and produced a knife in a sheath. She shrugged. "I was nearly caught once, remember." Grief flitted across her features and then Emmy straightened and braced her shoulders. "Lead on, soldier boy."

"You might do better taking Hazel, she should make them feel safe." Liz might have been right but one look at the alarm on Hazel's face killed that idea.

"No, but if the women, all of them, were to come outside and stand where the Army could see them it might help. Let them see who needs protection if trouble arrives." Harold turned to the youngster. "Hazel, can you ask Sharyn, and help to spread the word please?"

"OK." Hazel giggled. "Soldier boy." Then she headed into the girl club carrying the weapons very carefully under her jumper.

"Cheeky." Harold growled it after her but he was smiling, then he wiped the smile off. "No mention of soldier boy to the squaddies up there. Some of them think I ran away." Liz muttered and grumbled about that all the way down the street and onto the main road. Though she shut up once the soldiers with rifles pointed her way were clearly visible.

"Stop there. What are the presents, and who are you three?"

"Hello sergeant. I'm Harold Miller, and I've been elected to come and talk to you. These ladies are Liz and Emmy and here to help carry the presents. The dishes are full of fresh chips and the salt and vinegar are here as well." Harold put a hand over his dish. "Can I remove the cover? It's only there to keep them piping hot."

"One of you young ladies can do that, then bring the dish up here nice and steady. Why the chips?"

"There's an Army widow down there. She'd have brought the chips up but she's got a couple of youngsters who don't like being left." Actually both children had so far been relatively unaffected by all the trouble and were happy to be left with people they knew, but Harold was working the sympathy vote.

"All right. Stop there." Liz stopped. "Thatcher, leave your rifle and go and check that dish. Then search the young lady without getting your face slapped."

"Yes Sarge." The young private came over the sandbags, looked at the chips, picked a few up, grinned, and put them in his mouth. "Need salt and vinegar Sarge."

"Not eat them, you stupid, er, soldier. At least we'll know they're poisoned if you go green and puke your guts out. Now search the young lady."

The squaddie couldn't see Sarge's smile and looked stricken, then nervous as he patted here and there on Liz and asked her to open her jacket.

Harold reckoned he could have hidden an armoury in the bits not patted so Sarge wasn't too paranoid. Thatcher looked a big startled after Liz leant forward a little bit and then he turned back to the sergeant.

"Nothing Sarge, except the chips."

"What did she say?"

"Ah, well." The private stopped and visibly braced before replying. "I'm a bit young and not her type, Sarge."

"Then you'd better check the other young lady. Perhaps you'll have better luck." There was some sniggering and even laughter from behind the sandbags and the visible soldiers were smiling. The sergeant didn't even look back. "Anyone who finds that funny should remember there's miles of kerbstones up here that need polishing." Silence and straight faces followed his words but Harold had to smile, just a little one. After all he was safe from the kerb polishing.

Harold's search was a bit more robust but eased off after Harold whispered "you're not my type either." The three moved up and Sarge inspected the chips himself. Then he looked past Harold.

"What are they doing? The women down there."

"Just reminding you that they live there. So you understand if we get a bit violent over protecting them when trouble comes to call."

"When? Not if?"

"They'll come when the easy targets are all gone in the middle of the city." Harold looked at his bowl. "I may as well eat these if you don't want them."

"These have been commandeered now by the Army." Sarge smiled. "Since Thatcher didn't go green or puke. Hang on, let me check." Salt and vinegar went into the dish and Sarge chewed happily. "Thatcher, take the rest for the lads to inspect." The sergeant eyed Harold. "You're in charge then?"

"Sort of. You wanted one person so I'm it. You could have a committee?"

"No thanks. So what are your lot doing looting those houses?"

"Commandeering vital resources before they are destroyed by the elements." Harold shrugged. "Since normal services are not being resumed and you lot allowed the yobs to burn the supermarkets down."

"We didn't allow them to do it. We have orders to stay out and let the police deal with it." Sarge scowled. "Something to do with Human Rights." Harold stared and this time Sarge shrugged. "Lawyer crap but that's what we're told."

"You'll still shoot the bad guys if they're armed, right? Because we're relying on that." Harold hadn't expected Human Rights to get into this. That could mean any sort of lunatic regulation.

"Not if it's knives and hatchets or clubs. Those are allowed as civilian self-defence weapons. We will shoot anyone, even those women, if they're carrying a firearm. Providing we can confirm they are carrying one." Sarge gave Harold a long look. "That includes air weapons because it's difficult to tell the difference in a hurry. Though according to our instructions, bows and crossbows are allowed."

"Crossbows?" Harold was stunned.

"Not my decision." Sarge looked out across the houses. "The women can go back in now. We've got the message." Harold turned and waved at the women looking his way, and most waved back. Then he gestured 'go away' and shooed them indoors. Several waved again and Hazel produced a salute and an extra double handed wave before turning away. When Harold turned back Sarge had a smile. "Little sister?"

"No, probably an orphan and she's moved in with my sister and her two kids." Harold took a deep breath. "About ten of the girls and women are the only survivors of a whole block of flats. The looters came for women. The arses told the residents they'd trade, young women for the safety of the rest. The next night the bastards came back and insisted. Those ten broke out in a minibus, yes that one down there, when the door of the flats went in and the mob came through."

Sarge scowled again and the anger in it wasn't aimed at Harold. "We get strictly limited news. Seriously though, even knowing about those women we can't come off the bypass to help you." Sarge looked out over city. "If you knocked down the first row of damaged houses beyond the occupied ones, we could see better to shoot. Should we see a firearm." He shrugged. "Though I wouldn't suggest it."

"Though someone might just come up with it now. Thanks."

"We can still only shoot those with firearms, unless they come into the zone. That's why the bulldozers knocked everything down in the zone, so we can see to shoot. Your nearest back gardens are only just outside, so don't come over there for any reason." Sarge looked left and right. "You've got clear ground either side. It's a pity you aren't allowed a machine gun since that's a lovely field of fire. Ah, another little bit of a warning. If somebody does give you an AK or any other automatic weapon, don't fire it. Our orders are to use artillery if we hear automatic fire regardless of collateral." The look Sarge gave him left Harold in no doubt about how serious that warning was.

"Or bloody napalm."

Sarge nodded. "Or napalm. Please don't make me do that. Are you making one of those enclaves here?"

"What enclaves?"

"Our reports say they're springing up here and there. Groups of people, sometimes gangs who've seen a golden opportunity but some are just pissed off citizens. They build a barricade and maybe a wall around their patch and declare independence."

"Independence of what?" Harold had seen barricades, but that was a whole step further.

"How should I know? They stop anyone going in without a search and as far as I know the police ignore the whole thing. There'll be real trouble in the end." Sarge wasn't talking to Harold for just a few seconds, he was talking almost to himself.

"What about?" Harold stopped himself to get back to real information. "Doctors don't come anyway, nor the post. Are any of the hospitals still open?"

"One. I didn't tell you this but don't risk the trip. The Army are evacuating everyone and everything from there. No, I don't know where to. Now look what you've done. A couple of chips and I've got a loose mouth." Sarge gave a rueful smile. "That was a really clever move, getting the women out there. So was bringing those two." Liz and Emmy were chatting to the soldiers though they were being kept outside the sandbags.

"They volunteered, and I only asked the women if they'd mind." That reminded Harold of a request of Sharyn's. "The widow wants to fly a Union Jack. Is there any objection?"

Sarge went very stiff and formal. "I hope you are not asking if we would fire on the flag?"

"Christ no. I just didn't know if there was some new law or regulation."

Sarge relaxed again. "As long as it's flown properly. Don't take the piss. Ah, Army widow, sorry." Sarge smiled. "Don't put the flag where it gets in the way of shooting at an armed intruder. What regiment?"

"The Rifles. He was in the Ukraine and came home in a body bag." Both sighed at that because economies meant that soldier's bodies did come back that way, not in a coffin.

Empty dishes were being passed back to Liz and Emmy, accompanied by big smiles. Harold nodded that way. "Keep the salt and vinegar though we can't promise a lot of chips. The supply depends on how many we rescue or commandeer."

"Hah. Yes. In the British Isles chips might be considered a vital resource. Wouldn't want too many coming up here anyway." Sarge gave a little frown.

"The lads would brag and then there'd be questions and snap inspections, that sort of thing. Can't have those innocent boys fraternising."

"Really?"

"Yes. You are not actually described as the enemy, but the rules of engagement as in actually speaking to anyone in there are very close to that." Sarge nodded towards the city. "I'm relieved to meet you because your lot seem civilised. That's really why I wanted to see you, to weight up what the neighbours were like." Sarge looked over and raised his voice. "You lot, are you soldiers or schoolboys who've never met a real woman?" The soldiers were suddenly all official and standing straight. Sarge whispered "schoolboys" to Harold and winked.

"So are we square, Sarge?"

"Yes, Mr Miller. I suggest the ladies wear tightish jeans next time and no jackets if it's warm enough. If not they could take the jackets off when we stop them, it saves having to search them." Sarge had a little smile showing. "Then no more of the lads will get their horizons broadened." Sarge turned to smile at Liz and Emmy. "Thank you, ladies." Sarge went back over the sandbags which was a definite hint.

Liz waited until they were halfway back. "Did it work?"

"Which bit?" Harold grinned at her. "You're not my type and a bit young anyway?"

Liz sniggered and Emmy smiled. "He was being so careful not to touch anywhere even close to a bit risky. I could have hidden ten poncy pistols."

"Don't ever try it because some soldiers will enjoy searching. Though if we get that sort I'll send you back rather than put up with it."

Emmy glanced back. "They seemed nice enough?"

"That sergeant has those under control. I've seen some soldiers that would take full advantage." Three names came to Harold's mind immediately.

"What did the sergeant want?" That was Liz, she loved to know everything first.

Harold gave a short laugh. "To know if we're setting up our own little kingdom. There's a lot of it about he reckons."

"What?"

"I'll explain to everyone at once, OK?" The rest of the walk was in silence.

Chapter 9:
Berry Beer

"Are we doing that?" Harry senior paused. "We already are, I suppose. Though I don't want to declare independence. I'm British and proud of it."

"No need for declaring independence. In fact we'll be flying the flag to prove we're still a part of the Union. Even if we're a bit cut off from the rest." Sharyn smiled and gave Harold a thumbs up.

"More cut off than we thought. Toby has finally connected his computer and there's a problem with the phone lines." Faith, Toby's Mum, waved a hand at her son. "I've no idea why but he can't play his games or talk to his friends most of the time."

Toby knew his cue. "It's the speed on the lines. Maybe because the landline here is an old one, though I would have thought that posh houses like these would have a good connection." He frowned. "The government said there was a minimum established everywhere now, and this is too slow. It's as if everyone is using the system at the same time and they can't be."

The meeting was being held outdoors and everyone turned to look at the stretch of empty, damaged buildings. There were a lot less people on the system now than there had been for a long time. "Can you fix it, Toby?"

"No. It's to do with the line or the exchange. Some of the houses use the Virgin network, with the fibre optics. Those are all dead. Not a flicker." Toby looked around hopefully but nobody had any idea of how to help.

"Does it really matter if Toby can't play games?" Seth asked, but others were nodding.

"It matters when we need information from the internet and there isn't any. Medical help would be a blessing since I'm only a trainee." Patricia smiled. "I'm qualified up to Band Aid, and maybe bandages, but if it gets serious get on the www sharpish." She frowned. "Maybe Toby could download a lot of that sort of information now, so I don't have to wait?"

"Where to find a brewery would be a good bit of information if we are going to hide in here. The cans will run out and I'm not the only one who enjoys a pint." Seth stared back at the smiles. "I didn't see anyone throwing that wine-making gear away even if none of us can use it."

Casper looked over. "Didn't you suggest getting a brewer, Harold?"

Harold nodded. "Yes. We should try to recruit a builder as well, and any other skills that might come in useful."

"A real building type joiner for starters, or a cabinet maker. I can fix up shelving, handyman stuff but I don't build kitchens or put on roofs." Finn looked around. "We should double up where we can."

"We can take apprentices?" Rob looked round and smiled. "It might not seem glamorous, but when the loo is blocked, guess who you need?"

"Won't happen so much now we're rationing loo paper."

"Won't happen at all in our house, nor will a loo roll shortage. Oh." Susan blushed because she'd just announced what had been unofficial up to now. Rob and Susan were sharing a house but being very coy about how official that was. "Anyway, Rob has put in a bidet. Ladies, I recommend you get on the list." Susan hid her blush against Rob which caused a few more smiles.

Rob answered the question in a lot of eyes. "If we take out any bidets we find and bring them here, I can probably fit them everywhere in time. That really will cut down on loo paper usage." He smiled at Harold. "But I could do with an apprentice in that case."

Harold thought that was a good idea. "We could end up with two of every skill." Harold nodded towards at the trainee nurse. "Patricia had the right idea. Everyone make a list and pass it to the computer fanatics for downloading. That's Toby, Alfie, Hazel and Veronica, the young teens. Anyone older who is willing to carry out straight searches?" A lot of hands went up for that. "Good. We'll need lists and rotas for finding out since it will be a slow job according to Toby. Scrounge any printers and ink if we find them."

"What about the wall idea, all around the houses?" Holly was another of the rescues from the minibus, and keen on defence.

"We'll knock down any garages and sheds close to the edge and throw any loose bricks in a long heap along our boundary for now. It's more important to get the food out of the ruins. There's still no hint of when we'll have any fresh supplies." Harold looked over at Seth. "Though getting a brewer or any other skillset will get some priority from me at least."

"I want a crossbow." Gabriela's severe olive face showed exactly why. She was still going through a breakdown over leaving Abraham to die, and now the young woman wanted payback. The idea of a weapon she could use and the Army would allow had caught her imagination. "Then I don't have to hide it. That lot out there owe me a life."

"Not just you Gabriela, but we can't go hunting them. There are too many." Harold spoke gently because a lot of the survivors had at least some sympathy with that point of view. Others wanted to pull the covers over their heads and wait for it all to go away and neither were practical. "Though any sports shop that stocked them can go on the list. Ski clothing might be handy if the electricity goes off this winter."

"There's just too much all at once." Sharyn was looking despondent. "There's not enough of us. What if the electricity does go off? Half the houses don't have a proper fire with a chimney. How do we cook because you all saw the TV? The news said that the gas will be turned off if the pipelines can't be fixed."

"We can use bottled gas?" Liz pointed across the road towards the mobile home park. "Those things use bottled gas. Hell, I use it for heating metal. Put a gas merchant on the search and we'll nick the lot before anyone else gets wise." Liz looked towards the mobile homes. "We should strip those places of everything like that. I think there are gas fridges and I'll bet that office has spare gas bottles."

"Good thinking. Sort out a few people and start tomorrow while I start on trying for the brewer at least. If the right person still answers his phone." Harold looked around. "I know you hate this, and so do I, but we need those lists and someone to put them together."

"Collate them? I can do that." Hilda, one of the original residents, gave a brittle smile. "That was my job at one time until the pay stopped coming. I can't do this macho stuff and I'm not strong enough for scavenging, so at least I'll be useful."

"Everyone is useful, Hilda. Some of us must have brains considering the size of Casper's brawn, just to even up." Liz smiled and several others laughed at her comment. The meeting broke up though Liz spoke quietly to a few as they left. Harold walked back home with Sharyn because he had a phone call to make.

*   *   *

"Hi there Mr Pilsworth. It's Harry Miller."

"Hello Harry. I already know about the robbery. Someone took the weapons and the ammunition, everything. It must be one of the members because there was no sign of a break-in. Five members aren't answering their phones including you. At least I hope it was members, I wouldn't want criminals to have them."

Harold thought about that for a few moments and decided against confession. "I didn't answer because we had to get out. Our neighbours were burned out and we were next."

"Really? Are your sister and the children safe? Where are you?"

"We're on the outskirts away from the worst of it. You could join us?" Harold thought another man who could shoot would be a huge advantage.

"No, no. Our estate have barricaded themselves in. I don't like the people who have done it. They're a rough lot, but they won't let the rioters in here." Mr Pilsworth sighed. "I haven't told them I've got a rifle and a bit of ammunition because they're already waving hand guns about and, as I said, they are a rough lot."

"I'd hide the rifle in case things turn nasty if I were you, and not mention the club." That was a bit selfish but Harold didn't want some 'rough lot' in the city getting a man who could shoot and keep their weapons in good order. Though those with weapons probably already knew how. "What I really called about was for the phone number of the Dog and Stoat. Have you any idea?"

"Maybe. What do you want Sam for?"

"I thought he might want to get out of the city. The same offer goes for plumbers, builders, electricians, any of those types. We're trying to build a little community." Harold crossed his fingers.

"I don't know. Maybe. Sam was robbed you know. He got out of the back but they smashed the place up and stole the stock. Hang on, I'll have a look. We used to book the Rifle Club Christmas party there." There was a short silence. "Here you go. Have you got a pen and paper? You can give me your number as well because the recognition thing doesn't work on mine anymore."

Harold wrote down the number and gave his own. "If you change your mind don't tell anyone. Just phone up and then we'll arrange to pick you up without any fuss, from somewhere outside the barricades."

"I should be all right in here. Everyone is putting their food together and these men brought several van loads in and they're selling it to us all. Bye for now Harry. Best of luck."

"Bye Mr Pilsworth, and thanks."

Harold sat for a moment before phoning Sam. The people who had put up the barricades had weapons, and had brought in van loads of food.

Harold was a bit worried about what happened when Mr Pilsworth couldn't pay anymore, but there was nothing he could do about that.

Harold dialled, and the phone at the other end rang, and rang, and rang. Harold wasn't sure what happened if the phone was broken but the line was open so he waited. Then the phone was picked up. "Who is it?" The man's voice was hushed which was crazy if the phone had just been ringing away.

"Harold, Harry. I came in for a pint with Mr Pilsworth from the gun club and then for a pint of home brew now and then."

"It's been robbed. I've been robbed. What do you want?"

"I know, Mr Pilsworth gave me your number and the news. Some of us have got out to the edge of the city and we're building a community. Do you want to come? Better still, do you want to bring the brewers? That was really good beer."

"Are you crazy? There's only one couple still brewing and they've almost stopped now. All the rest were robbed and the biggest one was stripped of everything and the brewer went with the gear. Maybe voluntary but he didn't phone anyone."

"We're out next to the bypass so if the looters come with guns the Army will shoot them." Harold thought a moment. "We've got an electrician and a plumber and we're trying to build a real community."

"One of those gang things? All guns and do as you're told?"

"No. We all get a say." Harold gave a short laugh. "A brewer might get two votes when we can't find any more cans in the ruins nearby."

"Hah. Yes, probably. Personally I'd go for the plumber as my favourite. Have you got your rifle?"

"Maybe?"

"So yes. Good, you'll need it if the brewers come and someone finds out. I'll ask them. Where are you?"

"I'll give you the number. If you come with them you'll know. If not you can't tell anyone." Harold had suddenly realised that giving out the actual address might be a bad idea if someone knew he'd got a brewer. Luckily Mr Pilsworth hadn't pushed.

After a long pause Sam spoke again. "That makes sense. All right, I'll phone them but I'll need your number." Harold gave it and Sam repeated it back and then. "I might want to come but I'll need to talk to family."

"Any non-looters are welcome. There's spare houses at the moment and enough empty housing nearby to provide food for a little while."

"All right. Thank you. I'll call."

Harold sat for a while after putting the phone down, then started calling the numbers in the classified directory. Builders, electricians, computer repairs, sewing services, he worked steadily through them. About one in seven answered and none wanted to take a chance on a total stranger. After an hour Harold gave up. He couldn't blame people for being cautious, but the six out of seven not answering was more worrying. Surely they hadn't all got a pass and left?

*   *   *

"Harold, Harold, Sharyn has just had a phone call. They're calling back in half an hour." Harold straightened and stretched then smiled at Hazel. He had been helping to remove a gas fired cooker from a mobile home. Liz, encouraged by Sharyn, had organised a small gang and removed the easiest accessed gas fires or worktop stoves. Harold was here with some extra labour to tear out the seriously built in appliances, with Rob to supervise.

"Any idea who it was, Hazel?"

"No, it was a woman and she asked for Harry Miller."

Harold actually thought briefly of Cynthia but she would have probably ask for Corporal Miller, or, he smiled, Harry Corporal Miller. Though it was vanishingly unlikely Cyn got out of London, let alone found his number here. Hazel chatted happily on the way back, about the garden digging, and collecting new bedding from the mobile homes.

She was also enthusiastic about the stack of magazines that Alfie had brought back from scavenging. The fifteen year old teenager had curled a lip at the girly publications, but then they turned up in Harold's house. Though he hadn't shown any other sort of interest so maybe it was just Alfie's generally genial nature. Harold realised he was already getting Daddy syndrome over Hazel and vetting any boys who were nice to her.

Hazel was having a good day today. Sometimes she was weepy, and others she ranted or hid in her room. The fourteen year old was trying to accept that Dad was definitely dead and Mum was missing. The news reports showing more riots and gunfire didn't help with the missing part.

As soon as they came in Hazel went to join Daisy where she was greeted by complaints that Hazel had left with the pirate ship half drawn. Daisy came for an Uncle-hug and to confirm that there would be an Uncle-Harold story tonight. Those alternated with Uncle-Casper stories, some of which Harold was half-sure Casper made up.

Sharyn had a mug of coffee ready, and a list. "This is from Hilda. The twenty most common suggestions though she's ignored a pub or a tank and a few similar ideas." Sharyn smiled. "It'll keep you busy while you wait because no, I don't know who it is and she wouldn't say."

The list worked. Harold actually jumped when the phone beside him rang. "Hello?"

"Hello, who is that?"

"Harry Miller. Who are you?" Harold certainly didn't recognise the voice. Definitely a local accent, and a woman, but that was all.

"I'm a friend of a friend who said you might want recruits. What do you drink and what pub do you use?"

Harold was now fairly sure who this was. "None now. I used to have a pint at the Dog and Stoat with Sam, and drank home brew. Is that the right answer?"

The sigh of relief was an answer all by itself. "Are you really set up somewhere safe?"

"Safer. The Army shoot people with guns if they see them and know we are law-abiding citizens. Apart from taking food from the ruins." That was a bit of a stretch, since the Army didn't seem to care about law-abiding. Though they didn't like violence aimed at or near them.

"So where are you exactly?"

Harold had already decided he wasn't giving that out. "Where are you?"

"Ah. Right. Awkward. Hang on." There was a muttering of voices in the background. "Can we meet?"

"If we have to bring a convoy into the city, even in broad daylight, it'll be just once. We either come to get you or not at all." Harold thought quickly. "If you load up your gear we can meet someplace and then come here? So you don't give me the location?"

"No chance. We haven't got... Hang on." More noises in the background followed. This time the woman's voice was resigned when she spoke again. "We've only got one van left. The other two were, are, gone." She sighed. "It sounds awful but we're sort of relieved that the drivers must be dead, or we would have had visitors."

"I do understand, but we can't risk the trip twice."

"We understand that. I'll give you a place and a time. Someone will be there and I promise we are near and want to come. But D.., Nigel wants to look at you first, all right?"

"Fair enough, but we might be late." Harold distinctly heard 'two hours, tops' in the background before the woman's voice was back. "He'll wait two hours, from midday until two o'clock. Can you come tomorrow?"

"Tomorrow? Hang on, let me think." Harold did think. That was a bit keen so was it a trap? If so, why? The vehicles? Surely there were still lots out there. Or were the brewers just very worried? Worried, he decided. "Am I right in thinking this will help with finding replacements for the cans of ale?" Harold was laughing at himself for not just saying brewer but the woman's paranoia was catching.

"For a long time. You're coming?"

"Two transits, a pickup truck, and maybe a car or possibly a minibus because we'll bring bodyguards. I'll have to check the fuel."

"Bless you. The car park in front of the burned out Halfords on Mortimer Street. Have you got a map?" The relief in the woman's voice was stark.

"Yes thanks. Are there any barricades nearby?"

"Not on the through roads, only in the entrances to estates or the industrial estate. You'll need the two transits to load um, supplies. We'll pack tonight. See you tomorrow." The phone went down and Harold realised he had neither her number or the woman's name. He sighed and stood up. Now he needed enough people to cross half the bloody city.

*　　*　　*

Harold looked them over. His crew, or gang? Mob of ruffians the way the women were muffled up. Nobody had said anything to Harold but all the women had carefully hidden what sex they were under big coats or jackets with hoods or woollen hats, or in one case a balaclava. No makeup, not even a bit of lippy, and three had smeared their cheeks in an attempt to look unshaven. It might work at a distance.

"Well you frighten me." There were some nervous giggles and chuckles. "We aren't looking for a fight so just look ready for one while we back off any opposition." He looked at the weapons three of the women had. "What are those?"

"My new project. I thought about those knives taped to sticks, and thought I could do better. It's a sort of sleeve socket and then I screwed it to the shaft and the knife handle." Liz was giving hers a critical look. "Maybe I could make a spear head if I've got some plate and enough gas to get it hot enough?"

"Hold that thought for when we get back. I want one of those in each van and the minibus to keep anyone ambitious from getting too close." Harold raised the big rifle with its long bayonet. "Harry loaned me his pig sticker for the pickup and the estate car can keep in the middle with a knife taped to a stick out of the window."

"There's several of those." Seven were waved along with an assortment of machetes and baseball bats. "Us girls are in the minibus." Casper brandished his machete and grinned. "If anyone gets anything inside there, it's coming off." There was a cheer from the women.

A group of residents not coming on the run had come to see the convoy on its way. "Don't worry Harold. If we get visitors I'll see them off." Karen was holding her air pistol and smiling and behind her Stewart was hefting a spade and nodding. Several of those remaining also had knives on sticks, garden implements and baseball bats. With the two rifles that should be enough if trouble came.

"Put two cars across the entrance once we're gone and take the keys out. We're giving ourselves lots of time so we should be back long before dark." Harold knew this was a risk, and would seriously weaken the little community if it went wrong. For that reason the route took in several other targets so there would be no need to go again. The Halfords might be one target depending on how burned out it was.

The drive into the city was stop-start. Harold was in the back seat of the pickup crew cab so he could shoot or stab either way, with Billy driving. A very determined Emmy with a baseball bat was in the passenger seat. Since Emmy was already tall and well built, the big jacket, pulled down woollen hat and heavy gloves made her look quite formidable. Emmy was nervous, as were most of the score of people coming on the run, but insisted on doing her part.

After turning into two blocked roads, one with a barricade and one with a building collapsed across it, Harold changed the routine. Reversing every vehicle out took too long, so now the pickup moved well out in front. By the time the second vehicle, the minibus, got to a turn the driver could see if the pickup was stopped. That speeded the job up but even so the diversions to look at prospective loot ate up time. Most of the premises were either emptied out or burned out.

A petrol generator was salvaged from one place, and four new car batteries from another. All the hardware stores were all already looted, though twice the convoy found wooden shafts for brooms, hammers and even pick shafts that had been left or dropped. A small selection of garden tools were also salvaged, and any scattered packs of torch or radio batteries were picked up. Then there was a good find, seventeen car batteries and a carton of bottles of distilled water. Everyone was worried about the electricity failing.

Two possible locations for crossbows were gutted ruins. At first Harold thought the third was as well. This was an archery store so he'd hoped the place had been missed but the gaping roof and soot-stained window on the end killed that hope.

The convoy drove into the car park and swung around to leave again and Harold asked Billy to stop. The other end was a showroom and had two broken windows but wasn't burned.

"I want six people please, but everyone else watch out for trouble." Men and women climbed out of vehicles and followed him towards the unburned end of the building. Harold stepped through the smashed door and was puzzled. There wasn't a bow or arrow in the store, but the showcases were empty, not broken. The glass doors had been opened but there was no sign of chaos, or looting. Apart from some boot marks on the floor, the place was clean.

"This is weird."

Harold agreed with Liz. "It looks like the place was evacuated properly, so why the fire?"

"This door should tell us." Matthew gestured with his knife on a stick. Harold walked over and gave the double doors a little push, and they moved. Everyone gathered round and Harold pushed them open.

"Now we know where the stock went." The shelves around the edges were empty and from the remains every item had been heaped in the middle and torched. Presumably with enough petrol to make sure they burned well since there was open sky above, where a roof should be.

"There's some arrows that dropped clear, but nothing to use them in." Matthew moved up one side of the mess of twisted shelving and bits of metal and charred wood and plastic.

"There's knife blades but all the temper will be gone. Are they worth picking up for spear heads?" Liz kicked one clear, picked it up and tapped it on a shelf. "I could make something to stick this on a broom handle?"

"Go and get a couple of those shopping trolleys, please, Bernie." Bernie went through into the shop again. Matthew's excited voice sounded from the back of the charred mess.

"Hey, there's some that fell off the fire. Some boxes caught but what's inside might be all right." There was a rush round and nine boxes had fallen clear along with a lot of arrows of various sorts and small packets. "This is a bow, but it's covered in little wheels and cords. There's another bow here, or it will be if we find some string."

A quick glance at the pictures on the boxes was enough. "Take them all, the arrows as well, and the easily retrieved knife blades." Harold looked round at Bernie and his shopping trolley, just returning. "Take all the little boxes and packets laid about in case they're useful. Put everything by the door and I'll get a van over here." Harold had barely started towards the side door that would lead into the car park when motors growled outside. Vehicles were pulling into the car park. "Keep collecting and loading." Harold moved to the side door and peered through the little window.

Two big estate cars, the off-road types, were backing across the exit and men were getting out. Four men armed with machetes and a couple of hand guns. A single barrelled shotgun poked out of one car window. One man was ahead of the rest and he spoke first. "You lot are trespassing."

"All right, move aside and we'll leave." Casper climbed out and he had the butt of a handgun poking out of his belt. As he'd told Harold, it was impossible to tell if the weapon was an air pistol or a real bullet type. The machete was very obviously what it was, a big chopping blade. Impromptu spears stuck out of windows and two rifle barrels appeared, one from each van.

"Not really. There's a fine for trespassing, so we'll take the weapons." The speaker was a burly, bald man in his mid-twenties and carrying both a machete and a handgun.

Casper grinned. "Not really. We've got you outnumbered and outgunned."

"The shotgun in the car trumps those little peashooters. Air rifles I reckon."

"Wrong, and fatally wrong if you find out. Toby, shoot him first." A rifle barrel moved across to aim at the big man.

"Kurt, shoot the big bloke first." The shotgun centred on Casper. "Guess who'll bleed most."

Harold was already moving because either this bloke was on something or really did think those were air rifles. Harold had eased open the door and now raised his rifle. "Him with the shotgun bleeds most. This thing will go through the windshield, Kurt, and the man behind him if there is one. It might go through the car door and one of those trees behind as well." The four men who had got out of the cars were now looking at Harold.

The leader spoke first. "What the fuck is that?"

"The real thing. Did you ever see any World War films and all those soldiers with big rifles and bloody great bayonets?" The double-take said the man had. "Better still it's got a clip so I get five tries. Those peashooters really are bullet rifles, not air rifles, so how about that shotgun points skywards?"

"Then what?" This man expected Harold to do what he would. Kill everyone and strip the bodies.

"Then you leave, we leave, and you come back and get the rest."

"Yeah right." Then his interest quickened. "The rest of what? The bastards burned it all before they left."

"We've found some blades and such that might be some use. I thought they were unclaimed. Since this is your patch we'll leave here with what we've got instead of digging deeper. Deal?"

"Maybe. Where are you from?"

"Nowhere near here. Just passing through and we'll be long gone if you let us. This was just a detour and a bloody disappointment." Harold waggled the rifle barrel just a bit. "Now let's see the shotgun moving and nobody needs to die today."

The man weighed it up, but he was outnumbered and the big rifle had screwed up his odds. "Kurt keeps pointing the shotgun at the big bloke until we're all aboard."

"Yes, but you get in the car with the shotgun. Then if Kurt fires I'll kill everyone in that car because the bodywork won't stop this." Which would then include this bloke, and Harold was betting self-preservation would keep baldy honest. "We'll be gone in ten minutes. Any attempt at an ambush and we'll hunt the survivors down."

"Listen to him." Casper put in his six pennorth. "He shot four like you off my ass the first time we met and then we beat the shit out of the other four." Casper laughed and waved the machete. "I only had a baseball bat then. He'll get three of you lot at least, but I want one to try this out. Harold, Toby, leave me one of those two." Casper gestured at the pair without handguns.

"Bollocks. He can't shoot that fast."

"Yes he can because he's Army, a real soldier boy, so he can shoot that and use the pig sticker." Casper's absolute confidence shone through every word.

Harold saw the leader make his decision, and saw the edge go off his stance. He wasn't calling Casper's bluff, if it was one, probably because it was already clear who Harold had down as number two target. "Deal. No sudden moves while we get in the cars, and you don't stop here looking for more gear."

"Deal."

Harold was really pleased when the second car with Kurt aboard followed the first out of the car park because the old rifle was bloody heavy held like this. Also because he hadn't had to kill another bunch of people and possibly end up with friends killed.

A hand hit him between the shoulder blades. "Again! And now you've got Casper doing it." Her voice deepened. "Pointing a gun at me? Pha! Put it down before I stick it up your ass." She hit Harold again. "Macho bastards." Harold was smiling because at least Liz wasn't crying this time.

"Finn, pull the van over here will you, just so they don't see what we load." Harold turned and let the rifle butt slide to the floor. Then gave Liz her wobbly-legs hug with the other arm. "Come on, get this lot loaded or I'll have to do it again." Liz gave him another thump on the chest and headed back to get the goodies.

Though as they were loading Liz moved close to Harold and murmured, "Shot four off my ass and then kicked the shit out of the other four? Some-one has been telling porkies." Then she smiled happily. "We'll gang up on Casper and get the truth."

Harold's answer was just as quiet. "Keep your trap shut and if nobody else noticed, you get the full story."

"Deal. Macho bastard."

Once the van was loaded Harold called out to the other vehicles. "No more detours. We got lucky this time so I'm not risking it again. Straight for the meeting now." There were no objections. As the convoy exited the car park and headed down the road outside, the two big cars were lurking a hundred yards down a side road. As the last van came past they started forward, keen to see what the fire had left. SUVs Harold remembered, those big estate cars were four wheel drive Sports Utility Vehicles. Off-road poser cars, just right for budding gangsters.

*   *   *

The Halfords store really was a ruin. There was a scattering of packaging and bits of metal and glass in the car park that crunched under the wheels, but there wasn't likely to be anything left worth scavenging. The twisted remains of cycles and a roof box for a car were visible in the wreckage where the roof had come down, all of it smoke-blackened. Harold was disappointed because he'd hoped for camping gear. Perhaps gas stoves or barbecues and suchlike.

A small spanner skittered away underfoot as Harold stepped out of the rear door of the pickup cab. He was only carrying a baseball bat but the rifle was laid across the seat in easy reach. "Hello?" The convoy was nearly an hour late because of detours. Forced detours were more common deeper in the city since roads were blocked by burned out vehicles and rubble as well as occasional barricades. The lower suspension on the estate car had most trouble over the rough sections and bringing it might have been a mistake.

"Casper, Matthew, and Bernie, have a quick look inside will you. See if there is anything that's worth salvaging. Then we'll settle in and give it until two." Harold was already wondering if the brewers had changed their minds, or had been found overnight and were dead or in hiding. The three men climbed out of the vehicles and had started towards the ruin when a voice spoke from inside.

"Stay right there." That was a man's voice and there was movement where a corner of the brickwork was still standing. "Everyone stay still while I work out if you're the right people." Twin barrels appeared round the bricks. "This is a shotgun so don't get ambitious."

Liz had followed Casper out of the minibus with her homemade spear. "Don't do that. If you threaten them one of these two will offer to shove it up your ass." Harold rolled his eyes and put his hand onto the butt of the rifle to slide it towards him.

"What?" The man had a perfect right to sound startled. "Hang on, are you a woman?"

"I hope so, or I've been shopping in the wrong clothes stores." Liz had a smile but it looked a bit manic to Harold. Her nerves had taken a beating once already today, and Liz looked a bit hyper, wound up like a spring.

"Why are you armed?" That seemed a stupid question but the man really did seem interested.

"So nasty bastards don't take liberties? We're all armed and dangerous." There was a round of sniggering from the minibus and Harold sighed because some of it was definitely female.

"Emmy, climb out and take off your hat please." Harold was relaxing a bit because this man seemed more interested in the females being armed than any predatory interest. Emmy opened her door and got out, then pulled off her woollen hat and her mass of thin plaits tumbled free.

"Blimey, you're big. Bet you don't take no for an answer. Er, sorry." The man actually sounded sorry, and Harold glanced over at Emmy's half-raised bat and set expression.

"Very bad thing to say since she's grieving."

"Oh shit, I really am sorry luv. It was just, well, I've never seen a woman dressed like that. Especially as big as you and armed with a bat. Sorry everyone. I'm pretty sure you're who I'm meeting but just in case? Who are you and where do you drink?"

"Harry Miller and I used to drink at the Dog and Stoat."

"I'm Nigel, and Berry is going to slap the hell out of me for my big mouth when she finds out. Sorry again, er?"

"Emmy. It's all right. I was trying to look like a man." Emmy's voice was clear and firm and she didn't sound angry. Possibly a bit amused now. "Is Berry your, um, girl?"

"Yes, literally since she's my daughter. We'd better get moving because she'll be worrying." Nigel stepped clear of the wall and lowered the shotgun, hiding it inside his long coat. He looked to be in his late thirties or early forties, a spare figure with a small bald patch at the front of his dark brown hair. He was wearing a pair of sunglasses which travelled across the vehicles and people. "Blimey, we'll be able to bring the sacks of barley and hops as well. Brilliant."

"Jump in here and you can direct us, unless you've got a vehicle?" Harold gestured to the pickup and climbed back in.

"No, I just walked here down the middle of the road with the shotgun under my coat. Our place isn't far away." As he walked over to the pickup everyone else climbed back aboard their vehicles. Nigel came round the door and his eyes went wide. "Bloody hell!"

Emmy laughed from the front seat, just a little laugh but Harold was pleased to hear it. The recent deaths were hard to take for the women from the flats and they could drop into tears or anger at the wrong word. "Everyone says that, or something like it, when they see that rifle."

Harold waved at the seat. "Jump in and stick your shotgun out of that window, Nigel. The driver is Billy and eager to get the hell home again."

"Too true. This is much too bloody exciting. Sorry Emmy." Billy was trying to stop swearing around the women and the rest of the men were following suit. Maybe it was a reaction to the profanity from the rioters and looters.

"Right Billy. Keep going the way you were before pulling in here. There's a left turn about half a mile down there." Nigel poked his shotgun out of the open window. "I'll bet nobody tried anything with you lot."

"One or two did but Liz frightened them off." Emmy had definitely cheered up. Perhaps because of meeting a man whose daughter slapped him for being rude to women.

*   *   *

"The driveway there leads to a garage. Stop short of the door and I'll open it. The vans will fit inside." The vehicles bumped down the driveway and the big old garage came into view.

"All the vans? That doesn't look big enough."

Nigel gave a short laugh. "It isn't. The back wall is a door into the flats behind. We knocked out a couple of walls to make a safe place when one of the other brewers was robbed." True to his word Nigel opened the garage door, walked to the back wall and banged on it with his fist. Then he pulled and the section of wooden wall swung forward. Nigel waved the vehicles in.

The last vehicle drove inside the large impromptu garage and parked next to a big square Luton van. Nigel had already been hugged by a young woman who towered over him. She had the same dark hair but was both taller and wider than her dad. The pair spoke briefly and then she cuffed him gently at the side of the head and came over to Harold, smiling. "Hello, I'm Berry." She looked over at Emmy. "Dad told me. I'm sorry about that."

"No problem, he wasn't to know. You actually did slap him?" Emmy was smiling back.

"I have to now and then. It's revenge for being beaten as a child." Berry's smile belied the words. "He says we can take everything because you brought extra transport? That'll make life easier." The young woman turned and pointed. "We broke the equipment down through there but it'll need a couple of strong men to carry some of the bits through." She smiled at Emmy. "Or you and I can do it."

Harold called out to the people climbing out of the vehicles. "Through there, everyone. This young lady will tell you what goes where. Let's get turned round and go home." Then he followed the rest.

*   *   *

There were a lot of stainless steel containers and electrical bits to load and even with the three big vans it only just fitted. "It's a real, semi-professional microbrewery. We set up in business four years ago and did well, selling Berry Beer." Nigel smiled. "What else could I call it? Berry helped right from the start but to be honest, when her Mum got the cancer, I might have let it go. Berry wouldn't hear of it."

The last bits of wiring and tubing were being tucked away in the estate car and minibus as they talked. Nigel was giving Harold a potted history. "She said her Mum would want us to keep it going, and that helped me through it all. Then the real trouble started." Nigel sighed. "I was worried about Berry getting caught up in all the violence, but she said it was just as dangerous working in an office."

Harold nodded. "We've got people whose partner or parent never came home from the office one day."

"I've heard similar stories. Though I insisted on taking off the labels when the first pubs were attacked, because Berry is an unusual name. We've still got a stack of labels through there, in the office." Nigel looked around. "We moved here nine months ago and fixed up the false door, because the bastards followed the vans almost back to the last place. The driver realised and diverted but he was too near to home by then. All they had to do was hang about until we had to use the vans again."

Nigel laughed. "The diversion cost us a lot of beer, but we couldn't take it all anyway. Half the neighbourhood had a street party and the bastards couldn't get their car through to follow. We've been half expecting a visit for weeks because we were the last ones supplying some of the pubs. We've been dropping the beer off at a pre-arranged spot and the landlord turns up there and picks it up. Berry kept changing the places by sticking a pin in a map." Nigel looked around again as the last sacks went into the pickup. "The Dog and Stoat won't be the only dry pub."

"What did the landlords say to you leaving?"

"We didn't tell them. I'll ring round and break the news once we're gone." Nigel shrugged. "Berry will slap me because I told her I'd done it, but one of them might have said the wrong thing in the wrong place. Several of them knew Berry's name."

"We're ready now. I'm travelling with the girl club in that minibus Dad, so you can talk grown up things." Berry was smiling, but the brutal truth was they were travelling separate for another reason. So that both brewers weren't lost if a vehicle was overrun. Berry climbed into the minibus and Gabriela came over and climbed into the pickup. She had a knife taped to a broom handle which she poked out of a window.

"You climb in there with Gabriela, Nigel. I'm going to sit in the back with the sacks." Harold patted the rifle. "It'll give me a good all-round view and the hops and such are like sandbags, I hope." Harold climbed aboard last and the convoy headed out. The garage doors were left wide open, and the first one inside would find two ten gallon plastic drums of beer that wouldn't fit aboard. The drums were covered in Berry Beer stickers, and more labels were in the front of the pickup with Emmy. So was a crate of beer, those were crammed in everywhere.

The return run was much quicker since this time the drivers knew the clear route. There was only one attempt to stop them. A van was obviously waiting to force a vehicle to stop, because it pulled across the road well ahead. Harold put a bullet clean through the body and the driver pulled out of the way again quickly. Apart from some shouting and a couple of thrown bricks, that was it.

The beer got a bit of a beating when the convoy arrived home and ten full pint bottles were sent up to the soldiers with Berry Beer labels on. Liz reported that the sergeant was a different one, and told her the beer was contraband. It would be seized and destroyed. Then he'd winked and said he hoped the Army widow was doing all right so the word about who lived here had spread. Two days later the washed, empty bottles were at the edge of the exclusion zone though technically the soldiers weren't allowed to come that far.

Chapter 10:
Enclave

"We've emptied about three quarters of them of most things, though we could still take curtains, bedding and suchlike. There's also carpets and some decent mattresses. A lot of the habitable houses here have broken windows and the curtains and carpets are ruins." Liz was having trouble with stripping the mobile homes. Mainly due to lack of workers.

"Sorry Liz but I want the sheds and garages taken down between us and the ruins, and some sort of barrier along the edge of our boundary." Harold waved his arm in a broad arc. "It's a hell of a job because every garden seems to have something built in it. We're taking down sheds inside the boundary as well to widen the clear zone." Harold looked round. "I never have asked, but why are so many windows broken?"

"Yobs driving through and throwing rocks though they've not come back since we moved in. Maybe because we've got those two cars across the road." Liz laughed. "A couple of the feistier residents want to let some of them in again. With the extra numbers we've got they want to beat the crap out of a few."

Harold frowned. "Some want to do a lot more than that to any they can catch."

"It's a worry. Maybe it'll ease off in time but Gabriela, Emmy and Holly are particularly angry. Holly really was sweet on Brodie but hadn't done much about it except a bit of cuddling. Fair enough since Holly is all of seventeen put now she's bitter over lost opportunities." Liz sighed. "Hopefully another lad will catch her eye in time."

"What about Gabriela?"

"Lapsed Catholic and she thinks that Abraham being killed is her fault. Because she sinned with him, lived with a non-Catholic outside of wedlock, used contraception, the full bit. So his death is God's vengeance or penance or some such crap. Her problem is that the idea is eating her." Liz frowned. "A priest would make her do some penances and that would sort it. I've tried to find one but the churches aren't answering the phones any more."

"No, a lot were shut down when I first arrived now I think about it. I'll ask the Army." Harold glanced up at the bypass. "I don't really hold out much hope."

"OK. What about my work parties then?" Liz grinned. "Will pretty please work?"

"After you've told me I'm too puny for you? No chance. I'm sorry Liz but anyone not on boundary building is scavenging. After all some of the houses over there have got no roofs, let alone no windows, so we need to get the food and gear before the weather does." Harold smiled. "Anyway, you can ask for people. It's not like I'm ordering them about."

"No but a casual 'would you mind' has half of them scampering about wagging their tails and eager to please." Liz shrugged. "Someone has to and you've done all right so far. Though be careful what you ask a couple of the younger ones because they've got very rosy glasses on. They'll take a stupid chance rather than report failure."

"I know." Harold gave a little smile. "Alfie thinks he wants to be a soldier boy. Not much I can do but I will be careful."

"Hazel as well in her own way. Toby is definitely that way and a few older ones have soldier leanings. Even a few women. As long as you're careful?"

"Yes Mum."

"Watch it or I'll give you a proper Berrying upside the head." Berry's habit of giving her Dad a pretend slap round the head was already a standing joke within a fortnight of her arriving. The brewers had been installed in a pair of semi-detached houses in the middle of the inhabited buildings, with a double garage so that all the equipment would fit. The scavengers were now collecting empty bottles that could be re-sealed as well as the full ones.

"I'll put you on collecting arrows in revenge." Three full sized crossbows, two children's and three pistol bows had been salvaged from the boxes. Several people were practicing because they could do so in full view of the Army and the arrows could be re-used. Unfortunately the accuracy was erratic, to be kind, especially with the two archery bows. Nobody could pull the one with all the pulleys.

Though everyone was having a go to find who could use that, or the crossbows. Practice cost nothing and the residents needed to learn as fast as possible. Even broken shafts could be replaced using lengths of wooden dowelling or other timber trimmed and turned to size. The searchers on the internet had pulled off several pages about archery and crossbows the last time the connection worked and those were being studied.

"Those children's crossbows are bloody disgusting. Fancy giving kids a weapon like that. At short range they'll do real damage." Everyone had been surprised what the children's crossbows would do.

Harold smiled. "But they had suckers on wobbly springs on the arrows until you fitted those nasty pointy bits."

"Nearest I get to artwork these days. Once the homes are stripped I'll get onto sorting out the knife blades as well, to make spears. There's an incentive to help me." Liz grinned.

"Nag, nag, nag." Though as he went off to help with heaving bricks about Harold was worried. There was so much to do and he didn't know which was most important.

Very high up the list was working until he was knackered. The sheer chaos of the escape had quietened Harold's dreams, but now they were back. There was a bloke who jumped off a roof in there now.

*   *   *

"We've been working our way down the lists and phone book and there's two suppliers within reasonable distance." Nigel had approached Harold but Berry was in the background.

"It's been less than a month. Surely we didn't drink all that lot?" Harold beckoned. "You may as well come over here as well in case your Dad needs a slap." Both Berry and Nigel smiled as she came over.

"No, we didn't even make it all into beer yet, but we're looking ahead." Nigel glanced at Berry. "We were already having trouble getting supplies, and now the city centre and our usual suppliers are cut off."

"Definitely cut off. I won't risk going that way again after we went after the dairy." Harold shook his head. That had seemed a good idea, to get any remaining milk stocks and freeze them down. "It wasn't somewhere we expected a war."

"You didn't get one."

"No, we were almost trapped by a mob who didn't care about milk. They wanted the petrol, weapons, women, or were just bloody nasty. Hard to tell which but we've three people who are still nursing bruises from bricks." Harold sighed. "So no more runs into the city proper. Nor to that big shopping mall we found. There was a big group in there when we came past and two bodies hanging from lamp posts. No Shoppers Allowed was blunt and to the point and spray painted on walls in letters about four foot high."

"These places aren't in the city centre. If we wait until we run short, someone else might get there first." Berry hadn't been able to keep quiet.

"What if we're too late anyway?"

"Then you ration beer, right now." Berry smiled. "Ration them and give anyone who finds beer a bonus bottle. They'll try harder."

"Seth couldn't try harder. He's in love with you just because you smell of hops." Harold grinned because it was hard to tell if it was because Berry was his type of girl or the smell of hops, but Seth was definitely a little bit smitten.

"Handy when I need a big strong man to help me." Berry was laughing because Seth wasn't as strong as she was, though he was working on it.

"All right, I'll look at the addresses, and think about it."

"You should do the same with other really important materials." Nigel looked a bit embarrassed. "Not telling you your job or anything."

"Not my job at all but it looks like I've got it, and all suggestions are gratefully received." Harold looked around. "Though as soon as you said about forward planning, it crossed my mind we weren't. Not long-range planning. I'll ask around and think, and see if we can combine this and that. Though we will make your supply run sooner rather than later."

Harold did think hard even as he headed towards the girl club. He went around the back to the shed, and the sound of hammering meant Liz was home.

"Now if I fancied blacksmiths I'd be sorted." Liz had her sleeves rolled up, a heavy apron on, and was beating seven bells out of a piece of glowing metal.

Liz straightened and rubbed her back. "Not really. I need a lot more muscle to qualify. Then an anvil, some proper tools, a forge..."

Harold interrupted the familiar litany. "We're looking. Actually we could look harder. If you can find a possible supplier or a place that might have them, let me know. Nigel has been long term planning for essential supplies and we need to do the same."

"For what?"

"I don't know. What sort of thing do you need, long-term? Not tomorrow but you'll run out in six months and it will be a bitch to get it." Harold was looking round. "Can you weld?"

"Sort of. Good enough but I haven't done so for a while." Liz thought. "A welder, a straightforward stick welder and some welding rods, might be a good investment. A lot of small engineering premises might have that."

"That's the sort of thing. Oh joy, another bloody list."

"Hilda will be happy." Liz waved at her hammer. "How many spears do you want before I can get back to my caravans?"

"Three dozen spears, or two dozen and thirty arrowheads for the crossbows. The bigger crossbow ones not the pistol bows. Then I promise you I'll pull someone off the scavenging and get the job done." Harold hated doing this, trading priorities with Liz, because it all wanted doing. "I've got four people measuring up broken windows and looking for replacements on the wrecked houses. Though putty will be a bitch to find." Harold sighed. "Glaziers go on the list."

"Good thinking. That will stop any further damage in the habitable houses. Right, back to the muscle building." Liz went back to hammering.

Harold was considering the arrow situation and what a relief it was they could make their own when it hit him. Bullets couldn't be re-used, or replaced as easily. Harold couldn't spare enough to train anyone to shoot even if he could do so without making the Army nervous, and that was a real problem. He had all the supplies to reload some ammunition for their meagre selection of weapons, but what about when that was gone? There was little or no chance or getting any replacements.

Gun clubs and gunsmiths had to go on the list. Though Harold expected them to have been robbed. Would the looters think of reloading the rounds they stole? He considered that and no, most wouldn't consider it. Which meant that moulds, primers and caps and possibly empty brass and some powder might have been left. Christ, how many more obvious things was he forgetting? Harold found out as soon as he arrived home and asked.

"Blackberries, blackcurrants, maybe gooseberries, rhubarb, anything along those lines."

Harold stared at Sharyn. "Why?"

"The kids, and the adults as well long-term. Lack of fresh milk is already a problem and thank goodness someone scooped up all those multivitamins from someplace. We all need vitamin C and there's no fruit now. That means when the bottles of Ribena and other fruit juice run out we'll all run short. Bushes like that will fruit the first year I think, but I'm sure trees for apples and plums and suchlike will take longer." Sharyn looked over at the phone book. "We'll need allotments and garden centres." She grinned. "An orchard in Orchard Close."

"Make a list and give it to Hilda." Harold went to scrounge another phone book and get the computer search team organised. Then he went to find their nearest thing to an expert in gardening.

"Trees take seven years from pip to fruit."

"Damn."

"A piece of an adult tree is usually grafted onto a stem to get round the wait, but don't look at me. I've no idea where to start with that." Curtis looked at the list. "Blackberries and blackcurrants are rampant if you aren't careful. They send out runners underground and they're a bitch to get rid of." Curtis glanced at the damaged housing beyond the boundary. "We could plant them among that lot?"

"Are blackcurrants prickly?"

"The plants? Yes, nasty little things, and bramble thorns are bigger and also sharp. We might find thornless blackberries?" Curtis was still considering the list.

"But that's good, thorns I mean. If they're out there, and the ungodly come sneaking about?"

"Ouch?" Curtis was laughing. "Though you'll want to cut them back periodically or an Army could form up behind them. Think of the thorn forest in the Sleeping Beauty." He gestured at the list. "If we get to a garden centre there could be fruit trees ready to plant. Then there should be seeds as well, so we can grow more veggies."

"Flowers as well. I've been told that flowers are necessary for morale." Harold smiled at the look from Curtis. "I can send you to the girl club to argue?"

"I'd love to go to the girl club, but not to argue." Curtis shut his mouth and looked away.

"Who?"

"Never mind because I've got a problem. Look, you won't say if I ask a question?" Curtis wasn't quite blushing but the colour in his cheeks was definitely high.

"I'm not disclosing information about underwear." Harold was trying not to laugh.

"No!" Curtis sighed. "Look, how long does it take, after a bereavement? Before a girl, a young woman might, you know, be interested? Elsewhere. I'll wait, but I'll be pissed off if someone else nips in." Curtis rolled his eyes. "Shit, that sounded gross. I don't mean a quickie, though she is gorgeous? It's, well I think I'd like to try for long-term?"

Harold took pity on him and stopped the floundering. "I get it Curtis. I think it depends on the bereavement. Boyfriend, husband, Mum or Dad will all get a different reaction and no don't tell me who. Then it'll be down to if she wants the same." Harold tried to work out something to say because

Curtis wasn't the only one to notice all those unattached women in the girl club. "Just be there. Not pushy but be a friend. If she needs a shoulder, pat her back and dry your shirt and be there next time."

Harold sighed. "I'm no expert. Just remember, if she decides to give you a thank you kiss that isn't an invite to stick a hand up her skirt. Take it steady. Kiss back just enough so she knows you're interested. Bear in mind it could be years, or so I've heard." Harold rolled his eyes this time. "We need a weekly magazine and an agony aunt."

"No good. The girl club would produce it and advice for men would well be down the list." At least Curtis had a smile now. "Be there, help out, don't push it." His smile widened. "No hand up skirt." Inspiration struck. "Maybe I can get her interested in gardening?"

"Squished up together in a greenhouse? It's a plan but remember the glass walls." Harold escaped and heaved a sigh of relief. He was a long way from being a father figure because some of those young women were definitely on his own attraction radar. Worse still, several of them were very grateful because they gave Harold the credit for recuing them. Even if he thought they might welcome a bit of interest, Harold couldn't really make a move if all they were offering was a thank you quickie. With a little smile Harold decided that Orchard Close needed a broom cupboard, one his sister didn't know about.

* * *

"Harold, Harold!" Deja vu but this was Sharyn not Hazel and her voice was low. Even as he opened his mouth to answer the telephone rang downstairs. "I'll get that, you get your soldier head on."

"What? Trouble?" But Sharyn was gone so Harold packed up eleven days of lists and put his jacket and boots on. Sharyn was still on the phone when he came downstairs and she held the receiver out. Harold put it to his ear.

"It's Emmy. I'm round here next door to Harry, visiting Sal. The bastard wants a blonde. He says his pal saw one here."

"Slow up Emmy. Who says?" Harold mouthed rifle to Sharyn and she headed into the study.

"Two cars full of yobs and they've pulled up in front of Harry's house and this one. They're out of sight of the Army and one of them is waving a bloody great gun about. Looks like a cowboy pistol." There was a voice in the background but Harold couldn't make out the words. "Harry is shouting at him, telling him to clear off."

"Can you get word to Harry and tell him not to go outside with that bloody rifle? He can't shoot the damn thing so if this bloke starts Harry will just get hurt." Sharyn already had Harold's rifle and a box of rounds waiting for him. "I'm on the way and I'll come in the back of number nine, the other side of Harry. Then I'll stop them, all right?"

"Shoot the bastard dead, Harold. He's on about searching the houses if he doesn't get a blonde. Sal is crapping herself. We've only got one of those kid's crossbows in here."

"Keep down. You can use the crossbow so send Sal to Harry. I'm on the way. If the bastard comes in wait until he opens the door, stick a bolt in him from behind the kitchen door, and scarper while he's yelling and bleeding."

Harold threw on his long coat and took the rifle and ammunition from Sharyn. "Keep everyone inside and quiet, Sharyn. Bullets can go anywhere and if the Army get nervous or spot a gun they'll open up." Harold hid the rifle under his coat and headed out and down the street. He could already hear shouting from round the corner. As Harold came past the two houses containing the girl club Liz stuck her head out of a window.

"What's happening, Harold?"

"Trouble. Yobs with guns. For Christ's sake don't turn up and give them any lip, all right?"

"Yes, I know. I said sorry. I'll let the rest know."

"Tell them to keep their heads down though if Casper is there he should bring his shotgun." Nigel the brewer had been happy to give Casper his shotgun because the thought of actually shooting someone had worried the hell out of him. Nigel didn't reckon he could do it except maybe to protect Berry.

"Will do. Go and gettem, soldier boy." Liz moved back and closed the window. Harold strode up the side of the last house on Orchard Close, Betty's house, and across the back garden into the rear of number nine. Hilda's startled face popped out of a door.

"Oh, thank God. I thought you might be more of them. Toby is in here and wants to shoot the one with a gun. Tell him not to be so silly, please?"

Harold raised his voice. "Don't shoot unless I tell you to, Toby."

"OK Mr Miller, Harold." Harold could hear the tension in the lad's voice but he was here and ready, which was what counted.

"I'm off upstairs to talk to them." Harold ran upstairs and to a front window, then looked round the edge. One man definitely had a cowboy gun, or a big pistol of some sort, and was waving it about. Harold opened the window just a bit to hear him, and put the ammunition on the windowsill. He flicked open the box and loaded as he listened.

"If you were going to do anything you would have started, you silly old fart. Now I'm coming up the path and if there's no blonde in there I'll slap you silly. Then I'm working down the row with my friends here." The man waved at the five men around him. "My mates in the other car will take the other side of the road and they don't care about hair colour."

The pistolero looked around at the eleven men who had climbed out of the two big estate cars. "I told you, old men and office wankers." The speaker turned back to number seven, Harry's house. "We'll take the keys to those motors across the road as well, since you don't use them. Last chance. Where's the blonde?" He took a step up onto the kerb towards Harry's garden gate.

Harold banged the window wide open and raised his rifle. Twenty yards, so the bloke might even hit Harold and with that weapon would be dangerous. Harold kept behind the edge of the window frame as much as possible. "Bad idea. Now get in the cars and piss off. You've been talking to the wrong person."

The short stocky man swung towards the noise. Then he brought his other hand across to take a double-handed grip on his weapon. "Who are you then?"

"The man with the rifle. The others were waiting for me. We're new residents and neither old, office workers or girls. Get in the cars and go." The rest of the group were looking to each side and a man by the rear car reached inside and pulled out a shotgun. Single barrelled, small calibre Harold automatically noted. Two others pulled out crossbows and looked towards Harold.

"Maybe not. " The pistolero was looking intently. "That's a very little rifle and this is a very big pistol. Hand it over and we don't kill everyone." The men behind him, those not already holding a weapon, produced baseball bats or machetes.

"Liar. You would still carry on and steal women at least. Last chance." Harold smiled internally because if Liz was here she would be muttering macho bastard about now. "Left eye or right?"

"What?"

"Do I shoot you through the left eye or the right one? Hurry up and decide." Hopefully neither.

"Bullshit. Nobody can shoot like that."

Harold wanted to rant a bit because every bloody member of the rifle club team could shoot the prat's sodding eyes out at this range. Christ, the A team could hit the bloody pupil.

"He's a soldier. He can do it." Emmy didn't sound too confident unfortunately.

"More bullshit, and now we know where you are, darlin. I'll be right there in a minute." The man raised the big pistol and Harold shot him through the left eye. At the sharp crack the shotgun wielder ducked behind an open car door and several men exclaimed as the gunman toppled. Harold ejected the brass and loaded another round, then slid the bolt home.

"Left eye, who wants to try for right." One of the group near the body leaned forward.

"Shit, he's right. He shot him through the left eye for fuck's sake." The nearer group looked uncertain but the shotgun wielder spoke up.

"Then don't stand looking at him, dickhead. If he shoots again, two of you run for the house and chop his bloody head off because that's single shot." Men ducked behind car doors or turned so Harold couldn't see their eyes. That didn't protect their throats and anyway, the bullet might actually penetrate a skull at this range. "Tough shit on Jamie, but we can get payback. When I say, we split. He can only shoot one at once and as soon we're in the houses he can't see us."

"But I can cut your head off. Unless your dick arrives first." Casper's voice was music and yes, he'd got the macho bastard thing dead right. "Of course you won't get here because I'll shoot you."

Even as Casper finished the man turned, still behind the car door, and raised and fired his shotgun in one fluid motion. There was the crash of breaking glass, a scream, and then Casper's shotgun roared. The man by the car came partway up and then over backwards, halfway into the back seat. The shotgun hit the road and his body slithered down to follow it. One of the yobs nearby looked, and was promptly sick.

Above the retching Harold could hear someone whimpering but he was watching the men in the road. He noted the sharp metallic noises as Casper broke the gun and reloaded, so chappie got both barrels. That explained the puking because he'd be shredded. Harold raised his voice. "Right you lot, who's next?"

"I've got the bloke with the blue shirt." Billy only had a crossbow, but the range was short enough for him to hit.

Holly's voice echoed Billy. "Mine's the asshole in the black jeans."

"Bagsy the fat bastard, I'm a lousy shot." Matthew really was a lousy shot but he was only forty feet away.

Berry laughed. "I'll double up 'cos I'm crap as well." Harold gave a little smile because the macho bastard thing was catching on. They'd learned the lesson from the flats.

"Him with the white baseball cap is gonna suck a crossbow bolt in a minute. Give us the word, Harold." Harold winced because Gabriela really was bitter, and right now sounded downright bloodthirsty.

While Harold was still registering which men and women had spoken up and was wondering how they'd got there, the downstairs window banged. "I've got one of those little rifles as well. I can hit heads from here." Toby was in on the act. Hilda would be having a fit. More voices were coming from the houses both sides of the street now, and Karen claimed 'the scrawny punk with the knife' as her victim.

Harold stepped into clear view because there were no guns in evidence now, and one of the younger men in the rear group pointed. "Fuck, fuck, fuck! We're all dead. It's the fucking SAS!"

"Don't be a twat." The speaker was looking hard and wasn't totally sure what Harold was.

"He is. He killed Currie and two others in ten seconds flat. With a fucking stick." There was a clatter as the man dropped his baseball bat. "Oh shit, he's got a fucking gun now." He turned and ran off down the road. Harold was trying to remember what the youths had looked like, the ones who ran back at the flats. That had to be one of them.

There was a lot of muttering among the men in the street, and a voice was raised from behind a car door. "We're leaving, right? No more shooting."

"We want some payback, Harold. That bastard hurt Emmy." Casper sounded as mad as hell and Harold was near to letting everyone open up. But if even one bloke made it to a house and used a machete on one of these people, people he knew, it would eat Harold up. He knew it. Better if they left without anyone getting hurt, but there would be payment.

"How is Emmy?" Because the sounds of pain had suddenly stopped and if she was dying then sod it, so were that lot. He'd deal with the dreams.

"She'll be all right. Just cuts I think and her eye is working." Susan's voice was a long way from firm and Harold could hear the strain.

Harold heaved a sigh of relief. Then spoke to the yobs. "You leave the weapons and the motors." There were some protests so he raised his voice. "This lot want to kill you. Don't give them an excuse."

"Yes please, give me an excuse." Gabriela wasn't joking and that was clear in her voice.

"What about the motors? We need transport."

Holly at least had an edge of humour in her voice, but it was a savage humour. "Steal some, the same as you did those."

There was muttering around the cars. "OK, but for fuck's sake don't shoot, all right? Don't let that bitch start."

"Calling her a bitch doesn't help. Ask your friend who ran off why she's so bloody angry. Now all stand up nice and slow, then turn and walk away with empty hands." Harold gave a short laugh. "You can run if you like once you're past the last car."

Nine figures rose carefully, hands going onto some heads as weapons clanged and clattered on the tarmac. They all hesitated for long moments and then turned and walked away. Some did run once they were past the second car, followed by whistles and jeers. Harold waited until the last one was out of the entrance, then he headed for number five to see Emmy.

*   *   *

"Christ Emmy, I thought you were all right." Half of her face and the left side of her head was covered in a big wad of cotton wool, bandaged into place.

Karen put a finger on Emmy's lips as the young woman started to answer. "Keep your face still and let it all clot." Karen turned to Harold. "It looks like just glass cuts. A lot of them. She told me that as he brought up the gun she turned and started to duck."

"He must have seen the movement and thought it was me." Casper was shaken but still bloody angry. "I should have just shot the bastard."

"We will another time. He must have been using birdshot and the double glazing took the power out of the pellets." Harold sighed. "We might not get that lucky next time. From now on, if anyone is inside the boundary with evil intent we kill them. From hiding and in the back." Everyone stared.

"Can we do that?" Harold looked at Holly and she gave a little smile and continued. "I'm good with it because, well, they owe me. It's just you've been saying we're better than them."

"We are. We don't go and attack their homes, and we don't torture or make slaves out of them or rape their women. We will kill them and burn the bodies if anyone threatens us, but that's all." Harold ran it through mentally. Yes, that made sense and fitted his sense of fairness. This lot weren't up for a real fight, so ambush worked better and he wouldn't get someone else shot doing the macho bullshit.

Harry came through the door with his big rifle. "Here. Take it. I wanted to shoot him and couldn't pull the damn trigger." Harold accepted the weapon and Harry slapped him on the arm. "I'm damn glad you came. Now next time you don't have to worry about hitting an eye."

"Hell no." There was true reverence in Casper's voice. "That'll go through the car first if necessary."

Harry held out two spare clips, and then fished in his pockets. "There's another seven loose rounds here but that's it I'm afraid."

Liz came in with her spear. "You'd better get home, Harold, before Sharyn bursts a blood vessel or something. She says there's someone shouting from the bypass but she's no idea which house you're in so can't phone." Liz smiled happily. "I heard the macho bastard bullshit. That's the left eye, who wants the right?" Then Liz saw Emmy and headed that way.

Harold left the big rifle until he could sneak it home. The weapon might be best left here so Harold didn't need to sneak it anywhere, since trouble would come through the entrance or from the city. Harold's house backed against the exclusion zone, at the opposite side of everyone. As soon as he stepped outside and heard the bullhorn properly Harold ducked back inside. He took the little rifle out from under his coat and propped it against the wall. "Liz, will you please phone Sharyn and let her know I've gone straight up to see the Army. They're getting impatient."

"OK. Go on, but remember they're macho bastards as well."

Harold headed for the exclusion zone boundary without going to the road entrance. He didn't want to go out that way with those yobs still about. He walked up to a warning sign and cupped his hands. "I'm here. What do you want?"

"What the bloody hell is going on? Who was shooting?"

"Some yobs came and tried to kidnap the women. They've run off." Harold was shouting as best he could, but the sergeant was using a bullhorn so it wasn't a fair exchange.

"Come up here nice and steady, so we can talk properly. Take off that coat first and give me a twirl." Harold took off the coat and turned slowly with his arms out. "All right you can come up, but no sudden moves."

"Can I put the coat back on? It's cold today." Which wasn't surprising since they were well into September now. Harold held up his coat and turned it to show inside and out.

"All right, Keep your hands out of the pockets."

Too true Harold would. The sergeant was on edge and Harold had been on the other end, behind those sandbags. One nervous finger and the rest would shoot as well. He walked across the exclusion zone at an angle and up the road ramp towards the soldiers at a slow, steady pace.

"Near enough. You know the drill or so I've been told. Arms out, turn round and someone will come and search you." Harold did as he was told and soon a pair of hands patted him down. Really patted him down, thoroughly and professionally. He heard the footsteps retreat to the sandbags and the sergeant spoke again. "You can come up to the barricade now, and explain what just happened."

As Harold approached he could see that the sergeant and men were new arrivals. He'd never seen them before and this squad had a wary look about them that spoke of bad experiences. "Hello. You lot are new. I'm Harold Miller, ex-corporal, retired to look after my sister and her kids. There's an Army widow under that flag and a lot of us are refugees from the violence." He stopped three paces short, near enough to talk without shouting.

"Yes, we were told that by the squad who moved out. They said quiet and law-abiding, or as near as it gets." The sergeant paused. "Not what we've found elsewhere. Then we've barely settled in and there's shouting and shooting, and a group of men running off into the ruins. Makes us wonder if there's been a change of management down there?"

"No. I can get the women to come out and wave spears or something to prove they aren't captives?" Harold gave a little smile. "I'd ask you to come down and look but you aren't allowed."

"Too bloody true. One or two idiots followed a pretty smile out of the exclusion zone in other places and never came back. As a hint about anyone else trying that, we burned the area to the ground." The sergeant's head came up further and he looked over the buildings below. "I can see people gardening so can we assume the excitement is over?"

"Yes, though we'll be burning a couple of bodies in the ruins."

"That's the sort of thing I want to know. Whose bodies, how did they die, and I still want to know who was shooting? One was a little rifle or pistol, the others were shotguns, weren't they?"

"Yes Sarge. Two cars full of yobs arrived and demanded a blonde woman one had seen. They threatened to come into the houses and take more women if the answer was no." There was no humour in Harold's voice or face now. "They had firearms and parked where you couldn't see them."

"I couldn't see anything except men and women, some with crossbows and spears, sneaking over back gardens. Spears for God's sake." Sarge actually sounded indignant.

Harold shrugged, then stood very still as a rifle twitched. "Rifle and bayonet since we aren't allowed a rifle? Stops the assholes laying hands on the women."

"Yes, I would imagine so." A trace of humour showed in the sergeant's voice for a moment but then disappeared. "So what about the shooting?"

"I am a very good shot with a two-two target rifle. When one of them aimed a big pistol at me I shot him." Harold hesitated but it was worth asking. "Do you know if two-two indoor target rounds will go through a skull? That wasn't in the training." He stifled another shrug. "I had to shoot him through the eye which was all right since it was only from twenty yards. I'm worried about longer ranges or if I can't see an eye."

Harold was a bit worried about admitting that but surely self-defence was allowed if the police had abdicated? "Then one of them shot at a woman with a shotgun, and one of ours had a shotgun and used it. We've ended up with two bodies, both bad guys from our point of view."

"I don't know if a target two-two will go through a skull either, and I've had more training. How is the woman?"

Sarge sounded as if he really was concerned about Emmy, more so than about the shooting, and Harold relaxed a bit. "She was behind a window and he was using small birdshot. She was lucky. Emmy was trying to duck and turn, and was only hit by flying glass. A lot of it but the double glazing slowed up the pellets. She's got a lot of little cuts and might have scars but her eye is all right."

"Good. Now if you just hand in that target rifle?" Apparently Sarge was concerned about the shooting after all.

"I haven't got it on me. You could come down for it?" Harold tried a little smile. "Come on Sarge. I've got women down there and you expect me to turn over the only protection?"

"What about the crossbows and spears?"

"Would you want a daughter of yours to face that type of asshole just with a spear and crossbow?" Harold really hoped that Sarge was a family man.

He was, or just a decent bloke. There was a real warning in the reply though. "No, but if we see that rifle, or the shotgun, we will shoot whoever is carrying it."

"Fair enough Sarge, and thanks."

"Now what about the weapons the dead men dropped? That lot running away weren't armed." The two soldiers pointing the rifles tensed and Harold was worried again. How far would Sarge push this?

"Not apparently armed Sarge. Maybe those men picked up the weapons and hid them while running? After all, they knew enough to stop the cars where you couldn't see them. They know the rules of engagement." Harold was half resigned to giving up the shotgun.

"Everyone knows the bloody rules because they've been told on the TV and radio. Time after time." Sarge sounded resigned rather than angry and the two tense soldiers relaxed a little. Though they kept their rifles aimed at Harold. "We've even dropped leaflets because their human rights say we have to warn the assholes even if they're shooting policemen."

Sarge turned to the riflemen. "Keep ready but don't shoot him accidentally, all right?" The rifles moved just out of line and Harold was suddenly very relieved. Shot accidentally sounded a lot like code for remove suspicious looking character when said that way. Characters such as ex-corporal Miller. He wondered just how many people were being shot accidentally these days.

Sarge looked at Harold again. "I was told you were a smart-arse but good people. Fair enough, but be very careful. We've been shot at from the ruins elsewhere so any mistake will be fatal." He paused and looked down at the houses. "What happened to their cars? Why did they run away on foot?"

"We asked them to leave the cars as compensation for wounding the young woman. The rest of the women were very angry and the yobs thought it was a good option." Harold waited to see how Sarge took that and noticed that one of the riflemen had developed a very small smile.

"The poor defenceless women with the crossbows? You aren't helping your case, Mr Miller. Still, under the circumstances, I'm relieved to know that your women get scary when they're angry. Go on, sod off and see to that lass."

Harold could hear the humour in Sarge's voice so he made the offer. "My name is Harold these days. Since it won't be a bribe now, do your lads prefer impounding beer or chips, or possibly hot soup when it gets colder?"

"Cheeky sod. Any such items, such as Berry Beer, will be immediately confiscated. Just what is Berry Beer made of?"

"Hops and such I'm told. Berry is one of the young ladies down there."

"Really? Good job fraternising isn't allowed because she sounds like a perfect squaddie's girlfriend." Sarge looked over to the side. "What are you two grinning at?" The little smiles on both the riflemen disappeared. Harold was treated to a small smile from the sergeant. "Better get down there and look after her then. Try not to disturb my sleep again, Harold."

"I won't, but I can't speak for the neighbours. Is it all right if I cut across to the back gardens again, in case of lurkers?"

"Not a problem since you asked."

Harold turned and walked back nice and steady, and without putting his hands in his pockets. Those soldiers were definitely not the young, relaxed recruits he'd seen up to now.

*   *   *

Harold explained the conversation to those waiting in number five when he went to get his little rifle. "Pass the word to everyone as fast as possible please. Make sure everyone keeps firearms, even air pistols, well hidden. That lot up there are very tense."

"What about the bodies? The one Casper shot is a real mess." One look at the speaker, Holly, and Harold knew one person who didn't want to move that body. She looked very pale.

"If nobody fancies it, I'll get Casper to give me a hand to put him in a rubbish bag. Then both of them go into the abandoned housing and we build a bonfire over them."

Casper's voice sounded from behind Harold. "Don't worry, I'll clear up my mess. Makes a change from tidying up after you. Though I will take a rubbish sack. Sort of appropriate. Taking out the trash." Casper put his shotgun down against the wall. "That's loaded so everyone leave it alone. You go and see the rest Harold, I've got this."

Harold made sure the little rifle was well hidden under his coat and headed off home. He stopped to answer questions from several other people on the way back and soon there were messengers spreading the warning.

Then Harold explained the whole meeting again to Sharyn and several of his nearby neighbours. Though the latter was after the evening meal because Sharyn insisted on eating on time. Because of the children and because, according to her, someone had to act civilised.

It was getting dark outside before Harold could relax and get back to his lists. But not for long. Deja vu mark three was Hazel banging on his door. "Harold, Harold!"

This time Liz was downstairs and almost weeping with rage. "The bastards, the stinking rotten bastards. Shoot them all, Harold."

"Christ, why?" Harold also wondered why Sharyn hadn't got his rifle out if something was that urgent. He kept the weapon locked in the study with all the ammunition and reloading gear so the kids never got near it.

"They've burned my caravans, Harold. They're shouting bloody insults from the darkness, in the ruins nearby. The bastards say they'll burn us all. All that lovely bedding. Dry mattresses, and at least two settees, Harold." Liz grabbed Harold and shook him. "Shoot the bastards!"

Harold wrapped his arms round her and hugged. "I can't, Liz. The Army will go crackers if I open up on unarmed men, even if they're assholes." Harold hugged a bit tighter as Liz finally cried, to release either her frustration or anger. "I'm sorry we couldn't find the people to get everything out in time." Liz sobbed some more and hugged back and Sharyn mouthed 'shall I go' and mimed leaving the room.

Harold smiled and shook his head. Then he spoke to Liz. "Sharyn thinks we need some time alone. She doesn't know that you think I'm a limp-wristed weakling unworthy of your affection."

Liz stopped crying. She gave a couple of sobs and a sniff, then raised her head off Harold's damp shoulder. She turned her head towards Sharyn and managed a shaky little laugh. "It's true. That's why I cry on him. If he takes advantage I can slap him silly."

"Thank all and any Gods for that." Sharyn seemed to like that phrase. "I'm his sister and I'd hate to see anyone sensible get taken in by his boyish charm. Not only that, but if you'd snogged him I'd have been sick on this lovely carpet."

Liz was rallying nicely with a bit of banter to distract her, but now she remembered her caravans. "Can't we do anything, Harold?"

"I doubt it. I seem to remember lots of scare stories about those places when one of my mates lived on a caravan site. They burn like hell once they're really going. We can't risk it anyway since those that ran away might have found friends." He turned to Sharyn. "I'll go down to number five in case they get ambitious. Lock the doors and I'll get one of the girl club to nip over with a crossbow for protection."

"I'll do it, Harold." Liz sniffed. "I'll get a crossbow and then Sharyn can tell me all about the sort of women who actually fall for that act."

Harold smiled, gave Sharyn a hug and headed down the street. He could see the flickering of the flames above the houses now. Harold went into the back of number five and retrieved the big rifle from the cupboard under the stairs. When he went into the front room Emmy was at the broken window, sat to the side with her child's crossbow. Liz had been right, the modified bolt did look damn nasty.

Emmy turned as Harold came into the room, one half of her face and head still covered by a bandage. Though a clean one now, and a lot neater so Patricia had probably been at work. "Oh good, it's you. Do you think they're coming back?"

"No. Don't worry, Emmy, they won't risk it."

"I wasn't worried. I want some payback for the scars. Bloody bastards. Er. Sorry." Emmy didn't swear at all usually.

"I was thinking something a bit stronger. Don't worry about the scars. I doubt there'll be many. What did Patricia say?" Since Harold had no real idea about scarring and Patricia was a trainee nurse and might have.

"She said the deepest cuts were on my head, not face, and I might get away with just a couple of little ones that showed." Emmy sighed. "She shaved off all my plaits on that side so I've got to grow them all over again, or cut the rest. It'll take ages. That's another reason for payback."

Harold gave a little laugh, of relief really. "There you go then. In this day and age, among all the bad boys, a couple of little scars will only enhance your already stunning beauty. Leave the plaits on the other side and you've got a statement hair style. Like the models used to have, or pop stars. You'll knock 'em dead."

Emmy's teeth gleamed in the gloom, and then she laughed. "Blimey Harold, with a line of patter like that, how come you haven't got a girlfriend? Oh, sorry. Did you lose someone?"

"Not really, not like you. I've been abroad since I was seventeen. Three years of sand and Dads who would use a gun or a big knife if you looked hard at their daughters." Harold gave a little smile. "I met a girl when we came back." Then his smile went. "I had to leave her in London. It never turned into anything but maybe she got the nearest to me. Now? Well, under the circumstances?"

Emmy's tone softened. "There's a lot of us grieving." A bit of mischief sneaked into her voice. "Though a few of us aren't, and one or two have wondered about showing you a bit of gratitude, for the rescue." She giggled. "That's their excuse anyway."

"Which is a bit of a problem. Gratitude instead, of, well, attraction." Harold shut up because this wasn't a conversation to have with a wounded girl in a damaged house with nutters dancing round a bonfire outside.

"I'll tell them."

"What!"

Emmy gave a little laugh. "Less gratitude and more attraction. That should liven things up."

"Christ no. Are you on pain medication?"

Emmy laughed again. "A couple of pills but I am sort of happy. I saw that gun aiming at me, and then there was a boom and pain, and then all the blood." She sighed. "Now it's just a couple of scars and short hair and I'm really happy. Sorry about the teasing."

That made Harold chuckle. "Don't worry about teasing. I've got an older sister who still practices."

"I've got a brother who headed to Jamaica to look up his roots before travel became difficult. About three years ago. I haven't heard from him for over a year now. I wouldn't mind him being here to tease me now and then." Emmy peeked out of the window. "The noise is dying down."

"No fun for them if nobody is answering. It's cold out there as well and they'll want to find somewhere warm for the night." Harold knew his annoyance showed in the next words. "Somewhere I can't find them in the morning."

"I don't think I'll sleep anyway."

"Nor me, just in case they do get brave. Maybe we could move to a warmer room? One with a window?" The cold was definitely biting now all the excitement was over.

"Good idea but I'm bringing my seat." Emmy's half smile flashed round the dressing. "A crate of Berry Beer."

"Full ones?"

"Of course. I might share if you're a gentleman and carry the crate. After all I'm wounded."

Harold spent a pleasant night, under the circumstances. They chatted about this and that, history and relatives, and sipped beer now and then. Harold had his shoulder re-dampened at one stage when Emmy was talking about David, her man. Harold also found out that despite everyone thinking so, Emmy wasn't married to David and they'd been together less than a year. But they had been sort of making plans.

He patted her back and Emmy mopped her eye and they moved on to the last news out of Jamaica. Then Alfie being so nice to a Hazel still interested in dolls rather than boys. They both agreed that the interest was Alfie's good nature, and Hazel being near his age and an orphan.

Though the choices when the young teens started thinking of romance were going to be very limited. Alfie and Toby were also being nice to Veronica, who was a very quiet girl just as her Mum and Dad were, Kerry and Isiah. One of the few complete families from Sharyn's block of flats. They played a bit of who might like who about the four teenagers until Emmy pointed out that one might be gay and mess the whole idea up.

Sometime as dawn was breaking Emmy drifted off to sleep in an armchair, having abandoned the beer crate some time previously. Harold quietly headed upstairs and peeked into the two rooms with open doors. He brought quilts down and covered Emmy, then wrapped himself up in the other and slept in the other armchair.

He was greeted by Emmy and a cup of coffee when he woke up. Sharyn gave him a lot of teasing about where he'd spent the night. Emmy teased Harold on her good days, declaring that the last she remembered was the second bottle of beer. Then rolling her eyes and pointing out *anything* could have happened after that as she woke up under a quilt. Harold laughed along because everyone was well aware that Emmy was still grieving and no man was on her agenda. No living man anyway.

Chapter 11:
Setting Boundaries

Ten days later Emmy's bandages were off even if her head was still half covered in stubble. Just in time for her to reclaim her shotgun seat in the pickup when the first convoy set off to get long-term supplies. Emmy insisted on coming along as Billy's guard and this time had one of Liz's spears.

The spear heads were the burned hunting knife blades recovered along with the bows. The tang was socketed onto the end of the broom shaft and even spirited stabbing of a door failed to dislodge the experimental model. After a dedicated session of hammering Liz had produced twenty three of the spears, and eleven came on this convoy.

"This looks more promising." The convoy was parked at the front of a big warehouse which hadn't been burned. There was the usual evidence of looting, so when Harold led the group through the broken doors the empty shelves weren't a surprise.

Berry pushed past and bent over scattered packaging on the floor. "Good, they were idiots. We want this lot."

"What is it?"

"Yeast for wine making. They've looted the kits for making beer and wine but they'll run out of yeast." Berry was throwing packets into a wire basket and Billy and Seth both went to help her.

"Do you need the yeast for beer?" Harold was sure beer needed yeast but it wasn't on the list.

"We keep our own going. The brew is more consistent and no need to go shopping." Berry glanced over to Billy and Seth. "Take any wiggly bits of glass tubing, corks even if they're rubber with a hole in, and any tubing or filters."

Now Harold really was puzzled. "So why take this? Unless you've got a grapevine you're keeping quiet about?"

Berry delivered a patent beaming smile. "Blackberry wine will blow your brains out. We can make wine out of potatoes, rhubarb, and even tinned fruit, just for a change." She turned back to her task. "Though beer is best of course."

"So that's it. No beer supplies?"

Berry stood up and looked around. "Maybe. The looters also left those sacks, so maybe the store at the back has more?" Berry was pointing at four sacks that had been pulled off the shelf and then abandoned. "We want those anyway." She headed for the big doors at the back of the shop area but Harold and Emmy got ahead of her as quickly as possible.

"You have a bodyguard, Berry. Let us go first or your Dad will slap me round the head." Harold smiled to take the sting out of it because Berry was too young to be needing an armed guard for shopping.

"Bodyguard? I'm just here to help carry things." Emmy pushed the door open and Harold poked the rifle inside. Emmy's big torch lit up the large room and there was a stack of sacks at the back. Berry pushed through.

"Brilliant! Someone has been at them but there's loads left here." She pointed. "Those and those are what we want."

Harold turned around. "Billy, get the vans here now and everyone loading, Someone is already taking this stuff and they might be back. Send the vehicles round the side to the loading door, there has to be one." Billy left at a run. "Seth, get all that little stuff in baskets and bring the lot through there and help with loading. Everyone, hurry."

The loading bay door was still locked so Harold used the butt of the big rifle on the lock. The first van was pulling up outside as the shutter door went up. "Casper, keep the guns on the vehicles and watch for annoyed neighbours. Someone has already been taking this gear. The rest of you, all of you, get loading."

Thirty minutes of intense effort later and Casper called out. "Here they come. A mob not a gang, waving sticks and suchlike. They're all on foot."

"All aboard, leave the rest of the sacks. Casper, get someone with a two-two to fire a warning shot over their heads. Seth, take someone else in the Luton van because it's going first, so Berry isn't going inside. That's the biggest vehicle so make a hole in that lot. Run them down."

Seth stared, white-faced, and hesitated.

"I'll do it." He switched his stare to Liz when she shouted. Harold opened his mouth to say he would, but didn't get the chance.

"No." Seth swallowed hard. "I can do it." He turned and raced for the driver's cab, beckoning, and Bernie followed with a spear. The big square-backed van lurched into motion as the rest clambered aboard their own transport and the six other vehicles dropped into line. Seth took Harold at his word and kept his foot on the accelerator. The approaching crowd spread across the exit, wavered as the vehicle kept coming, then most scattered at the last moment.

That decision was too late for some. Men and at least one woman were bowled over as two tons of fully loaded goods vehicle brushed them aside. At least two went underneath because Harold felt two big bumps when the pickup went through the gap. The convoy roared off down the road pursued by a hail of half bricks and lengths of timber, but the shocked crowd reacted too late.

Five minutes later, on an empty stretch of road, the Luton swerved to the side of the tarmac and Seth climbed out. He tottered three steps and was violently sick. Harold made his way forward past other vehicles. Seth glanced up, still bent at the waist.

"Christ, Harold. I saw her face. Oh Christ, Harold." He retched again, trying to be sick when there was nothing left.

Harold patted his back. "It had to be done, Seth. If you'd said no I'd have done it. Otherwise they'd have ripped us to bits." He offered the white-faced driver a bottle of water. "Here, rinse and spit, then drink a little bit."

Seth half straightened and did. Then he looked at Harold again. "She froze. So I shut my eyes and kept my foot down. Oh shit, Harold."

"You might have missed her. She might have jumped and you didn't get her. You might have hit someone else. I'll get another driver for the rest of the way." Harold didn't think she, whoever it was, had made it. At least one woman didn't, but Seth needed the doubt.

"You think? Oh God. I kept thinking, it's her or B... the rest of you. Oh Christ, Harold." Someone came past Harold and gathered Seth in her arms. Berry!

"Thank you Seth. I was so frightened. It must have been awful." She held him tight for a while, murmuring, then as Seth straightened up Berry gave him a gentle kiss. The young woman turned and headed back along the vehicles, giving Harold a big wink as she passed. The first aid certainly worked because Seth was staring after her and some colour was back in his cheeks.

"I'll get a driver, Seth."

"Er, no, um, I'll be all right now." Seth drank more water and climbed back into the truck, then wound the window down as Harold waved.

"The pickup will come to the front now Seth. Hang well back the same as usual, all right?" A white-faced Seth nodded. Harold headed back, re-assuring those who asked after Seth. The young man had made himself a lot of friends today.

Berry leaned out of the girl club minibus as Harold passed. "Did it work?

Is he all right?"

"Yes, but he'll be chasing you round the brewery after that."

Berry smiled. "No he won't. Seth is a bit frightened of me so he'll be a gentleman. Anyway, I might let him catch me eventually if Dad isn't there. I just haven't decided yet because some of the others are very sweet."

"Hellfire. Whoever it is won't stand a chance." Harold shook his head and walked away from the laughter in the minibus. Some of the laughing was close to hysteria because their escape had been shocking and a close thing.

*   *   *

The next two places the convoy visited were useless, one was empty and the other was ashes and twisted metal. Then a collection of garages produced an old welder and several boxes of welding rods that Liz seized with glee. The route zigzagged to take in industrial estates, warehouses, groups of shops and small industrial units. Some were burned but many were now being protected. So were many small groups of houses.

Firearms were aimed from upstairs windows in a street lined with shops. A barricade across the street to a warehouse consisted of two vans on their sides and several road sign poles. Behind it were people with garden forks, machetes, and a couple of crossbows. A small group of archers with the complicated bows were holding a boarded up supermarket. It had been looted but they were protecting what was left, aiming their arrows down from the roof. Sarge had been right about the enclaves.

*   *   *

Harold told Billy to sweep in a wide half circle across the car park of the garden centre. He wanted to weigh up the store, but also see into the outside area. The place where the greenhouses, big pots and trees were kept, and the raised beds of plants. The big front windows were smashed and boarded up but the building itself was intact. Better still there were trees, brown and withered, showing over the low fence at the back. Billy stopped and Harold climbed out, leaving his rifle on the seat.

"Go away. There's no food or booze." The man's voice was muffled and came from inside the building.

"What's out the back?"

"You can't have the spuds and stuff. Go away."

Harold could see the movement inside now, behind a gap between the sheets of plywood boarding the door up. "We want trees, and maybe bushes. Can we trade?" He said it without thought because Sharyn had been really worried about getting fruit.

"Trade what?" Harold was still wondering what when the man's voice spoke up again. "We'll trade for spears."

Harold looked at the wall of points poking out of various vehicles. They did look vicious things, somehow worse than a knife taped to a stick. He faced the store again. "We could do with some seeds, and maybe bushes. Can someone have a look?"

"Not in here. Someone can look in the garden but leave the growing things, the veggies, alone." Harold looked round as a door opened and Berry was out of the minibus and heading towards Harold. So much for staying with her bodyguard.

Before Harold could object, Berry started. "He said they had no booze. Trade some yeast and the expertise to brew wine, with a few traps and tubes." She smiled. "But not until we've got some fruit bushes."

Harold faced the boarded door. "We can show you how to make booze and trade supplies to start you off. We'll also discuss a couple of spears depending on what is worth taking. Those trees look dead."

"Not completely, we've put the fruit ones in water but there's no spare soil. Those others are drying out for firewood." This time Harold heard a woman's voice from inside. "The woman can look."

Harold wasn't sending any woman on her own. "A man with each woman or girl. Two of each. Just so we can get done quickly and leave."

This time Harold had to wait as a real argument erupted inside, then the man was back. "All right but the rest of you stay there. No vehicles come any closer."

"Deal." Harold turned to the convoy. "I need two women, Curtis and a man. Casper, you're the man, not a girl." A ripple of laughter ran down the convoy as Casper climbed out and waved his machete. Curtis joined him and they moved towards the pickup truck. Berry opened her mouth and Harold beat her to it. "No, Berry. Get in the pickup please and stay there. I will not take your body back to your Dad."

Berry opened her eyes in surprise, opened her mouth, and then shut it. She sighed.

"I'll go." Emmy climbed out of the pickup. "You sit in there Berry, and look mean. Ooh look, that pout should do it." The two young women laughed at each other as Berry climbed in and sat down. Then she produced a ferocious scowl.

Sal was heading over with a spear and a baseball bat and the four lined up ready. Harold pulled the rifle out and showed it to the garden centre. "Don't try anything or I'll shoot the shit out of the whole place. The boards won't stop this." He had all of twenty two rounds so he wouldn't affect the big store very much, but the effect was just what Harold wanted.

"Bloody hell, point that somewhere else. There's women in here." Another argument broke out in there and this time Harold distinctly heard 'but they've already got women' before the volume dropped away. "All right. There'll be no trouble if they don't try to take anything." The four inspectors headed for the gate in the fence.

Harold could see the four heads moving about in there, so he didn't get worried as the convoy waited. Eventually Sal came back to report. "There are some fruit trees that Curtis says are still alive. He thinks four apple and two plum, and one cherry are worth taking. The rest are a bit touch and go. There's blackberry and several of the other bushes, and rhubarb though it's planted. They may not want to trade that."

Sal glanced at the store and lowered her voice even if she was a long way away. "Curtis says if they dug holes through the tarmac, they've probably got enough compost in there to grow more. Trees will send roots clean through the rubble and such underneath and into real soil once they're started. Brambles will for sure."

Harold thought about it. How did he work that into a trade because once said, nobody needed to pay for the information? "Thanks, Sal. I'm going to go and have a chat to the man at the door. Ask Curtis to sort out everything we want and put it by the gate. Inside. Then I'll make a deal with this lot."

Sal headed back and Harold spoke up. "We can help you to grow more, but it's worth plants or seed. We'll sort out what we want, and I'll come over to the door and talk."

"Not with that cannon."

Harold smiled and gave the rifle to Billy, who got out and stood holding it. Then he walked over. "We can teach you to make wine and leave some kit, and we can tell you how to grow some trees and bushes. Those are both worth something. We'll also trade two spears. What seeds will you offer?"

This time Harold could hear four distinct voices arguing, and at least one was a woman. "Go round to the back and we'll bring the seeds."

Harold tried to keep the relief from his voice. "We'll want veggies and some flowers that will seed again for next year."

The bartering was intense, but eventually there was a sort of agreement about the value of knowing how to grow more. The same with the wine making but two booklets and sight of the gear helped with that. Berry did come across to explain the wine making, with a scowling Bernie standing guard. In the end three spears were also traded, and the deal was done.

The locals were disgusted with themselves when told they could just punch holes in the tarmac or take the lot up, but agreed the information was worth the extra seeds and two rhubarb plants. In the end three of them stood by the gate, carrying their new spears, and waved goodbye to the convoy. The convoy headed home, pushing hard, because the days were shorter now.

*   *   *

As they came around the roundabout and headed down the road towards the bypass, and the entrance to home, gun flashes rippled up on the bypass. The Army were shooting! "Foot down Billy. Get home now!" Billy did. The pickup screeched and swayed around the turn into the estate and mounted the footpath to go round the cars on the road. As the vehicle bumped back off the kerb Harold could see a group of people heading across the back gardens towards a figure on the ground.

Harold was out of the cab as soon as the pickup stopped, leaving the big rifle on the seat. Emmy was right behind him as he headed across the garden, and the group parted. Gabriela was laid there, covered in blood but still moving a little. Beyond her, across the boundary and near the ruins, two men lay. "What happened?"

"A lot of men came from the ruins. They demanded booze and women." Holly's face was white but her eyes were alight with rage. "One of them came forward to the boundary and Gabriela went to meet him." Holly averted her eyes and her voice dropped. "She tried to do your thing. What Liz calls macho bullshit."

"Gabriela told them no and to back off or they'd be shot. We could hear it clearly." There was no fight in Karen now. She looked frail, and Stewart was holding her. "He said she would do for a start and came over the rubble heap we made. He had a machete. We opened fire. I tried, Harold, but this gun didn't do any good."

An amateur with an air pistol wouldn't hit much at over twenty yards so Harold wasn't surprised. "He stopped in surprise and Gabriela hit him on the arm, with her machete. He dropped his machete. But then he pulled a knife with the other hand and stuck it in her." Holly was almost shaking with rage now. "He said the rest should rush us and then our lot fired again. One of them screamed and held his face."

"One man pulled a pistol at that and the Army opened fire. They hit him and three others. Two of those left with the rest but they were wounded. The one who stabbed Gabriela picked up both machetes and went as well." Stewart looked frightened but determined. "He said they'd be back tonight. He said there would be more of them, and they'd run right over us and share the women round. He claimed Holly."

"Father." Everyone but the two knelt by Gabriela whirled as she called out. "Father, forgive me." She coughed and then whimpered, curling around her belly.

Harold headed over and knelt beside her. One glance and nothing, no medical help he could get her, was going to save Gabriela. The knife had cut across her belly, ripping her wide open. He took her hand and Gabriela's skin was already cold.

"I tried to stop them Father. It was all my fault they came. Forgive me."

A low voice spoke right near Harold's ear. Sal? "Tell her God forgives her."

"What?" Harold was startled, but managed to keep his voice low.

"She thinks you're a priest. Be one."

"Forgive me Father, for I have sinned. It has been too long since I last confessed. I loved him Father, my lovely Abraham, and I am sorry because he was an unbeliever and that was a sin. I wanted him so much and we sinned without marriage. Is that why he died? I have taken life, Father, and I can't forgive them, those who killed him. Will I see him Father, will he be waiting?" Gabriela was rambling now but holding out her other hand, so Harold took it in his.

Sal nudged Harold as both Gabriela's hands grasped tighter.

Harold tried. "Abraham will be waiting. God is merciful." Not likely, or she wouldn't be laid here.

"Father?"

Sal whispered. "Wrong words. Tell her she sinned, but has repented and she must say a Hail Mary."

Harold's head spun, but he tried for it. "You have sinned, but you have repented. You must say one Hail Mary." Whatever the hell that was. "Then you will see Abraham again."

"Hail Mary, full of grace, the Lord is with thee, blessed are you among all women and blessed is the fruit of your womb, Jesus. Holy Mary, mother of God." Gabriela stopped and whimpered. Her eyes were open, but whatever she was seeing wasn't in front of them. "Pray for us sinners now and in the hour of our death."

Sal murmured again. "Now repeat this." Harold did, word for word as she said it. It was completely wrong, and had to be blasphemous, but as he spoke Gabriela's face cleared. Much of the pain went from her features though she was still twitching and whimpering sometimes.

"I absolve you from your sins, in the Name of the Father, and of the Son, and of the Holy Spirit."

Gabriela's bloody hands grasped harder as she finally heard the words she had needed for too long, her absolution.

Sal nudged and whispered, "Now repeat this."

Harold did. "Go forth, O Christian soul, from this world, in the name of God the Father Almighty, who created thee; may thy place be this day in peace, and thine abode in holy Sion. Through Christ our Lord."

"Amen." Harold nearly jumped out of his skin as four or five other voices joined in. Sal whispered on, relentless.

Harold tried to keep his voice level. "O merciful and gracious God, mercifully regard this Thy handmaid Gabriela and grant her a full discharge from all her sins, through Christ our Lord."

"Amen." More voices now, and they were stronger. Sal whispered again and Harold spoke.

"I commend you, dear Sister, to the almighty God, and consign you to the care of Him, may you be placed among the company of the blessed and enjoy the sweetness of the contemplation of your God for ever." This was all wrong because Harold didn't really believe this stuff. But Gabriela did, and so he carried on as her grip began to slacken.

"Amen." At least a dozen people now, and maybe more.

Sal whispered again. "Keep going while she can hear. It's working." Then she fed Harold the next line of this travesty.

"Receive, Lord, Thy handmaid into the place of salvation, which she hopes to obtain through Thy mercy."

"Amen." That was a deep, solid response by a lot of voices. Then apart from Sal's voice, the only sound was Gabriela's laboured breathing. Harold repeated the next lines as instructed.

"Go forth, O Christian soul, from this world, in the name of God the Father Almighty, who created thee, may thy place be this day in peace, and thine abode in holy Sion, with Abraham. Through Christ our Lord." Harold stuck the Abraham in because he thought Gabriela needed it.

At least half the residents must have arrived. "Amen."

"O God, mercifully regard this Thy handmaid Gabriela and grant her a full discharge from all her sins, who with a contrite heart most earnestly begs it of Thee. Through Christ our Lord."

"Amen." Harold knew most of the residents blamed God for the mess if they even believed, but they were still doing their part. He was praying to a God he didn't believe in, asking forgiveness for something he didn't consider a sin. Some part of Harold accepted that if Gabriela was right, then he would burn long and hot for this. Sal was whispering again.

"I commend you, dear Sister, to the almighty God, may you be placed among the company of the blessed and enjoy the sweetness of the contemplation of your God for ever."

"Amen." Harold had never been in a church but now this felt like some sort of Holy. Maybe religion worked better, out in the open. Sal whispered again and Harold spoke the words.

"Receive, Lord, Thy handmaid into the place of salvation, along with Abraham, which she hopes to obtain through Thy mercy." Harold stuck another Abraham in. It couldn't hurt because Gabriela was still listening. Her failing grip tightened briefly when Harold spoke her man's name.

"Abraham." So softly that half of them missed it. Those that heard could never decide if it was prayer, or a greeting. Though the smile that came afterwards should have melted any God's heart.

"We commend to Thee, Lord, the soul of Thy handmaid Gabriela, and we pray Thee, Lord Jesus Christ, be pleased to admit her to thy bosom."

"Amen." There were a few sobs after this one.

"She's gone." Sal spoke but Harold knew because Gabriela's bloody fingers had released his hands.

He turned, still knelt. "What the hell was that?" Harold almost choked getting it out, and rubbed away the tears so he could see Sal.

Sal's face was harsh, with tears streaming down her drawn cheeks. "That was the most half-baked, messed up, blasphemous parody of confession and the Catholic priest's prayer over the dying you will ever hear." She sighed, and her face and voice softened. "But look at her, Harold."

Harold did, and Gabriela had died totally at peace with her God. He figured that alone was worth the possible hellfire. Though others needed some of that first. Harold's eyes moved down to her terrible wound and his face hardened. "Who's with me?"

"I am." That was Holly, and she understood immediately.

"For what?" Liz didn't.

"Who is coming to hunt the bastards down?"

*   *   *

Harold didn't need names. A dozen faces hardened and their backs straightened. Those faces went from grief to anger or determination and people turned back to get firearms. "I'll get your big rifle, Harold. You clean up so you can shoot properly." Sharyn turned away and yes, it would fit under her long coat.

Then Toby was there, cheeks wet and his two-two rifle tucked under his coat. "I tried, Harold. I hit one but it wasn't enough."

"You got them to draw a gun, and that brought the Army in. You might have saved everyone with that one shot."

"It's not enough." Toby looked down at Gabriela and then up at Harold, now on his feet. "I want more. Can I come?"

Harold knew it was wrong to let a fifteen year old boy go on a vengeance manhunt. But so was some arse knifing a young woman because she wouldn't let him do whatever he wanted. Toby was going to live in a very bad world so maybe this would help him one day. "Stick close to me. Only shoot if I tell you to."

Toby nodded and did just that, stuck close as Harold washed his hands with a bottle of water someone handed him. "Here. Ah. I'll take it to the first ruins." Sharyn had the rifle under her coat but it wouldn't fit under Harold's jacket.

"Then go back to the houses immediately. Where are the kids?"

"Betty's got them. She was going to take them into the exclusion zone if it all went to hell, and hope the Army didn't shoot children. We'll sort out Gabriela. Get her cleaned up and all that." A snarl came into Sharyn's voice. "Get them, little brother."

"On my list. Right at the top." Harold looked around at the group who had now gathered. A dozen, all with hidden rifles and pistols or displaying crossbows and machetes or spears.

"No macho bullshit, right? This time we just kill them." Liz had a pistol crossbow and a machete, and a determined look.

"I want him. That bastard. I'm gonna cut him into tiny pieces." Harold should have said something but he needed them all ready to kill, and not thinking too hard. Even a slim seventeen year old blonde girl.

"Which way, Holly. Where did they head off to?"

Her arm came up without hesitation. "At least one was yelling because he was wounded. A couple have crossbow bolts in them and two were shot by the Army. At least one of those is limping badly. One was holding his face. They disappeared that way." Harold was actually impressed by how well the defenders had done.

"Right. We must move as quietly and quickly as we can. Keep an eye open for blood sign and we spread a bit to catch a change of direction." Harold was heading for the ruins already and as soon as he stepped inside one Sharyn gave him the rifle. She also had the two spare clips.

"All of them brother, and stick their heads on a post as a warning."

"Good thinking. Send someone up to the Army, will you?" The bullhorn had started demanding and Harold simply didn't have the time or inclination to answer.

"Go." Sharyn pushed and Harold went.

The group moved quickly but hadn't caught up as the light dimmed. Harold would have thought he'd missed them but at least one was still bleeding enough to leave signs on walls and bushes. Casper's hand went up off to the left and then everyone heard the complaining. Someone wanted a rest to sort out his leg, and another wanted a breather. A loud voice was pointing out that there'd been a lot of bloody vans turn up, they had to keep going.

Harold's group gathered and went through the next line of overgrown hedges together. There was a shout from further down the road. "It's them. Charge, they've only got pissy little single shots."

Harold saw the man who was shouting and smiled. His rifle came up, then he hesitated and moved the muzzle just a bit, towards the shoulder opposite the rough sling. The big three oh three bellowed and the man was spun and flipped off his feet into the garden behind. "Pissy?" Harold breathed as he worked the bolt and swung his whole body, looking for the next target.

The noise caused a few to hesitate and scrabble for pistols, which gave Harold his targets. Casper was prioritising as well though Harold needed to do something with the shotgun loads. One man staggered and dropped his pistol, but kept coming with his machete. The other one Casper hit was closer, already shooting, and the packed birdshot knocked him straight down.

Harold shot three before he had to defend himself from a machete. All were men who had stopped to aim properly and the heavy, high-powered bullets took each one off his feet. Harold grinned as he took the machete blow on the solid wooden forestock of his rifle. Déjà vu except for the lack of sand, and it wasn't a plastic and tin rifle this time. Harold stepped into the blow, hooking the butt round to smash the big brass plate into his opponent's face. The man staggered back two steps spraying blood from his mouth and nose and Harold followed.

He brought the rifle back over his shoulder, butt foremost, and this time drove the brass into the man's forehead. He went over without a sound. Harold turned and saw Liz and he was going to be too late. Her attacker already had a machete raised. Liz turned her head away from the attack as she took a wild swipe, and the man avoided the blade with a smile. He stepped in, machete already coming down and Liz was still looking away.

Harold was pulling his rifle round as fast as possible, working the bolt to feed in a round but too slow, much too slow. Then the man's eyes went wide in surprise as he was plucked off his feet. Casper had him by the collar and heaved, and man flew backwards and down. Casper's batting arm was already well into its swing as the man landed, and the target barely managed a short scream. Liz looked round, eyes wide and horrified, but Harold was already looking for more targets.

Four of his people were down, but so were all the others, the enemy. All of Harold's wounded were still moving, so Harold ran forward along with Casper, Holly, Toby, Sal, Emmy, and Seth, machetes and spears raised. There was no mercy as they worked through the wounded. Though two with crossbow bolts in their legs put their hands on their heads, and the machetes halted.

Holly went past them heading for where the leader had fallen, with grim determination and a raised spear. "Don't kill him yet."

She paused at Harold's voice, glanced back at him, and looked down. A voice was raised, either pleading or plain begging. Holly bent down and picked up a discarded machete. She swung and it came down hard. The man screamed, and then whimpered as Holly looked over at Harold. "Not dead. Not yet, but he won't be using that damn knife again."

Casper was dealing with the captives, using belts to tie their arms behind them. Harold, along with Emmy, Toby, and Sal, went to look at their own wounded. Matthew had a bullet in the shoulder which Toby and Sal started plugging and wrapping up. Liz had already strapped her sheathed machete as a splint for Curtis's shin. He'd passed out as she did. Liz moved over to help Emmy with a sling for Finn's arm, avoiding looking at anyone else.

Harold knelt next to Rob. "Good job you didn't duck or it would have been your head."

"Yeah. Though I need to lose weight, not be such a big target."

Harold was looking at the hole in Rob's front and out the back. "I'm not Patricia, but that's well to the side of the vital stuff I reckon. Though we'd better give you the luxury trip home."

"How? Ow."

"Just cleaning it. Wait until Patricia starts." Harold chuckled. "The luxury trip is we carry you."

Rob winced, and not from pain. "Seriously? Are gut shots really bad? The TV films always go on about them."

Harold smiled and hoped he was right. "Not out to the side like this. Through the middle is a problem, where the aorta and intestines and kidneys and such are. This has probably missed the lot. One really good thing, it went right through and out the back."

"Two holes is good? Aargh. That bloody hurts."

"Think yourself lucky the bullet isn't still inside or Patricia would dig it out. Anyway, if it makes you feel better, you aren't hurting anything like as much as that asshole who started it."

That stopped Rob worrying about his wound, for a moment at least. "Holly didn't kill him?"

"Not yet. I asked her not to she only hit him once, with a machete. He's alive because I heard him scream afterwards." As Rob smiled, Harold jerked his belt tight over the dressing.

"Ooh. Ow, I really hope it hurts more than that. Now what?"

"We put up a boundary marker."

Harold stood and went over to the two captives with Casper. "Tie them to lampposts, Casper, leave an empty one in the middle." Casper looked puzzled. "Boundary markers." Casper grinned and he and Seth got them on their feet. The captive pair hobbled to their lampposts as Harold went to see asshole.

Asshole wouldn't knife anyone ever again, even if he lived. Harold had, as he'd intended, hit the man's good shoulder. The transfer of energy when the bullet hit the bone must have ruptured or shattered everything needed to make it work again. Holly had done something similar to the other shoulder with the machete. The sling the man had fashioned after Gabriela hit him had been removed, and Holly was folding it up.

"I thought Gabriela might like it, to take with her. I considered his head but she wouldn't want that on her pyre." Holly looked down. "Can I start chopping yet?"

"No." The man shouldn't have looked relieved at Harold's reply. "He needs tying to a lamppost with his friends." Holly was puzzled but perfectly happy to help the man to his feet. She pulled him by an arm which elicited a scream, and the man's enthusiastic compliance with getting up. He tottered across to the lamppost in a haze of pain, then cried out again as his arms were tied back with his belt.

Harold looked at the three. "We need something tight round their waists."

"Why?" Holly looked from one to another.

"So the bodies don't slip down." Harold knew he should just shoot them, but somewhere inside he wanted a bit more. Execution at least. So they knew what was coming. So they could know they were dying, like Gabriela did, if only for a few moments. Holly, Seth and Harold soon cut shirts and jeans off bodies and bound all three firmly so they wouldn't slip down.

One of the men with a wounded leg had to ask. "What's that for?"

"So your body doesn't slide down and spoil the message." The man stared at the young blonde woman with the vicious smile and bloody spear and machete.

"We surrendered. You can't do that."

"Why not? You do what you want. Tell you what, we'll make it legal." Holly turned to Harold. "We should try them. We've got a jury."

"They're a bit biased." Though the idea appealed to Harold.

"Only jury we've got." Casper raised his voice. "You lot are sworn in as a jury. You heard the prosecution evidence back there with Gabriela." Casper turned back to the lampposts. "Anything to say in defence?"

"I didn't kill her."

Harold smiled. "Aiding and abetting. The sentence is death."

Holly smiled and pointed at the blood spatter from the man's leg wound. "Littering the pavement. The sentence is death." She turned to the other two, "Any defence?"

"You can't do this." That wasn't too clear because this man must have been Toby's victim, and his cheek was torn open.

Holly looked at the one who had just spoken. "Of course we can, you stupid shit." She glanced at the next lamppost. "The one in the middle isn't interested in answering." Holly was right, he was only half-conscious. "Verdict everyone?"

"Guilty." That rolled back from everyone without hesitation.

"So how do we execute them, Harold, bearing in mind this one still owes Gabriela?" Holly gestured at the centre man and hefted her machete. "I should do it, because after all you claimed me didn't you?" The eyes looking at Holly were glazed with pain, but Harold could see the shock hit as the man realised who this was.

Harold called out to those around his own wounded. "Toby, can I borrow your rifle please? To save on the big ammunition."

The youngster hurried over. "Yes, of course Harold. Here's some rounds."

"I only need two. Remember to pick up any brass on the road so I can reload them."

"I'll look around, Harold. Once you're done." Toby stepped back a little. "I want to see them die."

Harold loaded and stood in front of the left man, about ten feet away. He aimed the rifle. "Hey, look up." The man did and Harold shot him through the left eye. Then he walked down the street and repeated that with the one at the other end, through the right eye. "Pull the crossbow bolts out of their legs and his arm, so we can use them again."

"This one tried to take Gabriela. Attempted rape so I should cut his nuts off. That would be a clear message to any others?" Holly's suggestion got through and the man raised his head despite the pain in his shoulders.

"No!"

"I wonder how many said that to you." Harold decided his evil half had played enough today. The asshole was dying of blood loss right now, but Holly was right about the message. "You can cut off his nuts, but cut his throat first. Pull his pants down before you cut, so whoever sees him understands." Harold walked away before he was tempted to torture the bastard first.

The man's voice was loud behind him, protesting, and Harold paused when there was a long, sobbing scream. Then it was cut off and Holly's voice sounded from behind Harold. "Sorry, I got confused. I cut off his nuts first." There was a world of satisfaction in Holly's voice so Harold let it ride. When she joined him in stripping the bodies of weapons and undamaged clothing, the manic glare had gone from the young woman's eyes. Perhaps that scream had been enough revenge.

Chopping off the heads on the other bodies was a messy and gruesome chore, but those doing it agreed heads helped mark the boundary. The nine heads were placed in a line in front of the three lampposts. There wasn't any paint to write 'Keep Out' but hopefully the message was clear enough.

*   *   *

Those still unhurt used timbers from the houses and jackets from the bodies to make a stretcher for Rob. When Emmy offered her arm and shoulder to help him get back, Curtis developed a massive smile and Harold a small one. Harold was remembering being asked how to deal with a grieving woman. Being her patient could work best of all. A patient in a greenhouse would be bonus, since Curtis would no doubt keep up his gardening.

Harold and Casper carried the stretcher, with comments about people going on diets. The return trip was slow and once he thought they were near enough to risk it, Harold sent Holly and Toby ahead to let everyone know what had happened. Almost full dark had fallen when the group arrived back, and Gabriela's body was nowhere in sight. The two men had been stripped of boots and anything else useful but they had been left among the weeds.

Susan came running across the gardens to see Rob as soon as the stretcher broke cover, and Harold had to warn her to leave the jackets covering him. Harold's rifle and the captured firearms were under there, and an Army scope would be able to see them even in the dark. Patricia was waiting in Rob's or Susan's 'our' house. Maybe this would finally settle the pair's reluctance to admit their relationship, since according to Patricia any woman willing to deal with a man's bedpans wasn't a platonic friend.

The group split up with people going off with small groups to explain what happened and Harold tried once again to talk to Liz. Once again she avoided him, which was worrying. Harold understood. Liz had found she couldn't hack at another human being. Given everyone's background and upbringing that wasn't strange, but Liz needed to understand that.

*   *   *

Harold had to fend off invites to this house or another before he could go home. Sharyn made him a cup of coffee while Daisy bounced all over him. "Uncle-Harold story tonight."

"I know luv. Just let me have my cup of coffee."

"I've drawn a dog because Betty used to have a dog. Can we have a dog? Please?"

"I don't know if there are any for sale now. I'll look out for one."

"A big, fluffy one. Can you draw dogs?"

Harold looked up and smiled at Sharyn as he accepted his drink. "I can probably learn, Daisy." Though he was wondering about dogs. Apocalyptic films all claimed that packs of them should be running about hunting people. Apart from an aged poodle there were no dogs on the estate. There had been a general drift towards cats in recent years but a complete lack was still strange. Then Harold was too busy learning to draw dogs to worry about where they were.

Sharyn was waiting after Uncle-Harold bedtime story with a bowl of soup, bread, and questions. "Now I want to know, little brother. Did you set the boundary?"

"With a line of heads, sis. I think Holly finally got it out of her system."

"Good." Sharyn thought a moment. "Maybe good. How did she do it?"

"She got to the right man. Nearly hacked an arm off and tied him to a lamppost, and we had a trial. There were enough for a jury."

Sharyn had a little smile. "What was the verdict?"

"Death for the three we caught alive. I shot two of them." Harold gave a little laugh. "Through the eye with a little rifle to save big ammo."

"The other one?"

"He's the one who killed Gabriela. I told Holly to cut his throat and then cut off his nuts for attempted rape." Harold smiled. "Her idea but without the throat cut."

Sharyn winced a bit. "Ouch, but appropriate. Did she do it?"

"She did it the other way round, but didn't leave long between them. Sort of a compromise." Harold sighed. "I was tempted to do much, much worse."

He received a sister-hug. "We would all have helped tonight, and felt bad tomorrow. How is Holly now?"

"A lot better. Can you keep an eye on her please?" Harold wanted some-one watching for any reaction.

"I'll ask Liz."

"Liz has a big problem. She broke. When it came to it Liz can't carve up people, which makes her a nicer person than me but she doesn't believe it. I'll bet she's worried about letting us down." Harold sighed again, it was that sort of talk. "I'll ask Casper, though she'll be embarrassed with him as well. He saved her life."

"I'll do what I can." Sharyn wounded doubtful. Liz wasn't really the weepy confiding type.

"Explain that making nasty sharp stuff is actually more useful to us. We've got others to beat heads." Harold sniggered. "Oh, don't say much but watch how Curtis responds to Emmy nursing him."

"Oh? Really? Is she coming out of it already?"

"No, but he's sort of manoeuvring to be there when it happens." Harold explained the advice.

"Pretty damn good for a thick squaddie. Are you offering shoulders?"

"Firstly I'm worried about taking advantage. Secondly I wouldn't tell you in a million years." Harold went for his third sigh. "Where is Gabriela?"

"In number six where she lived. She's laid out in the front room, all cleaned up and made up and dressed pretty. A couple of her friends are sitting with her, and I'll bet Holly joins them once she's cleaned up. Possibly Emmy as well if she can get clear of her patient."

"Holly's got a present for the pyre. She brought the sling he needed after Gabriela hit him."

"Yes, despite Gabriela's anger, she went for his arm." Sharyn sighed this time. "She was too nice, deep inside. You wouldn't have hit his arm and he'd have never reached the knife."

"Training and bad experiences."

"Yes, so you've said. Want to talk?" Harold did, for a while, and explaining him losing his temper to someone else helped. So did admitting that killing was easier now which was worrying.

"As long as you don't do that stuff without emotion. Freddie used to say that was really bad."

"He was right." Harold explained dreams, and that he was going to see dead people when he slept, and Sharyn hugged him long and hard. Then they sat a while and chatted about Daisy, and Wills, and very little of importance. Peaceful and normal things. Harold dozed off for a while until he was shaken awake.

"I was going to wake you to go to bed, but now there's a phone call."

That woke Harold up properly. "Who?"

"Casper. He says he'd like you to go to the terraces at yon end, near the big car park. No need for a rifle, but you should take a look. Wear a jacket, because they've still got broken windows."

"Broken roofs as well, some of them. I can't take the little rifle anyway because Finn still has it I think." Harold put on a winter fleece. "I've no idea how long I'll be. Don't wait up."

"All right, see you in the morning."

*   *   *

The night really was chilly as Harold walked through the inhabited houses. The next buildings were habitable but empty so a sentry sat at the end of them to stop yobs starting a fire. One day, hopefully, there would be people to fill all the houses. There was a light on in the upstairs of one of the terraced houses and someone waved so Harold waved back. The curtains were then closed, cutting off most of the light.

Harold went up the stairs and into the back room, a little bit puzzled. Though he realised what the reason for privacy might be when he went in. Misplaced shame. "Hello Liz."

"Hello Harold." Liz looked embarrassed. "I needed to talk to you, sort of private. Do you fancy a beer?"

There were two open bottles on a little table and two chairs. Harold could take a hint that big. "I'd love one, though that's a bit cloak and dagger. Has prohibition arrived?"

"No, idiot." Liz sat as well. She was also wearing a thick jacket against the cold. "I couldn't face everyone so I was going to hide here tonight. Then I realised some people deserved an explanation."

Harold shrugged. "I don't need one since I can more or less guess. But if you prefer to say it I'm listening."

"I should have known." Liz gave a little, sad smile. "Macho bastards understand us little mice."

"No you idiot. It's us macho bastards that aren't normal, that should explain ourselves to normal people. It isn't normal to hit people with sharp or blunt implements, not in our society." Harold sipped at the beer and put the bottle down. "I can do it, but couldn't until about two years ago. Then I lost my temper and learned the knack."

Liz stared. "Seriously? You seem like some bloody death machine when you start."

"Angry, I'm angry. I'm a pussycat otherwise. It took a sodding great bomb and a horde of maniacs to finally annoy me." Harold actually managed a little smile, putting it like that.

"Then I suppose you upped and slaughtered them." Liz had a tiny smile now.

"Sort of. The bloke with me got a few but he was entitled. Stones really was, and hopefully still is, SAS." Harold smiled at those memories, of drinking rather than shooting.

"Cripes. We could do with him here."

"Stones would be out there with a knife in his teeth, looking for the rest of that lot." Harold laughed. "Actually he'd have a machine gun, shotgun, two pistols and a grenade. They're a real good bunch most of the time, but very, very bad if necessary. Most of them like a quiet drink and suchlike same as anyone else. You'd be disappointed."

"Relieved." Liz sighed. "I'm a mouse, remember."

"Not really Liz, you're normal. The world needs the normal people, more now than ever before, I think. Some of you need to survive or life becomes some computer game apocalypse with everyone running around killing everyone." Harold tipped the top of his beer bottle a bit towards her. "There's another reason you in particular must survive. You're our armourer. Who else would put sharp things on sticks for us?"

"Not very well. They pulled out the bolts and arrows. I need to put barbs on them." Liz sounded disgusted.

"See?" Harold smiled and raised his beer in salute. "You make them, then I'll stick them in someone."

"Don't miss, I'll charge you for wasted ones." Liz chinked her bottle against Harold's. "Truly? You don't mind? It's just than I pound metal and I'm probably the strongest woman here, physically. I shouldn't be relying on a slip of a lass like Holly to defend me."

"Ask Holly if she wants another head pounder, or someone passing her a fresh, sharp spear when hers breaks." Harold sipped again. "Holly might be a bit less manic now anyway. I think she got something out of her system."

"Good." Liz drained her bottle. "Right, I'm ready for my breakdown now. It's another reason I wanted you here. Your shoulder is just the right height." Liz's voice had a real catch in it so Harold stood and offered his arms with a smile. Liz pulled down his jacket zip and hers "because I'm not hugging a fleece" and her arms went round Harold under his jacket. He returned the hug, then Liz's head went onto the front of Harold's shoulder and the first sob arrived.

"Christ, Harold. This bloke was coming at me and he was going to kill me." Liz sobbed and shuddered. "I couldn't move. Then I just waved the bloody machete and looked away." Tears were flowing properly now and the words were being gasped out. "So I didn't see it coming, death." There was a prolonged period of sobbing. "When I looked you'd seen it, and Casper was just pulling that damn great chopper of his out of the bastard so he knew."

Liz produced another flood of tears. "Then you were both gone, hacking and stabbing like maniacs." Her sobs carried on for a while, gradually becoming less intense. Harold kept hugging, and stroking her back as Liz's breathing finally steadied. "You really are reassuring you know."

"Unfortunately I'm also a puny weakling."

"It's a problem. If I need a real man to hug me it's a puny one, or I can have a big one who's also a big girl. Story of my life." Liz was relaxing now, reviving a little of their usual banter even if she still sniffed a bit. "Though you are a warm puny weakling."

"Well it's not my fault you chose to meet in a fridge."

"I thought nobody would bother me here. Now it's a good reason to keep hugging. You give good hugs." Liz hugged a little tighter for a moment.

"One of my minor talents."

"Emmy said so."

"Emmy?"

"Yes. She said for a big rough acting bloke you hug real nice and you're absorbent. Soak up the sobbing." Liz giggled. "Sort of comforting and safe."

"Great, just what a bloke wants as his reputation. Safe."

"Oh, there's a few want to tempt you into danger." Before Harold could answer Liz swayed a little bit. "If we're going to hug, since we have music I want to dance. I haven't been to a dance for ages." The little MP3 player had been playing quietly in the background, sad songs and lonely ones. Liz raised her head and gave a bleary smile, then used a sleeve to scrub her face. "Sorry, they're a bit slow and weepy. They're my mood music."

Harold kept his arms round her and Liz sighed and put her head back on his shoulder and the arm back round him. They stood and sort of swayed a little bit while Harold stroked her back and Liz returned the patting and stroking a bit. She was singing along quietly to the music and the 'dancing' was really restful. The third record came on and Liz sang the opening very quietly. "I need a man with slow hands." Then she giggled. "I'm a slut you know."

"You must have an odd definition because as far as I know you've been celibate since I've known you." Harold was mystified.

"Ah, but that's because I can't commit and I'm particular. I'm a sooty iron-beating butterfly, flitting from one-nighter to one-nighter. I learned to weld and beat metal so I could go to trade fairs. To meet all those real, honest to God beeeg, muscly smiths." Liz laughed and hugged a little bit tighter for a moment. "I would drag one off to see my artwork, or nip over to inspect his anvil. Then kiss him goodbye in the morning and leave him smiling, and be all sorted until the next fair."

"Shouldn't this be a girly confession? To Casper for instance?" Harold liked Liz and didn't want her all awkward with him next time they met.

"Casper knows. We traded vice confessions." Liz snuggled in a bit. That was getting to be a bit of a problem for Harold since he hadn't been sorted out for a while either. He really did like Liz but if he started thinking of her that way, and caught her at a weak moment, then the friendship would be gone. Harold didn't have many friends outside the Army, and not that many in. Not enough to waste one on a night of sex.

"My problem is, I like you." Damn. He'd thought sex and Liz and now she was telling him she liked him. "As a friend. A lot." Liz sighed and wriggled in a bit, which wasn't helping friend thoughts. "So here I am, all down and feeling useless and you do that stroking thing." Harold stopped. "Don't you dare stop now, or I'll make an ornament for your bed." Harold carried on stroking and so did Liz. Though as always, the stroking was strictly north of the belt line. Crap, why had he thought that?

"After all the blood and such I need to feel really safe tonight, and right here I am. I've got the big bad soldier boy all wrapped round me. It's very reassuring." Harold was just going with the flow now, until Liz worked out whatever she was working on. "But now I'm considering finding out the answer to a question. You see, the girls have been wondering about that hugging and those gentle hands. They are wondering how that feels if the girl isn't crying."

Liz gave another little wriggle. "I can tell them because I stopped crying a bit back. It's really nice. Now I'm wondering what it would feel like if a hand strayed a bit." Her hand patted Harold's bottom gently as a hint.

"Liz?"

"Don't worry, I don't kiss and tell and I never hate them in the morning." Liz sniggered. "I told you, no commitment. Though should this turn into something tonight, promise you'll stay my friend? No awkward looks and silences."

"I was a bit worried about the same thing."

Liz lifted her head and there was a gleam of mischief in her eyes. "So you were considering being a bad boy?"

"Thinking of consequences if I did." Harold gave her a little smile. "I don't exactly get a lot of action either."

"But yours is choice because there are definitely volunteers waiting for a hint." Liz kissed him quickly and gently on the lips and put her head back on Harold's shoulder. "I was handling all this very well until this damn song came on." She sang it again, slowly. "I want a man with slow hands." Then sighed. "Tell you what, why don't you stay here and hold me tight tonight? I really don't want to be alone, Harold."

"It's a bit chilly." Which was a long way from no, Harold thought. His hand had also strayed just a little bit south. Liz's little wriggle was encouraging, not objection.

This time Liz's giggle was pure delight. "I was planning on staying tonight, so I made preparations. Which also works out well for a basic lesson in slut 1-0-1."

"How?" Harold was really getting interested now, but wary of more than gently stroking what he had confirmed was a firm, rounded ass.

"Get the bloke into a cold room. Point out that the bed is warm. Very warm since the electric blanket has been on full for a couple of hours." Liz somehow cuddled a bit closer. "So will you hold me close tonight, soldier boy? Keep me safe?" Her head came up and there was a definite twinkle in her eye. "I promise not to throw you out into the cold if those gentle hands stray a little bit in the night." This time her kiss was a bit firmer and Harold kissed back, just a bit.

Liz put her head back down and Harold chuckled. "Straying might be difficult to control. It all depends on your nightie."

This time when Liz lifted her head her eyes were dancing and she had a big smile. "What nightie?" Harold was still looking for a reply when Liz's next kiss removed all ambiguity.

*   *   *

"Good morning. I bet the girls don't know how warm you are on cold nights."

"Blimey, don't tell them that." Harold opened his eyes and hugged because, well, Liz was there and had proved to be very huggable.

"Mmm. It's a good job I'm a callous slut who won't need another fix for six months or so, otherwise I could get to like that in the morning." Liz did that damn wriggle to get an impossible bit closer. "I'm not telling the girls a thing. Casper will stay quiet because I know things about him. Drunken confessions."

"Casper knows?" Harold couldn't see the daft sod being able to resist making jokes.

"No. I realise it spoils my slut reputation but I planned on waking alone, crying into my pillow. This is much better." Liz smiled quietly. "I told him the truth. I wanted to clear things with you. I even brought your little rifle, and my crossbow and machete to turn them in." True because Harold could see them from here, against the wall where the door opened. Liz kissed him on the nose. "Then I got my hug, which I really did want. Then I really was feeling frightened and lonely, and you really are a hell of a bodyguard."

"So you just wanted a bodyguard for the night? If this is how you treat them you'll have a queue of volunteers." Harold grinned.

"No idiot!" Liz thumped him on the chest, which was a lot more personal like this. "Then I was enjoying the cuddle, and the stroking, and got to thinking. That's dangerous especially when it moves to wondering." Liz poked Harold in the ribs with a finger. "But now I know the answer so I'm immune. Don't expect that cuddle approach to work again."

Harold gave a huge mock-sigh. "So that's it? I'm to be thrown into the cold cruel world, all used up?"

"No. Well yes, but not until you're all used up. I said I leave them with a smile, but not why." Liz produced a wicked smile and that twinkle was back in her eyes.

Harold could take hints, sometimes. "Why were they smiling?" He had a big smile already so it wouldn't be hard to do. The smile was at least partly because Liz was still Liz, thumping his chest and teasing.

Liz slid over until she was lying on top then kissed Harold hard. "This is what you're aiming for, just so you've got the end result in mind." Liz slid slowly off to the side without losing any contact. "Now, can you remember that slow hand stuff without the music? I don't want to freeze my butt turning the player on."

"I could warm your butt up again? Or I can just work from memory. Hmm, now, how does it go?"

"Typical, the girl does all the work." Liz put her mouth against his ear and sang very softly. "I need a man with slow hands."

*　　　*　　　*

"Do you need breakfast, or did you get yours with cream? As in the cat with." Sharyn greeted Harold with a big smile.

"Breakfast would be lovely. What cream? Did we find a cow or a goat?" Harold returned the smile.

"Do I have to find out when some simpering girl swoons as you come by, or sniggers and you blush?" Sharyn was already putting coffee in a mug. Harold started cutting bread for toast. "Will I be tripping over strange undies in the bathroom?"

"Sister questions. Prompted by baseless assumptions on the morals of both your little brother and the fairer sex of this parish." Harold was sure there'd be no hints. The Liz who had pushed him out of the door was the same woman he'd been exchanging jibes with for months. She'd told Harold he must leave first. So that Liz could wipe the cream off her chin and then deal with the trauma of having weakened and bonked a wimp.

"Well it wasn't Casper, because he phoned to say something was taking longer than expected and not to worry. So what or who was it?"

Harold smiled sweetly. "Soldier boy business."

"I'll get a confession eventually. I'm a sister and we have ways." Sharyn was happy, she had a mystery and a way to tease Harold.

"Ha yes, I want to talk to you about that. Confession, the Gabriela one. I do not ever, ever, want to do that again."

Sharyn came over and treated Harold to a sister-hug. "That was one of the most terrible, and the most beautiful things I've ever witnessed. You did good, bro. I heard her last word." Sharyn's eyes filled. "And saw her smile. That single moment has made us a community, somehow. Possibly your community. Almost everyone was there at the last moments and complete atheists were saying amen." Sharyn sniffed and rubbed her eyes. "Then you sealed the deal by turning into that nasty soldier bastard and hunting them down."

"But never again, right? I'm not too comfortable with the leadership thing either. I'll kill the nasty bastards all right because someone has to. The other things send me crazy." Harold stuck the bread in the toaster. "I'm not religious, Sharyn."

"I know that, you fool. You'll never do it again for two reasons. I doubt anyone else will need that sort of release, and now we would know it was you so the same thing wouldn't work." Sharyn shook her head. "I'm not religious but that was special, a one-off, and really was holy in some way. Perhaps sort of pagan holy considering the heads and such, but it's helped us all somehow. Though you will have one duty now."

"What's that?"

"Light the pyre. Everyone was saying the same thing, they want a pyre because nobody out there will respect a graveyard. The nasty sods will piss on the markers. All those present want you to send them on the way so you'd better figure out some words." Sharyn had a little smile. "Not religious. Someone else will sort that and anything that needs saying about them. Just a few words of goodbye at the end and stick the torch in the wood."

"I'll ask Casper."

"I thought you might. Try Liz as well." Harold kept his face straight and smiled after he'd left.

Casper didn't even hesitate. He thumbed through a dog-eared book and then threw it over. "Here, page a hundred and twelve."

Harold read it. "That covers it. I was thinking of just saying 'Fare thee well, whoever' and sticking the flame in. How many will recognise this?"

"Nobody I know has ever heard of the poet, let alone the poem. Except me because my Mum was given it as a kid, or her Mum was. I've always wanted that poem read to anyone curious or morbid enough to attend. Just as my box lurches into the furnace." Casper laughed. "Now I want Fare thee well Casper as well. It has a nice touch."

"I'm going to run it past Liz as a sanity check."

"She's out the back, beating metal. Whatever you said worked. That and the soggy shoulder thing." Casper grinned. "It doesn't work for me. Blokes don't break down and want sympathy the same." He smirked. "Just make sure they're crying before you open your arms, or that the curtains are closed."

Harold laughed and headed round the back of the girl club, towards the sound of hammer on iron. "If I had a hammer." Liz was singing along and beating in time.

"Hi Liz."

"Hi wimp. Do you want to try this? Maybe build some real muscles?" Liz was smiling happily. "I'm working out the best way to make a crossbow bolt impossible to pull out without losing the limb."

"I want some advice."

Her smile widened. "That's new. A few insisted on making begging phone calls, but advice? I'll warn you I don't do critiques because I don't take notes at the time."

Harold smiled back. "No thanks. I'm trying to wipe the whole terrible experience from my memory." He waved the book. "Apparently I'm pyre-lighter in chief."

"Too true. I expect a real flourish if you do mine. Oh cripes, that's Casper's lost poet book. He's got strange tastes, except in men. What's he picked out?"

Harold showed her. "I was going to say fare thee well whoever as well."

"Better use their real name, not whoever. Ghosts can be damn vindictive according to the sort of films I saw. Say that at the beginning, then give this bit out to the audience as the smoke rises. Accompaniment for the snap crackle pop." Liz grinned. "Will we be having a barbeque?

"Gross bitch, but what can I expect from a woman who thinks sweat is classy?"

"Hmm. Yes, a bit over the top. I'm in a good mood today and can't think why. Now sod off before you spoil it." Harold walked away with a big smile. Liz was definitely on top form and still Liz. He was in a damn good mood himself, or was until he thought of Gabriela.

Harold really didn't want to see her laid out. He asked Sal at the door about the timing, and if there was anything special he had to say.

"No Harold. I'm a failed Catholic so I'll see to that part. That mish-mash I whispered was from when my Gran died and being forced into confession until I rebelled. What are you saying at the pyre?" Harold explained and showed her. "Nicely non-religious. Perfect. I'd rather you just used Gabriela Mary and no surname this time. She wasn't married to Abraham but wouldn't want that made clear. That's my opinion." Sal gave a little shrug.

"Good enough and thanks."

"No, thank you, Father." Sal gave a little smile. "Really thank you for that, and sorry for lumbering you. There aren't any female priests so I couldn't fake it."

"It's all right as long as that was a one off, and more to the point because it worked and helped Gabriela." Harold headed home to copy the wording and then learn it.

*　　　*　　　*

The weather was right, as was the timing. Both suited the sombre mood of the mourners as they gathered. Early evening, with ragged grey clouds scudding across the sky and a cold wind whipping light rain against everyone. Truly everyone because Rob was there on his stretcher, and the children were standing with Sharyn. Only fifty mourners, now Gabriela was gone. Ten men and women carried the board with Gabriela laid on top, and placed it on the huge pyre of mainly dry timber.

The pyre was carefully built and the centre, the part that Harold would light through a slot, was packed at the last minute. There was precious petrol in there so it caught and oil to help the fire take hold, as well as dry kindling. The main timbers were from roofs and the whole edifice was at least twice the width of the actual board and corpse. Some internet research said a truly fierce blaze was needed, so one was provided.

Several people spoke of Gabriela, of before the troubles, of her and

Abraham, and her grief, and some spoke religious passages. Then Sal handed Harold a length of timber with wadding around the head. A plastic bag was pulled off and an electric paint remover applied intensive heat. Moments later the torch was blazing fiercely. Harold had been warned that it was very flammable and wouldn't last long, so he walked straight out to the pyre and stood alongside, facing Gabriela.

"Fare thee well, Gabriela Mary." The torch went in and flame licked eagerly at the centre. Harold stepped back two paces and turned to everyone.

"Atoms reborn into grass
Fire and passion stilled at last
Clouds of happy what night be's
Scattered clouds of grief and tears
Fading memories, not quite true
One day, my friends, this will be you."

He gestured towards the pyre on the last words. Then Harold marched as steadily as possible back to join the rest. There were some assessing looks, maybe wondering if he'd been taking the mickey, but more were pressing Harold's hand or patting his back.

He joined Sharyn at the back, and lifted Daisy as asked, and watched the flames roar up. Flames and smoke from the wide sides that hid Gabriela for which Harold was really grateful. He had been assured that the construction was designed to do so, but still worried. He really didn't want to actually watch Gabriela's body burn.

After fifteen minutes Sal called out that if anyone wanted a warm drink or food, there was something waiting in number six, and the crowd gradually dissipated. Not all left. Sal and Holly stayed. Many went to number six, some gathered elsewhere or just went home. Harold went home and had an interesting evening trying to explain what had just happened to Daisy. He tried very hard to explain death and beliefs to a four year old without sticking preconceptions into her head.

Daisy seemed to conclude that Gabriela had gone to a special place that was made by everyone she loved. There she would meet them all again someday, because love is magic. Near enough for four years old and the special place Daisy described included bits from various fairy tales, including fairies and a unicorn. Harold assured Daisy that Daddy was in a place like that while Sharyn went in the kitchen to cry. Harold and Daisy tried to draw special places with lots of rainbows and flowers, until a red-eyed Sharyn came back in.

*   *   *

"But I wanted a real pumpkin like last year." Daisy was practicing her pout.

"There aren't any. Sorry. We could draw one?" Harold was flummoxed because Halloween hadn't been much of an event in Kuwait. Anything like that, or Christmas, triggered riots, bombs and showers of rockets.

"But I can't put a candle inside a drawing. We had one with biiiig eyes and gnashy teeth." Daisy was drawing them in the air as she spoke.

Sharyn gave a stage cough and when Harold looked up she was waving a big empty container and mouthing 'tin' at Harold. Harold looked at what she was holding. Probably the catering size for coffee or drinking chocolate. "It doesn't have to be a pumpkin. We could use something else with eyes and scary teeth?"

"What? Where? Can we do it now?" Daisy turned. "Oh, that's not scary."

"Just wait until we get the paper off. Then it'll be shiny and we'll make a shiny metal head monster face."

At least half the next thirty minutes consisted of Harold trying to avoid stabbing Daisy as she helped. "Come on, Uncle-Casper will have a candle and Aunty-Liz will put a handle on it for hanging up."

Uncle-Casper produced a pink candle when asked. He really did love clichés. Then Aunty-Liz set into making a handle. "I hope your Uncle is ready for trick or treat."

Harold stared while Liz continued bending wire. Then she glanced at him with a little smile. "Though he's going to have a problem deciding on trick or treat. Both are likely to be a bit more personal than the usual."

"I'm not allowed to do trick and treat until I'm older." Daisy was swinging the result of Liz's efforts back and forth. "This is definitely wicked." Wicked was a new word.

"Your Uncle's trick and treat will be as well." Liz smiled happily at Harold and stuck out her tongue. "It's probably best your mum doesn't answer the door." Then she shepherded Daisy out of her workshop without another word.

The lantern was hung at nightfall and duly admired, and then admired several times after tea. Harold walked Daisy down the road before bedtime so she could get the full effect in the dark. There was definitely music and laughing from the girl club, and two windows were opened to shout 'trick or treat' at him. Though it wasn't until the TV went off that Harold heard laughter outside.

"Trick or treat, trick or treat."

"That's for you. With all that giggling I'm certain that a sister shouldn't even see who's on the doorstep." Sharyn was grinning as she pushed Harold into the hallway. "I was warned. Please try not to wake the kids." Sharyn closed the door into the lounge.

"Well, which do you want?" Liz opened her coat. She had 'Trick or Treat' written on her white tee with black marker so that each breast was labelled, with 'or' written in her cleavage.

"Naughty. If I wasn't a gentleman, and didn't know how you despised me, I might be tempted." Harold sighed. "Then you'd break my arms and leave me to the rest."

"Ooh, yes please. Leave him armless and defenceless." Sal pouted. "I wanted that tee shirt." She sighed to make sure everyone could see where the words would have been. "Instead I had to settle for this."

"Which is?" Harold was eying the really tight top and tight, short skirt, with huge high heels. Sal was also wearing what looked like a homemade Viking hat with cardboard horns.

Sal turned to waggle her bottom. Which demonstrated the length of cloth with a point on it coming out from under her skirt. "Devil of course." She smirked. "The angels are coming later because they're shy."

The group broke up laughing. The devils included a few who were definitely non-devilish. Louise was usually quiet, but tonight she was wearing really tight jeans and a blouse that had been glittered. Trish was rarely seen outside of work parties. She was thin and frail but did her best at scavenging. Now she had on a red dress and more of the homemade horns. Both of the latter two looked decidedly embarrassed as did a couple of others.

"So what is the trick, because I've got a suspicion what treat is." Harold looked along the smiling faces. "Hugs, perhaps?"

"Oooh, a bit more than hug. We want to practice for the mistletoe." Harold wondered if Sal had been at the beer. They wanted kisses?

"What's the trick?" Harold was grinning as he asked. He really had been set up this time but in a bunch so it wouldn't get out of hand.

"We kiss you. Now you've got to decide which one will be nicest." Sal licked her lips very slowly. "Fair warning, soldier boy. I'm going to be kissing you either way." The rest dissolved in laughter again and Harold wondered how much beer had been imbibed.

"Oy you lot, get on with it." That was shouted from the girl club.

"Me first, just to get him warmed up. Not only that but he can't resist. Come here wimp." Liz hugged and so did Harold. Then she planted a very firm and slightly beery kiss. Liz put her head forward to whisper in Harold's ear. "That was trick, so if you don't find a blacksmith in time, I'll want the treat." Then she turned and high-fived the rest. "OK girls, he's all warmed up."

Trick and treat got a bit confused since both meant hugs and a kiss. Louise kissed Harold very lightly and hugged quickly and chastely. Trish hugged hard but kissed Harold on the cheek. There was a bewildering variety working up to Sal, who waited to be last. "This has got to be memorable so you remember after the angels have been." She licked her lips thoroughly while the rest gave her hints on making it memorable.

Harold was a bit worried because Sal was decidedly unsteady on her heels, and he thought that might be drink. He was a lot more sure when Sal's lips swallowed his and her arms wrapped around his head. The cheering from behind was egging her on. As he had with the others Harold started by kissing back. Then he tried to check a bit because Sal was going for a full lip lock.

She had plastered herself up his front and then her tongue started. Harold might have welcomed that if she was sober, but not on the doorstep with witnesses. When he pulled away, or when Sal finally let him, both were breathing heavily. Harold smiled. "That should do it." Sal did the high fives and then tottered. Two of them caught her and Harold raised an eyebrow at Liz in a question. Liz grinned and made the sign for lifting a bottle to her lips, then helped the rest steer Sal home.

Harold went back in, bemused. Had Sal got carried away because she'd had too much drink, or had a drink to get over her nerves and get serious. In Liz's words, cripes. "At least that's not a smug smile. That might have meant losing my tea." Harold's head came up to meet Sharyn's smile.

"It was Sal. She, well, I'm not sure. Cripes, this is awkward."

Sharyn laughed. "Cripes? You've been around Liz too much. What did Sal do?" Harold stared at her and Sharyn struck her forehead with the heel of her hand. "Silly me. Why would I want to know that? Yeuk."

"Not yeuk, but maybe beer."

Sharyn laughed. "Oh, that sort of cripes. I'm sure you'll find out on Guy Fawkes."

"Why?"

"Because the silly sods are dressing up again then and want a bonfire and dance, with potatoes in the embers and toffee apples." Sharyn smiled. "Or dried apple and banana slices dipped in melted toffee the last I heard."

"Sal won't be dancing in those heels."

"She might if she's sober. You'd be surprised what a girl can manage in high heels. Oh, yeuk." Sharyn mimed putting her fingers down her throat. "I've just realised why she's worn them. Were Emmy, Berry, Liz and Holly there?"

"Only Liz, the angels are coming later. Oh." Those four were tall enough to get lip contact with Harold without heels or him bending.

"Emmy, Berry and Holly are angels and are coming later? Please, grim reaper, take me now?" Sharyn waved at the settee. "You'd better rest up. So what was Liz dressed as?"

"A bloody tease of course."

"I'm not asking about any more." Sharyn turned up the music on her MP4 player. "I could hear some of that, and I really don't want to hear the angels."

The angels left it all of five minutes. They knocked and started singing trick and treat, not angelically. When he opened the door, Harold found that most angels wore white but the amount varied. He was really startled to see Celine there, in a long white dress. A real evening style one down to the ground. Celine gave him a little smile. "All the rest came, so." She gave a little shrug.

Harold was very, very careful to barely hug Celine, and even then she tensed a little. Celine had been raped on her way home from work a month before Harold arrived in the flats. The man put a hand over her mouth, a knife to her throat, and pulled Celine into the ruined children's playground within sight of her flat. Now Celine pecked Harold gently on the cheek and then stepped back with two tiny spots of colour in her cheeks.

Alicia couldn't manage a real smile. She had become very withdrawn so seeing her here in a flared white dress and a halo was a real surprise. Her kiss was quick but on his lips and her hug was brief. Berry had a big smile of course. She was dressed in white jeans and a long sleeved white blouse. Berry produced something close to a bear hug but her kiss was quick.

Emmy grinned and did a twirl. She was wearing a short white pleated skirt and a white tank top, and the effect was stunning against her dark skin. Emmy definitely went for a proper kiss without getting really serious, and her hug was firm and held on a bit. "No soggy this time."

That left Holly who looked startled and then apprehensive that she was last. Holly was wearing pink, a tutu but without tights. She had a pink tee on top with Fallen Angel across the front. Harold had already noticed that the regular exercise was toning up the girl club. Now he realised that either

Holly had been covering up before, or really had got in shape recently. Oops, he'd looked a bit long, maybe. Harold opened his arms. "Last but not least."

That meant Holly actually smiled though she looked startled again when Emmy said "Now live up to it. Honour of the girl's club." Then pushed her friend forward. Harold was very gentle given Holly's apprehension, but both her hug and kiss were decidedly firm. The kiss wasn't sexy, or rather it became sexier because the soft, warm contact kept going.

Harold had started to pull away when the pressure lessened, but Holly must have been taking a breath. Her lips came back firmer and Holly tightened her hug. When they parted she wouldn't meet Harold's eyes, and then went scarlet. That was because all the rest had turned away and were covering their eyes. When they turned back laughing, they all hugged her.

They'd set Holly up. In that case. "You missed that, Emmy. But for the record, the honour of the girl club is intact." Holly high-fived all round, and started into pretending to beat them all, and the laughing group left. Now Harold really was confused because Holly didn't show any interest in blokes normally. She was still angry about Brodie dying, and it wasn't booze because he didn't taste any.

He wasn't less confused when Matthew phoned to ask if Harold had been trick or treated. He'd had four women on his doorstep asking if he preferred devils or angels. The following day all the younger men had been visited by a group, and all were trying not to talk about who or what the women wanted. Though they were all definitely intrigued about what Bonfire Night would bring.

The general mood as everyone, male or female, set into their tasks was definitely happy. Casper complained about the lack of male devils or angels. Harold grinned at him. "It was a superb exercise in morale boosting. The MOD should employ that lot to go round the Army units."

"Yes, but I doubt they'd put as much into it. Just so you sleep at night, Sal had a drink for her nerves and got a bit carried away." Casper smiled at Harold's face.

Harold had to ask. "What about Holly?"

"Holly?" Casper was definitely curious. "They all turned away because it was planned. She'd been a bag of nerves about hugging you in that getup." Casper smiled. "So what about Holly?"

"Just that, the turning away." Harold shrugged. "She went scarlet." He smiled. "That getup, as you called it, was definitely eye catching."

"She only put the tee on at the last minute, when someone said the cold air would make her stand out a bit. That would have been even more eye catching." Casper gave a huge mock sigh. "So when do I get to trick or treat someone?"

"When I can kidnap a lumberjack?"

"Cripes, yes, Liz really wants her trees for charcoal. Aargh, she's got me started with cripes." Casper rolled his eyes.

"Me too. Liz can have trees when we've got all the food we can find, and the wall is built." Harold yawned. "Now I need some beauty sleep because I'm off out tonight after a bakery. We need the flour and any yeast, because Berry's Beer yeast is the wrong type."

"Are you still finding enough to warrant the risk?"

"Yes, especially since only six of us go. Though I'm having a night off soon to ride herd on Daisy at the bonfire."

"Cripes, Daisy and a Guy Fawkes bonfire. That'll be fun."

"Definitely cripes."

*   *   *

"That is what, exactly?" Harold eyed the handful of what looked like rags. "Stuffing for the Guy?"

"This is your fancy dress, since you blokes didn't dress up at Halloween." Sharyn grinned. "The girl club produced the Guy for the fire. This is a Rambo costume."

"Rambo? Come on, sis, you know I'm not that keen on the blood and guts stuff. This just encourages the rest to think of me like that."

Sharyn burst out laughing. "I was too busy producing a Womble for Daisy. They really are recycling old kids programmes now." She waved the rags. "These were delivered, so hard luck. Now get them on."

Getting them on was both difficult and easy. Easy because it consisted of tee shirt, jeans cut off at the knee, and a stocking for round Harold's head to represent Rambo's bit of rag. Difficult because he had to get feet and arms in it while avoiding all the holes and slashes. Harold's Army boots and a huge cardboard knife finished the look, by which time Daisy was bouncing around shouting "Guy, guy" so it was time to go.

Keeping track of Daisy round a bonfire was a cripes job that took two Uncles and her mum. She was entranced by the Guy, a creditable attempt at a Wild West cowboy with a bandana over his face and big cardboard six-guns. Luckily racing around and trying all the various attempts at toffee this and candied that wore Daisy out. An hour later Harold carried her home and

Womble was put to bed with Karen as babysitter. Stewart must have been there as a Karen-sitter.

The dancing afterwards wasn't quite cripes, since both Sal and Holly were careful not to get into a clinch. Or not a proper one, though all of the girl club except Celine, Alicia and Trish claimed a slow Harold dance. Trish was an honorary member as she lived alone. All the men claimed slow dances here and there and Jon and Billy probably managed to dance with the entire girl club. For the only two eligible but unattached teenaged lads that was a real triumph.

The rest of the men had also made an attempt at a fancy dress so Harold didn't feel too conspicuous. Casper went for fairy lumberjack. Harold's cardboard knife didn't outlast the highland fling, reel or whatever it was. Then some halos and horns and Casper's wings were shed during the attempts at a Russian kicking dance and a can-can. Liz sniggered when she claimed her slow dance.

"Worked out who volunteered this?" She tugged the stocking round Harold's head.

"Cripes. It's actually someone's stocking? I thought it was, well, a new one?" Harold tried to decide if it was or not, and tried to remember if it looked used. Though he wasn't sure how to tell.

"Not a chance. Maybe we all wore it for a few minutes, just so there weren't any fights?" Liz tugged it again. "You'll have to look properly afterwards, to see what sizes it might fit."

Harold was still wondering if Liz was winding him up when the bonfire burned down and everyone collected their baked potatoes from the ashes and went home. He wondered hard enough to not have bad dreams.

The following day everyone went back to serious scrounging and building, though the whole of the enclave seemed more settled. Halloween, Guy Fawkes and dancing were normal, even without fireworks.

Chapter 12:
Armageddon

Casper inspected the stretch of wall between two houses. "It's not very strong without any mortar, even two bricks wide. A couple of kicks and it'll fall down."

"So don't kick it." Harold looked out over the stretch of cleared land to the first ruined houses. "That bastard came over the rubble line too easily. If it had been a wall he might not have tried."

"You can't bring Gabriela back, Harold. This way we've lost these back gardens." Casper kicked moodily at the house wall. "I sweated buckets digging some of that."

"We'll still plant crops, Casper. This way we've got twice as much open ground to shoot the bastards because that side of the gap, the ruins, is the boundary. Anyone who steps out of there is a target." Harold waved at the houses either side. "Once we've boarded the windows facing that way and maybe bricked them, we'll be a lot safer."

"I know." Casper looked along the wide, clear stretch. "Though this took a lot longer than expected without machinery. Nearly two months."

"Not non-stop, because we had both Halloween and Guy Fawkes." Harold smiled in recollection, because he still didn't know quite how much of the Halloween kissing was real. Nor whose stocking that might have been. "We also brought in a lot of food and also all those fridges and freezers. On top of that my little group have brought in a lot of vital supplies. I certainly feel a lot happier about winter now."

"So does everyone else, because they might have bitched a bit but everyone has helped. Even most of the wounded."

"According to Patricia we were insanely lucky with that. The bullet that hit Curtis must have hit a brick or something first because it barely broke the skin. Emmy says that Curtis is wondering if he actually broke his leg falling down." Harold crossed his fingers for luck before continuing. "Finn's left arm might never be right again but so far he can still use the fingers of that hand. Patricia says he should be clear of any risk of infection now. Straight through the meat and not deep is a lot better than through a big blood vessel or bone." Harold had seen that sort of hit.

"Matthew must have been living right as well because the hit wasn't his shoulder, just the big muscle above his collar bone. Ha! Just! A fraction of an inch down and it would have smashed his collarbone and Patricia says she can't deal with that sort of injury." Harold sighed. "Not even from handguns."

"Yeah, I saw what that big rifle of yours did. Scary. Maybe Gabriela's guiding angel was one of the swords and hellfire lot and gave us a hand?" Casper sniggered. "Or maybe one of the old gods of lust considering how Curtis is luring Emmy into his greenhouse with that limp of his."

Harold thought that if any god was involved it was one of old ones, the nasty interfering sorts the Romans, Greeks, Norse and Celts had. "However it worked, I was really pleased to see everyone out and about so soon."

Casper grinned. "Well not Rob and his nurse, though maybe he's ashamed of the wound."

"Maybe he's really enjoying the nursing. Anyway, being shot through the love handles is a cause for celebration, not shame. If Rob had been a lean mean type that could have hit something vital or at the least he might have got blood poisoning. Though he still reckoned the cleaning hurt like hell." Now Harold smiled.

"I can only sympathise. If I'm wounded just finish me off. Don't let Patricia clean the wound." Casper gave a mock shudder.

"She apologised profusely, but that was the only way to wash through and make sure there was no crap in there. Patricia just hasn't got the facilities and she did keep the wounds, all of them, clean." Harold thumped Casper gently on the bicep. "So hard luck, wimp, you get doctored."

"Fairy, not wimp. You're the wimp. Liz says so. That talk of yours really did wonders. She's fitting spikes to a length of steel to put across the entrance at the moment. In case someone tries to ram the improved barricade aside. That or she's started an artwork project." Casper looked down the line of houses now connected by lengths of impromptu wall. "Someone could ram a car through here."

"Not a car, because the rubble would stop them. Maybe with a van." Harold looked out across the gap. "If we manage to tear the houses down, we can lay a low heap of brick about twenty yards out."

"I thought we'd just removed one heap because it was a bad idea?"

"We used that to build the wall. Now we want a wide low one we can shoot right over even with the crossbows. One that will strand a van like a giant sleeping policeman would." Harold pointed to the entrance. "We need those garages down next, so there's a gap from the main road to our first houses."

"Hellfire Harold. How bad do you think it will get?"

"Maybe like the continent? You saw the news. Most of the major population centres in the UK are fenced in now, but over the channel is worse." Harold looked back at the houses and people behind him, and the bypass looming over the lot. "You saw the TV, I assume. The last pictures out of Lille showed it burning. Skinheads from Germany are invading France to help their brethren, and several immigrant areas in Paris have declared a Holy War. Plus half of Europe are starving and heading for the only country that grows its own food, France."

Casper grimaced. "Yeah, the TV said that and about the Navy making sure none of them get across the Channel or North Sea. The religious war thing and the colour wars will be ugly. We've got areas of Britain where there's a lot of immigrants so what do you reckon?"

"There's not so many here, or anywhere outside London." Harold fell silent because London was bad news. The Army had blown up the junctions on the M25 and literally walled London in.

"Bradford or Leicester could be bad." Casper grinned. "For the skinheads and general race hate assholes. I reckon they'd be really outnumbered in Leicester and some of those Sikhs and suchlike are feisty buggers."

"Maybe the minorities will make enclaves? A lot tend to live in communities anyway. Sort of local majority to offset being a minority?" Harold smiled. "You're a minority."

"What, an Orchard Close of fruits? They'd die out in a generation." Casper chuckled. "Though they might not. A lesbian friend of mine had a kid without a father. She found a donor, then used a turkey baster to get her girlfriend pregnant during a night of passion."

"They'd never find enough basters."

"You might on your travels. Are you going out again tonight? I still don't like the idea for two reasons. First because you go at night and second because only six of you go. Though you do bring some good stuff back."

"Essentials. I've found lots of bits needed for loading bullets, for instance, even if a lot of the powder has gone, and a good bit of dowelling for arrows. Last run we found needles and gut for Patricia to sew up wounds. Patricia doesn't care if those and the instruments were from a vet's. She's going through the drugs to see what's useable on humans."

Harold tone darkened. "So far we've found enough medication to keep those like Karen and Mary, Finn's Mum, more or less all right. That's getting harder and already some people are deteriorating. Patricia sorts through what we find for equivalents but she's not a doctor."

"I already know the answer to the second objection. You won't take more people because you won't weaken this place again." Casper had a little smile. "So are you going tonight?"

"No, because I have been told very firmly that it's Daisy's birthday and there will be Uncle-Harold story and also Uncle-Casper story tonight. Or else. Kids are damn scary when they're determined. Even at four – oops, five." Harold grinned. "I found a dozen colouring books and some crayons a couple of trips ago so the present is sorted."

"I have donated candles for the cake, from my personal stocks. Pink ones. Put candles for cake on the essentials list because others will want them." Casper grinned. "Pink for me because I have a reputation to uphold."

"We can render them from tallow? That's how they used to be made. I wonder how bad this will get?" Harold almost swore in disgust at the current state of things and remembered that he didn't do that now. Manners were important in a small community and swearing was dying out here. "It's awful out there now."

"The local radio reckons it's got bad enough for civil action." Casper nodded at Harold's look. "Yeah, shooting on the streets and the people are going for civil action. There's talk on the local radio of a mass march on the city centre to demand food supplies and payment of redundancies and unemployment pay. Toby's got his CB working and there's the same messages on there, and some are from places like Manchester and Liverpool."

"Christ, good luck with getting here from there."

"The local radios from nearby cities are talking of the same idea, a day of action in all the cities, not travelling. If there's enough people marching the assumption is that yobs will leave them alone. Most of the ordinary folk who'll march probably already live in some sort of protected estate or a similar arrangement, so they'll have baseball bats and suchlike." Casper looked up at the bypass. "If the government sent in the Army they could clean the place up by running over the worst enclaves. The ones where the real assholes are concentrated."

"Finding them would be easy because the news keeps putting pictures of the worst ones on the TV. If there's enough Army left to actually deal with them." That depressed Harold, since he knew the government had deliberately run down the Army. "Well, now this is done, I'm off to help with the orchard."

"Be careful. Part of it is the back garden to the girl's club and several are wondering out loud." Casper had a big grin now. "About just what sort of hugs you give when there are no witnesses."

"Don't you start. I'd dearly love to know where the speculation started. I've already given two hugs where there was a bit too much happy afterwards for how sad they were supposed to be. Sal looked bloody triumphant." Harold frowned. "She was sober this time as well."

"They're taking bets on who gets a hug next." Casper's eyes widened. "Ooh gossip, is it only hugging?"

"What do you think? I've got a nosy sister remember? Now stop winding me up." Harold grinned. "Or tell me what the betting is and we'll clean up. You place the bets and I'll hug."

"That's prostitution, being paid for it." Casper laughed. "Or I think so, even if you're only hugging."

"Is it prostitution if I enjoy it?"

"That just makes it a vocation instead of a profession." Casper smirked. "I'll listen out for the odds. Now go on, get off to the orchard. At least Emmy is occupied now she's got her patient. She'll be all fixed up for hugs now."

"I'll remember that." Harold headed off with a smile because it really was funny. He wouldn't ever bet on doing so but Harold had now ended up hugging four more of the girl club, all in tears when they 'found' him.

Though none wanted hugging in the prospective orchard with all the rest around, it seemed. Harold spent several hours digging and planting, and headed home for the party.

A party attended by a dozen adults as well as Hazel, Toby, Veronica and Alfie. The guest of honour loved her home-made cards and the musical chairs. Followed by jelly, some precious, rare ice cream, and sponge cake with butter icing and five pink candles. Butter and sugar were both getting scarce, and all the real milk was gone so the milkshake tasted a bit odd. Daisy didn't care. It was a party, her party.

After her two stories Daisy finally settled down, or at least she went to bed with a colouring book. Hazel, Toby and Alfie went off with Betty to play computer games which was their version of a party, while Veronica went home. Harold, Sharyn, Casper, Liz and Sal settled down to watch TV and relax. Or as much as possible once the news came on. "That's Leeds. I recognise Leeds castle. Oh crap."

*　　　*　　　*

"What the hell happened?" Casper had asked but they were all wondering the same thing. On the screen a mass of screaming marchers were running right over a line of police despite the gunfire. Men and women went down and then the police were buried in a mob. Moments later the captured police weapons were turned on the reserve lines behind, and the rest of the police broke and ran.

Liz was incredulous "They're just wrecking the place." A section of the mob had charged across the approach and into the castle, and flames leapt from the windows. "The council have their offices there, so how can that happen?"

"It's a rebellion, an uprising. Worse than rebellion, they're not trying to take over. The bloody lunatics are burning the whole city." Sharyn's voice was quiet and horrified because the camera had pulled back to give a wider view. Lines and swathes of fire were moving across Leeds, clearly seen in the darkness. Here and there the lines stopped and spread out, engulfing a whole area.

"It's Armageddon." Harold was aghast. "This doesn't happen in England. People march and protest and yes, these days they riot. But not like this. Yobs and hopheads shoot at police. The coppers aren't overrun by a mass of ordinary looking men and women with guns and pikes. Christ, they really have got medieval pikes." From the castle no doubt but the long sharp blades and vicious points just looked all wrong even in England.

"It's Lille, and Paris, and Toulouse, and Antwerp. Those cities we saw burn, when the ethnic and religious violence broke out." Sal frowned. "That isn't ethnic violence in Leeds. There's all colours in that crowd."

"Maybe that comes after, when the survivors try to live in the remains." On-screen a retail park was a blazing chaos of burning vehicles and superstores and a swarm of running figures. "See, they've started already." Harold was right. Among those looting or burning, two groups had clashed and people were sprawled on the floor as they parted.

Casper was pale. "We've got a march tomorrow, according to the local radio. The day of action. Surely they'll call it off after this." Onscreen a fireball rose, and a caption came up.

"Analysis suggests a gas mains had been broken and ignited. The gas pipeline into the city is being turned off as a safety measure."

"Gods, this is recorded. It must have been happening while the radios were talking about the marches. That means they'll go ahead." Sal's voice was hushed.

"The police will meet them with barricades and blocked streets and weapons locked and loaded. It'll be a massacre." Sharyn shuddered. "Then what happens to the places the marchers come from? When darkness falls and there aren't enough people to man the barricades?"

"The smarter ones will run for the boundaries. They'll try to slip through the fences, or maybe storm an exit." Harold swallowed hard. "Tomorrow, first thing, we seal the entrance properly. Forget the moving road block, the vehicles. We take the metal doors off the garages out there and build a wall."

"Then what? We can't just hide or we'll run out of food." Liz glanced at Harold. "I hope you aren't going into something like that with six people?"

"No, we do actually sit tight. That mob can't keep that up for long. They'll run out of food as well as being just plain knackered, and some will have families to get back to. It'll break up come morning though Leeds will be a hellhole afterwards." Harold tried to look reassuring. "Remember, we've got a wall, and the Army just behind us." They all sat in silence for a while, watching a city burn until the TV closed down with the usual platitudes.

"Remember, keep calm. The government are working on a solution to the oil crisis. Civil unrest will only disrupt those efforts."

For a moment Harold thought Liz was going to spit. "A line of soldiers to pen us in until we're eating our young, more like." She gave a sigh, then a big grin. "After that I need a hug, Harold."

Sal actually opened her mouth to say something, and then shut up. Casper grinned as Liz wrapped her arms round Harold and put her head on his shoulder. Harold hugged her, it wasn't exactly an unpleasant task.

"That's better." Liz turned to the door. "Come on then, I want to get home while I'm feeling better."

"No chance, my turn." Sal stepped forward and opened her arms with a big grin. As he hugged her Harold could see Casper trying not to burst out laughing. Worse, Sharyn's eyes were alight with glee. She was going to have a lot of fun with this.

"Lovely, just as advertised. I'm nothing like as upset now." Sal and Liz high-fived each other.

Casper held out his arms with a big grin. Harold shook his head. "Piss off. Go and hug a tree now we've got some."

"Curtis will tell you if any of them have a preference. Apparently some plants have a male and female." Casper took a mock swipe at Liz and the three left, laughing.

"Right little brother. I'm trying to fight back the nausea at that exhibition, but I'm also curious. Just as advertised?" Sharyn had her hands on her hips, but the frown was losing out to the glee. "Exactly how many innocent young women have you been molesting like that?"

"Innocent? Those two?" Harold settled for trying to divert her though Sharyn would be asking elsewhere now. If she found out what the actual game was, Harold would like to know himself.

*　　　*　　　*

Laughs were in short supply the following day. Everyone turned out to barricade the entrance to the little community, so that anyone heading for the exit wouldn't be tempted to divert and overrun their cluster of houses. "Get the welder Liz. Make sure the front layer can't be pulled apart." The metal garage doors were nailed to timbers, which were jammed firmly into the three wrecked vehicles towed from the main road.

"That serious? How do we get in and out with our vehicles afterwards, Harold?"

"We don't, not until things get better. Seriously better." Harold looked towards the bypass. "We'll put the two pickups and both vans along the boundary on that side. Just this side of the exclusion zone. I'll get the hammer mob to bash out the back of a garage and drive them through."

"What about the minibus?"

"Yes, good idea, just in case we do have to go somewhere mob-handed." Harold sniggered. "Peacefully." One of the girl club had carefully painted 'we come in peace' on the sides and front of the minibus. The effect of that and the flowers and big cupid bow lips here and there was spoiled by the rear. There, 'we shoot to kill' was just as carefully painted on the back doors with a selection of spears and crossbows. All with pretty bows on them.

"Make sure the rear is towards the road, so any passers-by get the message." Liz wasn't joking at all. The comfort hug hadn't lasted long and many of the girl club and most of the residents had been discussing Leeds deep into the night.

"Will do. Try to use as few welding rods as possible, because there aren't many out there."

Liz looked thoughtful. "Will do, but something else came up last night. If the gas goes off but the electricity keeps going, we can manage. But that will screw up heating metal. Once this is over, we want every tree out there," she waved at the ruins, "to turn into charcoal."

"Remind me afterwards."

"Harold, Harold." Hazel was running down the road, waving.

"I'm having my name changed to that, Harold-Harold." Liz laughed at him and left to get her welder.

"Harold, the radio and TV died. All of them. There was just a buzzing noise. Then the TV and radio came back but a bit crackly. Only the BBC. Nothing else." Harold stared, trying to get his head round that while Hazel hopped from one foot to the other. "Sharyn wanted you to know straight away. What does it mean, Harold?"

"Why didn't you just phone?" Harold pointed to the house on his left. "Number two is right here."

"Oh." Hazel stopped hopping about for a moment. "I forgot. The phone doesn't work. That was part of the message. Sorry. What's happening, Harold?" She was on the move again, too nervous to stand still.

"It's just to stop the bad people in the city centre from getting organised. Don't worry about it Hazel. The radio and phone will probably start up again once the marching is over." Harold had a terrible suspicion they wouldn't. "Will you collect Toby, Veronica and Alfie as runners, and go to every house please. Ask them to turn off their gas, just in case the pipes get broken somewhere?"

"What about the heat, Harold? Some of the houses use gas heating?"

"Just get it all turned off, Hazel. Ask Harry to go round and check the main tap is off in every house, even the empty ones." Harold smiled at her, because Hazel really looked worried. "Just to be safe. We can use extra blankets for a day or so, and electric blow heaters."

"I've got an electric blanket now. Liz gave me one for emergencies."

Harold had no trouble with a smile now. "There you are, all fixed up. Now off you go and spread the word. If you can do that for me, I can keep working on this. Thanks Hazel."

She gave a big smile and was off like a whippet, shouting for Toby. Harold had a moment to think it through, when it didn't matter how grim he looked. The thoughts weren't any better the second time round. Without local radio coming from nearby cities, this one was isolated except for government information. Without local radio within the city, or phones, each enclave was isolated. Without gas, petrol or oil, the electricity supply was a knife at everyone's throat.

Harold straightened his shoulders and put on a not-so-grim face, and got stuck into making this little enclave as isolated as possible. He spread the news as he worked. At lunch time Hazel, Veronica, Alfie and Toby became official runners. One would be at the gate at all times, and one near Harold, to pass any messages.

"I'll still be there if needed, with my rifle."

"I know Toby, and I'll be pleased that you are. It's just that you four run fastest." They were also least capable of the heavy lifting and heaving bricks, though Harold would never tell them that. Though Alfie was packing on muscle now. He was pumping iron, or using gym equipment anyway, to build up his shoulder muscles. Muscle was going on elsewhere at the same time and Liz complained that it was totally unfair. Alfie was too young so even if he kept going for a couple of years and gained the right body, she'd still feel like a child-snatcher.

It turned out that Alfie was the right size for the compound bow, but needed more shoulder muscle to pull it. Nobody had any intention of trying to alter the way the bow was set up. The bits of information gleaned from the internet insisted that resetting the bow needed specialist equipment. Three people were the right size, or rather had the right pull according to the internet, and Sal had no intention of bulking up like that. Bernie couldn't, he just became more wiry and lean with exercise though he was getting fitter.

Harold thought of things like that rather than what might be happening in the city centre because if there was a march, it was happening now. They could all hear popping noises from towards the centre, but it was hard to tell just how bad that was getting. Mid-afternoon several helicopters gathered over there, and two thick plumes of smoke rose into the sky. Soon afterwards, by common consent, they all went home to look at the TV. By then Harold was only throwing extra bricks on the approach road to impede vehicles. They'd done what they could to make the place safe.

*   *   *

"This is a recording Harold. If you watch they'll skip forward, and there's lines and circles drawn to highlight things that happened." Sharyn came through and brought the smell of chips and warm bread with her. "Here you are, quick and nasty so I can watch."

"Thanks sis. Quick and scrumptious, chip butties." Salt and sauce landed on the table next to Harold. They sat side by side watching and munching.

"There, see." On the screen a circle appeared around a group of men climbing out of vehicles and disappearing into the crowd. Harold thought two of them were carrying what looked a lot like long weapons. The commentary switched from describing the complaints being presented to the Mayor.

"The group just highlighted were not noticed at the time. With such a large crowd it proved impossible for the forces of law and order to be properly vigilant."

"The forces of law and order are too busy messing themselves." What was probably every policeman left in the city was lined up between the crowd and the Mayor and officials. Behind the first rows with riot shields and batons, the rest were clearly carrying firearms. A close-up highlighted that.

"Be fair, Harold. I have never seen such a big crowd." Sharyn was right, there had to be tens of thousands of protesters spilling over the roads and the big open market area and car parks. There was no sign of the market or any cars now, just a seething mass of humanity that spilled into the surrounding streets. More were still pouring out of the underpasses, and gathering on the raised roadways nearby.

"Nor have I. I really hope they don't start a riot because there aren't enough police. What idiot told the Mayor to meet them there instead of in front of his offices?" The car park in front of the Mayor's office wouldn't have held a tenth of this crowd. The picture onscreen highlighted another large group of men arriving and disappearing into the crowd.

"The reduction in broadcasting facilities and the temporary closure of the telephone system was instigated in response to these armed groups. It was hoped that such actions would prevent any co-ordinated attempts to harm the Mayor."

"Oh crap. This is recorded, so that statement is preparing us." The picture zoomed in to show a group carrying a big banner with rough lettering. 'Give our children their milk' in big red letters. Behind the women with the banner three hard-faced men were passing, carrying shotguns. "The lunatics are going to start a Leeds."

Sharyn looked at Harold aghast. "All those men and women won't allow it, surely. Those women won't charge the police to get milk, for God's sake."

"No, but if the ones with guns shoot at the Mayor, one of two things will happen. The best result is that someone sensible will order the withdrawal, and the police will get the hell out with the Mayor. Then sharpshooters will start on the gunmen." Harold sighed. "I've seen the other result as well. Someone in charge shouts 'shoot them, you idiots' and one of the policemen pulls the trigger. Then the rest of the police will do the same. Then the only way for the crowd to survive is to trample the police."

"Where?" Sharyn's voice was soft. "Where did you see that, Harold?"

"Not quite that. In Calais there was a crowd, and soldiers, and then either us or the French killed the women and kids."

Sharyn stared, aghast. "What? How?"

"Planes came in low and dropped napalm on the refugee camp. We might still have stopped them with bayonets because reinforcements were coming." Harold grimaced. "Then an officer panicked, and someone opened fire." Harold stopped, and Sharyn took his hand in one of hers and patted then stroked it with the other. Harold gave a short laugh. "It's been a while since you did that, sis."

"It's been a while since it was needed. So we sit and wait to see which way this goes." There was a short silence. "We were shown pictures of Calais, on the TV. There were close-ups of weapons on the bodies and dead soldiers but nothing about a camp burning."

"Whatever we see here might be a bit that way. After all, we can't really check it can we?" Harold really had that bad feeling now. He'd never mentioned Calais because Harold preferred to never think about it again. Now the same thing might be happening in England. "I'm really worried, sis. Make sure the kids get onto the exclusion zone if necessary?"

"Hazel and Veronica will be here with Betty, and Finn's mum in her wheelchair, and Harry at least will be here to take the kids. I'll collect as many of the frail as I can persuade, but I'll never get Toby and Alfie to come." Sharyn sighed. "They both want to be you."

"No, they want to be what they think I am, some shiny superhero. Toby has already claimed his place at the gate, with that rifle. I'll tell him to run if they get over the barricades but I'm not sure he will." Harold patted Sharyn's hand this time. "Get them out, sis."

"Nope. It must be that soldier boy thing in my blood. I'll run when you do, Harold. If they get to the kids it's over me." Sharyn's voice was bleak, because on the screen the recordings had reached the moment the overhead cameras noted the armed men. They were zooming the picture in on group after armed group as they worked forward in the crowd. Then the pictures showed soldiers marching up and standing in ranks each side of the mayor's party. Harold made it about fifty, and no more appeared.

"You run when I say, Sharyn. Don't do the last stand thing."

"You will though. If you get angry you won't run, Harold." Sharyn wasn't asking, that was a resigned acceptance.

Harold knew she was right. "But I'll be doing it so you can run sis, so don't waste it."

"When you tell me to, I'll run, but wait until I'm no help anymore. I can use a crossbow well enough to hit a crowd, and for the kids I really will shoot anyone." They hugged, and Harold found that a big-sister hug was still very reassuring. "That does feel better, though I don't think I'm getting the benefit that makes those women smile."

"You give good hugs as well sis, you always did."

"Family talent then." They both watched with sinking hearts as the gunmen began to congregate near the front of the crowd, four or five ranks back.

"Why hasn't someone told the Mayor?" Harold was puzzled because on the screen the Mayor was receiving a deputation from the marchers. "That plaza thing he's on is only six or seven steps high but it means everyone up there can see what's coming. They could get him clear and pull back the police. Then the cameras could zoom in so the marksmen and soldiers could kill those bastards." Eerily the TV seemed to answer Harold.

"Mayor Turnbull has been warned but believes that if he meets with the marchers, peace can be restored. He will not allow the police or Armed Forces to fire on a peaceful gathering of British citizens."

Onscreen the Mayor stepped forward, past the deputation. He raised both hands to quieten or address the crowd. Gunfire rippled and the Mayor went down along with most of those with him. That included the deputation of marchers. The cameras zoomed in and the Mayor was on the ground but still moving. Police and officials rushed towards him. The soldiers moved forward and formed a single line in front of the casualties, then raised their rifles.

"Fortunately, although wounded, the Mayor's protective vest has saved his life."

Onscreen someone was bandaging the Mayor's leg. Then the picture flipped to the lines of police and some were already down. The ones behind, the armed police, started shooting. Then the soldiers followed suit. Single shots, Harold was pleased to see.

"The forces of law and order are attempting to keep the peace by shooting the armed assailants, but the crowd are giving them shelter. Members of the Armed Forces that had been airlifted in to reinforce the local police are assisting."

"Giving them shelter? They're trying to get the hell away." Sharyn was starting to cry now and Harold offered an arm for a brother-hug.

"It's the excuse, sis. The official reason for shooting unarmed people because now that's the only way to get to the others. Too late now for a few sharpshooters to stop it. Too late for a few soldiers to make a difference with single shots." Onscreen men were falling in the front line of riot police where the armed men in the crowd were shooting through between their human shields.

"That's organised as well, the bastards are breaking the police lines up. Unarmed police, except for the batons." Harold saw a distinctive shape before the man went down, presumably shot. "Crap, that's an AK and there's other automatic weapons. There, where groups go down and create sudden gaps in the riot police." The armed police went to rapid fire as those gaps opened in the lines of riot shields.

"The cowardly assailants and their accomplices have conspired to kill unarmed policemen. Unfortunately, and with true regret, the officer in charge has no option but to give the order to open fire on the front ranks of protesters."

The officer was a bit late in some places as some police were already shooting as fast as they could reload, but Harold couldn't blame them. Now the soldiers were firing short bursts. Probably only Harold noticed the first squaddie to lose it and fire a long indiscriminate burst into the front of the crowd. Too little, too late. Even above the popping of weaponry that could be heard by the circling camera overhead, the deep roar of the crowd was clear.

"The ones behind, up on the walls and steps and on the overpass, will think the police and Army are shooting unarmed people. They'll tell the rest." Harold was saying it but Sharyn could probably follow the eddies in the seething crowd as the news spread. Then most of the mass was moving forward. Those in front were fighting to get away and just briefly the whole mob stalled.

Then more shots tore into the front of the crowd, more of the riot police went down at the same time, and the juggernaut ran over them both. The only benefit was that any gunmen in the crowd were too busy staying on their feet to shoot. The camera was zooming in here and there, or the controller was flicking from one camera to another as rioters and police died. There were close-ups of ordinary unarmed men and women going down and under the front of the crowd without the rest slowing at all.

There were brief pauses in the advance here and there as knots of riot police put up a valiant resistance and then the first marchers, rioters now, were surging towards the armed police beyond. Some policemen ran like hell and maybe got away, others tried to defend the Mayor and died. All the soldiers emptied their weapons into the crowd in long bursts and stopped them. Then many had to reload and in those moments the volume of fire dropped. One surge and any hope of stopping the mob was gone.

Missiles including bricks and wooden posts flew into the soldiers. Men in the crowd were firing again from close range and now the soldiers were the only target. More began to fall, enough to create gaps and there were only fifty to start with. Even as the soldiers emptied their weapons again they, and the group around the Mayor, died. They were beaten down with protest signs and captured batons and trampled.

The crowd surged and eddied over the place where the Mayor had met the deputation. Moments later the ambulance that had arrived rocked, then went over. Army rifles were brandished in triumph as the mob moved on, blindly looking for more targets.

"Despite their valiant attempts to stem the tide of savagery, the Armed Forces have been overrun. At least partly because right until the end they tried to avoid hitting unarmed citizens. Such consideration was wasted on those who have no concepts of common decency."

Tight knots of men were deliberately shooting down the remaining scattered armed police, then looting the bodies and moving on. "That's organised as well. Who the hell are those people? Whoever they are, they've just started another Leeds. Deliberately. Who would want that?" The screen zoomed in on an armed group, all dressed as old-fashioned teddy boys. Then on another group in hoodies who riddled an escaping police car with bullets and swarmed over it.

"The authorities have been able to identify several criminal organisations, who have apparently combined. There are streets gangs, and also criminals involved in drug trafficking and robbery. There are also political insurgents and religious zealots, who may have employed the criminal element."

"They're claiming this is political? Milk isn't political. What religious zealots? This is England. We don't get excited over religion, let alone kill people." Sharyn's hands were knotted together, shredding a clump of tissues she'd used to try and clean her face with. As the commentary continued the camera zoomed onto different armed groups.

Men went down in one group wearing studded leather jackets, and they all looked at a block of shops and charged inside. Harold couldn't get his head round it. "Where are the gunships? We see the tracers coming down at night so they're somewhere near. A couple of those would chew the armed groups up in no time."

"Marksmen are still attempting to stop the attacks. The criminals and the rioters are targeting the buildings with marksmen in. These murderers have no regard for the innocent during their attacks."

Another burning shop was shown with windows above. A man was leaning from an upper window and shooting carefully and deliberately into the crowd. Smoke was already billowing out of the window and around him. Eventually one of those who were shooting back from the crowd hit the man and he slumped back inside. A family dashed out of the burning shop and were beaten to the ground by the crowd.

"The forces of law and order are resisting to the end, giving their lives to protect the innocent. Ordinary people are now being targeted in their homes."

"It's a script. The bastards are reading from a script." Sharyn was right. The theme was there, and the commentary wasn't spontaneous. The delivery was too measured, too controlled. "A real reporter would be weeping and screaming." Someone had watched these pictures and produced these words, to write the history.

"You're right, there's a time delay. The message is that criminals and religious nuts were aided and abetted by the marchers. Together they have attacked a Mayor trying to make peace and solve the problems, then attacked the police and Army. The police and then the Army have been forced to open fire, but because they tried not to shoot unarmed citizens they died. The mob are now on a rampage, killing innocents and burning buildings. Not the fault of the authorities or the police, certainly not the fault of the government." Harold fell silent. An announcement that the gas supplies were being cut as a precautionary measure was almost an anti-climax.

"Oh crap. There were supposed to be marches in all the other places that have been sealed off. All today. This is national TV so why aren't we seeing them?" Harold hugged Sharyn close as he thought a bit more and carried on, answering his own question. "Because when the radios were blanked out, what we got back wasn't national TV. It might be some of the time, but I'll bet we've got our own transmitter now. Manchester, or York, or wherever, all have their own news on tonight."

"I wonder if they'll ever know what happened here?"

"Maybe the version we heard on the commentary, with these pictures. Suitably edited of course to show that no police opened fire early. Pictures showing that the front marchers were obviously sheltering the gunmen. Pictures proving that the soldiers tried to only shoot armed men right to the very end" Onscreen a small block of flats was burning and as the occupants came out they were attacked. A group of men dragged a woman away, kicking and screaming. "That will be shown."

"It's the flats all over again, only now the nasty bastards have got an Army."

"Maybe not." The cameras were showing two groups of the armed men shooting at each other. Bullets that missed went into the crowd, who surged forward and trampled them underfoot. Their weapons were soon being waved by the crowd alongside battered protest signs. "Not an Army and the original bastards may end up as targets. I hope."

Sharyn and Harold sat in some sort of shock as they watched their own city turn into a copy of the Leeds footage. Familiar landmarks burst into flames, or formed an impassive background as groups of supposedly sane people slaughtered each other. Not even over loot because there wasn't any in municipal offices. There were fights between armed gangs, and now some which were definitely racial. In places the bodies were actually heaped up. Finally flames bloomed among the rioters.

"The RAF are being forced to use napalm to destroy captured Army weapons. The criminals are shooting at the helicopters and due to the all buildings, gunfire is ineffective."

Harold never even saw a helicopter trying to use a cannon or machine gun. They dropped napalm though, and jets screamed over Orchard Close. Half an hour afterwards the screen showed explosions that blotted out whole swathes of rioters. That was a clear indication of the delay in broadcasting.

The TV closed down and Harold and Sharyn, still with their arms around each other, went outside. They stood in the street and watched the glow of the fires in the city centre bloom and fade, bloom and fade. The fires faded less each time and soon a permanent glow sat on the horizon, above the intervening buildings. As they watched more and more people came onto the street, most of them hugging someone. Casper had Liz on one side and Holly on the other. Hazel came running up the road and claimed Harold's other arm, sobbing into his coat. She wouldn't look, and wouldn't leave.

Eventually several people came up the street to Harold and extra sentries were agreed and set off. Then gradually everyone else made their way back inside and tried to sleep. Harold sat and hugged Sharyn and Hazel and they tried to make sense of the night.

Harold woke up sat on the settee, stiff and still tired. Hazel was curled under one arm and Sharyn tucked under the other, and none of them had even taken off their coats. That took some explaining when Daisy appeared to point out she had been awake for *ages* and was starving hungry.

Harold left Sharyn explaining that they'd been celebrating Daisy being five and fallen asleep. "Go upstairs and try to sleep before you wake up properly." Hazel gave Harold a tired smile and headed upstairs. Then Harold went to see the sentries. The columns of smoke on the horizon were definitely closer than the city centre.

Chapter 13: Making a Stand

"Hi Toby, what are you doing here? You look shattered."

"I thought you might need a runner or my rifle, Harold." Toby looked tired and drawn, not at all his cheerful fifteen year old self.

"Go home and sleep. I'll need you sharp if there's trouble. Collect Alfie wherever he is, and tell him the same." Harold looked round. "There's enough people here to raise the alarm."

Harold worked his way around the perimeter, sending the most tired looking home to sleep. He also accepted a small two-way radio from Bernie. "I had them as a kid, and then just boxed them up. There's four and they might still reach the gate from here despite the jamming. We need a proper CB."

"We've got one, Toby's. We actually need three or four CBs to talk to each other. Toby's isn't powerful enough to hear anyone through the jamming, or to talk to anyone else."

Harold tried the button once he was outside and sure enough he could contact Bernie. "Just what we need. Will you take one to the gate, and one to the far end sentry please? Leave the other one where you are. What sort of batteries do they use?"

"Ordinary AA, we've been picking them up everywhere we found any so there'll be no shortage." Harold could hear Bernie inside, already coming down the stairs. "I'm on it." He saw Harold waiting and spoke directly. "There was even a GPS facility originally. That won't work now of course." Bernie frowned. "You're ex-Army. The TV has stayed solid on blaming that on the Chinese. Did the Chinese really launch millions of ball bearings into space, into orbits to destroy the satellites?"

"I've heard exactly the same thing, and never a hint of another reason, so maybe they did." Harold took another radio from him. "I'm going to yon end anyway so I'll take this and test from there." Harold looked at the little plastic toy as he went. Because that's what it was, something for children to play with though useful elsewhere no doubt.

The reception was bit crackly but as long as everyone spoke clearly, the little radios would work. That was a big relief. "Hand this on to the next sentry Emmy. How long have you been here?"

"All of ten minutes Harold. Matthew just headed homeward. He said he could stand guard but not swing a machete or use a crossbow. Well he can but says he's useless left-handed."

"Where's Curtis?"

Emmy grinned. "I've no idea. I'm his nurse, not his keeper." Her face fell. "That might be a problem. I think Curtis wants me to be his keeper, sort of. You know? But I'm not ready, and I don't know when I might." Her face crumpled a little bit. "I don't know if I ever might." She moved forward and Harold knew his cue these days. A little later Emmy patted his back. "Thank you Harold. That's taking advantage and a bit mean."

"How?"

"I want a hug because of what happened in the city and David." Emmy raised her head and scrubbed her eyes dry. "But you could be hugging some-one who would be a lot more grateful." Emmy produced a tiny smile. "Or rather someone who was up to showing how grateful she was."

"That's not why I gave you a hug."

"I know. Do you want the names of those who aren't really sad but still want a hug?" Teasing was an improvement over weeping. Liz and Sharyn encouraged all the girl club to tease Harold now and then. It was a recognised sport in Orchard Close.

"No thanks. Let that sneak up as a really nice surprise when I hug the wrong girl." Harold smiled as well. "Just as long as Sharyn never finds out."

Emmy's little smile grew a bit. "That depends on how smug the girl looks I suppose. Which could increase the number wanting hugs or put the rest off?"

"Which is a good reason to just hug. Otherwise I might lose even that."

Emmy managed a little laugh, and took the radio. "Go and find out then because a lot of them are a bit down today." She waved the radio and her face fell again. "Don't worry, after seeing the TV I'll mention the slightest hint of some oik lurking. I've got my crossbow and a machete, but a bloody great shotgun or rifle would be better." As Harold left Emmy was putting on a motorbike helmet. Another item Harold had now put on the list of essential items, along with cycle rider's hats or horse riding hats.

"Harold, Harold."

"That's my name" Harold murmured with a smile and turned to meet Holly. "Yes, Holly."

"Do we all have to stay inside the boundary? What about the traps?"

"Damn, I forgot them. You can go, right now, and take at least five people. Don't set them again because we really are pulling in and staying put. Be quick." Harold had been intrigued when three of the residents had asked about trapping game. There were already some rabbits in the ruins, and a lot of fishing line, wire and twine had been collected here and there.

"We'll bring all the loops and sticks back in then, in case someone does arrive and nicks the lot. Bunny stew tonight with luck. I hope there aren't any cats or rats today. Learning to skin and gut bunnies has been gross enough." Holly set off to collect her guards. Harold hadn't mentioned cats and rats being edible. Not yet, not until the food supply got worse.

Harold called into Betty's house next. "Hi Veronica. Still nothing on the web? No sign from the satellite?" Harold still hoped the big dish would pick up a signal one day.

"No Mr Miller. Um, Harold. Dad says that with both the phones and radio connections down, the web will be finally broken. How will we get information now?"

"We have to go back to old style now, Veronica. I'm afraid we'll be looking through heaps of books, if we can find the right one. Searching the pages instead of clicketty-click." Which was worrying but the disgusted look on Veronica's face was enough to bring a small smile to Harold's face. "You'll love it. You'll find out lots and lots of useless information while looking for the bit you need."

"I will?"

"No need to look so worried. We've got archery information and how to cure rabbit skins and all sorts of other stuff you downloaded. Now all we need is for me to collect books and make an Orchard Close library." That caused a little pang, because he'd already kitted out one library the other way, as a refuge.

"What about the computers?"

"They'll still work, won't they? Everything you've got will still be there, won't it?" Harold hoped so.

"Yes, but do I really have to sit and read boring books?" If her expression was any indication, Veronica would have a magnificent pout when she was older.

"We all will. Though you will have time, because your runner duties won't be as often. I've got this now." Harold waved the radio.

"Dad says you need a field telephone system between vital places."

Harold chuckled. "I'd love one, if someone has a spare setup tucked away. Then an engineer to fit it."

"Er, Dad is one. A telephone engineer. From what Dad was saying, he could probably fix something up?" Veronica gave a little embarrassed wriggle. "Dad has been very quiet since the redundancy. He doesn't say much even to me and Mum. Dad was actually a bit excited about the telephone idea. Do you think, you know, without mentioning me?" Veronica was blushing now.

"Of course. Don't worry. I'll just call round two or three others first and ask if they know anything about telephones." Harold did the zip motion across his mouth. "My lips are sealed. Now, you are supposed to be sleeping."

"No, Mum sent me to my room when the shooting started so I slept all right, thanks. Though everyone has told me what happened." Veronica sighed theatrically. "Where are these books?"

"I don't know. Your first job is to check the empty houses and see which ones have books in them. Then we'll collect them all up. Though if you hear someone beating metal together, you get home because that means an alarm. You know the code?"

"Emmy told us about the iron bars. Triple bash and stop, pause, triple bash and stop. That tells everyone there is an alarm, and to get to their places." Veronica blushed again. "Dad is really embarrassed about his leg, that he can't help much."

"If he can fit me up with a telephone it'll be worth more than him turning green and throwing houses." Harold really meant that because the loss of internal telephone communications had been a nasty shock. "Just remember to listen for the continuous bashing to tell you where the actual emergency is."

"Yes Mr Miller."

"Harold, you're fourteen and I'm not that much older."

"All right." Veronica hesitated. "Harold."

Harold looked around as he left the house. If the estate was still intact after the rioting died out, one of these houses would have to become the library. It was a pity none were stone built because those books might be incredibly precious eventually.

*   *   *

Harold's radio crackled. "There's cars on the main road, coming closer but not quickly."

"Thanks Billy, I'm on the way. Bash on the gong. Even if this turns out to be nothing, it'll give everyone practice in turning out." As he headed for the gate Harold could hear the clanging of an iron bar on a bit of steel tube hung from a chain. A Liz special. The other three started up, and whoever was bashing had remembered the impromptu code.

"All right Billy. Give it a break so I can hear these cars." Silence fell at the gate though the other gongs could be heard behind the houses. "Those cars must be going very slowly."

"No, the cars I heard stopped just before I started beating this. Now there are more of them."

"What is it Harold?"

"Hi Casper. Cars coming up the main road. From what Billy says they had a scout out but now they're all coming." Behind Casper determined men and women with crossbows and spears were coming along the road from their homes. Others were heading for positions on the wall in case this was a feint. "You take your group into number two. I'll stay here but move into number one if there's real trouble."

"Is that where you want your rifle, Harold?" Holly had a long coat on and was carrying her crossbow and the rifle bayonet in one hand. The other was clutching her coat, holding the hidden weapon. "Sal is coming but she wanted you to have the big rifle. It's heavy under here. Can't you make something to go over a shoulder?"

"I'll fix up a sling later. Good idea Holly." Harold glanced at number one. "Take it upstairs will you, and put it in the small front bedroom. You take the loophole in the big bedroom but don't let anyone see you."

Holly smiled. "Yes sir!" Then she headed through the door followed by four more men and women.

"We can't see with this barricade here, Harold." Emmy had a spear and her child's crossbow. "How can I test this for Liz?" This was a flat point on a crossbow bolt, with deep serrations down the sides.

"If someone charges the barricade, Emmy, you do as we discussed. Stand here and shoot an arrow in them as they stick their heads up. Stab the ones that get over."

"I know, but now it's real I can't see and that makes me nervous." It had, Emmy was decidedly jittery.

"If you can't see them, they can't see you to shoot. I'd give you a hug to settle you, but you'd cut me to pieces with all that lot you're carrying." Emmy had two kitchen knives in her belt.

"By the time you'd hugged everyone who's nervous it would be all over." Sal pouted as she went past to her position. "With my luck I'd be last and miss out."

"Hey, send him in here, we're nervous." Harold looked up at Holly, who had opened an upstairs window to join in.

"You should be in the front bedroom, not the bathroom." Harold tried for severe but it bounced off all the smiles.

"Ooh, I want my hug in the bathroom. In the shower?" "Hey, I'm in a bedroom and willing to hug?" Harold tuned out the banter. At least they were all laughing about that now instead of worrying about the cars out there.

Harold stepped up onto the box put there so he could see over the barricade, and waited. The front of a Bedford van appeared and stopped where the driver could see up the side road. The driver or passenger would be reading the clear writing on the garage doors. "NO ENTRY without Invitation." The last bit was because they might want some visitors to come in. An experienced joiner for starters, or a blacksmith.

After a long inspection the van drove slowly past the turnoff and on towards the bypass. Harold relayed what he could see to the group around Emmy. "Six cars have followed that van, and now another van. They've all got the side windows painted out except for small clear patches."

"Women aboard?" That was Emmy's suggestion.

Billy chipped in. "Or maybe they're coloured?" A sharp crack stopped the speculation.

Casper called from his vantage point upstairs. "That was a warning shot from the bypass." He paused. "Some of them are getting out of the vehicles. Billy might be partly right, because one of the men is definitely black. Hang on, Emmy is right as well or one bloke is wearing a skirt."

Everyone could hear the bullhorn. *"This is MOD property. You will be shot if you trespass."*

"Let us through. There's women and kids for God's sake. You can't shoot women and kids." The man's voice was weak compared to the bullhorn.

"My little girl is here. Don't let that lot get her." The woman's voice was almost lost in cries from others of her party as they protested.

"All trespassers will be shot."

"Casper, is that Sarge?" Harold was wondering if Sarge really would shoot kids. Sharyn was relying on him not doing so to save Daisy and Wills.

"I can't tell Harold but there's a lot more soldiers up there. At least twenty I reckon."

"That many will have an officer." Harold swore silently. An officer could go one way or the other. So could a sergeant but the man Harold had met wasn't a child killer.

"What can we do? Where can we go?"

"Take shelter in the houses. We will shoot any rioters and criminals with firearms." That wasn't really reassuring since the size of the mob on the TV didn't need firearms.

"But they've burned our houses. Nobody will let us in." More pleas rose from the small convoy.

The next words from the bullhorn were unexpected. *"Have you asked for sanctuary?"*

"What?" "Where?" "Nobody will talk."

"Over here you bloody idiots." That was Casper, bellowing at the top of his voice. Casper spoke lower. "Sorry Harold, but there's two kids now, about Daisy's age. This lot aren't yobs."

"Fair enough." Harold turned to look at the defenders waiting behind him. "I'm going to let them in if they look all right. Does anyone object?"

Bernie was worried about how, rather than against the refugees. "We can't move the barricade!"

"Not a chance, Bernie. They go round the side and over the wall one at a time, and get searched."

Emmy stepped forward. "They have to obey the rules."

Harold was baffled. "What rules?"

"Treat women decently." "No foul language." "They help with the defence." "Everyone works." "They do as Harold tells them." "No stealing my hugs." The last one raised a ripple of laughter.

"Treat women decently, watch their language, and all pitch in. Does that cover it?"

"They do what you say, Harold. After all I do and I'm bigger than you are." Casper paused. "Get ready, there's four on the way."

"We all do what you say, little brother, even if it isn't orders. This way any newcomers get the message. Otherwise one of them will try for the job." Sharyn had arrived with a crossbow and six Liz specials to use in it.

"All right. I'd argue but it wouldn't be good for my image when you beat me up." Actually there wasn't time. Harold pointed at the crossbow. "No last stand today, sis. You can go and put the kettle on."

"I'll go when this is all settled. Until then I'm stopping right here. I brought your little rifle and Alfie has got it because he can't pull that bow yet." Sharyn gave Harold a tiny smile. "Yes, I told him to keep it hidden."

"Here they come."

Harold turned round at Casper's voice and six people came around the corner and hesitated. Harold called to them. "You can walk up nice and slow with empty hands if you want to talk."

The group inspected the houses either side of the barricade, and would be seeing little except blocked windows with Xs cut for shooting arrows from. One of the men cupped his hands. "You won't shoot?"

"Why? That would waste arrows and we aren't the type anyway."

A woman spoke up. "It says shoot to kill on the van. We could see it from further down the road."

"It says we come in peace on the front and sides but some people don't like that idea. Then we shoot to kill. So who are you?" Harold wasn't so sure about this now. A couple of the men looked rough types, though Casper hadn't looked great when he arrived.

"We're from the Ashcroft estate. This morning a big mob appeared outside the barricade. At first they just demanded to be let in, and then they wanted food. Someone started shooting and I don't know who." That was the spokesman again, a short slim man who looked to be in his twenties except he was almost bald.

"Sadie said to get ready. If they came over the barricade we should drive out over the gardens and get away." The woman looked around. "We don't know who else made it. The place was already burning behind us so we headed for the bypass."

"We had bricks thrown at us and twice we were shot at but not a real attempt to stop us." This was from the taller of the two rougher men. Something indefinable caused Harold to mentally tag them rougher, something about how they held themselves. Arrogant, confident, and both were keeping their coats closed, but a hand near an undone button. "Now you can let us in." That sounded more like a demand than a request.

"Maybe, or maybe only some. Who ran your estate?"

The other of the rough pair answered. "The Minutemen ran the estate. We kept out the gangs and went foraging and the residents paid us. How much does it cost to live here?"

While Harold was processing that the other woman, the younger one, spoke up. "Some of us? You're not taking just the women, no chance."

"No. Or rather yes. We'll take the women and anyone else who obeys the rules."

"What rules, and who are you?" That was the taller Minuteman again.

Holly's voice rang out. "That's our very own Soldier Boy. Just like those up there but this one is ours and you'll do what he tells you."

Harold spoke up before people got too contentious. "That's one rule. The others are that you treat the women with respect, and we don't allow crude language. Everyone helps with running the place, doing whatever they are good at."

"What extras do the guards get, the fighters?"

Emmy's voice sounded. "None, we're all fighters if we have to be."

"Too true" and similar sentiments sounded from various voices.

"Sod that. I'm not putting myself on the line for fuck all. Come on you lot, we're moving on. We'll fort up someplace." The taller Minuteman turned to the group which had now grown to eight.

"You wait a minute, Pierce. This place is already forted up. I can handle not swearing and I don't abuse women anyway." The original speaker, the small slim man, turned towards Harold. "I'll do whatever work you want. We've got some gear in our vehicles. How do we get in?"

"Zip it Conn. I'm running the convoy and I say we leave." Pierce put a hand inside his coat and glanced towards the bypass to check that the house was blocking the Army's view.

"Leave it!" All eyes turned to Harold. "You use what's under that coat and you die. I warned you. Come in peace or we shoot to kill." Harold reconsidered. A hand gun would be better this side of the barricade than in this man's hands. "Take it out nice and slow with two fingers and it goes on the floor." The man tensed, as did his companion.

"She told you he's a soldier. He taught me to shoot. Tell me when, Soldier Boy." The men on the approach might have laughed at Toby's young voice if it hadn't been so utterly serious.

Casper knew how the macho bullshit worked. "I'm up here with a lovely view so any time you like." Harold hoped not. Even after Harold had used grease to try and tighten up the spread, the shot would probably get the women as well.

"Me too." Holly's voice didn't leave any room for doubt. Nor did Alfie's, Bernie's or Curtis when he joined in.

"How do we defend ourselves if we disarm?" The Minuteman was glaring at Conn, who had quickly moved away from him.

"With whatever your friend has under his coat. This is your fine for foul language after being told the rules. You also take your coat off and put it down over the weapon and the pair of you stand over the other side of the road, hands on heads. Are any more of the Minutemen here?"

"Two more in the last van." That was the older woman, and her glare was directed at the two with hands on their heads.

"Someone tell them to back that van up to the other side of the turning. They can do it now, or not at all because I've got a rifle that will go clean through a van." Harold paused. "Now you, fella, put your coat and whatever that is on the floor." Once again the man hesitated, weighing up the distance to the corner and cover.

"He is a Soldier Boy just like we told you, and he really has got a great big rifle." Harold sighed as Holly spoke up. He had to stop them doing that, though it worked this time. The man complied, slowly, and moved away from his coat and a handgun. One of the group went around the corner and voices were raised. A head appeared and looked at the two with hands on their heads. The Minuteman jerked his head and a few minutes later the van backed up and just out of sight past the opening.

"What about my coat? Not only that but I've got gear in the other vehicles." The tall man was edging back a little towards the centre of the road.

"No. You've got your van, and some weapons. Take them and go, and don't come back. Just remember next time. If you charge people to protect them, they won't back you up." Harold paused. "The next time someone tells you the rules, pay attention." Somehow he doubted this one would.

The two men moved slowly away, and the taller called to the young woman. "Come on Bess, we're leaving."

"You are. I'm going in there with that big strong soldier type."

"Bitch. You'll be sorry."

"I doubt it. Piss off, loser." She grinned. "You'd better get moving before that mob arrives."

The pair of men turned and went around the corner. Harold called to the rest. "Send a spokesman or woman forward, and tell the rest to get ready. Park the vehicles on the rubble across from the entrance."

There was a quick consultation and Conn called out. "We really can't bring the vehicles?"

"Not yet, maybe later when things calm down. This barricade doesn't move." There was more consultation. Meanwhile Harold, and the rest, heard the van reverse off up the road. Then there was the stop-start sound of a three point turn and the vehicle roared off.

Conn, Bess, the older woman and another young man moved up nearly to the barricade. "How do we get over that?" Behind Conn the first car was backing up and bumping over the rubble in the front garden of the ruined house Harold had indicated. A woman and young girl climbed out and began pulling out bags.

"One at a time. You walk through where that garage has no back and round the boundary." Harold smiled. "Past the shoot to kill sign. You come in one at a time and are searched. No drugs except medicinal and they go to Patricia, our nurse. If you need any, talk to her."

"We'll be searched?"

"We'll only take weapons and drugs until you're settled in. Then you get the weapons back or something else. Hide any firearms or ammunition for them so the Army never see them, and warn the searchers."

The older woman scowled. "The Minutemen didn't allow us to have firearms. These searchers. What about the women?"

"They'll be searched by women. I suggest someone goes to the Army and explains since you'll be walking between our boundary and theirs."

"What?" That was the younger man, but all four looked worried.

Harold tried to sound reassuring. "Safe enough. You're outside the exclusion zone, but telling them helps with those nervous trigger fingers."

"Ah, right. I'll do that." Conn turned and went back down the road.

"Do we have to be searched by women?" Bess was smiling up at Harold. "You can search me if you want to?" Damn, she'd obviously been the Minuteman's girl and had switched targets.

"Get in line, girl." Emmy was trying not to laugh.

So was Sal. "There's a queue."

"It's a long one." Holly actually giggled. Harold thought hers might be relief.

"Before that you've got to pass inspection from his sister." Sharyn smiled up at Harold's incredulous look and added very quietly. "Unless you don't want her backed off, bro?"

Harold grinned and turned back. Oops, Bess was still smiling "I can work to the rules. My name is Bess and that van just drove off with my worldly possessions."

"We'll fix you up. I'm sure I can find you something." There was a ripple of laughter as Casper spoke, which puzzled Bess but she turned and made for the designated path. From the humour Harold thought a lot of people were relieved, and he certainly was.

Some of the new people had to go back to the cars and the van several times for bags, while others had little more than what they were wearing. The evacuation of the Ashcroft estate really had been rushed. Harold couldn't place the name, which meant it wasn't one that had been on the TV as a trouble spot. Just another group of houses trying to survive. He glanced towards the city centre and was sure the plumes of smoke were nearer.

Once the dozen adults and two children were inside the boundary, they lined up while Harold spoke to them. "Hello everyone. I'm Harold. This lot do more or less what I ask, and you'll have to do the same. I will listen to suggestions, and I mean listen. Please don't waste my time though."

Harold gestured at the dozen residents stood about with bats and crossbows. "These people behind me are some of the residents and will be fixing you up with houses. We've got plenty of empty ones but they'll need airing out. Tomorrow we'll sort out what help you can be in keeping the place running."

Conn was still the spokesman. "What's the rent for the houses?"

"Nothing." Harold smiled. "They're not my houses. I didn't pay for the one I'm in which is the one with the flag."

"Are you really a soldier?" Bess was giving Harold, and then the rest of the men in the group, a close inspection.

"Ex-soldier, yes."

"Where do I sleep?" Bess made that an offer with her body language and smile. Some of the girl club needed to talk to her, Harold decided.

"Most single women, the younger ones, sleep in the girl club." Harold gestured behind him where Sal and Emmy waited. "These ladies will explain. They might even find you some clothes." He turned to Emmy and murmured "Back her off for Christ's sake."

"You could pick one of the girl club as a girlfriend?" Emmy's voice was just as low and she headed Bess-wards with a big smile leaving Harold open-mouthed. Others moved in and began to talk to families or single people, and then help them move their gear further into the estate.

"What is this place called?" Conn waved his arms to encompass the housing.

"Orchard Close." Matthew had come to help with the new influx but paused to answer.

Harold turned to answer. "That's just the street I live on."

"So what? We need a name for the enclave and half those in the other houses say they're Orchard Close residents. Your old group." Matthew shrugged. "It's easier than 'this estate' or 'our group of houses' or a list of streets."

"I can see how you boss them about." Conn had a little smile now.

"We get the job done. I'm the go-to man for sorting out soldier trouble. I'm hoping your lot have the go-to man for a few other things. We've got a plumber, an electrician, and a brewer."

"Really? A brewer? I'm going to love this place!" Conn was thinking. "We've got a general handyman, and Pippa is a genius baker. Cakes mainly, but she can rustle up a lovely loaf of bread as well." Conn looked round. "It was all a bit rushed, and I'm not sure what some of these did. The mob came over the barricade and then vehicles were going over the gardens in all directions. These cars and the two vans sort of congregated and the Minutemen dropped in front and rear as guards."

The older woman from the original negotiators spoke up. "I'm Janine. The guards weren't exactly welcome though they were a comfort. Those who didn't bring much were a bit worried about how we were going to pay them." She looked around. "I worked in a laundry so I'm afraid the best I can offer is nicely ironed clothes."

"Get a settled in, sort yourselves out, and we'll all talk tomorrow. I really would appreciate anyone who can use a crossbow properly, or a firearm, and people who will stand with a spear if necessary."

"You sent the four best at that away. The rest of us were discouraged from that sort of thing. We really can just pick a house?" Conn was looking at the houses with more interest now.

"Yes. We prefer more than one living in each one though it isn't a rule. We've found that two or more stops people getting depressed in the evening." Harold knew that worked for him. Living with his big sister had downsides, but he was sure the incessant cheerful chatter from Daisy kept him from brooding too much. "Choose one with electric heating or ask for Betty and she'll fix you up with electric fires. Then look for a TV or kettle if there isn't one."

"The gas is off?"

Harold shrugged. "The TV says so and we're not risking it going out and coming back and something going boom. So we've turned the gas off to every house."

"OK." Conn hesitated. "Are there rules about the single women all sleeping in this girl's club?"

"No, why?"

Conn glanced along his group and spoke quietly. "I've sort of got a friend. Maybe it's time to make it more permanent?"

"Only if she agrees."

"Bloody hell yes. Look at the size of me." Conn smiled and went off, and the woman he was talking to soon afterwards was definitely in no physical danger from him. She was big enough to beat him up instead, or tuck Conn under one arm and carry him off.

"Come on sis. You can apologise to Liz on the way back. She'll have to wait for her test subjects."

"She's already here. She followed me to hear the macho bullshit. Liz says it's reassuring." Sharyn sighed. "How many more groups like this will we see, Harold? How many more can we take in?"

"We've just taken fourteen including the two kids. We can take more without leaving the originals in a minority and perhaps making someone ambitious." Harold frowned. "Maybe I need a quiet chat with my sister about how many we can take." Sharyn hooked her arm through his and they went home.

They decided that another dozen wouldn't be too much strain, and would help with the defence if it came to that. By nightfall five had already been admitted. One couple and two women with a four year old girl. All five were perfectly happy to accept the rules and were shown to houses. All were running from a mob that had overrun where they lived. Their cars were parked in the front gardens on the main road and the fuel tanks were drained.

*   *   *

Hazel had been sent upstairs to read, or just worry, and hopefully sleep. "She doesn't need to see this." Harold gestured at the TV where the line of fire stretched and contracted, swelled and faded, as more of the city died. "Veronica was spared last night because her parents wouldn't let her watch. Hazel might worry about it, but that won't be as bad as seeing just how bad the riots are getting."

"That's beyond a riot, but not an insurrection either though that's the government line." Sharyn watched in disgust as the blurb came up at the bottom of the screen for at least the fifth time.

"The authorities have ascertained that the cowardly attacks last night were an organised rebellion. Criminals and other unprincipled citizens including religious zealots combined in an attempt at taking over the entire city. The valiant attempts by the representatives of law and order averted this, at the cost of their lives. The mass of accomplices are now leaderless, lashing out blindly at the innocent citizens around them. Because of Human Rights legislation, the Armed Forces are not allowed to intervene. We are attempting to modify the laws to allow the Armed Forces to rescue the innocents."

Harold raised his fist but hitting the settee wouldn't help. He'd tried it. "Lying bastards. I was in the Army. We formed lines and bayoneted civilians in London. We went into housing estates with snipers and machine guns backing us up. The lying bastards."

"You're right, it's bullshit. Human Rights doesn't say that the Army should shoot people trying to escape from this lot." Sharyn was close to weeping, again. "For some reason they want this to happen. Why, and who is running the country? There's never a mention of a politician's name now, just the government." Her voice sharpened. "What about the King, or Queen? Christ, we don't even know which we've got now."

"In practical terms they're powerless anyway. We've spent years gradually making the monarch powerless. A Head of State responsible for everything but who can't interfere. A politician's dream." Harold gave a short laugh. "Unless, according to what some barrack's lawyer said after a couple of beers, there is no government. Then the Armed Forces answer to the monarch." His smile was grim. "We still swear allegiance to the monarch, not Parliament."

"So where are they? Last we heard there'd been a terrorist attack on the Royal Family. That was a year ago, and there's been nothing since." Sharyn turned to Harold "Seriously? The King, or the Queen if none of the men made it, can order the Army about?"

"Theoretically, and most of the squaddies I knew would rather follow them into a bad place than the bloody politicians. After all, a good few of us served with or near a Royal at some time. Not so many bloody politicians' kids up on the sharp end."

"Ooh, you're a Royalist."

"Well I know which I'd rather have at my back when it hits the fan. Definitely HRH Harry for starters even if he's a bit old for it now." Harold watched the TV, where the blind monster of fire and death had lunged south. Now the estates that had been torn apart on that first night, when the city was sealed, burned again. "Not that I reckon the Royals would have much say anyway. I reckon they're dead, or somewhere that is sealed off for their own protection and, guess what, has no phones or radio links."

"If they got Charlie's whole family, it could be Queen Beatrice or Eugenie." Sharyn paused. "Hah, it could be Princess Anne. She would pin some ears back even if she's a bit creaky now. I suppose we'll never know." Sharyn gestured at the TV. "If that lot heads this way we'll be dead anyway."

"I know sis. I'm actually reassured by that officer on the bypass and the extra soldiers. That mob hasn't hit the Army yet. They keep swerving away from the boundary. I fervently hope that the lunatics keep doing that until they run out of energy or rage or food. If not I hope that the Army has some sort of master plan." The next part was in a much lower voice, almost a whisper. "I'd even welcome a tank up on the bypass, and I've seen what they do to crowds."

"Enough. We go to bed, we try to sleep, and catch up tomorrow. I'm not watching another hour and a half of this because that's all they're showing." Sharyn stood up and turned off the TV. "That's if you actually get undisturbed sleep."

Five times during the night the little radio called Harold down to the barricade. Another seven people were admitted, but two heavily armed groups were sent away. The fighters and weapons would have been welcome, but neither group would agree to the impromptu rules. Both wanted preferential treatment and first pick of resources. One group also wanted women for the fighters as part of their pay.

*   *   *

By four am the escapees stopped coming and everyone not on sentry duty slept. Harold woke at seven but stayed in bed for a little while trying to get back to sleep. He gave up eventually and got dressed because although tired, he was too wound up to relax. The view out of the bedroom window didn't help.

This morning the columns of smoke were much closer, and spread across much of the western horizon, across much of the city. There was a taint of burning in the air itself now even if the light rain seemed to be keeping the smoke from reaching Orchard Close.

After breakfast Harold went down to the barricade. "Where is Karen?" He'd suddenly realised that neither Karen's blue rinse nor Stewart Baumber had been at the barricade yesterday, or last night.

"She's having a bad time. The last lot of tablets aren't doing the job. Patricia is doing her best but she says there's not enough specialist medicine." Betty shouldn't be here on the barricade anyway, but she'd brought hot coffee.

"Christ, Betty, why didn't she say?"

"Because you can't fix it, and you've got enough problems just now. Just to stop you running off to Patricia there's three, four now, in trouble. Mary, Karen, and Harry need something stronger than Ibuprofen and Paracetamol, and one of the new men is a diabetic and out of insulin. Sandy, another new one, is borderline with his arthritis but can manage. Both Mary and Karen have other problems as well as pain and their medication has run out. Switching to something else has caused them a lot of problems."

Betty patted Harold's arm. "Now you keep us safe while Patricia does her best. The rest of us can manage on the pills you brought. Once things settle down, we can all try to find a proper solution." Betty collected empty mugs and headed back up the road. Harold turned back to the barricade and tried to clear that news from his head.

"Harold, what do we do about that?" Holly provided a distraction.

"What?

"A dog. It's hanging about at the end of the lane. It seems to want to come up here but it's frightened." Harold stepped onto his box and a chocolate Labrador was at the end of the lane, trotting back and forth on the main road. The dog sniffed the cars, and started to follow the scent of the occupants. Then it stopped, looked at the barricade, and backed off. "It keeps doing that."

Harold frowned. "Maybe it's frightened of the barricade. Who had a dog, before all this happened?"

"I did, why?"

"Sal? Do you fancy a chocolate Labrador, second hand and decidedly wary of barricades?" Harold kept his voice light but he'd always had a soft spot for strays. Birds with broken wings, dogs with three legs, that sort of thing.

"I might. Is it a he or she?"

"Bitch." Holly sounded certain, then Harold remembered she'd got the binoculars up there.

"That was uncalled for. I'd make a good mummy for her." Sal sounded happier now. "What have we got to tempt her in? Oh, what do I feed her?"

"Rat and cat? At the moment Holly and the trapper squad take them out of the traps and throw them away." Harold hadn't thought of food when he made the offer. "Is there dog food in any of the houses?"

"Some. I think number seventeen still has a stack of tins and some packets of dog food. I was waiting until we ran out of meat before putting it in the stew." Rob looked round at the faces glaring at him. "Joking, I was joking for God's sake. I was saving them for Rascal." Rascal was Hilda's ancient poodle, much too old and creaky to be rascally now.

"Never mind." Harold wasn't sure it was a joke and if not, Rob had the right idea. Food was food. "Nip up the road to seventeen, Sal, and get a tin. Tip it in a dish and go out round the side to tempt her closer. Look around for a lead and collar or some rope." As Sal set off Harold called after her. "Hurry, because if someone comes up the road you leave the dog, right?" Sal started trotting.

Harold watched the dog. She really didn't like the barricade. Once again he wondered about the lack of feral packs. "I'd expected more dogs."

"Maybe out here on the edges, but there won't be many in the middle of the city. The council banned them from their estates ten or eleven months ago." Harold stared at Billy as he continued. "It started with flats because there was a health scare. Too many dogs were crapping near the people, even if it was cleaned up. A year after that the ban was extended to everywhere the council owned and social housing."

"A lot of private landlords followed suit. Dogs weren't allowed in any of the parks, or in the city centre, or any pedestrian precincts." Seth sounded grim. "My Mum had to take hers to the RSPCA and they were absolutely packed out."

"There were a lot of rumours about what happened to them. About even the RSPCA putting dogs to sleep in job lots with mass cremations. The dogs must have all gone somewhere." Billy scowled. "There were marches and some people probably kept their dogs anyway. We were expecting cats would be next."

Seth disagreed. "No, because people would just turn cats loose and the place would be overrun."

Harold thought that had happened, in effect. "We're getting them in the traps, so there are cats out there."

Billy looked thoughtful. "We should tempt some in. Rats and mice will be a problem so cats might be dead handy."

"But how do we feed them, to keep them here?" Holly sounded reflective. "I wouldn't mind a kitten. We had one once and they're funny."

"We can use the bits taken out of the rabbits when they're gutted, and there will be rats and mice to catch. After all we want hunters, not another Fluff." Harold looked at the dog again. "Anybody who works out how to catch one without losing fingers, let me know."

"Sandy could make a trap. If we catch something else it becomes cat or dog or human food." Billy smiled. "We could keep rabbits as well. For food."

"It's a plan." Harold listened to everyone talking about what animals could be kept and why. The dog had already been a bonus because there wasn't so much speculation about the riots. Though there were still plenty of glances towards the smoke hanging over the city even if that was partly obscured by the rain.

*   *   *

"Rover." "Chocolate." "Mutt." "Sal's bitch." "Lucky sod." "Greedy." "Fang." "Wags." The suggestions rolled in. Sal, now inside the barricade with a thin Labrador bitch on a collar and lead, looked up and smiled. Looked up because Sal was on her knees stroking a happy, wriggling doggy back.

"Lucky. Definitely Lucky. Aren't you girl?" Lucky thought so from the tail wagging. Once around behind the barricade the dog had become very, very friendly. She wanted to say hello to everyone and didn't mind the attention even while bolting down a tin of dog food.

"With luck, once she's settled, Lucky will also be a guard dog. Her ears will be better than ours." Billy had a big smile as did everyone else nearby. It was something about that frantic wagging and sheer happiness.

"First rule. Pick up the crap, right?" Harold didn't want to be scraping his boots clean. "Second rule, we find out nice and slow how Lucky is with kids, because Daisy is going to want to swarm all over her. So you don't let the two meet except when Daisy has a minder."

"No problem Harold. I'll take her to the girl club."

"Well she is a bitch." Matthew mock-ducked as a couple of female hands threatened a Berrying. "Taking her there should make sure a lot of blokes want to spoil her."

"Good idea Sal, take her there as soon as that dish is licked." Harold gave a little smile. "Someone off-duty can keep an eye on her until she's settled." It was a subtle hint that Sal was on duty just now. Licking took mere seconds. From the way Lucky bounced around on her lead and followed Sal up the road, settling might be a done deal.

*   *   *

The good mood lasted through two sets of arrivals. One was a small convoy and didn't like the setup or the rules or maybe losing their vehicles. They went back to the roundabout and headed south. The second was three people on foot. Two men and a woman, who had simply run with what they were wearing. They brought a warning. The younger man looked up at Harold from just outside the barrier. "They're about a mile away. I don't think this place will stop them."

"We had a barricade and they came right over it." The woman was late teens, maybe early twenties, and the marks of tears were clear on her face. "We could hear screaming and fighting behind us. So we ran."

"We've got nothing." The second man was in his twenties, maybe, and had an arm around the woman. "We've got nothing but the Army won't let us out, so you're our last hope. Give me a club or something and I'll stand on your barricade and fight."

This trio had attempted the bypass and been rejected by the Army, as had all the others. They had also been told to seek sanctuary and now that was part of the opening speech from the bypass. One man, earlier, hadn't believed the warnings. His body was laid in the roadway just inside the exclusion zone.

Harold couldn't turn them away even if the numbers were climbing too fast. "Come round the side, past the van with the painting on it. You'll be searched."

"If you can find anything, you're welcome." His smile was bitter with no humour at all. "We really do need sanctuary."

Sharyn came to take Harold home to eat and rest. Harold agreed after she said he should, because he probably wouldn't rest tonight. "We're already past the agreed number, Harold. How do we feed them all?"

"That lot, that roaming mob, has to reach a crisis point soon and break up. Then the new people can spread out in the damaged houses and bring in more food. Until then they'll dent our stocks." Harold looked back at the three just being processed. "How do I turn them away?"

"You might have to in the end. We have to feed the ones already here and winter is closing in." Sharyn was in a sombre mood. "It might be a choice between Daisy or some stranger before spring."

"Daisy, Sharyn. If it comes to that we'll throw people out to fend for themselves. I'll throw them out." Harold tried hard to un-think that idea while he ate and watched the latest news.

"Thank all and every God for that."

"Thought you didn't believe?" Sharyn had a little smile until she looked at the screen. "What's good about that?"

"They've split. If we get one of the smaller ones, and the Army chip in, we might stop them." On the screen the huge blind monster of destruction had split, becoming a many-headed hydra. Each head writhed across the city, spreading out from the latest huge conflagration, leaving a trail of flame and smoke in its wake.

"Oh God, they're heading for the outskirts, for the bypass. They're really coming for us this time." Sharyn had gone pale as she realised.

"Only one of them Sharyn, and they might hit one junction north or south. I really hope they hate the Army enough to go for them, not us." Harold was paying particular attention to two of those heads when the screen showed their positions. The one that would be the first to strike Army positions, and the one that would come nearest to Orchard Close. Unfortunately Harold was sure the one heading his way would arrive after dark.

As soon as he finished eating Harold arranged for everyone possible to rest. He warned them, tonight could be really bad. "Did you mean what you said, Tim?" The latest recruit, the younger man, nodded. "Then here's a baseball bat. This is Matthew. He can't use a bat but he'll try with his air pistol. Have you ever used a firearm?"

"Christ no. But I promise to do my best. I won't let them get to Toyah." The young woman clung to his arm.

"What about you, Toyah? You can use a bat and stand with Tim? That or go on fire-fighting, or help with casualties. Everyone has to help out." Toyah's pale face became paler.

"Fire fighter. I can do that, but nothing to do with blood, please." Half the residents felt the same, which was fewer than Harold expected. Desperation and some terrible experiences were hardening attitudes.

"Go down there and ask for Betty. She'll give you a position, and a bucket and something to beat out flames." The mob were using fire so Harold was doing his best to prepare for that.

"I'll fight with you. I can shoot a hand gun." Bess wasn't smiling at all now, nor was she trying to flirt.

"Really? Don't mess me about Bess, not on this." Harold had no intention of fighting alongside Bess because she'd distract him. The backing off wasn't working and Bess would be trying to attract Harold at the wrong time. But he'd be damn pleased of someone who wasn't frightened of a firearm.

Bess looked grim. "My, um, ex. He showed me and let me shoot a few times because he thought it was, well, sexy. I've fired five shots and I can keep the barrel down though I'm not accurate. Not unless they're real close." Her smile came back but not at full wattage. "If I shoot someone, I might need a hug?"

"If you shoot some bastard trying to get into Orchard Close you'll probably get a queue wanting to hug you." Harold gave her a little smile. "Some might be blokes." He thought quickly. "Can you put a fresh clip in?" Bess gave a quick nod. "Since you know how to use this gun, you go in the middle house on the side towards the city." Harold handed her the Minuteman's weapon, recovered along with two full clips in his coat.

Harold turned and called. "Matthew, another one for you in the centre strongpoint. One who can use this handgun. There's two clips as well so over forty shots. Use her to break up any groups that get close." Harold turned back. "You understand Bess? You shoot when Matthew says so, at groups. No wasting the bullets. One shot at a time and aim." Harold relented a bit since

Bess really did look apprehensive. "Are you OK with that?"

"Yes? I think so? I will shoot, I promise. I don't want a mob like that to catch me, not ever." Harold gave her a quick hug and Bess smiled and then pouted. "That wasn't a proper one."

"See your new boss about hugs though they'll be one-armed." Matthew looked startled and Bess looked speculative.

Harold worked his way through the rest of the new arrivals and they all went to their new homes to wait for the alarm. Harold checked the handgun he'd kept, one taken from the gang who attacked Gabriela, and Sharyn shooed him off to bed as well.

Chapter 14:
Firestorm

"Harold, Harold!" Hazel needn't have bothered because the alarm outside the girl's club was clanging and his radio was crackling and shouting.

"I'm coming Hazel. Go to Betty's." Hazel and Veronica wanted to help so they were going to supply warm drinks if the volunteers, half the population, were out on the walls for a long time. Though they were to run for Harold's house if told to. Harry, Finn's Mum Mary, and the three new children would be coming here straight away. Harold put on his boots, and his long coat for hiding rifles. The pistol went in his belt, the spare clip in a pocket.

"Ready Sharyn?" Even as Harold spoke there was a knock on the door. Karen was stood there, her face drawn with pain.

"I'll make sure the kids have chance to run, Harold. I'll do the punk thing and wave this." Karen waved the poncy air pistol. "I won't stop them long but maybe long enough?"

"Get out if you can, Karen, if it comes to that." Harold gave her a hug.

"An old woman's dream come true. I've made the girl's club jealous." Karen tried for a smile. Sharyn gave her a hug as well. Karen had one serious request. "Tell Stewart not to do anything silly. He's on about over his dead body and silly things like that."

"I'll tell him to come and follow you if it gets too bad. That you'll need him so he's not to get all heroic." Harold turned to Sharyn. "You go in the middle strongpoint with Matthew. No arguments. It's a straight run from there to here, all right?"

"If I have to."

"If Matthew says I'm screaming it down the bloody radio, all right?" Sharyn answered with a hug. As they left Harry was coming in with a little girl holding one hand and a young boy the other. The adults nodded to each other and kept going. At the end of Orchard Close Harold hugged Sharyn again. "I'll be down there, the other end to the gate because it's a weak spot." He turned to go and a voice spoke.

"Hey, no fair. Come on."

Harold turned and seven women and Casper were stood with their arms open. "No bloody chance, there isn't time." There certainly wasn't. The sentry at the far end was reporting fires springing up and moving this way.

"Remember, you owe us all." Holly turned to the others and them all had a quick group hug. A careful one because of all the sharp metal. Then seven of them headed for their positions.

"I'll be in Betty's house, Harold. I'll throw things if they get that far, to slow them up a bit." Liz gave a wan smile. "To give the kids more time." She turned and headed back in. "It might work since I'll throw the spare spear heads. Then I'll run like a bunny."

Harold took the big rifle and ammunition from just inside Matthew's house, and slung it over his shoulder under his coat. Then he ran down the road, because he could see the flames now and they were definitely nearer.

*　　　*　　　*

"It's me, don't shoot."

"I hope it's you from that direction." Seth wasn't joking. He gestured to the crossbow. "That's only got one shot."

"Two." That was Berry from the next room, and she wasn't laughing for once.

"Plus however many are in this thing." Harold had taken Nigel at his word. Nigel had said he could shoot to save his daughter, Berry, so Harold gave him a captured firearm. He now had the big revolver from the first group to invade.

"Six, Nigel. Count them and then try to reload. But wait until they're really close and aim each one because there's only another four rounds." Harold checked the other upstairs room on the corner house. "I'll be in there if there's an attack from the side, Seth. You warn me if anyone tries to cross the big car park." Harold took out the big rifle and patted it. "I'm hoping to hit some of them at the other side, to make them afraid to cross over all that open tarmac.

"But we wait until they reach the white bricks because that's crossbow range, right?"

"Right Seth. That's where they'll be close enough for the bolt to go through a jacket we think." There'd been some experimentation because in range didn't mean the bolts would penetrate.

Harold checked downstairs where four more defenders waited with spears and clubs or machetes. "Try to keep them out and we'll do our best up there, OK?" Four tense faces nodded. "Berry has taken bricks up there in case she runs out of crossbow bolts." One face smiled, better than Harold had hoped for. "This is why you came to us for sanctuary, remember. So we stand together and survive." This time the nods were firmer.

"We can do it." "Last chance." "No retreat." "Shoot the bastards." The comments followed him up the stairs and at least one sounded confident. Outside the flames were closer still and Harold was hoping their light would allow him to see any attackers. The area of tarmac suddenly lit up and a few moments later his radio crackled.

"Harold, the Army just lit up the road outside the gate, the one going past the end."

"Calm down Billy. That's good. They can see to shoot but so can you. Just warn everyone again, keep the gun barrels inside the windows. Tell everyone not to look at the bypass or they'll be blinded for a bit." Harold pressed the next button. "Have you got a light as well Matthew?"

"Yes Harold. We can see the first row of damaged houses really clearly. The beam is going backwards and forwards along them."

"Good. Don't let anyone look at the bypass or they'll be blinded. The gate has got light and so have we, so be doubly careful about showing firearms." Harold put the radio on the sill and knelt by the window. He rested the rifle barrel on the folded blanket over the wooden table just inside the slit and worked the bolt to load a round. Lastly he stuffed the cotton wool in his ears. Everyone near a firearm was doing that. They'd have to shout, but hopefully wouldn't be deafened.

Then Harold waited since some of the flames further in towards the city were already level with the car park.

*   *   *

"There, Harold."

"Thanks Seth." A group of five or six were running towards the small building near the far end of the open tarmac. Harold led them a bit and then put a round into the middle of the group and one dropped. The others paused so Harold shot again and another went down. Four men retreated, dragging one man with them.

Very little happened for a little while until someone started shooting from the damaged buildings nearby, towards this house. Behind the gunman more flames rose in the already damaged houses. Harold waited because nothing was hitting near the windows. A larger group ran out onto the tarmac heading for that small building again so he fired into the middle of them, twice. Gunfire came back from at least two weapons.

"Christ!" Seth's voice was a mixture of shock and awe.

Harold couldn't have put it better. A line of fiery streaks descended on the group from the direction of the bypass and tore into the men. "No, just the Army but probably more use right now. Those Army reinforcements brought a machine gun."

At the other end of the car park the men broke and ran, many limping or staggering. Seven or eight still shapes were left on the ground. "That's worth a crate of Berry Beer." Harold could hear the relief in Berry's voice.

"Let's hope the Army earn some more tonight." Harold picked up the radio. "Matthew, they're coming your way. Shoot at the first ones out of the houses. With luck they'll shoot back. They did here and the Army opened up."

Matthew sounded relieved. "They did? Great. Will do." Harold repeated the information and instruction to Casper, who now had the gate radio, with a similar response. For a few more minutes there was nothing but shouting from the damaged housing, and more flames rising here and there.

"Let me know if they try the car park again, Seth. Nigel, come through here will you, as backup for Seth. In fact it's probably better if Berry comes through as well. You can use the firing slots for crossbows alternately while the other one is loading." It had occurred to Harold that both Seth and Nigel would fight harder with Berry in here to protect.

Harold settled into the little bedroom, which had a small window in the side so he could see two ways. The larger window faced across to the damaged housing, where he expected the rioters to come from. The small side window gave him a view along the cleared strip in front of the Orchard Close defence line. Figures moved in between and inside the damaged houses, ducking for cover as the searchlight swept back and forth.

As the light swept back towards the gate end, a group of about thirty broke cover heading for the corner house. Harold shot the first one before he'd taken three steps and the rest scattered back into cover. Harold put in a fresh clip. The reloads this time because it was short range. He'd reloaded the rounds used when laying down the boundary but they were soft lead not metal jacketed. Real man-killers but not as accurate at long range, or so Harold was assuming.

"Get ready." Harold shouted as he began to fire. He aimed at belt height and put all five rounds into the bigger group that came the second time. This time they fired back which was what Harold had been hoping for. Harold put in the third clip but didn't need it.

"Go Army" came from the other room, and Berry whooped as the tracers hammered in from two angles. Harold had been worried that the house would mask the attackers from the Army, and maybe the attackers thought the same. The Army had certainly considered it. They must have spread along the bypass so the only blind spots would be in near the Orchard Close houses. The squaddies had also brought plenty of machine guns.

The attackers broke apart and ran for cover, leaving a swathe of dead and wounded out in the open. Crossbow bolts rattled against the side of Harold's house, fired from the damaged housing. "Don't waste bolts unless there's a clear target." Harold was sorry he'd never had time to knock down some damaged housing and make the clear zone wider as Sarge had suggested.

Several gunshots sounded and Harold saw flashes. Bullets hit the house but most were nowhere near the windows so the shooters were probably using handguns. "Keep to the sides of the windows in case one comes through." Harold was wondering why the Army were ignoring the gunfire when there was a crack from behind and a scream from in front.

"Why don't they just blast the houses?" Seth sounded indignant but Harold had realised what was happening.

"It will be the rules of engagement Seth. A group can be fired on if there's weapons among them, but they can't shoot indiscriminately into the buildings. So the marksmen are shooting at confirmed targets. Something along those lines." Harold would settle for what he could get since the shooting from the derelict properties dropped off rapidly.

Only temporarily. Gunfire rattled further down the line and Harold took a look out of the little side window. "Seth, Nigel, one of you let me know if they come again. I'm looking out the side window."

"I'll do it." Nigel sounded shaken. "I'm probably best watching there anyway in case they get across the gap. I can use this bloody thing on them."

"Good thinking Nigel. There doesn't seem to be any real organisation so I'm hoping the mob keep moving down the line."

"Me too." That was Berry. "I did my best but I'm not sure if I hit anyone."

"Near misses are scary as well. Just take a bit of time and get the range right." Harold forced a laugh. "At least Liz will get to find out if her new points work." Unsurprisingly, nobody else laughed. Harold moved across and knelt by the side window. His third clip was in the rifle and while he waited Harold loaded the loose rounds into an empty one. He'd used ten out of twenty-two and this had barely started. So much for trying to preserve the original jacketed rounds.

When a charge started across the open ground Harold held his fire. He only shot twice, at men stopping to raise weapons, and then the tracers were flying again and the charge came apart. Not completely because up to a score kept going and made it close enough to Orchard Close to be hidden from the bypass. Four went down to crossbow bolts or possibly the two-two rifle, and more stumbled so were possibly wounded.

Harold was waiting for any to show again because now the line of houses masked the attackers from him. Flame blossomed from about four houses along and there was shouting and the clash of metal. Then a storm of gunfire broke out. Three men broke away from Orchard Close, lit by the flames and the edges of the searchlight glare, but none got far. At least one two-two rifle cracked and crossbow bolts studded the men as they fell.

Someone was using a larger weapon from a derelict building near where that attack came from. Someone in a spot that the marksmen couldn't be sure of because he kept shooting. Harold settled down and waited. As soon the weapon fired he put a round just behind the flash, far enough behind to hit the shooter. Then Harold was ducking and rolling across the floor, away from the window.

"What's that?" The sheer terror in Nigel's voice was echoed by Berry's and Seth's yells, and Harold wasn't much better.

"That was a bloody automatic!" The attackers had automatics and that meant they'd shoot the defenders to pieces at these ranges. Especially if they had jacketed ammo. "Keep down, those might come through the walls." Harold rolled back towards the window and raised his head a little.

The weapon fired again but not at Harold and a second one joined in. Harold raised his rifle. His few rounds weren't going to be enough because others would pick the weapons up. Harold laid the sights on one of the flashes and moved the point of aim back a bit. "Shit!" Harold almost fired in pure reflex but now he wasn't going to be required.

There were less tracers, but the brick walls flying apart explained why. There was serious weaponry up on the bypass. A light cannon for starters. Harold felt a cold chill up his back. If there were tanks as well then he hoped the Army were worried about collateral. The muzzle blast alone could hurt people. Especially if the Army came off the bypass and started firing between these houses.

The cannon fire moved along the line of derelict housing and the previous reluctance to fire without a clear target had disappeared. Harold mashed the button on the radio. "Matthew. Cease fire, tell our lot to not fire anything! One muzzle flash right now and some trigger happy oik up there will blow the house apart." Harold gave the same message to Casper, who reported movement at the far side of the caravan park.

Then he said "Oh shit" and the radio went quiet. Harold tried to see or listen but the cannon was still hammering, and had been joined by another. Several machine guns were lashing the places smashed by the cannon with short bursts of tracers. Harold relaxed just a little, because nobody would be charging out into that.

Harold winced and raised his arm, but the light and heat were about sixty yards away. A large section of the housing that had been smashed by the cannon caught fire. Not caught fire, it ignited into an instant inferno and Harold didn't need the smell. Napalm had been dropped on them.

"What's that?" Berry was terrified and there were shouts and a scream from below.

"The RAF are burning the bastards. Keep down in case it drops nearer." Harold kept down and passed the same warning over the radio. Then he sat and hoped the RAF were only using helicopters. If the jets came in napalm wasn't precision, the canisters bounced all over the place. Collateral was even more scary when you were the possible subject.

"They're coming Harold. Hundreds of them, maybe thousands." Casper's voice was sober and didn't have much hope. "We'll hold as long as we can. Cheers mate. Get the hell out with who you can and good luck."

Harold half-rose to go and help, but a group broke from the wrecked houses opposite. "Harold, they're coming." Nigel's warning was heeded because seconds later one of the group stumbled with a shaft sprouting from his chest. The damaged housing this end wasn't on fire and this lot weren't waiting for napalm. Blind panic or just pure hatred drove them out across the open ground and Harold emptied the clip in a roll of four quick shots.

"Save the pistol." Nigel had fired but he'd probably missed as the remaining men were still twenty yards out. Two more toppled with shafts in them though one was struggling to get up with a crossbow bolt in his leg. Harold got the next clip in, his last, and took a second longer for each shot now. Five men went down hard when he hit them as did three men behind them.

Another five or six went down, some with shafts in them, then three more and Harold wondered where the extra bullets were coming from. The Army marksmen, maybe, since they weren't needed elsewhere? The last four broke and ran sideways, off across the car park. "Leave them, save your ammo. If any of the wounded try to come this way or use a weapon, take your time to make sure and kill them."

"OK Harold. Do you think they'll come again? I've used up over half my arrows." Seth sounded worried and had the right to be. Orchard Close didn't have the firepower or ammunition to stop these numbers if they didn't attract Army fire by using firearms. Harold was down to two shots in his rifle.

Above the roar of the flames Harold could hear firing from the other end, the gate. He took the rifle into the other room. "There's two shots left in here. Wait until they're close and they'll go through two people. I'm going to the gate."

"Why Harold? What if they come again?" There was no hint of the cheery brewer left in Berry's pale face.

"All those bodies should put them off trying here again. There's a big attack on the gate so I'm going to try and help." Harold showed the handgun. "It's going to be close and furious and this will help." He scooped up his stick and headed down the stairs.

"How's it going?" "Is it over?"

"Not yet but we stopped the attacks here. I'm going to the gate. If anyone gets over the wall here just keep them out of the doors, OK?" Harold grinned at them all. "If that happens I'll be coming up right behind them." He turned as the relieved smiles bloomed on worried faces, and let himself out. Harold really hoped he'd be coming back. Then he ran towards the gunfire.

Fifty or sixty yards along the street he passed the broken section of wall and scattered bodies where the attackers had briefly made it over. Four figures were trying to build the wall back up. "Get indoors. If that crap splashes over here you can't put it out." Startled faces looked at Harold, glanced at the flames and billowing smoke forty paces away, and ran for the houses.

Ten steps later Harold stopped, aghast. The deep bellow and the vibration right through his bones meant that there was a real battle tank firing up there. He pulled out the radio. "Casper, Casper. Get away from the windows. Duck, everyone. If they use a bloody shell Christ knows where the crap will hit." There was no reply. Harold pressed Matthew's button.

"What the f...what the hell was that, Harold?"

"Tank. Heads down, right down." There was a whistle and a deep moaning noise overhead. "Really down, kiss the floor." Harold turned and started to run back. Then he more or less kissed the tarmac as the road did it's best to smack him silly.

The artillery or mortar rounds crashed down, then again, and again. Harold felt a wave of relief since they were well over, deep inside the damaged housing. He lurched to his feet as the radio crackled and Berry's voice came on. "Harold. Harold! They're coming Harold."

"I'm coming Berry." Harold ran flat out, cursing himself. He dived for the road again and the ground kicked back as more rounds ploughed into the houses, but still across that narrow gap away from Orchard Close. He was up on his feet straight away and running, and now Harold could hear shouting ahead. He really hoped the shots were Nigel. Then there were other shots, just a few, and Harold could see the corner house.

A crowd were around the door, trying to get inside while others were attempting to pull the boards from the ground floor windows. Harold stopped thirty feet away, propped the stick against his leg, and raised the pistol two-handed. "Oy, bastards!" Harold bellowed as loud as possible and then emptied the twelve rounds, six each side of the door. He didn't want to hit the defenders. Harold got the other clip in and repeated the process as the men around the door turned and a group ran at him.

Then Harold grabbed the stick, dropped the gun, and went for them with blade and club. A line of fire bit his leg, and something hit his shoulder. Harold jerked his head back as a machete tried for his head and kicked a convenient leg bloody hard. Then stamped on an arm reaching for a dropped machete. Meanwhile he thrust and slashed and clubbed and flailed in a combination of training and ice cold rage.

Four loud shots from overhead and the bodies were thrown forward past Harold. The group hesitated as men went down, shot from behind. Someone shouted 'charge' and there were now spears and machetes stabbing and hacking into their backs. Bricks landed from above and attackers spread out. As they did spears and clubs reached past Harold to get at them. Reinforcements had arrived from the neighbouring houses.

Harold chased two of the attackers down the side of the house and got one before the other got over the partly broken wall. As he stood, head bowed and gasping for breath, the escaping man raced across the open space until he pitched forward with a shaft in his back. Behind Harold there were cheers and jeers, and they were voices he knew. Harold cleaned the blade and wiped off his stick, then used it to limp back towards the door.

"Hey, Harold. You're crazy, you do know that?" Nigel was looking out of an upstairs window."

"So is that daughter of yours with her bricks." Harold smiled up at Nigel. "So are you, sticking your head outside with that bloody lot still flying overhead. Get indoors." Harold came in sight of the door and paused.

"I'm just dealing with the wounded. The bastards killed Sue." Isiah might be reclusive and have a limp, but he was methodically wielding a spear right now. He put the point about where the fallen man's heart would be, then threw his weight on it until the point sank right in. Then he wrenched the spear clear and moved to the next, regardless of if the next target was moving or not. Beyond him Kerry, his wife, was performing the same task using a machete and going for necks. Both had faces like stone despite the tear tracks gleaming in the firelight.

Isiah's limp was more pronounced because he'd got a big cut on his left leg, and his wife had her left arm tucked inside her coat. Sue was laid across the entrance with dark stains on her front, and a coat across her face. Harold assumed it was Sue, because the fourth defender was by the wall at the end of the house, trying to rebuild it. Beyond him scattered figures were running across the car park as if the Hounds of Hell were on their heels.

Harold looked around and five figures were heading back down the road to their original positions. One was limping and another was holding an arm but there were no friends among the bodies lying here.

Finn came along the road from nearer the bypass. He'd been there with a pistol crossbow and a baseball bat as a last ditch defence. "Pippa and Robert are still back there with that little crossbow and clubs. I tried to get here, Harold."

"It was all too quick, Finn, go back and get under cover." More rounds moaned and whistled overhead. "One of those could still land short."

"Crap. Really?" Finn looked at the debris being tossed up in among the ruins. Definitely ruins now.

"Go, scat, we've just been tidying up and now we're going indoors." Finn turned and walked quickly away, nursing his arm. Harold called out to the others. "Come on, indoors now where we're safer." He walked back to pick up the handgun and the empty clip. The empty brass could wait.

Sue had been pulled inside and the door was propped shut as soon as he got back. As well as possible since the door had been broken in and both the lock and hinges were torn free. The other three defenders were huddled together, bandaging and murmuring, and in Kerry's case crying softly. "Thank you. All of you. I'll be upstairs." Harold hobbled up to the big corner bedroom.

Upstairs Seth was curled up in the corner, hunched around his upper arm, and Berry was trying to stop the blood. She was getting there but Seth had lost a good bit already. A cut off arrow shaft on the floor explained why.

His white face looked up. "Oh good. Berry set off with bricks after I got hit trying to use your rifle. Nigel followed, with that gun." He winced. "Then there was screaming." He gestured to a loaded crossbow. "I was waiting to see who came through the door."

"If you'd shot me I'd have slapped you." Berry gave her efforts a critical look and kissed the bandage. "There, all kissed better."

"My face hurts as well?"

Berry looked at Seth and smiled. "You finally asked. All it took was being nearly killed."

"Hey, steady on there. Father present." But Nigel was smiling. So was Seth when Berry straightened up again after making his face better.

Harold looked through the firing slits. "We all need to keep down and away from openings until this stops. You may as well sit and hold hands, Berry. I'll send your Dad out if you like."

"Not a chance. I'm not leaving her alone with him. She's a pushover for a wounded hero." Nigel ducked as he was quickly Berry'd. Then the three sat in a row along the wall. Harold limped downstairs to check on the rest and scrounge a bandage himself. The wadded cloth he'd stuffed through the rip in his jeans leg needed binding in place.

Then he came back up and settled down in the other bedroom to wait until the Army was done. The most worrying thing was no response from the gate, but neither was there any alarm from Matthew. Matthew reported that the rioters weren't pouring down the inside road so the gate had held.

Twice Harold went to look out of the side windows, back into Orchard Close, when an explosion was in the wrong place. One house now had the roof blown off and the upper floors shattered. Harold tried to remember who lived there, and hoped they were with the defenders. The second short shell landed the other side of a boundary house so Harold couldn't see the damage caused.

Occasional bullets or shrapnel and debris clattered as they hit the roof, since the Army were still firing into the chaos beyond the narrow boundary strip. Forty yards seemed a long way until someone was throwing fire and explosives about. Once again Harold berated himself for not knocking down those houses. Also for going off to the gate. Maybe Sue would be alive if he'd stayed? Or maybe the shrapnel whizzing about would have killed one of those repairing the walls?

Eventually the explosions stopped, though there was still gunfire from down by the gate. Harold had a good look out of all the upstairs windows. Berry was indignant. "The nasty gits fired the building as they ran." The single story office on the big car park was burning.

"It's just that Berry. Sheer nastiness because they got whupped. I don't mind really because they missed the garage at the side. That was what I was worried about or I would have let the first lot get on with it." Harold smiled. "We haven't got many vehicles so the fuel should last for ages."

"Sal said the underground tanks were empty because the petrol pumps said so."

"Technically, because someone must have pumped until it said empty before breaking the pump itself. There's a lot still in there but it will need straining. We've got diesel and petrol for a while if we're careful."

"Can't you bring it inside here?" Seth seemed a bit better, the hand holding must be healing as well.

"We would need too many cans and then one spark and we've lost the lot. With that wide open tarmac we can stop anyone nicking it." Harold grimaced. "We can when I reload all the empty shell casings. I've got two left."

"I used all mine up." Nigel looked at the floor. "I'll do the housekeeping in a bit and collect them."

"There's more on the road outside and probably outside the wall. With luck we'll now have a tomorrow to sort all that out. Or maybe day after tomorrow because none of us will sleep tonight." Harold went to the door. "Nobody will be coming across the cleared section tonight because the houses at the other side are a raging inferno. I'm going to the gate."

"Why?"

"I can't get a reply on the radio. I'll take mine and get back to you. I can't reinforce them because we've got nothing left." Harold waved at his rifle. "You've still got two in that."

Seth pointed at three shafts. "We've got some arrows for the crossbows."

"They're bolts according to the internet."

"Yes dear."

"Dear!" Berry glared at Seth. "Do you want a slap?"

"Please?" Seth was grinning.

Berry looked at her Dad. "Hey, I've found a volunteer. You might get a break."

"As long as you keep holding his hand so it doesn't get into mischief."

*   *   *

Harold left them to it and limped down and out of the door. The three downstairs were actually asleep though one roused as Harold scraped the door open and jammed it shut again. He limped down the road, looking at the houses either side. There were more broken windows but not too many, and there were broken tiles here and there.

Harold paused where the shell or mortar round had landed between the boundary houses. The original broken down section of boundary wall had a big bite out it and a chunk of the house wall nearby had been blown in. There was a body hanging over the edge of the exposed upstairs floor. Harold thought of going up there, but not yet. Not until he found out the problem at the gate.

Matthew was stood outside the house he had been defending. His good arm was round Bess and both hers were round Matthew. "Hi Matthew. How is everyone?"

"Sharyn is fine. I'll let her know you're hobbling but mobile. We've got one dead and four wounded in here, mostly from when that machine gun thing fired from over there. There's more dead and wounded along the way." Matthew gave a little smile. "If there's more trouble I'm standing behind Bess. She's a maniac."

"Not really. I think a lot missed. I'm sorry Harold but I got frightened and forgot the single shot thing." Bess looked sorry, and shocked, and was hugging Matthew tightly. "I used them nearly all up."

"But she scared the hell out of those she missed, and we got those." Matthew gave Bess a hug, and smiled at her. "We made a good team."

"Still nothing from the gate?"

"No, I was considering going there but didn't want to leave here." Matthew glanced back up at the house. "We managed to hang on to this place and I wouldn't want to lose it now."

"Fair enough. We'll stay in position until dawn at least. Take turns to get some sleep if you can." Harold left them with a little smile. Being under fire together seemed to be breaking down boundaries.

*   *   *

The gates looked reassuringly intact. The smoke beyond was thick and as it drifted over stank of napalm and burning meat. To Harold's great relief Casper stepped out of a house. "Hello Harold. Lost your way?"

"No you lump. I can't seem to talk to you on this anymore." Harold waved his radio.

"Ah, sorry. My fault." Casper gave an embarrassed shrug. "I put the radio down because I thought we were about to be overrun, and it dropped to the floor."

Casper waved a hand upwards to the house. "It popped open and the batteries rolled out, and one went down between the floorboards. We've been too busy to rip up the floor to find it."

"Yes, busy, I heard you. How many have been hurt? What happened?"

"We've got five in here with holes in them. None that will kill them straight away but we need lots of disinfectant and bandages and recovery time. I don't know about over there." Casper waved at the opposite house, then pointed to the barricade. "Look over there first. We've been redecorated."

"Hang on, let me tell the others that the place is still standing." Harold used the radio to do so then stepped onto his box, still here, and looked over the boundary. "What the... heck happened?" There were hundreds of bodies, starting almost at the barricade and stretching right across the caravan park.

"A bloody great mob gathered on the caravan park over there. I didn't fancy annoying them but you'd said to get the sods to fire if possible. Toby did it with that little rifle. He must have hit something since after the second shot some of them started shooting back. Then another mob came down the road and past the end here, heading for the bypass." Casper gave a little smile. "About four million of them according to my quick count. I screamed cease fire to everyone so we didn't annoy them."

"Harold." He turned and had his arms full of Emmy. "Ooh, I really need this." She stepped back, smiling. "I'll get a full breakdown soggy-hug later." Emmy turned to Casper. "Have you told him about the explosions?"

"Not yet Emmy, because we were rudely interrupted." Casper grinned at her, then sobered and turned to Harold. "The Army were shooting at those in the caravan park, shooting the ones with weapons. We could see well enough from here because that light was on them. Meanwhile there was firing from up there towards the bypass. I reckon the four million opened fire."

"Four million? You counted? Sorry, carry on." Emmy waved up at number two and beckoned.

Casper carried on. "If they did it was a mistake. There was this bloody great boom."

"Tank, Casper. That's when I nearly messed myself."

"I'm pleased I'm not the only one because I need to check my undies as well." Casper grinned.

Emmy looked to the side. "You're just in time, Holly. They're checking undies."

"Ooh good. Will you check mine please, Harold?" Holly stopped, mouth open as the other three turned and stared. A bright scarlet blush crept up her neck and covered her face. "Er, um, I mean. Oh." She turned and fled.

"I blame the excitement. That was decidedly un-Holly like. Though if you are checking undies I'll let the girl's club know?" Emmy raised an eyebrow.

"Not until Casper or you finally tell me where all the bodies came from, and why the garages seem to be mostly knocked down?" Harold hoped that the invitation was just the excitement and a slip of the tongue. Seventeen year old Holly was still mourning her boyfriend and definitely didn't need to be getting sudden crushes on twenty year old ex-soldiers. Not the sort that invited knicker inspections.

"The tank, as I now know, did something bloody awful to the crowd going up there. Some of them were actually fighting to get back, away from it." Casper was still impressed by that idea.

"Was there an explosion?"

"No?"

"Think of that tank gun, then think of one of your shotgun rounds blown up to that size. One thousand nasty little bits of metal someone once told me."

Casper went pale "Crap." He swallowed. "Anyway, the Army got fed up of shooting those in the caravan park one at a time. About then they started using something a lot worse. I think some were machine guns, lines of tracer like on films. The others were tracers but exploded. Not big ones but men out in the open were being torn to bits."

Casper had a minute to recover and take a drink after that memory. Harold left him to do so because that would have been bloody, and shocking. Then the big man took a deep breath before continuing. "The big gun went boom again and suddenly the mob at the end of our road were all trying to get away. A lot turned up here. I yelled for everyone to open fire. We sort of slowed them up but it wasn't going to be enough. Then one of the tracer things that exploded ripped lumps out of the garages, the road, and the crowd coming at us."

"Light cannon, probably on a personnel carrier or an armoured car."

"Whatever it was is terrifying and I'm glad they were accurate." Casper waved at the house. "I hope you can make refills for the weapons because apart from the little rifles we used most of it up. That didn't take long which is worrying. I shouted for everyone to get their heads down because bullets and arrows were coming at us and even our crossbow bolts were getting a bit short." Casper glanced at the barricade. "We could do with nipping over there and getting some back."

"Not a good idea tonight. Maybe tomorrow depending on the Army?"

"Definitely up to the Army because I'm not annoying them. There were some big explosions out there. When I peeked there were heaps of bodies on the main road. Those cars parked over there in the gardens? Well, you've seen them, they're scrap." Casper looked around him. "There was stuff pinging off everything so we kept low and waited. Several houses down there on the main road caught fire eventually. I was worried something would hit one of our houses."

"Something did back there. Twice and we've lost at least one person but I couldn't see who."

"Oh, the rotten bastards." Casper looked towards the bypass where a searchlight still illuminated the main roadway.

"Not really, in the cold light of survival. Without the Army chucking big stuff we'd all be dead, Casper. There were more than I imagined. Christ, this was a small mob, can you imagine that big one?" Harold was angry about the deaths as well, but he wanted the residents thinking rationally about the two shells. He looked at the swathes of bodies on the approach road and they would have swamped the barricade. "Shifting that lot is going to be a lousy job."

"Leave the bastards to rot." Casper stopped. "We can't, can we? The stink would be appalling."

"Not to mention flies, scavengers, and possible diseases. Let's hope we've got enough people fit to shift them all." Harold turned to the other house, number one. "Come on, let's find out."

*   *   *

"Shit, shit, crap and I really want to Army swear." Harold went to his knees next to the body. Barely marked except for the hole on his forehead. The mess at the back of his head was disguised by the bundled jacket.

"He was really proud you know. That you trusted him with the rifle, and let him stand with the rest of us." Sal had a hand on Harold's shoulder. "Toby was doing what he wanted, Harold. He was at the window, shooting as fast as he could."

"It'll kill his Mum. Oh crap, I'll have to tell Faith."

"I'll get one of the girl's club to do it."

"No Sal. This really is my job. Anyone else?"

"Chris. One of the big group that arrived with Conn and Bess. He was hit in the chest with something big that came clean through the plywood. He only survived a few minutes. We've got three wounded but they're all wrapped up and not bleeding much now. They'll be all right until they can get to Patricia. One needs an arrow digging out."

"They're all walking?"

"Ours as well." Casper shrugged. "I reckoned it had to be the height of the window sills. Nothing came through the walls so everyone got hit above the waist."

The door burst open and Holly came in "Oh, no, not Toby. I didn't know. He was so young!" She came across to look at Toby and then buried her head in Harold's shoulder. Nobody smiled this time. After a while Holly raised her teary face and then went scarlet as she looked at Harold's face. "Oh, er." She fled.

They heard her clattering down the stars. "Hello what's the matter?" The voice on the stairs was Hazel's and Sal was immediately moving to catch her at the top, on the landing. Before she saw Toby.

The voices were clear through the almost closed door. "What have you got, Hazel?"

"Hot coffee. Betty thought everything had gone quiet so she sent Veronica up towards Harold and I came this way. It's in a teapot so I can carry it and the mugs are tied together by the handle. I'll bring another one for the other house." There was a chinking noise outside the door. "I've got a tin of milk here in my pocket and a clicker full of sweeteners. Betty says we're saving sugar."

"That's great, Hazel. Just what we need to keep us going."

"Is everyone all right because fifteen, the one in Meadow Lane, has been all blown up."

"Nobody was in there Hazel. Off you go." Sal came in with the coffee and tears were starting to trickle down her cheeks. "I couldn't tell her."

Harold straightened his back and braced his shoulders. "I'll do it when I get home. Will Holly be all right?"

"Yes. She just forgot you were there." Harold kept looking and Emmy sighed. "Any other time this would be funny. We make jokes in the girl's club. Holly made a girl's club joke but you were actually there."

"Jokes about, er?" Harold felt the blush work up his face. "Oh." Because there were those sorts of jokes in the Army, about certain girls that the men fancied and didn't expect to get near to. He turned and went to the door. "I'll check on the wounded, to thank them. I'll come back for Toby in a minute, and take him home."

Harold went across to the other house after talking to the three wounded, and spoke to the wounded there, and the rest of the defenders. Nothing profound, just agreeing the whole night had been bloody awful, and thanking them all for standing firm. He explained the tank and napalm to those who wanted to know, and the light cannon that had chewed up the garages and the attackers. "How's Toby?"

"Come over with me, Alfie, and you can see him."

Alfie looked around. "Will that be all right? I don't want to leave this house short-handed."

"No problem. That mob is broken for tonight, and maybe forever. The Army blew the hell out of the houses where they were gathering, then burned them." Harold gestured at the two-two. "Leave the rifle."

Alfie propped the weapon against the wall and took a box of rounds out of his pocket and put them with it. "It's the only gun with ammunition, except maybe a few for Casper's shotgun." Alfie followed Harold across the landing and down the stairs. "I really need to sort out that bow. It'll be a lot faster than the rifle. For me at least."

"Not the same range though, or accuracy at range."

"I'm useless at range anyway as yet. Toby is a lot better." They were outside now and Harold turned and took a deep breath.

"Not any more, Alfie. Toby didn't make it."

Harold watched that sink in and caught the young man in both arms for a solid hug before releasing him. Enough for support without offending his budding masculinity. "He was at the window, doing what he was supposed to. Shooting that little rifle like a maniac. He's upstairs in number one." Alfie headed that way in a sort of daze and Harold walked alongside.

"But how? Why? If he was behind the plywood? It's not right. Toby was better than most of the men with his rifle." Alfie cleared his throat as a warble came into his voice. "He really liked that rifle. He was going to be, er."

"I know. A soldier. He would have made a damn good soldier. In fact he already was one."

"How?"

"Toby stood on the line, and he defended his people, and he died doing it. You can't get any nearer." Harold sighed. "If he'd been older the Army would have been lucky to get him."

"Oh no, he wanted to, well, be a soldier here. Protect everyone." Alfie stumbled over the words, and now he stumbled over the stairs a little and scrubbed at his eyes.

"Let it go Alfie. Cry. It's not wrong, and I cry when that's what I need. I will cry over Toby, probably a few times before I'm done." Harold still expected Alfie to hold it in because of his age and sex, but hoped he'd let the grief out later. Emmy put her head out as she heard feet on the stairs, and spoke over her shoulder.

As Alfie reached the top the room's occupants came out but Harold caught hold of Sal's arm. "Stay please, because mine is the wrong shoulder. He won't accept it." Sal's eyes opened in alarm and Harold gave her a sad smile. "Your turn kiddo."

"OK." Sal watched Alfie go through the door and her face softened. "Fair enough. Though I'll want a shoulder as well sometime."

"Won't we all after this, Sal."

*   *   *

Harold waited outside until a red-eyed Alfie came out. He saw Harold and straightened up. "What so you want me to do now, Harold?"

"Go back over there, and tell everyone to sleep in turns where they can. We'll stay here until morning and then see what happens." Casper came out of the other room with the walking wounded following. "Casper will organise sleep shifts."

Harold tried to lift Toby but the wound in his leg wouldn't allow it, so in the end he pulled the door off the airing cupboard. Harold put a sheet from the airing cupboard over the lad and his stick alongside him, and called for assistance.

"I'll do it. I've known Toby for the last year so better than a stranger." Billy glanced at Emmy and Sal who had both volunteered. "No offence meant. You're not strangers but." He gave an uncomfortable shrug.

"I've only known most of you for a few weeks and none of you are strangers, but I understand." Emmy produced the ghost of a smile. "A soldier should have a couple of big rough blokes anyway."

Billy glanced at her but Emmy wasn't taking the mickey. Emmy and Sal did help to get the improvised stretcher down the stairs, then stayed in the house as Harold and Billy took Toby home.

The news had spread because there were people on the side of the road with their heads bowed. Louise, the reclusive graphics designer who was a long-time friend of Toby's Mum followed them up the road. By the time they turned up the path Liz was waiting to open the door, and Hilda arrived and followed Harold inside.

When Harold left, fifteen bruising minutes later, Faith was surrounded by five women she knew. Karen had just come in. As he left Harold could hear the same question again, the one he couldn't answer. "Why Toby? He's only a boy, what was he doing facing those men with a gun?"

This time Harold heard a clear calm answer, from Karen. "He was protecting his Mum, Faith. What else could he do?"

Harold spent the next few hours working up and down the line between the boundary houses, checking how everyone was. Two dead at the gate, one in Matthew's strongpoint, three where the mob came through the wall the first time, two in the shelled house, and Sue. He sent the wounded to Patricia, and Sharyn home to the kids. He also sent Pippa, Olive and Suzie, Sue's sister, up to the big house to look after their children. The last three had all arrived over the last couple of days, but had stood on the boundary to do their part.

*   *   *

Since more batteries had been sent to the gate, Harold now had his little communicator back. Which meant that Casper could pass his worries along. "I think you need to get your soldier ass up here. There's big engines revving up on the bypass." Harold could soon hear the noise as he headed that way and had a good idea what was revving up.

At least the limping was easier after Patricia and her team had stuck a proper bandage on Harold's leg. He would be pleased when he got home to change because he'd lost the bottom half of his jean's leg in the process. Patricia had found a diversion for Faith's grief. The entire group of women had been seconded as nurses, along with Hazel and Veronica. According to Patricia, in a quiet aside to Harold, it would help them get through the night.

"What are they doing, Harold?" Casper might have slept, but he looked haggard so maybe not.

"I reckon those are tanks. Tell everyone to put their weapons on the floor and do not pick them up. We've nothing that can scratch one, and if you annoy the driver he'll run over the house." Harold met Casper's incredulous look. "Not over, but right through will do the same job. Tell anyone with a loose mouth to shut up this time." Casper headed into the house on the run and Harold went to the other one.

"Who's in charge?"

"You are, I hope." Emmy was trying for cheeky but was a bit rough looking as well. The strain and lack of sleep wasn't doing anyone any favours this morning.

"Silly sod. In here I mean because big rough soldiers surrounded by armour are coming to call and I don't want them annoyed." Harold glanced at her crossbow. "Put that down and the spear for starters. Then get everyone to do the same until I tell them different."

"We could offer them a bottle of beer? Blow kisses?" Emmy frowned. "No, because if any of them took me up on it I'm too knackered." She sighed. "I'll tell the rest."

"Tell them seriously. All and every weapon on the floor and don't even look too hard at the soldiers. I'm going to be stood on that box and hopefully talking to someone and really don't want them nervous." He smiled. "Resist the impulse to shout this time, please?" Harold looked round. "The beer is a good idea. Where is it?"

"Here, there's only a couple of bottles."

"Perfect. I want them happy, not drunk." Harold headed outside and stood on his box.

The engines were growling closer now. Even though he expected it, sort of, a full sized battle tank crunching and clanking past the end of the Orchard Close entrance road was a bit of a shock. Harold had the same feeling as he'd had in London. Those things shouldn't be allowed in built-up areas. The armoured personnel carrier that turned up the road towards him was almost an anti-climax. It stopped twenty feet away and the hatch popped open.

"Who are you?"

Harold weighed up the lieutenant and decided on playing down the Army part. "Harold Miller."

"Are you the gang boss, or head of security, or whatever?"

"No, or maybe a whatever. Nominal leader by impromptu vote of the residents." Two thirds anyway, Harold thought. The rest had been told.

"All of them?"

"All except the kids under fourteen."

The officer looked at the houses, and then the barricade. "There was a lot of fire coming from here."

"Briefly until they ran out. There's a few arrows and a few two-two rounds left and nobody is aiming any at you."

"Good. We are clearing the road and moving into the city. Please don't obstruct us."

"You must be joking. We've been praying for it." Harold paused but he had to ask. "What will happen to us?"

"Nothing if you keep out of it. We have a list of enclaves, and yours isn't on it. What is yours called, just for the record, and how big an area do you claim?"

"Claim? Look, can we talk sensibly instead of shouting. After all if anyone does something silly we'll last as long as it takes to pull a trigger." Harold looked each way. "I can come round but it will take few minutes. This doesn't open."

The lieutenant talked on his radio for a moment. Behind him another tank crunched past and then a personnel carrier. "I've got clearance. The sergeant claims you are decent people." The officer clambered down and walked up to the barricade and read the sign. "Without invitation? If they get one how does that work since you can't open up?" He seemed more relaxed now and genuinely interested.

"They have to walk through a gap in the garages and round the side past the vehicles. Then we search them." Harold looked at the wrecked garages. "You've made that easier."

"Is that a problem?"

"Not really, since you sorted out that lot laid in the road. I was going to knock them down to give us some clearance but we never had time." Harold looked at the bodies and grimaced. "They're going to take some clearing away. None of this lot are used to that sort of thing."

"You are, aren't you?" Harold stared and the officer gave a little smile. "It was the way you said it."

"Ex-Army, and I came back from Kuwait straight into riot control in London, and then Calais. Then the Army offered, so I left all legal and proper. I left because my sister is a widow with two kids and the Army weren't helping her much." Harold gestured, slowly, towards his house. "The place with the flag."

"The Army widow? We were told, but not about you. Are the rest all civvies?"

"Yes. We've got people from seventy six down to four. About these bodies. Can we retrieve our arrows now just in case some of that lot come back?"

"They won't. We're chasing them home. If nobody does anything foolish we could clear the road for you?" Behind the officer the next rumbling and clanking was an armoured bulldozer. The blade was pushing a mess of bodies and some masonry. The machine swerved to push them, and the wreckage of the cars, through the ruined house opposite the entrance. Then it reversed out of sight.

The officer looked where Harold was watching. "That's the only practical way. We'll be heaping them up at the far side of that open space." He looked at the road up to the barricade. "He can clear this lot as well?"

"I'd be really grateful. Though I'd still like to collect the arrows, unless you lot are staying and getting serious about protecting us?" Harold glanced to the side, to the house. "I've already told them to put all weapons on the floor and not touch them until the armour is a long way away."

"Sorry. We're just passing through." He looked up and down the road. "All right, you can collect arrows. Inoffensive people and they do not, repeat not, pick up any firearms."

"Young women?" Harold smiled just a little. "They'll put skirts on instead of jeans if you can control the soldiers. A couple might put on short skirts as a thank you."

The officer smiled back. "We'd better not risk that, Mr Miller. The lads haven't had much leave lately and there's a dearth of young ladies."

"Can they collect baseball bats and machetes, please? We don't have many and every nutter out there has one."

"Hmm. The baseball bats, yes. I'll have to check about the sharp stuff. How did you get on in there? I was told that your lines were breached." The officer hesitated. "Also that there were some short rounds."

"We lost two and some wounded to the artillery, and two houses. We have another seven dead, men and women including a fourteen year old lad who wanted to be a soldier. We've got a lot of wounded and one probably won't make it. Can the Army spare any wound dressings? Antibiotics would help, our trainee nurse tells me?" Harold sighed. "Otherwise we might lose more."

"I really am sorry but no." The officer braced to attention. "There will never be any official recognition that it happened, but the Army is truly sorry about the casualties we caused."

"I understand, and the rest will do so in time. Some already realise that you saved all our lives and the shorts weren't on purpose." Harold thought the apology deserved some recognition. "If you're going to clear the road, I've got something for you or the driver." Harold smiled.

"What would that be?"

"If I threw two bottles over would anyone shoot me?"

"Not if I warn them. Bottles of what?"

"Berry Beer. They will explode if opened too soon after being shaken which would be a crime." Harold held them up.

The lieutenant gave the personnel carrier a hand signal, and turned back. "One at a time, very carefully. There was a rumour about Berry Beer. What berries are they named for?"

"Who. The perfect squaddie's girlfriend, I was told. A pretty, seventeen year old brewer called Berry."

"I'd better not mention that or there could be a riot, and a tank through the gate." The officer was smiling as he put the first one down to carefully catch the second bottle.

"If you clear that lot far enough away so we can't smell them, there could be a couple of crates left in yon house?"

"We'll do that, don't worry. Some of us will be back this way and would probably appreciate the beer, but we'll clear up properly anyway." The officer looked over at the still-burning ruins. "We can't do much about that but most of the nearer bodies will have burned. I still need a name for your enclave, and the number of residents and an area of influence. For the record."

"Orchard Close, and we have seventy residents that but might be sixty-nine tomorrow. We only set a border once in reaction to an attack and that was more of a warning. We want leaving alone, that's all." Harold was puzzled about the area part, were others doing that? "We really might lose more people if the wounds can't be kept clean so the number might not hold."

"I really am sorry but we aren't allowed. We are specifically forbidden in fact by the rules of engagement." The officer shook his head a little. "Those are comprehensive." He glanced towards the city. "I'll include a mile each way, all right? Just it keep it all tidy." The officer went back to his vehicle and spoke into the radio before returning.

"Up to ten women can come out, and they can take edged weapons and bows as well since those are permitted for self-defence. You've got an hour at most until the bulldozer comes to sort this out." The officer smiled. "The ages of the women are your concern but they must not pick up firearms."

"I'll warn them." A thought struck Harold. "Can we get rid of the bodies of the ones we, and you, killed in the clear zone? We can throw them onto the fires the other side, since the buildings are already burning. It'll stop them stinking the place out?"

"That sounds like a really good idea. Bring us any firearms you discover?" The officer had a little smile so Harold assumed he wasn't expecting any. Harold could take that hint.

"Of course, if we actually find any. Thank you."

"You're welcome." He gestured with a bottle of beer. "Your little community is a pleasant surprise and I wish you luck, Mr Miller." The officer climbed onto his personnel carrier and the vehicle reversed to the end of the street.

"Emmy, Sal, Holly!" Harold looked up as the first window opened. "We've got an hour. Ten women can go out there and collect arrows, baseball bats, knives, bows and machetes and then the Army are clearing the road." By now all three were looking from windows. "Please do not touch a firearm no matter how tempting." Harold smiled. "Dress in jeans and don't look too tempting since those soldiers aren't allowed to fraternise." Harold dropped his voice. "We'll get some firearms from the other boundary so don't take risks."

"No problem Harold. Can we smile at the soldiers?" Tired and strained or not, Emmy managed a lovely smile.

"Yes, but stay clear. They haven't seen a woman close up in months and might have no manners at all." Emmy laughed.

"That's a shame. Soldiers give great hugs." Sal waved at the personnel carrier and closed her window. The other windows closed and moments later Holly was running up the street shouting names.

Harold caught Emmy as she ran past. "Just throw the lot over the barricade and we'll sort them later."

"OK, but you'd better move from there or you'll get flattened." Harold did after asking Casper to keep an eye on things, then he set off up the street at a fast limp.

Bess and Berry came past him along with Liz, heading for the gate. They were soon followed by Holly and a slim intense looking young woman with long black hair. "This is Gayle. Gayle, this is Harold." Then the two were gone at the run. Harold needed to catch up on who actually lived here.

*   *   *

Harold went to the centre house of the boundary defence. "We'll need teams, Matthew, to get rid of the dead assholes out there. Maybe four people per team and strong enough between them to throw a body on a fire. Someone with a wound can go as well to help with collecting. We'll take boots, shoes, undamaged clothing, and weapons. Retrieve our shafts either from the bodies or the misses."

"What about any wounded?"

"What wounded? Use crossbows in case they lash out." Harold eyed Matthew. "Are you all right with that?"

The normally mild mannered man produced a fairly good snarl. "Just now most of us will happily nail them to trees for target practice." Then Matthew smiled. "I'll give Bess a full sized crossbow for that job."

"Bess is looking all sweet and innocent for the Army, and collecting allowed weapons and arrows from the bodies outside the gate." Harold glanced that way. "If you get chance before the bulldozer clears them, go and have a peek over the barricade. We were lucky here."

Matthew had started to smile at the comment about Bess but now his face paled. "Really? Christ." He rallied. "I'll get Jon to use the crossbow. He's limping but both hands work just fine."

"Fair enough. Be really careful with firearms if there are any."

Matthew frowned. "What should we actually do about retrieving the guns? There's at least one shotgun I can see."

"Cover them with clothing, then bring them back all bundled up. Make sure you get a person between the weapon and the Army while you cover them up." Harold grimaced, "Search the bodies as well as you can for ammo and anything else useful. Lighters, penknives, whatever."

"Cash?"

"Good thinking, if we can ever find anywhere to spend it." Harold tried to think but that more or less covered it. "Pocket any used ammo as well and I'll refill them."

"Really? You really can?" Matthew smiled. "We thought it was only the little ones for the rifle."

"I can reload some of the others." Harold grinned. "Then your girlfriend can go crazy again."

Matthew shuffled his feet a bit and looked uncomfortable. "About that. I wouldn't mind, and Bess seems interested? It's just when we dived for the floor I banged my shoulder, and she came to see if I was all right." Matthew shrugged with his good shoulder. "Then she wanted a hug because that banging and fire really was bloody scary and you said it was my job." He gave a little smile. "She hugged back and we talked a bit. Bess says it's nice to have a choice."

"Just be sure how far you want it to go. I mean as in permanent or a fling. Bess might have different ideas." Harold was smiling for two reasons. Matthew was a bit shy and if Bess had shifted targets Harold was off the hook. He didn't think Bess would use the hand holding approach.

"Er, right. Oh! How far? Bloody hell!" Matthew looked stunned. "Er, right. Teams." Harold left him to it and went to check on the rest.

*　　　*　　　*

An hour and a half later the last body and most of the rubble from the approach road and the front gardens of the main road were in a heap. A large heap at the opposite side of the caravan park, which Harold still thought would be too close when the bodies rotted. The Army thought the heap was too near to their people on the bypass, or were being very tidy, because they solved that. Or rather the RAF did when the whole lot was inundated in what smelled like oil, and then napalm. That stank, but not of rot.

The heap was still firmly ablaze as the bulldozer and the last armoured vehicle headed into the city. Behind the barricade there was a crowd of busy people sorting out the scattered bats and arrows and suchlike. There weren't a lot of machetes and some were bent, and most of the bats were wood, but the collection was a primitive armoury. There were only two crossbows and one had been run over by the personnel carrier.

"I can straighten these if I'm careful." Liz was inspecting a bent machete. "Though it will need a lot of charcoal." She looked over at the ruins where fires still blazed. "Now the tree thing is really serious. Even bushes with thick stems will do, Harold. Then we can make charcoal ourselves."

"What about the roof timbers? Further back there were more explosions and less napalm and roof timbers will have survived." Harold looked at the bent blades. "We could make as much as you like."

"No thanks. Those timbers will be treated and the fumes could be lethal. Do you know all the gods of the forge and old smiths in legend were crippled? That's because the real smiths were, due to fumes and lousy ventilation." Liz crooked her back and hobbled a step. "Nope, my fair body stays unsullied by chemicals, ta. So you need lumberjacks."

"I'll put one on the list with a blacksmith. Blimey, I'd better stop the barbecue brigade and those who like a log on a fire." There weren't many logs being burned yet but some had been gathered. The simple solution to barbecues was to impound all charcoal.

Emmy came over with a big shopping bag. "There you are Liz. We're cutting the broken shafts off like you said." She waved a particularly spiked arrow head. "This was a bitch to pull out."

"Good. Typical though, those are also a bitch to make. Did you save the other end?"

"Yup, someone else is bagging them. Though there's plenty of plastic for new ones laid about."

"Ah, but Toby… Oh cripes, that will take some getting used to. The, um, info from the internet says the originals are curved to spin and they work better." Liz sighed. "That's gonna be a real problem for a while." She bent over the machetes again.

Emmy went back to sorting, and Harold went to find something to occupy himself other than thinking of Toby. Berry fixed that.

"I've got a bit of a question, Harold."

"If your Dad doesn't mind, Seth can move into the brewery."

Harold ducked but was still lightly Berry'd. "Stop it, we're only holding hands. Well, a bit of snogging as well but definitely not moving in yet." Berry sniggered. "Dad would have a heart failure. I'm still about twelve in his head." Then she straightened. "No, this is a serious question, because I'm not sure of what I saw."

"When?"

"When you turned into what Liz calls the alien killing machine. That wasn't a machete, and you don't carry one anyway. Then it was gone. I've been trying to persuade myself you were using your sheath knife." Berry sighed. "Tell me that it was so I can forget the whole thing. The whole attack was confusing and all over so quick and I'd rather not keep replaying."

"Who did you tell?"

Berry narrowed her eyes. "Nobody, because I might have been imagining."

Harold debated lying. But Berry was smart and she'd not believe sheath knife. "Will you keep a secret from Seth and your Dad?"

"Keep a secret from Dad?"

"I'd prefer it." Harold smiled. "Practice for if Seth gets beyond snogging?"

"Hey! Stop that!" Berry gave a little smile. "I will need to tell Dad a porky or two about someone eventually. All right, yes."

"Seriously?"

"Very. Cross my heart. Now tell me or I'm going to slap you." Berry was smiling.

"All right. Step this way just out of sight." Harold showed her the weapon, quickly. "Now you say nothing, but you'll sleep in peace. Very, very few people know."

"Christ, Harold, why? People would feel safer knowing."

"If that's a secret and things go very bad, the assholes might think I'm more or less disarmed. I trained a long time to do that stuff and still do, so let that make you feel better. But also keep it quiet." Harold smiled. "Or I'll tell your Dad I saw you nipping into an empty house with Seth, and Seth that you were snogging Billy."

"Yeuk. Don't you dare. My lips are sealed." Berry looked closer at the stick. "What do the words say?"

"The pen is mightier than the sword."

"Some pen. All right, Harold. Thanks." She left with a cheery wave.

Harold worried about Berry for a while, which was a bit better than thinking about Toby and the others.

*   *   *

Eventually everyone ground to a halt and headed home, defeated by sheer exhaustion. Almost everyone. Harry senior, along with several of the others unable to fight such as the arthritic Sandy, stood guard. They all claimed to have managed some rest in the night and early morning. Harold checked one last time that the impromptu sentries were all clear on the radio links and alarms, and headed home. Fatigue and grief were eating at him now, because despite everything he'd lost a lot of people. One in ten. One in five of the actual defenders.

Harold came round the corner into Orchard Close and stopped. Fourteen women were lined up at the front of the girl's club houses and none were laughing. Harold didn't even know the names of two. Many were dirty or dishevelled and some were wounded. Casper spoke up. "We thought you needed the hug this time. Sort of thank you and sympathy all combined."

Harold walked up the road trying to work this out. Were they serious? What he wasn't prepared for was one of Casper's arms round him and a quick hug. "Well done, mate." Then Casper smiled. "Liz is right, you are scrawny." Harold felt a little smile form.

Bess was next. "This is your first and last, soldier boy. You missed your chance." Matthew was stood nearby with a bemused smile so Harold didn't need an explanation.

Harold received thirteen more hugs without any of the usual teasing. They all murmured things like 'well done' or 'thanks, Harold' and there were eleven little kisses. Though several couldn't resist pointing out that they would need a proper soggy-hug at some time. Holly was next to last. She blushed a little bit, but still hugged Harold firmly and gave him a gentle kiss.

Liz was last. Her hug was thorough. "I know you feel like crap," she whispered, "but we, Orchard Close, survived. As a mouse I am very grateful, and even the ferocious ones feel the same. Now go and sleep, wimp." A firm kiss was applied to Harold's lips. "I'll need to wash that off, but it's a small price." She pushed Harold towards home.

Two steps inside the door and Harold had two more hugs, from Sharyn and then Hazel. Hazel's was very teary and she definitely needed some hugging back. Then Harold's leg bandage was inspected by Daisy. "I want an Uncle-Harold story about that. Are the bangs all finished?"

"Yes Daisy. All done."

"So why is everyone crying?" Harold was still trying to come up with an answer to that when Daisy moved on. "I've got some new friends. Georgina is *seven* and she's got a real Cindy doll. She says I can play if I'm careful."

"Good. Now I'm going to go to bed, because I forgot to sleep last night. I'll be awake in time for stories." Daisy headed for her Mum, and Harold went upstairs and more or less passed out on his bed. He roused later, enough to get a shower, and eat a meal, and read Daisy a story that wasn't about leg wounds. Then Harold taped the replacement pad over his leg wound, climbed into the bed and went to sleep. The sleep was helped by reports that Army vehicles were still going back and forth past the entrance. That was very reassuring.

Though according to those who watched, the evening TV didn't give any close ups of that type of action. The pictures of the night's fighting were from far overhead. The lines of fire were shown striking the boundary and spilling out sideways into huge swathes of destruction. The reports didn't mention actual fighting, but none of the rivers of fire passed over the boundary. There was certainly no hint that the conflagrations were being stoked by artillery and napalm.

The morning TV went back to showing two hours of repeats of children's programmes. The later news reports showed very little of the city because, it was claimed, the cloud and smoke obscured the view. Harold was damn certain that the cameras would get plenty of pictures if they came a bit lower. The remaining inhabitants of the city were true mushrooms now. Kept in the dark and periodically fed manure. His mind skipped quickly around mushrooms being cut and removed, diced and fried.

*   *   *

Harold was still hesitating at lunchtime. "What do you think? Will his Mum object? Is she still mad at me?"

"Go and see her, dummy. She'll go one way or the other. Karen and a few of the others have been talking to Faith, and she's accepted that Toby was where he wanted to be. Strangely enough the two killed by the Army helped. Sort of proved it could happen anywhere. Especially with Susie and Sukie losing their house, and Sue." Sharyn looked at Harold and his burden. "Won't you need them anymore?"

"No, I'm Orchard Close's soldier now."

"Well get off then, or I'll get Liz to come and beat sense into you." Sharyn smiled. "I'm glad one woman has sense. I had to close the door to protect Hazel from the sight of you coming up the street and those shameless hussies." Sister-love. Just the right thing to get Harold back on his feet and sort out his head.

Though he was still hesitant about the battledress. Eventually Harold left the clothing with Faith and told her that was her decision.

*   *   *

There's still plenty of wood in there." Casper was looking out at the ruins, which were still smouldering in places. That was despite a rainy night. "A lot will be charred but that won't matter for a pyre. Quite a bit will be wet though because most roofs have gone."

"We'll use some petrol or diesel if we have to. This is a better use than swanning about in a car."

"Fair enough. We've got out a gas-fired barbecue and Liz will be cooking bacon to supply butties for the mourners."

Harold stared. "Why on earth is she doing that?"

"A couple of people reckoned it was a way to cover the smell. If someone is burning bacon, your head will blame that and not the pyre." Casper wasn't totally happy with the bacon, but perhaps he was right.

"Practical, in a somewhat gross way. How many do you think will eat?" Bacon butties were popular usually, but maybe not at a funeral.

"Not many. She's going to burn a lot of the bacon deliberately. To cover any smell blown from the pyres?" Which was a waste, but nothing like the waste of good people on the pyres. "Is the Army square with this?"

"They should be, considering their version of a pyre is still burning and the smell will probably overpower anything from ours." Harold sighed.

"I'm just going up there to talk to whoever is in charge. We will burn our dead but I'm being polite. I'm letting them know, not asking permission. Has the beer gone down the road?"

"Yes, Berry helped take four dozen pints down herself but kept the crates covered. So only the armoured lot get it, for clearing the approach road. Pity they won't trade beer for medicine." Casper looked up at the bypass. "It's not like they need bloody bandages and there must be heaps on those armoured vehicles."

"I'll try, but I reckon the armoured type was as helpful as we'll get and he was a no. He reckoned it's forbidden under the rules of engagement." Harold frowned in thought. "Those must be a new set of rules."

* * *

"Stand very still until you have been searched."

Too damn true he would. Harold had seen the weapons on various types of armoured vehicles plenty of times. He'd never had them pointed at him. The various sized black holes he was staring into weren't at all reassuring from here.

"Come ahead." The captain looked at a paper in his hand "Harold Miller, ex-Army, running Orchard Close. Is that you?"

"It is."

"Right, what do you want and no, nobody can leave."

Harold stood up very straight and bit back a snide reply. "I came to let you know we will be lighting ten pyres this afternoon. To send our dead on."

"Are you lot Pagans?"

"No. We don't fancy some hopped up cretin pissing on our gravestones sometime in the future. Though we would appreciate being able to spread the ashes in the exclusion zone. Nobody will be pissing there, and the victims might not mind if a few assholes bleed on them." Harold took a breath.

He'd let the bitterness show for a moment and the captain looked decidedly frosty. "If you can spare a padre that would be a big comfort to the relatives and friends." Already Harold wasn't feeling hopeful about the medication.

Though the first sign of any softening of tone followed the request. "Ah. No, sorry, we aren't allowed to do that. Aren't there any priests?"

"Not here."

"How do you manage?" That seemed to be prompted by genuine concern.

"Those of the same religion say a few words, and I light the fire." Harold sighed. "I actually had to take confession from one lass. I'm not religious let alone a Catholic. She was past knowing who was there and just wanted to get square with God. Are you sure there's no way?"

"Sorry. Really sorry. That is specifically forbidden in the fraternisation rules."

Harold skipped the first question that came to mind, what fraternisation rules? There shouldn't be any with English citizens. "What about medication? We've got bullet and arrow wounds and some nasty cuts from machetes and shrapnel. Our nurse is a trainee and we've no proper medication. She lost one patient overnight." The captain blinked at the shrapnel part, but shook his head. "Also specifically forbidden." He hesitated. "There is something I can do for those needing regular specialist medicines or treatments."

"There is?"

"We had a memo saying that there is a facility in the Derbyshire Peak District. If someone is suffering because they can't get their prescriptions, diabetes or something similar, there's a concession. We, the Army, can accept their surrender. The patients will be picked up by ambulance and taken to the facility." The captain frowned. "I have no first-hand knowledge of the facility but presumably they have the drugs and staff."

"I will ask because there are people down there in real need. It will be their choice. Will they be able to write to those back here?" Harold couldn't see Mary, Finn's Mum, leaving under any other circumstances.

"I don't know but I doubt it. Normal services don't exist anymore, and might not for some time." The captain looked past Harold, down at Orchard Close. "Please pass on my condolences and regret, though they aren't official I'm afraid. I'll let the men know there's a service, and they will keep quiet while you deal with your dead. Was there anything else, Mr Miller?"

There was a huge list that was needed, but Harold went for generalisations. "Food, hospitals, schools, all that sort of thing? Do you have any idea when one or all might come back?"

"We've been told that steps are being taken. Once the armour comes back from the city centre the authorities will regularise the situation. No, I don't know what it means but the Army will stay here. That means that the exclusion zone remains in force, as does the ban on firearms." The captain looked at the paper. "Was it you using the cannon?"

Harold stared. Cannon? The Army were using cannon, not Orchard Close.

"Sorry, I meant a heavy rifle, one with a magazine." He gave the ghost of a smile. "Some of the more cautious thought it was an automatic but those of us with sanity opted for fast bolt action."

"Five rounds rapid fire. 1914-18 style as is the weapon. I've no idea what happened to it in all the chaos. All the ammunition was used up anyway." Harold couldn't do much if this bloke decided to come and search the place, except hope to warn everyone to hide the weapons.

"Of course it's missing, silly of me to think otherwise." The captain wasn't smiling now. "It's just that we aren't supposed to allow any weapon that can reach us accurately, and a Lee-Enfield three oh three will certainly do that." There was a real question there and Harold didn't know what it was.

"We consider the Army to be our protection, so if it turns up it won't be aimed this way." Harold remembered what he'd said about using up. "Even if someone finds ammunition."

"Good enough I suppose, since you left us on good terms. If you get hold of an automatic weapon, please turn it in. You saw what happens if some fool uses one."

"Christ yes."

"Good. I won't keep you any longer Mr Miller. I see some of your people are looking anxious." The captain gestured down towards Orchard Close.

"Right. Thank you." When Harold turned there were half a dozen women in the back gardens in plain view. He smiled to himself on the way back down. The residents were reminding the Army who lived here and this time it hadn't been planned.

*   *   *

"You can't resign, you lummox. A third of the people here joined under the assumption you ran the place, but the rest are volunteers. Anyway, you aren't a dictator or gang boss. If you started that we'd throw you out on your ear." Sharyn raised a hand and lowered it. "I'll send for Berry."

Harold shook his head. "All the planning and they got over the wall, Sharyn. Twice, and once was because I was chasing off down the road instead of defending the building I was in."

"While you've been running about I've had visitors. People coming to point out that they wanted to apologise. For grumbling about losing the gardens to give us that clear strip. For complaining about the time spent building the wall. About sealing off the roadway. About the practice and the time spent making up squads and practicing running to positions. People who weren't happy about looting, or rationing what they found." Sharyn hugged Harold.

"Now they are all very pleased you did those things Harold. You can't give the job away. As long as you listen to your big sister, and various other people with two brain cells, you'll be fine. Even those hussies in the girl's club have their good moments. What do you think that exhibition was about? It wasn't your manly body." Sharyn nudged him. "We've even got people who like paperwork so you don't have to do any."

"So I'm the figurehead. You lot run it all, and if it goes wrong I get the blame?" Harold tried for indignant but the relief probably showed through. He could beat on people if necessary, and hug, but organisation wasn't his strong point.

"All good systems of governance work like that. You're a big tough soldier so you can stand the punishment, and might enjoy it." Sharyn smiled. "Now write your speech."

"Speech? Why do I need a speech?" The change of tack left Harold confused.

"We've survived. We lost a lot of people. Now the fearless leader gives a speech to pull us together and make the losses all worthwhile." Sharyn wasn't smiling now. "They were worthwhile, Harold, because we're all still stood here. I was in that house on the boundary, and crossbow bolts weren't stopping that lot fast enough. Then they were through the boundary and Matthew led five people down and out the door to deal with it."

Sharyn gave a little giggle. "I'll kill you if you ever mention it, but Bess wasn't invited with them. Matthew was too chivalrous to take a woman. She said something about Matthew not getting away that easily and went after them. When they came back Matthew had his good arm round her and Bess had cream all over her chin, so to speak."

Harold nodded soberly. "She went barmy. Matthew said she saved the day."

"Oh yes, we heard that part. We didn't hear what was said while they snuggled during the shelling. It wasn't commentary on her shooting." Sharyn put a pad and pen in front of Harold. "You've got three or four hours. I'll give it a sanity check." Harold opened his mouth and Sharyn interrupted. "I'll get a couple more to do the same." Harold picked up the pen. Paper and pens, he thought. We'll need them. Then he tried to work out what to say. About Toby for starters.

Chapter 15:
Goodbyes

Harold wondered if this was now a tradition. Evening was coming, and the low cloud and occasional spatters of cold rain were a lot like Gabriela's funeral. Though this time he had to do it ten times. Toby came out on his board and was put on his pyre and Harold had a big lump in his throat. The fifteen year old looked even younger in Harold's battledress with the cuffs and trouser bottoms turned up. The beret covered his wound, and the lad looked as if he was asleep.

That settled which speech to use. Harold had tried to memorise both versions, but had the paper ready in case. When the last body was placed on the long pyre Harold stepped to the front. He raised his eyes to the bypass and the captain had been true to his word. No vehicles were moving and the men standing along the barrier were doing just that. Standing quietly.

"Toby wanted be a soldier. He is wearing an Army uniform because Toby made it, he became a soldier. A soldier is a person who puts their body between their homeland and the foe, and will stand and die to protect that homeland and people. It doesn't need a uniform, or an oath. So everyone who lies here deserves a uniform, and a flag, and a military salute. Without their bravery and sacrifice, none of us would be here today." Harold checked his paper, just to steady himself.

"Before armies, in times of trouble the farmer would bring his pitchfork and the butcher his cleaver. We are nearly back to that, so we have to live and if necessary fight as a community. Some will stand on the barricade, and others will make the cleaver, and patch up the farmer's wounds, or look after the cook's children." Harold tried to look at the right people as he did that. He wanted them to understand that everyone wasn't expected to be a fighter. That wouldn't work.

"We have to do it together. We will argue, because all families do, but this family will hug and make up afterwards. Because out there is much, much worse, and our disagreements will be nothing compared to the alternatives.

You have asked me to lead this family and I'll try. But not on my own because I can't. I'll need help, advice, criticism, a Berrying now and then, and hopefully a hug or two." Harold was relieved to see some little smiles, even if they were through tears.

Harold moved along the line of bodies and stopped opposite a young man, one killed by the artillery. "Now I'll say a couple of words for Vince because there's nobody to speak for him. He came in with others but they didn't know each other. We don't know Vince's story, or his religion, or even his age. We know what is important. He stood with us when we needed him. Because we don't know his religion, I'll use something my Gran used to say. May your God go with you, Vince."

Harold stepped back and the mourners stepped forward for the rest. Some were family, though very few. Others were friends or had become friends in the last few months or even weeks. There were prayers covering several faiths, and then the last one, Faith, stepped back. She picked up an unlit torch and waited.

Harold didn't spin it out, he walked to the end of the pyre. Suzie handed Harold the torch after pulling off the cover and Casper was there with a gas brazing torch to set it going. "Fare Thee well, Sue." Ten times Harold repeated that, one torch going in under each person, and then he marched back to the middle. Though his step faltered for a moment as Faith straightened and saluted, briefly.

Harold stood to attention, his best Army version, and recited the words. He couldn't look at all those faces while he did, so Harold looked over them, at the bypass. There, some of the soldiers on the rails had straightened and a few were saluting. That was tremendously reassuring because it meant, to Harold, that despite the new rules those soldiers still identified with the people down here. Then his eyes blurred.

When he'd finished Harold turned to the flames and saluted as well. This time he stayed at the front of the mourners. Harold held his salute until Sharyn's arm came round him and took him back into the crowd. There people did the same as before, patted his back and said well done or spoke about one of the victims. Nobody seemed ambivalent about the words this time. Maybe that was a tradition already. Everyone watched, deep in their own thoughts, as the flames took firm hold and a wall of fire hid the ten people from sight.

*   *   *

"Come on, Harold. Time to go home." Sharyn hooked her arm in Harold's, and Daisy caught hold of his hand. Hazel had Daisy's other hand and Wills was on Sharyn's other arm as they made their way clear of the crowd. The mourners were breaking apart a little now, though Faith, and Suzie, and probably a few others would be here for some time yet.

Liz offered a bit of charred bacon on a plastic fork. "It's a bit overdone, Harold." Tears were still trickling down her face. "I'll be giving you your hug later, since you asked."

"I'll skip the bacon thanks, but the hug will be welcome. See you later, Liz. Where's Casper?"

"He's staying to keep an eye on those who aren't likely to leave for a while. In case they need a safe hug or someone to scream at." Liz looked past Harold at the pyre. "Making cleavers? You did all right, wimp."

"You too, mouse." They walked up the road and into the house. Daisy and Wills ate, but nobody else had an appetite. Harold spent an hour drawing pretty places for Toby, and Sue, and Vince, and everyone else to live in. Then he had to read a story of course. Though from the bright eyes watching him leave the bedroom Harold thought there wouldn't be any sleep yet. Probably colouring, since a quick look later sometimes found Daisy fast asleep still laid on an open page, crayon in hand.

*   *   *

The TV was showing more action this evening. In fact the damn thing was showing edited highlights of the fighting from the night before. Highly edited, as could be seen when Orchard Close came on the screen.

"The Army is being forced to act to defend the surviving enclaves of decent citizens who are being besieged by rebels and terrorists."

Onscreen a tank lumbered past the end of the access road and 'NO EN-TRY Without Invitation' was clear on the barricade beyond. So was the clean tarmac, or clean if nobody looked closely at the stains or the potholes the cannon had created.

"These citizens will not be disturbed by the Armed Forces. Instead, measures are being taken to help them. Before that it is essential that the violence is contained."

Onscreen, tanks ran through a barricade and personnel carriers followed, spitting fire. The rear doors opened and soldiers swarmed forward, shooting at the defenders.

The next clip was of a shopping centre with 'No Shoppers Allowed' and 'Shoppers will be Hung' painted on the walls in large letters. A line of women were standing along the roof, waving at the soldiers. Some had machetes and baseball bats.

"Where there is resistance, we will be ruthless. Where the inhabitants are acting purely in self-defence, they will be left in peace. Steps are being taken to regularise the situation for the law-abiding."

Harold was worried. "This could be a real problem. The TV is showing the assholes where we all are."

"Maybe not. There was no indication where we actually are, or that shopping mall." Sharyn sighed. "In some ways it's a pity, we could do with finding our neighbours."

Onscreen a crowd swarmed over a personnel carrier. The camera pulled back to show a tank was aiming its main gun at the personnel carrier. There was a gout of flame and smoke, and the crowd were swept away. Literally plucked off the armoured vehicle and thrown in heaps on the ground.

"The Armed Forces will be ruthless when faced with any attempt to interfere with attempts to restore order."

"What the hell was that, Harold?"

"What they used out here to clear the road out there, Sharyn. Canister. The tanks used it when we put up the road blocks in London. I saw them fire canister twice and I never want to see that for real again." Harold was frowning a little. "That shopping centre was the one we came past on the run into the city. There were bodies swinging from lampposts. I don't think they're all that innocent."

"You tied people to lampposts once, Harold. Then shot them. Actually Holly gelded one and he might have preferred hanging."

Harold winced. "Fair enough point. Whoever is in there has also had the idea of putting women on show."

"Seems to work for them as well. The place was left alone." Sharyn gave a little smile. "A shopping mall? What are the chances of taking us all for a bit of retail therapy?"

"Close to nil. It's a good distance and regardless of what the TV says, the Army won't get all the, what do they call them, terrorists and rebels." Harold scowled. "There could be scores of them out in those ruins over our wall."

"What about our lippy and such, and when someone wants a slinky new dress?" Sharyn looked pointedly at the ragged cloth showing Harold's knee. "Or maybe a new pair of jeans."

"Lippy and eye shadow aren't a problem. The women who came on runs with me stuffed their pockets with that sort of thing, and other women's products. They headed for the bathroom at the run when we went into a house, and I didn't hear any flushing."

Harold gave a little smile. "They also brought hundreds of those little disposable razors. Not just for legs. I was told that regardless of stereotypes most women prefer their men smooth for the up-close action." He looked at his knee. "I'm wearing clothes to destruction because the shops are shut. Once I've got two tatty pairs I can patch one with the other."

"You've got a pair with blood on and half a leg missing. I reckon they classify as tatty. Ask Kerry to sort it out. She can embroider and she brought her sewing machine as her luggage allowance instead of clothes." Sharyn's little smile was back. "Who wants you smooth for close-up and what's wrong with electric shavers?"

"They were worried about the electricity going off, and so am I." Onscreen a building crumpled as the tanks blew away the corners and the troops and armoured vehicles moved in. "One solid hit on a substation or one of those things giving a pylon a nudge in passing and we're frying dinner over a candle."

"Yeuk, no. No more barbecue for a while. The stink from across the road would turn some of us vegetarian if there were enough veggies." Sharyn poked Harold's waistline. "This is your paradise. Burgers and chips because a lot of the freezers had both. Not so much frozen lettuce about."

"Nor freezers now." Harold stretched. "I really don't want to watch another couple of hours of the whole city dying building by building. I'm going for a walk to plan soldier boy things. Those damn walls need to be stronger for a start." Harold stood. "Don't wait up sis. I'm going to sit in the study and clean guns and make new ammo for a bit when I get back. It's a sort of therapy."

"Definitely soldier stuff. I'm going to bed soon because Daisy will be up at the crack of dawn. Where did Hazel go?"

"She asked if it was all right to go to Betty's. Alfie and Veronica are meeting there to have a memorial game on the computer. Toby's favourite game." Harold frowned and sat down again. "Is that normal, because at the pyre I wondered about something that captain said?"

"What exactly, apart from no and hard luck."

"When I said about pyres, he asked if we were Pagans. I said no but just now some people were putting locks of hair on the pyres." Harold sighed. "There were also mementoes, like the grave goods that were found in old tombs, and a few threw food on there."

"The food was Liz's bacon which was only fit for the fire. People often used to put something in a coffin anyway, before the lid went on." Sharyn thought a moment. "You may be right in some ways. That was more brutal, not like the clean, quiet, antiseptic service and carefully concealed furnace."

"Even Faith put something on there, though she sort of sneaked it on."

"If you mention that I'll do sister things to you. That was a toy soldier. Toby liked soldiers long before you turned up." Sharyn sighed. "Now get off and check sentries or whatever, or you'll be fretting all night."

"Yes sis. I hear and obey."

Though tonight the therapy didn't work. There were faceless people among those Harold shot and stabbed in his sleep, and now he actually had lost count. Or rather, he couldn't count if he wanted to because he didn't know who he'd hit in the chaos. Somehow, that was even more horrific.

*   *   *

"Harold, Harold." Harold smiled.

"Yes, Hazel?"

"Can you go to the gate please? A big tank thing stopped and Emmy thinks they took the beer."

"Good."

"No, it's not that. She says the man stood at the end of the building where he was hidden from the bypass. He pointed inside the house. Then he blew her a kiss, then he pointed again. She doesn't think it was just thank you."

Harold could picture Hazel. She'd be hopping from one foot to another out there. "All right Hazel. Please tell Emmy I'm on the way." Harold heard footsteps racing away. Harold had told those with radios to not use them for anything regarding the Army, and this qualified.

All the way to the barricade Harold wondered what the hell they'd left. It could be anything from frilly underwear to a sack of spuds so he gave up. "I'm coming with you." Emmy preened. "He blew me the kiss, after all."

"Bitch. Only because he couldn't see me." Sal pouted, then laughed. "Come on, it's ages since a strange man sent me gifts." Emmy and Sal bantered as the three of them walked down the access road and Harold peered into the shadowed interior. The present wasn't easy to see since it was covered in sacking. Harold pulled the cover clear and stood speechless for long moments.

"Well, what is it?"

"Possibly life for one or two inside Orchard Close. These are exactly what I asked for. They've even taken them out of the big boxes with red crosses so nobody will realise what we're carrying." Harold held up a packet. "Antibiotics, wound powder, dressings, oh bless them. If the tanks come back all of you line up and blow them a kiss."

"Patricia was talking about those, antibiotics. If they get near enough I'll give them a real kiss. Come on, let's get them shifted." Sal reached forward for the heap.

"Not yet. Just wander up there and fill half a dozen carrier bags with bricks or something else you can dump here. Get Casper to help you bring them down here. Then we amble back up with the same filled carrier bags, but full of goodies. Otherwise those nice soldiers will get into a lot of trouble, because this isn't allowed." Harold shooed Sal with both hands. "Put those down or in your pockets and get gone."

"What if someone comes before then, so see what we've been doing?"

Harold smiled. "They won't come in. Fella and young woman in private place? Heavy breathing and suchlike if they get close? They might peek round the door but won't interrupt if the couple are hugging." Sal laughed and turned to go.

"Take your time, Sal. After all I've just been told there will be hugging, and heavy breathing, and I want time to find out about suchlike." Emmy smiled happily. "Who knows what we could be up to when you get back. Just knock before entering, please."

"I said only if someone is coming." But Sal was on her way, laughing, and a smiling Emmy was advancing. The hug was a nice gentle one and then Emmy stepped back and turned to the heap of medication.

"Right, let's see what's here." Emmy glanced at Harold and winked.

"I'm confused. Possibly relieved but after the build-up possibly a bit let down." Harold was grinning because he really had been worried about just how full on some of the girl's club seemed to be. Now he knew they were just winding him up.

Emmy stepped in close for another hug and this one was a bit stronger. She whispered in his ear. "There are at least five of us who would love to get you somewhere private. Just to see what a hug might lead to. Some, like me, are still grieving and aren't ready to try that yet, and maybe never will be. Some are definitely ready right now so be careful who you suggest suchlike to."

Her breath was warm on Harold's neck as Emmy giggled. "You have been warned." She pulled back a bit and her lips were soft on Harold's just for a moment. "There, so I can claim some suchlike went on. Just to wind the rest up a bit."

"What about Curtis? I thought, well, you seem to get on." Harold had thought the pair were getting along better than it now seemed.

"Ah, well. A lot of us girls get a bit tempted by a bad boy, if one is available. Maybe not to settle down with and raise rugrats, but perhaps to get her fingers singed a bit." Emmy became dead serious. "I like Curtis, but I also wonder about singed fingers." She turned back to the medication.

Harold stared at her back. Bloody hell! He definitely wouldn't mind a private hug or two with some of the girl's club, including Emmy. Maybe some suchlike eventually if the hugging went well, but that sounded like a hunting pack. Worse than that, if he got caught by the wrong one, was he ready for rugrats? Just what a bloke needed with his sister watching from the end of the road. Harold started wondering which five and quickly abandoned that. Inspecting medicine was safer.

*   *   *

"Knock, knock. Can we come in? Do you need time to adjust anything?" Harold stood up from where he was bent over the heap, sorting it into smaller piles.

"Just a moment." Harold turned to see why and Emmy wrapped her arms round him. Harold hugged back and suddenly this wasn't at all chaste. Warm lips connected and Harold kissed back because, dammit, he wanted to kiss Emmy. Especially with what she'd said still buzzing in his head. Then Emmy leaned back and slowly licked her lips. "There, that deals with heavy breathing. After Halloween I wanted to find out if I'm ready and sorry, not yet. Though once I am, you'd better start running."

Her second kiss was softer and then Emmy turned away and called out. "All right, my whatevers are straightened and tucked in. You were a bit too quick though."

Sal came in with Casper, then stopped and a big smile spread over her face. "Only just too quick from the colour of his face, and how long you took to tuck." She sniggered. "His breathing is a bit heavy as well. You'll have to explain about whatever later."

"My lips are sealed. Come on, give me a couple of the bags."

Casper was looking questions so once they'd delivered the carrier bags to a delighted Patricia, Harold pulled him to one side. "Emmy sort of wanted to test the water, so to speak. It's too soon for her."

"I could have told her that." Casper was smiling but still curious. "So you've decided on making a play for Emmy?"

"Not really, though I do really like her. It's just that I don't know which ones want some fun, which ones want a permanent arrangement, and which ones are winding me up. I'm not very good with commitment, especially the rug-rat type. It doesn't make for restful sleep, especially with Sharyn at the end of the road." Harold chuckled. "I shouldn't complain, should I? I should be bloody smug with two or three girls interested."

"You can't count. It's nine, though some are only teasing and some of the others are doing what Emmy was, wondering how they feel. Not all of them have you at the top of their list, but there's a competitive side to that now." Casper sniggered. "No, I'm not telling which are which because Liz would kill me. She's rolling about laughing at them, or winding them up. Now get going before they think I'm competition for their bad boy."

"I'm not really a bad boy."

Casper patted Harold on the back. "Dangerous works the same, apparently, so hard luck. Liz agrees with that assessment. She says you're an alien killing machine, but it's reassuring having one parked at the end of the road."

Harold got going, though in quiet moments he did start to wonder who was serious.

*   *   *

After four nights of watching tanks and armour smash barricades, and days where the TV showed a ring of steel around the city centre, everything changed. "They're pulling out."

Harold came through to look at the TV and Sharyn was right. Every last vehicle and man was pulling out of the city centre and heading towards the boundary in small convoys. Behind them they left a charnel house. "They could have burned the bodies." Harold knew his disgust showed but this was disgusting. "It's probably an economy measure."

In the background as the vehicles pulled out heaps seethed with crows and ravens and buzzards. The black heaps were mottled as seagulls joined the feast, and even at a distance the scurrying dots of rats were visible.

Sharyn winced, then thought about it. "You might be right." She stared. "Look at those heaps, there must be thousands of bodies. Why didn't the idiots surrender?"

"I told you what the tank man said. The armour was chasing them home. The other armour coming in must have done the same until the mobs were neatly bottled up together. Right back where they started in one big mob." Harold hesitated over the next bit, but pushed on. "We've seen how the pictures of what happened here were chosen. Who can say if that lot tried to surrender in the end and were killed anyway?"

"Surely they tried to negotiate at least? Regardless of numbers they never stood a chance." Sharyn was staring at the heaps. "Do you think they actually caused any Army casualties? I thought the Chinese or someone used human waves to destroy tanks?"

"That was why those canister rounds were developed for modern tanks. To sweep infantry off an armoured vehicle without harming the vehicle. Though they work well on crowds as well." Like a giant hammer swung by a God, smashing big groups of people into bloody ruin. "There might have been Army casualties when the soldiers got out of the vehicles to finish the job."

"Out of respect for the dead, the City Centre is declared off-limits for every-one. The RAF will enforce the exclusion zone with napalm."

Onscreen, flame blossomed on a heap of bodies. For a moment the watchers thought the RAF were going to burn the bodies after all, but that was just a warning.

"It has proved impossible to eradicate the subversive and violent elements in the city, so the area must remain quarantined from the rest of the country."

The screen showed small groups still shooting at each other here and there in the wreckage. "That's bullshit. They've not carried out a proper sweep to root them out."

Sharyn's reply reeked of her bitterness. "No Harold, they haven't. Now, conveniently, that means the authorities can leave us all in here to rot." She scrubbed her eyes with her sleeve. "All the killing, all the terror, and they had no intention of letting us out. Why?"

"There were too many people for the resources? People who were conveniently, as you say, grouped together in cities that were already getting more violent and generally lawless. They've cured unemployment at a stroke." Harold hit his forehead with his palm as he realised his reply might be exactly right. "Of course. The gas and oil. No bloody ships, so no food. What's the betting that the population will level out when the country is self-sufficient?"

"Can we do that? Be self-sufficient?" A shocked Sharyn was thinking furiously. "But won't the farmers want us to help with the growing if there's no fuel for tractors?"

"Plenty of fuel for tanks." They both filled in the next bit. So maybe there is enough for tractors.

"*Since the city will remain sealed, measures have been taken to alleviate the suffering of the innocent.*"

"What measures? Nerve gas?" Harold wasn't joking, gas would finish this farce neatly and right now he didn't discount anything.

"*Secure stores have been constructed and fortified. Here the inhabitants will be able to purchase the basics for survival.*"

Harold and Sharyn were silent now as the view changed to a huge building surrounded by a wire fence. A fence with watch towers along the length and coils of barbed wire along the top.

"*Precautions have been taken to repel attacks on the peaceful employees. These are non-lethal as long as no firearms are used by the assailants.*"

An armoured car used a water cannon to sweep away a series of dummies wielding baseball bats. More dummies fell as men in sandbagged positions on the roof fired shotguns at them, and the cameras zoomed on the non-lethal rounds. Then other dummies with guns were torn apart by a machine gun above the main doors.

"Have a nice day, please visit again?" Sharyn's voice was a whisper. "Surely not, Harold."

"*Any miscreants who are arrested will be sent to work camps to help grow your food. Any shoplifters will be also sent to these work camps. Criminals will no longer be a burden upon the citizens.*"

Lines of men and women in orange overalls were shown hoeing or digging. Grim faced guards with shotguns and batons watched over them. The scene shifted to show an armed group running from a bank. Banknotes scattered across the street as they ran.

"*Many banks and shops have been robbed, and many credit cards have been stolen and used fraudulently. The perpetrators will not benefit from these crimes. All banknotes are now deemed worthless. All electronic accounts are frozen. Vouchers will be issued to every inhabitant on an individual basis.*"

Harold laughed. He couldn't help it. "We'll steal anything the criminals didn't get in other words." His smile remained. "I'll bet a lot of the fraudulent use is actually people like us, using up our credit to buy food. At least we'll never be prosecuted." Harold held up a hand as if taking an oath. "The criminal elements did it, m'lud. The government said so."

The TV was now showing a convoy consisting of an armoured personnel carrier, a bus, and an armoured car. The picture zoomed in on the heavily armoured single decker bus. Then the picture jumped to desks with computers and clerks sat behind them.

"*These buses will visit each area noted by the Armed Forces as containing peaceful residents. Each resident will enter the bus and give a thumbprint and state their name, sex, age, and previous occupation. This includes every child. Those too young to answer for themselves will be identified by a parent.*"

"*Please be warned that if the coupon bus is attacked, the weekly service will be stopped. There will be no coupons at that location until the local residents have restored order.*"

"Wonderful. We deal with our own local assholes or starve. Who needs police because hungry residents won't need a judge or prisons if someone stops that bus coming?" Sharyn nodded unhappily. Onscreen the line of people were very definitely not from the city. They were clean, happy and well-fed. As they gave their thumbprint each one was handed pieces of paper which they placed in their pockets. A picture of the paper came onscreen.

"*This is a coupon. As you can see the recipient's thumbprint is printed at the bottom left. To use this coupon in payment, the other box at the bottom right must also be thumb printed. The Marts, the new stores, will have machines to automatically check one print against the other. Anyone attempting to pass a forged coupon will be arrested and sent to the work camps.*"

The happy citizens were now shopping in a Mart, and seemed to have brought their own designer shopping bags. None were being provided even for loose vegetables. There was a good selection of canned and fresh food, cleaning materials, detergents, and plain clothing. There was one aisle with washing machines, kettles and games consoles.

Nobody would be doing the trolley dash in there. Steel grills were slid up by hand to allow the shoppers to remove items, one at a time. Except for loose veggies, where there was a scoop being used through a grill. Then the purchasers were shown entering long narrow lanes with high sides. One at a time the shoppers went through a door.

"*Please bring your own bags or boxes to carry goods. The checkout will be in a sealed room. The bags and customers will be scanned to ascertain what they are carrying, and someone must supply coupons to cover the cost. The electronic tags will then be cancelled.*"

The close-ups showed bar codes printed on even the teabags. Every tiny item had the line of bars and numbers. Then the customers were thumb printing their coupons to pay and leaving, smiling happily.

"*These coupons can also be used for barter between citizens. Those receiving* coupons with both thumbprint boxes filled can use them in the Marts. If you are engaging in trade, please ensure that the purchaser actually places the second thumb print while you are present. If the prints do not match, you will be arrested when trying to use them in a Mart."

"Where are these places, and how do we get there? I don't fancy trying to run a convoy into the city and coming back loaded with groceries." As it had once before, the TV answered Harold. A map of the city came on the screen and routes were highlighted. All led onto the ring road, the joined-up bypasses that the Army used to seal everyone in.

"The Armed Forces will continue to control the ring road. Unarmed citizens will be allowed to walk along the bypass to their nearest Mart to shop for supplies. To ensure that they are unarmed, there will be scans. Please remember that the carriageway is MOD property and any armed intruders will be shot."

The happy shoppers were walking along a wide road and being scanned by smiling soldiers. "What about anyone who can't walk?" This time the TV answered Sharyn.

"If any group of residents wishes to send a few representatives to carry out the shopping, all they need to do is thumb print their coupons before handing them over. Then the representative can use them to make purchases."

Happy old people in wheelchairs were sticking their thumbs on bits of paper and handing them over to people with empty shopping bags.

"Unfortunately, the Marts will not be able to sell prescription medicines. Any person reliant on prescription medication should contact their nearest Army post. Arrangements will be made to take them to a facility where trained staff and medication is available."

Occupied stretchers and wheelchairs followed people who could barely walk onto ambulances. The same people were then shown in a clean room with comfortable chairs and a TV, and one woman had a cat on her knee. Nurses bustled about and then hot meals were brought in on trays. A view of the outside showed wheelchairs moving through manicured gardens and more nurses.

Harold pointed. "The captain mentioned this. For if some of the residents here couldn't manage."

"William is worse, and won't get better without insulin. Mary, Finn's mum, is in a bad way though she keeps smiling." Sharyn was thinking hard. "Karen doesn't come outside much now, though Stewart is making sure she's all right."

"I'll ask around. Someone might still be using their stocks and need to take advantage of this option before they run out. Betty mentioned that old Harry is running out of something Patricia can't supply." Harold frowned. "I don't know what the effect will be on him. Sandy, the carpenter from the Ashcroft estate, has a lot of arthritis but Patricia says he's managing on what she's got. He might not want to face winter without something better. Hang on, more news."

"Convoys will be escorting tradesmen to repair major breaks in electrical supplies and water mains. Any attempt to attack these will result in the break being left unrepaired. If you know of a break that is easily accessible, please notify the coupon bus."

The scene showed an electrician hard at work on a big junction box him. Behind the man an armoured car, personnel carrier and soldiers watched over him. "That's actually a big relief. Though hopefully our supply comes from outside the city so we'll be all right. After all the shelling didn't cut us off." Onscreen the TV showed the progress of the Army convoys leaving the city. There was a knock on the door.

It was Liz. "The armoured lot are nearly here according to the TV. A lot of the girl's club want to go to the barricade and take boxes and steps. We want to blow kisses." She grinned. "A couple are putting on frilly undies to give the lads a flash, just as a thank you."

"Be careful or one of those big tanks might be climbing the barricade. Those lads haven't met many friendlies of late, and definitely not any flashing their frillies." Harold smiled at Liz. "You'd better go and warn them since I might lose control if I'm there."

"Hard luck, Soldier Boy. Half of them are putting on short skirts and frillies on the assumption you are there. Since you're in charge of Orchard Close, you should be out front waving." Liz turned and headed for the girl's club but not without a warning. "They'll come and get you?"

"Unfortunately she's right, you should be up there waving. Not only that but I'm not having this place inundated with half-dressed women. What will Hazel think? Go on, scat." Sharyn shoved him towards the door.

Despite a lot of threats the women restrained themselves to standing on the garages that still had roofs, and the barricade, and blowing kisses. Though several did have their skirt hems high to show a lot of leg. Harold realised that really was very deliberate. He hadn't seen a miniskirt worn since the attack on the flats. Apart from Halloween and Guy Fawkes night, when some of the 'disguises' were very short or tight.

The soldiers who could see waved back very enthusiastically, but none of the vehicles turned up the approach road. When the convoy had passed every single one of the girl club insisted that they couldn't climb down. A laughing Harold lifted each one down as requested while a group of other residents laughed and shouted advice.

Nearly all of the women had to be hugged and several took the chance to steal a kiss. Holly seemed to have got over her embarrassment and delivered a real smacker before high-fiving Emmy. Berry was lifted down by Seth and was given a definite kiss, his first in public, and that raised a cheer. Matthew's face was the colour of his hair after lifting Bess down and being rewarded.

The girl's club accompanied Harold back nearly to his door, laughing and insisting on extra hugs because they were cold. Then they split off and headed indoors to warm up. Personally Harold appreciated the leg show but thought they were crackers. There was a real nip in the air and Curtis had warned of frost. Liz and Casper followed Harold home to talk about the news on the TV, and what it meant.

*   *   *

The coupon bus was there two days later and everyone filed aboard except William and Mary. The clerk advised the residents to send them to the nursing home, since otherwise they would not receive coupons. That would mean the other residents supporting them out of their own allowance. That bit of news led to the sick making their own decisions. None of them wanted to be a burden, not when there was an option. Though some had no option but to go, because they were dying.

Three days later Harold walked down the small line to say goodbye to five of their small community. Though each had at least one other person with them to carry luggage. The rest of the goodbyes had been said and an ambulance was already making its way down from the bypass. The armoured car at the end of the access road was to make sure nobody misbehaved, Harold had been told.

Mary was in her wheelchair. Harold had actually driven her up the road on the back of a pickup just once. For her bucket list, Mary insisted. Now Finn was pushing his Mum and talking quietly, possibly for the last time. Karen had renewed her blue rinse and was on her feet, but Stewart was more of less supporting her. He shouldn't be because Stewart had taken a machete blow to his shoulder and upper chest. But the erstwhile caretaker wouldn't hear of anyone else doing this last chore for Karen.

Harry was walking, but using Matthew's arm. The feisty old man's deterioration once his personal stash of medication ran out was startling. He didn't have any relatives here but a lot of people had stepped up offering to escort him. The last man was on a stretcher. William was only thirty-eight but was in a bad way. There was no insulin and his diabetes was out of control. Diet was no longer enough to keep him going. Robert and Zach, two of the people from the Ashcroft estate, were carrying him down the road. Lillian, Conn's girlfriend, was carrying William's bag because they had been neighbours.

The last woman was a surprise. Trish was one of the original inhabitants of the estate, here when Harold arrived. The small, thin, quiet twenty-three year old had stood at the wall with a baseball bat, but kept to herself as much as possible. Now she'd told them why. Trish had AIDS. Her friend Jane had been HIV positive. When Jane failed to return from a doctor's visit Trish had carefully rationed out Jane's and her medication to last as long as she could. Now it was gone. Harold gave her a hug and Casper carried her bag.

"Open the gate." The car with a garage door and sheets of timber across the rear backed into the access road, leaving a narrow gap.

"Let's go." Harold led the little procession down the access road. Most of the population had stood along the road inside to say goodbye because they weren't allowed out here. Not near the ambulance. The ambulance pulled up and two men removed a proper stretcher and dropped the wheels.

Harold pointed. "What about Mary's wheelchair?"

"We've got docking points sir. Not a problem." A lift came down, and then lifted, and Mary was inside.

She managed a smile. "When this is over I want another ride, Harold. On a motorway."

"You'll get one Mary." Harold moved over to give Karen a gentle hug while Finn said goodbye to his Mum.

Karen wagged a finger. "You keep sorting out the punks, all right?"

Harold smiled at her. "It's a pity you can't take the poncy gun. You'd be running the place in no time. Have you got plenty of blue rinse?"

"Ha, I'll be running the place anyway." Karen looked up at Stewart. "This fella has packed my blue rinse, so that I'm all pimped up next time we meet." Karen's slang would be definitely missed. "I've warned him. I'm skipping the gin for the next game and getting straight to the rum stuff."

Harold left Stewart saying his goodbyes. Harry's grip was failing when they shook hands. "I hope you'll look after that cannon?"

"When you get back I'll teach you to shoot it. Then you can scare the assholes off on your own." Harold stepped back as the bags were loaded and last goodbyes were finished. Casper gave Trish a hug and lifted her into the ambulance.

The ambulance turned and headed up the ramp, and the small group trudged back inside Orchard Close. The car pulled the section of barricade into place and Billy joined them. The rest were waiting along the road, but now they began to break up into little groups and head home.

Daisy claimed a hand, and Wills went on Harold's arm. Sharyn put her hand through the arm supporting Wills. Hazel took Daisy's other hand. Sharyn looked at the departing residents. "From a whole city down to fifty six adults, three adolescents and five kids. That simplifies a lot of things."

Harold glanced around. "Not everything. We need something better for the front gate, something that doesn't use petrol and a car can't get through. That wall wants strengthening as well."

"That's it little bro. You do the Soldier Boy stuff, and we'll deal with putting dinner on the table." Sharyn gave Harold a little nudge. "Tomorrow you can take me shopping to this TesdaMart. I remember how much you like shopping." Harold grimaced, then laughed because he never had liked traipsing around with a trolley. Now there'd be no trolley and already he was sorry.

Hand in hand, the little family walked up the road towards the big house with the flag, towards home. "Christmas soon Harold. Seventeen days. Have you made any plans?"

Harold laughed again. "Not really, I've been busy."

Though some of the eyes watching had definite plans for Christmas and one or another member of the family.

This ends Book One of

The Fall of the Cities.

Find out what happens next!
Book 2 will be available soon!

CHARACTERS IN
PLANTING AN ORCHARD

Harold (Harry) Miller – 20 – Corporal pay clerk with CGC Conspicuous Gallantry Cross. Civilian marksman even at sixteen but not comfortable with shooting live targets so won't take sniper training, or qualify as a marksman.

London

Arnold Tredwell – Lance-Corporal on supply runs.

Chris Wilson – Sergeant who considers Harold an aberration, unfit for the medal if he won't be a 'proper' soldier.

Cullen – Trainee cook in commandeered hotel.

Cynthia (Cyn) – 19 – Pretends to be kitchen staff because her home is a council estate and now a war zone. Daren't go home.

Davie Maynard – 20 – Squaddie – Harry's darts partner and a friend.

Forbes – Private, crony of Suggs.

Gallaher – Private, crony of Suggs.

Janina – Young Polish woman.

Lieutenant Symonns – Has a chip on his shoulder about Harry's medal.

Marcie – 17 – Young prostitute caught in hotel when rioting starts. Daren't go on the streets because of riots, so volunteers for kitchen duty.

Nita – 18 – Spanish woman – very religious – Catholic – cleaning staff. Pretends to be kitchen staff because her home is a council estate and now a war zone. Daren't go home.

Santos Menzies – Corporal that Harry meets on the way home.

Stones – 24 – Nickname because he has the 'stones' to tackle anything. SAS soldier who knew Harry when he was younger, and has been Harry's friend since they were in a shooting club together.

'Suggs' Young – Corporal – All around trouble-maker.

The flats:

Bethany – 46 – Widow who has children elsewhere in the city.

Billy – 17 – Newly arrived resident.

Casper – 20 – Big well-muscled gay man who becomes Harry's friend.

Clarence – Old resident who has difficulty with reality.

Daisy – 4 – Harold's niece.

Faith – 35 – Short stout woman with light brown hair. Probably a widow since husband didn't return one night. Toby's Mum.

Finn – 48 – Electrician resident.

Isiah – 34 – Reclusive – telephone engineer – redundant.

Karen – 68 – Feisty blue rinse from the ground floor.

Kerry – 32 – Shy – Isiah's wife and sold embroidered patches on the internet.

Liz – 21 – 5 ft 11 woman who does arts and crafts in iron and bronze. Strong, she pounds metal but is wiry, not bulky.

Logan – 17 – Quiet youth who is grieving for his parents.

Louise – 29 – Quiet small time graphic designer on internet.

Mary – 73 – Finn's Mum, needs a wheelchair.

Mr Baumber (Stewart) – 56 – Caretaker for the flats.

Mrs Burren-Croft – Ground floor resident with big furry cat, Fluff.

Rob – 38 – Divorced Plumber resident.

Sharyn – 24 – Harold's sister – newly widowed.

Susan – 31 – Divorcee living in flats.

Toby – 14 – Interested in computers and soldiers. Faith's son.

Veronica – 13 – Quiet – daughter of Isiah and Kerry.

Wills – 2 – Harold's nephew.

From next door flats: (10 stay)

Alicia – 21 – Small dumpy woman who retreats into herself.

Celine – 19 – Slight skinny redheaded typist. Shy and very frightened as she had already been raped coming home late from work a month before Harold arrived.

Emmy – 20 – Jamaican – newly widowed, tall, well-built woman. Lost David in the flats.

Gabriela – 23 – Southern European – maybe Spanish origins. Short and stocky. 'Failed' Catholic who lost her man, Abraham, in the flats. She hates looters with passion.

Hazel – 14 – Orphan whose parents were killed by looters in neighbouring flats. Second refugee with Patricia. Prefers to keep close Harold and his gun.

Holly – 17 – Tall and a little overweight but slimming rapidly through grief and fanatical exercise. Almost blonde with pale blue-grey eyes. Bitter because her boyfriend Brodie was killed.

Patricia Elliot – 27 – Trainee nurse. First refugee escaping from looters.

Original Orchard Close residents: (16 in total)

Alfie – 15 – Probable orphan since his Mum didn't come home from work. Living with Betty. Absolutely hero-worships Harold.
Bernie – 26 – Slim bit not fit. Wants to work out with girl club.
Betty – 59 – Older woman on the 'committee'.
Curtis – 25 – Short and stout, amateur gardener.
Harry – Spry 76 – Resident with his dad's WWII rifle.
Hilda – 41 – Ex-clerical worker. Loves collating lists.
Matthew – 24 – Red haired ex-traffic warden.
Sal – 24 – Blonde woman who wants to tone up and join the girl club.
Seth – 25 – Tubby and unemployed. Likes chips, beer and watching videos.
Trish – 23 – has AIDS – her friend (HIV) Jane didn't return from the doctor's.

Collected from the city:

Berry – 17 – Daughter of Nigel. Taller, stronger, and also a brewer.
Nigel – 43 – Brewer, widower.

New Refugees pre-Armageddon: (29 in all)

Bess – 19 – Ex-girlfriend of one of gang running her estate (Spyke).
Chris – 23 – Man killed defending.
Conn – 22 – Short slim man, prematurely bald.
Gayle – 18 – Thin, long dark hair, dental trainee.
Georgina – 7 – Zach and Olive's daughter.
Janine – 34 – Laundry assistant.
Joey – 6 – Pippa and Robert's son.
Jon – 18 – Wounded defending the wall.
Lillian – 19 – Tall overweight woman who moves in with Conn.
Olive – 29 – Part-time cleaner – Zach's wife, Georgina's Mum.
Pippa – 22 – Genius baker.
Robert – 24 – Pippa's husband.
Sandy – 56 – Carpenter but retired with bad arthritis.
Sue – 22 – Killed defending.
Sukie – 4 – Suzie's daughter.
Suzie – 20 – Sue's sister and Sukie's single Mum.
Tim – 22 – Refugee with nothing but his fiancé, Toyah.
Toyah – 19 – Refugee with nothing but Tim.
Vince – Young man – friendless – collateral.
William – 32 – Diabetic.

Zach – 32 – Ex-office manager.

OTHERS:

Mr Pilsworth – Looks after rifle club.

Sam – Publican at the Dog and Stoat.

Spyke Pierce – 'Minuteman' rejected by Harold.

VANCE HUXLEY

Vance Huxley lives out in the countryside in Lincolnshire, England. He has spent a busy life working in many different fields – including the building and rail industries, as a workshop manager, trouble-shooter for an engineering firm, accountancy, cafe proprietor, and graphic artist. He also spent time in other jobs, and is proud of never being dismissed, and only once made redundant.

Eventually he found his Noeline, but unfortunately she died much too young. To help with the aftermath, Vance tried writing though without any real structure. As an editor and beta readers explained the difference between words and books, he tried again.

Now he tries to type as often as possible in spite of the assistance of his cats, since his legs no longer work well enough to allow anything more strenuous. An avid reader of sci-fi, fantasy and adventure novels, his writing tends towards those genres.

Printed in Great Britain
by Amazon

61820715R00210